THE FALL

PROPERTY

Cemetery

✕

Emily's
larch

INDIAN RIVER

◼ ← Final site of Buttes house

◼ ← First site of Odder's house

PROPERTY LINE BETWEEN BUTTESES AND RAYMONDS

▦ The Raymond
mansion

Coswell
swamp

Odder's
Island

Raymond
Island

LAKE

Sedge Island

THE
WINDFALL

◼ Worth Hart's house

◼ Crane's blacksmith shop

BLACKWOOD HOLLOW

BEAR COUNTRY

*One
of the
Raymonds*

by Jean Rikhoff

Buttes Landing
One of the Raymonds

THE TIMBLE TRILOGY
Dear Ones All
Voyage In, Voyage Out
Rites of Passage

The Quixote Anthology

Mark Twain: Writing about the Frontier

Robert E. Lee: Soldier of the South

One of the Raymonds

Jean Rikhoff

The Dial Press   New York   1974

*Material for the Reconstruction
was partially accumulated through
a summer grant from the National Endowment for the
Humanities in 1972 for research in Black Literature.*

*Library of Congress Cataloging in Publication Data
Rikhoff, Jean.   One of the Raymonds.   I. Title.
PZ4.R573On [PS3568.I377]   813'.5'4
73–19617   ISBN 0–8037–6674–2*

*Book design by
Paulette
Nenner*

For
Helen Taylor,
who tried to make me a writer, and
Joyce Engelson,
who is trying to keep me one,
two great editors; and to my agent
Barthold Fles,
who lent the encouragement
and (often) money to keep me going,
this book is dedicated in admiration and affection

*A note
of thanks to
Harold Worthington
for his help with the dogs;
Bill Gambee,
for his woods lore;
Joe Delong
for the basics of balladry
in the Adirondacks and the Appalachians;
Joyce Shuman,
for her reading, typing, and suggestions;
and to
Carolyn Hemmett
for suggesting the three-line frog poem.
And to
Elizabeth Gambee Osborne
for her help with life in general.*

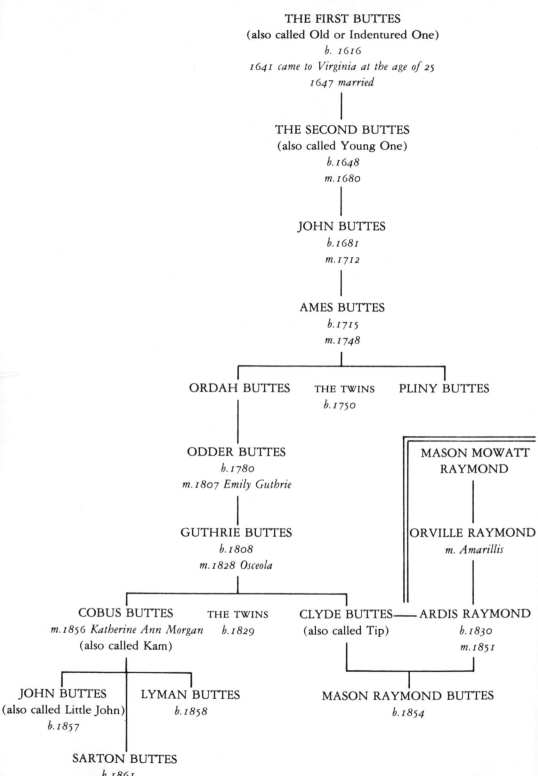

THE FIRST BUTTES
(also called Old or Indentured One)
b. 1616
1641 came to Virginia at the age of 25
1647 married

THE SECOND BUTTES
(also called Young One)
b. 1648
m. 1680

JOHN BUTTES
b. 1681
m. 1712

AMES BUTTES
b. 1715
m. 1748

ORDAH BUTTES   THE TWINS   PLINY BUTTES
b. 1750

ODDER BUTTES
b. 1780
m. 1807 Emily Guthrie

MASON MOWATT
RAYMOND

GUTHRIE BUTTES
b. 1808
m. 1828 Osceola

ORVILLE RAYMOND
m. Amarillis

COBUS BUTTES   THE TWINS   CLYDE BUTTES —— ARDIS RAYMOND
m. 1856 Katherine Ann Morgan   *b. 1829*   (also called Tip)   *b. 1830*
(also called Kam)   *m. 1851*

JOHN BUTTES   LYMAN BUTTES   MASON RAYMOND BUTTES
(also called Little John)   *b. 1858*   *b. 1854*
b. 1857

SARTON BUTTES
b. 1861

One

Buttes Landing, 1869

I went into the woods because I wanted to live deliberately, to front only the essential facts of life, and see if I could not learn what it had to teach, and not, when I came to die, discover that I had not lived.

Henry David Thoreau, WALDEN

I

"**S**trung *hisself up*, let his wife and boy come in and find him swingin' over the stairs, gittin' hisself all dressed up in a fancy suit, then go 'nd pin a psalm to hisself, them Raymonds always did consider theirselves on an equal footin' with the Almighty. Clyde Raymond even wanted to be governor, that's what he had in mind, you don't fool me."

Mason Raymond stopped, his hand on the door. The men inside were talking about his father, the Landing boy who had gone away and been a big success in Albany, and then hadn't been so successful and finally hadn't been successful at all, and four months before had hung himself in the front hall of the house at the Landing. A sign on Frank Lite's store said in crude letters: OPEN. But nothing was ever really open in the Landing; people talked (as these old men were doing) behind closed doors.

There was a bell attached to the sign; if Mason Raymond moved the door the slightest bit it would sound an alarm. He could picture Lite standing in the middle of his cheeses and bolts of goods, his kegs of nails and bins of sugar and flour, talking casually about a man hanging himself on Christmas

Eve; Mason Raymond could see Lite's cronies listening politely. Lite's store was Buttes Landing's clearing house for information; Lite tolerated anyone making his store a headquarters so long as that person agreed with its owner—a big handsome man, pretty and smiling, a man you instinctively trusted; but while Lite was smiling and leaning forward gracefully to pay you some compliment, he was measuring how big the rock, how sharp the knife he needed to be King of the Castle. He's going to say, "Pride comes before a fall," Mason Raymond thought. He hated my father because he married rich and got away and for a while was A Big Man, and he envied that and coveted it and—worse—knew it and now he'll make a lesson out of it, to show how smart he is, how much better than The Big Man.

"Pride goeth before a fall," Lite said. "A man who puts on airs and puffs hisself up bigger than he was meant to be," Lite philosophized, "ain't gonna do no more then blow hisself up so big he's bound to bust. Pride's a puffer," Lite said pontifically, an expert—after all, it takes one to know one.

Though nearly a third of a year had passed since his father's death, nothing nearly so interesting had happened in the Landing since; people would keep on entertaining themselves on the suicide until something newer, more exciting occurred. "Uppity," Lite said now as Mason Raymond knew he must have said a hundred times before in the past three months. "Them that's uppity git their comeuppance jest like Clyde Raymond got his."

Clyde *Raymond:* that's how they thought of him. His father was a Buttes, but he'd married "above him" into the Raymond family, the rich Raymond family, and the Raymonds, like most of the rich, absorbed into themselves all with whom they came into contact. Thus, his father had become a Raymond.

Inside his mind Mason Raymond read the maxim, repeated again and again at the Academy by fat Mr. Morphis, whose sin it certainly didn't describe: *Whom the gods wish to destroy, they first make proud.* H U B R I S, Morphis's fat fingers traced on the blackboard and Mason Raymond dutifully wrote *hubris* in his notebook and after that "excessive pride—arrogance," a phrase which those fat fingers also blocked out on the blackboard. Filled with *hubris*, his father had put on his good suit and pinned on his psalm and in his bare feet padded down the hall to the stairwell and plunged over, hanging himself with his silk bathrobe sash. A touch of elegance, his father was fond of telling the Albany cook who complained about all the company, can do wonders with leftovers.

Lite's sure, hard voice said, "Hang'd hisself, went 'n hang'd hisself, and put a prayer on his vest 'n done it on Christmas Eve, what kind of man is that? It's the Indian blood," Lite's voice said in a tone you would never in a million years argue with. "Clyde, he never looked Injun, not the way his brother Cobus does, but in the end he acted Injun. Blood *tells*," Lite said. "And more'n likely it was part *her* doing." *Her* was Mason Raymond's mother, rich and a Raymond, what might be called the only gentry in Buttes Landing, lumber people; that is, the money had been made out of the woods, *stripping* the woods, his Uncle Cobus said, and he ought to know, he was one of the ones who'd gone in and helped hack down the great primordial forests, "and don't think I don't regret it," Cobus Buttes would say, banging his fist on the table, a quiet man who was driven to emotion by the sins of his youth, pounding the table in penance and looking guilty, saying, "If I'd knowed what I was really doin', I'da never cut one tree, but you don't know nuthin' at that age, nuthin' at all." Mason Raymond's father and his woods uncle were twins, but no two men could have been further apart, one a big lawyer down in Albany, mixed up in politics, the other a mountain farmer ("It's nothing but rock and ridge," Mason Raymond's father would say contemptuously, though it was his birthplace too) who, since the Civil War, wanted nothing to do with any government—"They're all maggoty," Cobus said—and sometimes, Mason Raymond thought, maybe didn't want anything to do with anything except his own family, his wife and three sons. John, Mason Raymond thought, his heart dropping at the thought of his strong, resilient younger cousin, the boy whom the Landing said could do no wrong, just as he himself was the one who could do no right. "Two left feet and two wrong thumbs," they said of him while of John Buttes there was the enthusiasm for the golden and gifted. "Ain't a boy in

] 5 [

these hills got John Buttes' feel for huntin' nor his gift for gab. Ain't it odd," people would ask, "how them two twins could put out sech different branches? Takes after his mother, that Raymond one does—city sired."

In the Landing, Mason Raymond was nobody and John was everyone. What did people who lived by the land care about what went on in books? City bred also meant school wise, school sassy; people who lived with their hands always distrusted the dreamers. They weren't *workers*. Workers were those whose fruits you could see. Who could see an idea? Mason Raymond Buttes tried to take this knowledge and examine it objectively, not let it hurt him (why, after all, should what the people at the Landing have said hurt him, why should *he* care?), but the truth was that almost anyone had the power to hurt him, he was vulnerable to everyone else's opinions because he had no real convictions of his own that he was willing to fight for. His uncle said the only real things a man believed in were those he would take up a gun for. "It's that kind of world," Cobus Buttes said, "and the less you have to do with it, the better off you are—killin' to keep what you believe," he said, shaking his head in wonderment. And Mason Raymond's father, Cobus's twin, wouldn't fight—really fight—for anything. To fight meant you might get hurt.

He—Mason Raymond thought, seeing in his mind an image of his father, toying with his wine glass, leaning across the table—saying smoothly, handsomely (another finely cut man like Lite), with the recklessness of the debt-ridden: "It might be nice if we were *all* up at the Landing for the holidays."

"Takes nerve, pinnin' Holy words to yourself when you go 'n do a thing like that."

"Well—" There was a laugh—"Clyde Buttes was never one to hang back."

"You want us *all* to spend the holidays at the Landing?" Mason Raymond's mother had asked incredulously.

Smoothly his father sipped his wine, as if he saw nothing unusual in the idea, though he hadn't been to the Landing with them in four or five years; the Landing house was Mason Raymond's mother's house, just as the Albany house was his father's. His parents lived apart; Mason Raymond and his mother only came down to Albany for the winter so that he could go to school there, an arrangement made for his benefit solely, because on their own he was sure his mother and father would not have lived together in the same house at all. In Albany his mother had her "quarters;" his father never came up to that part of the house, just as he never came to the Landing for summers and holidays.

"I thought we could all spend Christmas together," Clyde Buttes said, putting his wine glass down under the candlelight where the flame fell in a ruby-red pool and lay, golden, like a dropped star, in its shimmering center. He was thinking of running for office again, he said, and it would be better—they all knew what he meant, but Mason Raymond's mother had insisted on putting it into words. "You mean you need some-one who looks like a real wife?"

His father had had the grace to look down at his plate, conceding, Mason Raymond supposed, all the other women there had been down through the years who had not looked like a real wife.

"Cain't put a good face on somethin' like this," one of the old men inside said, his voice filled with venom and envy. "I don't care how much money they got."

Why did she let herself be persuaded? Mason Raymond wondered. I suppose she just thought it'd be easier to give in, it didn't really matter, not any more. The years his mother had still been in love with his father were the hard ones for her; once she'd given over any hope of getting him to love her back and had accepted the uselessness of loving someone who would not love back, things went easier. She had put on weight, she didn't bother about pressing all her love on him, she had learned to laugh again.

So she had given in—all right, he could come up if he'd let extra help come up with her, one or two of the "girls" he usually kept with him in Albany, though there were no longer any "girls" at the Albany house because of his father's weak-ness, hadn't been for years; but out of concern for everyone's sensibilities, his mother still said "girls," one or two could do the cleaning, get the dust beat out of the furniture and the covers off the wing they never used and send over for whatever they were low on that he would want—cigars and liquor and things like that that the "girls" would know, so that when he got up there wouldn't be all that endless work getting him comfortable, if he'd do that, she guessed it would be all right.

Snow fell all the day before he was to come, seven, eight inches, enough to make the roads nearly impassable, but once his mother set her mind to a thing, even something she didn't want to do, she moved heaven and earth to see it got done. She sent Rivers, who worked the horses, down to the Falls so that his father could change carriages and have fresh horses for the last part of the trip, so that he would not be pressed to get through in darkness, even though the change in plans meant Rivers leaving in the bitterest part of the morning, the dull, gray dawn of day when the thermometer read seven below and footsteps squeaked eerily on the snow as his mother and Rivers and he crossed the courtyard to the sleigh. There was a full moon; it still hung like a big, blue-white ball in the gray sky. It was always coldest at the full of the moon.

Rivers was a mass of mufflers and blankets, his mother an encyclopedia of instructions; the whole sleigh was piled high with rugs and furs; only his mother's eyes gleamed out from under the velvety ruff of black fur (seal? lamb? he wasn't sure) that encircled her head. She was thick and bulky in her big fur coat, and her breath made plumes almost as big as the enormous ones coming from the horse's mouths, the big, matched pair stamping impatiently in the dove-colored morning light; they loved the winter, the horses, it brought back to them coltish ways, and their thick fur coats that nature had made with miniscule pockets that trapped the warm air and insulated them from the terrible effects of the sub-freezing temperatures and gave them a security against the cold that humans lacked, for all their coats and rugs. Now they pawed and pranced and in the air around them floated their feathery breath, full of the steamy fragrance of their stalls, released now on the piercingly clear, cold, full-moon air so that Mason Raymond, smothered in an old wool coat too big for him, breathed in an odor of horse sweat, horse excitement, horse heat.

They must just have been grained—though the rule was they were not to be hitched until an hour after they had been fed. Rivers had skimped on time; now, as his mother stood beside the first horse, leaning forward, sniffing its frosty breath, she said in a clear, tinkly voice, "When were these animals fed?"

She was very strict about her horses. About people she was often lax, irritable, and inconsistent, but about her animals she had set notions from which she never deviated: Mason Raymond waited, tense, for a scene.

Then something utterly unprecedented occurred. Although it was perfectly obvious Rivers had disobeyed her orders, Rivers was not chastised. She gave a tinny little laugh, almost child-like, and waved Rivers up into the sleigh. As they stood there, she and Mason Raymond, Rivers gave a shout and the horses strained against Rivers' efforts to hold them back. They wanted to run, and a lesser driver would not have been able to control them; Rivers would let them feel they were free, but in a mile he would have won their confidence, they would be behaving as they should, eager but obedient.

Rivers was driving toward a great persimmon melon, the rising sun, which blended with flashing crystals reflected on the crust of the snow; tears of cold stood on Mason Raymond's lashes, but he felt a moment of excitement and elation when the world seemed to him mysteriously beautiful beyond all understanding; possibly he was so inordinately happy because he loved the house at the Landing in a way he had never loved the big mansion in Albany and because his father was coming up and that might mean that there was a chance at last that his mother and father would get back together and be real parents to him instead of separate people in separate houses who took turns being formal with one another and especially formal and ritualistic with him.

In Albany, in the early years, there had been company almost every night, people to dinner, to drinks, wandering in after the theatre for a nightcap, browsing through the library at midnight, talking, laughing, someone playing a half-finished piece on the piano, too many staying way beyond the polite hour for departure. His father never hurried anyone on his way, even though Mason Raymond's mother often lay in bed exhausted the next day and then weakly rose to get ready for more company and another night of endless people wandering in and out.

Eventually she began sending down excuses—she was laid up with a headache, earache, eye trouble, what did it matter? The parties went on without her, lasting even later now that her pinched, tired face wasn't present to get people into their coats and out of the house. In his room upstairs she and Mason Raymond would sit over a simplified version of the lavish supper being served below and talk like two adult conspirators about the guests downstairs—who was going bankrupt, who was going to run for the legislature, who was dying of a fatal illness.

In the hot room her love was stifling. She took small, insect-like bites, her eyes pouring out her love, her hands fluttering now and again with a napkin while she choked back tears, fought for a smile, dropped the napkin, leaned over and gripped his hand, "Oh, Mason Raymond, you don't know how much I love you."

At seven o'clock Mason Raymond went down to go around solemnly holding out his hand. "How is your poor Mama?" the ladies asked. His mother was spoken of as an invalid although there was nothing wrong with her legs or her ambulatory powers; it was her pride that was in trouble, injured almost beyond repair, so that she sat upstairs silent and forlorn amid the gloom of Mason Raymond's dark-walled room, waiting for her son to come back up and make her life have meaning.

Often she sat hour after hour preoccupied with some absorbing scene inside her head, frowning, far-away, in a world all her own. For over a year she lived in the same house with them, but far away inside herself, a woman tortured by the bleakness of her life, but too proud to protest.

And then unaccountably she had packed her bags, taken Mason Raymond, and gone up to the house at the Landing, her grandfather's house, suddenly a whirlwind of activity, as if during the lassitude of the last years she had stored up enormous amounts of energy and now it was bursting forth in bouts of dusting, decorating, painting, pruning, even in buying a horse to ride herself. She began to eat, enormous breakfasts, bigger lunches, huge dinners. She had toast and jam and cakes with her tea. Half-emptied boxes of chocolates, toffee, caramels, divinity, bowls of fresh and preserved fruits, silver dishes of fancy nuts, little trays of nibbly snacks, dishes of colored mints were scattered all over the house.

Her color came back; she dropped ten years of unhappiness out of the expression in her face. Her figure rounded; she rode, bristled with excitement, clattered into the house in a jangle of boots, spurs, long riding crop, her happy, high-pitched laughter surging up the stairs where Mason Raymond, bent over his microscope, looked up disbelievingly, asking himself if this could be the same woman who only last winter wrung her hands in anguish and repeated endlessly, "Oh, you don't know how much I love you, baby. You'll never know. Oh, I hope you never grow up and go away."

She ordered bright-colored cloth out of which strange, savage new dresses, bold in design, almost brazen, were cut; she bought a new coach, too ornate for the Landing, in which she flashed about the streets, catching every eye. She took to visiting up at the New House where her husband's brother Cobus lived whenever the whim struck her, which was often. "He's a *good* man," she said in a definitive way that meant, No one argue with me about anything Cobus Buttes does.

When the war with the South came, she threw herself into sewing, bandage-rolling, knitting, collecting with a passion that left little room for anything else. The beautiful new dresses lay in boxes, moldering; the carriage gilt peeled and was not replenished; the handsome horses stomped impatiently in their box stalls waiting to be let out. She had even gone to church to pray for Cobus Buttes to come home; in many ways her husband's brother had become the center of her life.

Mason Raymond crossed between the barrels and crates, under the hanging tin and tools, past the big pile of skins, past lame old Eben Stuart, cataract eyes misty with blindness and old age, his liver-spotted hands trembling over the dirty blacksmith apron he always wore, although he was too blind to shoe anymore, and went through Frank Lite's store, forks and rakes swinging overhead, but Mason Raymond was not in Frank

Lite's store, he was far away at the bottom of his own stairs, seeing the bare feet swinging, his father didn't have shoes or socks on, it was the bare feet Mason Raymond had seen first and now always pictured in his mind, his father swinging out over the hall with his feet bare and the twenty-third psalm pinned to his breast:

> The Lord is my shepherd; I shall not want.
> He maketh me to lie down in green pastures: he leadeth
>   me beside the still waters.
> He restoreth my soul: he leadeth me in the paths of
>   righteousness for his name's sake.
> Yea, though I walk through the valley of the shadow of
>   death, I will fear no evil: for thou art with me . . .

"We should never have let him come up," his mother said. "He'd never have dared do it down in Albany."

Lite's hangers-on saw him, quickly turned the talk to what was going on down South. The conflict had settled the question of breaking up the Union, but peace had posed in some ways larger problems than the war. What was to be done with the niggers now that they were free? No one seemed to have any workable answer. The Freedman's Bureau was trying, but there were endless charges of graft and corruption, of favoring blacks over whites, a notion very few Landing people seemed to cotton up to. For most it was unsettling to hear the tales of black bucks shoving white ladies off the sidewalk into the mud, of niggers—as the people at the Landing still insisted on calling them—packing the state legislatures and voting through all kinds of unheard-of laws—things as crazy as blacks wanting to marry up with whites; blacks were taking over and acting biggety and thinking they were as good as, maybe better than whites, that was the long and short of it.

The North had freed the niggers; now let them fend for themselves, the way other Americans had to. You worked hard, you'd git somewhere: that was the American way. Let the niggers live like everyone else, that was the way Frank Lite and the people at the Landing thought.

"If they'd had any gumption they'd never have let their-selves be caught and carried out of Africa in the first place. Ain't a Christian in the bunch, worshippin' crocodiles and snakes and crazy things like that," Lite said, smiling and nod-ding at Mason Raymond.

"They don't need no forty acres and a mule," Eben Stuart said. "You don't see the government givin' me that."

"You too damn lazy to keep it up, even the government knows that."

"Old Andy Johnson, he knows a thin' or two how to handle them people, ought to have lissen'd to him, that's what I always say, but look what it got him, nuthin' but trouble and tarn'tion, that's what."

"Couldn't nobody git along with him, that's why, not even Grant. Things has come to a disgrace when the Secretary of this here government got to barricade hisself in office to hold onto his job." They were talking about Stanton. "Irascible, stubborn, prejudiced son of a bitch, just the wrong kind of man to be runnin' the country at a time like this," Old Doc Bronson said. He ought to know. He'd served in the war.

"Those men—what you call 'em?—those Klanners," half-blind, half-lame old Eben Stuart argued, "they got the right idear. Keep the niggers in their place, make 'em show a little respect. This is the United States of America, and it was started white and it's gonna end white. Son?" he said imperiously to Mason Raymond, who, scarcely believing his voice, heard himself saying, coldly, angrily, "There are 'niggers' smarter than any of us. Benjamin Banneker for one." He could have bitten off his tongue. They didn't have any idea who Benjamin Banneker was.

He walked through hostile silence to the counter where Lite (always smiling, even at a nigger-lover) leaned toward him, a handsome man giving a handsome greeting, even to a nigger-lover, "Mornin', boy," and Mason Raymond looked back at Lite, not saying anything, striving for some of that strength his mother had finally mastered. "I'm *glad* he's gone." She was furious at only one thing: that he'd done it on Christmas Eve. "Nails, string, cinnamon," he said to Lite, standing there at the counter asking himself, No matter how she hated him,

] *13* [

how could anyone be glad a person killed himself?

They're all glad he killed himself, all except me and maybe Uncle Cob. To be like his uncle: Strong. Sure. Self-sufficient.

A pyramid of staples was accumulating on the counter in front of him, and he read down the list, mechanically, his mind far away, up at the New House, where his uncle, his father's brother, lived. His Uncle Cobus had three big brown boys— his cousins, who neither looked nor acted like him, it was difficult to believe there was any blood connection. They were younger than Mason Raymond, but tougher, more resilient. They were being raised to do what their father and grandfather and his father before him had done: claim the land and their place on it. Their lives were all laid out for them like one of those thematic illustrations in his books, the carefully constructed history the ancients believed in, with man hanging halfway between the angels and the animals in a universe where the sun and stars and planets revolved around the earth and man hung, created out of God's glad plan, at the center of the spheres.

But the real world—at least Mason Raymond's world down at the Academy—was the next illustration, an earth floating lonely and free out on its own, part of no recognizable system or plan, just some chance casuistry in a system no one understood and out of which no one could make sense, aimlessly afloat in the vast, lonely, purposeless spaces of time.

His father, even when he was alive, had never cared much which way Mason Raymond was headed so long as he was polite, quiet, and out from underfoot. He had just taken for granted any son of his would grow up all right. But what "all right" signified remained undefined. No wonder, Mason Raymond thought, he had felt adrift.

His father did not give love unreservedly the way Mason Raymond's mother did, she who understood the need for the monthly packet of books from Albany and never censured him because he knew neither how to hunt nor shoot, even though he desperately wished to do both. His father said a gentleman should ride, shoot, gamble and drink well. His father preached a lot of things he didn't practice. Mason Raymond's mother never untied the parcel of books, never diminished his happiness at being first to unpack and unwrap the fresh packets, to feel the sweat of new paper, to touch the beautiful, specially ordered bindings that, grainy to the touch, promised an outside, far-away world; "an ounce of cloves," he said to the smiling face of Lite in front of him, a face suspicious of the world of words, one that distrusted the things of the mind, *"cloves,"* Mason Raymond repeated, stranded between what was, here, now, and what he could see might be, in some far-away place, where, when he listened to the secret voice in his heart, something lovely and mysterious, lonely and unknown, whispered clues that he might run and find.

Mason Raymond gathered together his parcels and stuffed them into the gunny sack, Lite watching his clumsiness with contempt only half-hidden behind his smile. Mason Raymond threw the sack up on his shoulder and turned without any acknowledgment of Lite's offer to help, showing, he hoped, that he knew what kind of man Lite was, even if he was only fifteen years old and city bred and the son of a man who killed himself because he'd run up debts he couldn't pay. Mama could have paid, he thought, as he passed the old men by the stove. *If she wanted,* a second voice inside said.

His father had sense enough not to ask. But he punished her for not paying. Disgracing her in her own house and all those mean people sending letters and even coming all the way up from Albany demanding their money. In the end she had to pay. He knew that when he pushed himself over the rail, Mason Raymond thought. That's why he did it, to have the last word.

The old horse was tethered to the hitching post. His mother had made him take the oldest, most patient animal on the place. Rightly, she did not trust him around nervous, high-strung animals, another sign of his insignificance. Young John Buttes, his cousin, had one of the finest horses for miles around.

Of course John could ride, the way he could do everything else. He swung into the saddle with the same natural grace he swung a gun to his shoulder and whistled down the road, his big, ugly dog trailing beside him. He used harsh language. He hitched up his pants like a man and swung his head around and spit as contemptuously as any regular, grown man. And no matter how hard he tried, no matter how long he practiced, Mason Raymond would never be like him; that was the awful, grief-stricken, long and short of it. A bust, that's what he was, while John Buttes—Young John Buttes now, who used to be Little John and by the time he was ten had outgrown that baby name, while everyone still called Mason Raymond by his double name which sounded so silly and babyish to him—Young John Buttes was a real, authentic bowl-over.

The lake glittered up at Mason Raymond, almost black under the April sun. The ice had not yet gone out, but it was ready to go; the stretch of frozen surface before him had a dark, brooding look. He stood beside the horse and gazed over the row of sheds and stores that led to the lake. "When the weather turns warm," Cobus Buttes had said, "and the dogs can git a track, the coons'll be out. Your Ma says you want to go with us."

Maybe he'd forgotten.

No, Cobus Buttes did not forget.

There was a little boy with bare feet scrabbling in the dust. He had shucked his shoes even though he'd kept on his thick winter coat, spring-led to test his bare feet in the April mud. Bare feet. Inside his head Mason Raymond's father swung out over the stairs.

Ahead Worth Hart was getting down from an old, dilapidated wagon. Everything of Hart's was falling apart or rusting out. The shutters of his house were wind-ripped away, his porch steps broken and pulled apart; the house itself gradually disappearing under a sea of debris because Hart never threw anything away, never turned anything down, never gave anything away, never traded or sold anything he had put his hands on. Eventually, he said, everything came into use. It was just a question of finding what you wanted when you needed it, there was so much stuff being stored up for future use.

Hart was sixty-one years old and all those sixty-one years had been hard; yet he was young and fresh-looking in the face, with innocent, boyish blue eyes and an ingenious, boyish smile. He was short and wore a battered straw hat; on either side tufts of thick, coarse, salt-and-pepper hair tumbled free.

He was red-faced, sunburned; he was sunburned all the time, even in winter, something to do with his baby skin which, like the rest of him, had stayed young even though six decades of his life had passed. Everything connected with him—his house, his porch, his barns—was falling apart, but he stayed young and untouched.

"No, no, boy, I can manage by myself, don't pull nuthin' out of shape in you with a weight you ain't used to." Hart hoisted the sack over his shoulders, sunk under its weight, peering up with bright blue eyes. "You sprung up consider-able since the last time I seen you."

That had been at the funeral. Mason Raymond remembered his surprise that Hart, whom he had never seen dressed in anything but baggy blue coveralls, owned a suit. It was black, rusty, and hung as if it had been bought when Hart weighed thirty or forty pounds more, but it gave its wearer a curious dignity, as if he were play-acting a part that frightened him but which, nonetheless, he had agreed was his payment for being allowed to live. The newly dead, his composure seemed to say, always throw fresh fear into those left living. He was so quiet it was hard to identify him as Hart (the tale-teller), a solemn figure standing in a corner across from the coffin, shaking his head while he turned his celebrated thirty-six coonskin dress hat around in his hands and muttered a prayer between his store teeth.

Hart had a history of bad luck; not bad, but *terrible,* none of which discouraged his valorous heart. He believed suffer-ing didn't maybe give you the good life, but it gave you the best, because suffering was the only way you could learn to understand what living was all about. If he was right, Hart ought to be just about the wisest man alive.

A slow boy whom Hart had tried to help by giving him work had turned on him one day and hit him across the back of the head with a hoe. Hart had a small ridge of scar in the middle of his scalp as a remembrance; he told the story every chance he got, he was a great talker, Hart was; when he came into sight, people said here comes tall-tale Hart; he was soon standing in their midst, saying—twisting his everyday straw hat in his hands and licking his lips, shaking his head quizzically—Worked for us a year and eight days and never a cross word between any of us, Mabel treated him like her own son, I'd a give him the shirt off my back if he'd aneeded it; he was out in the wood shed splittin' wood and carryin' it in, a coolish day, it was, first chill of autumn and we was fillin' the kindlin' box, at least he was, I was paintin', and he come up behind me and I said, You about finished, and he said, One more load, and went back to the shed and split it and picked it up and picked up the hoe and come up to the house and put the wood in the box and then come back out and hit me over the head with the hoe. I fell forward so hard I broke my jaw in three places and busted my nose. Weren't no rhyme nor reason to it, he jest took it into his head, he said, to hit me, so he went in and got the hoe and done it. When I fell forward, he left me lay and went and put the hoe back, there was blood all over the woodshed. Then he lit out. He didn't darst go home and he didn't darst stay where he was. He took one of my horses and headed north. God knows what he had in mind, a seventeen-year-old boy like that, we trusted him like he was our own son, even if he was slow, we figured that weren't *his* fault, never had one sour word between us, and Mabel, she didn't believe he done it.

She come out and found me laid out all covered over with blood. I had crawled up the steps and got myself onto the porch, don't know how. The brain was sticking right out of my head. The skull was broke just like a latch, there was a kind of hinge bone on it, and it had swelled so there was the brain popping right out of the top. Every time I took a breath the brains beat up and down jest like a heart. And the breath was rattling in my throat like the death rattle, Mabel says. It was the blood in my lungs. It stayed there five days and the second day she says I smelled so bad from that blood you couldn't stand stayin' in the same room with me long.

She thought sure I was done for. Weren't no one could live with a gap in his skull like that, but Old Doc Bronson come and he said, Mabel, I got to take the slivers out and if I do I'm sure to puncture somethin' vital in the brain and kill him but he'll die anyway if I don't try to take those splinters out; and Mabel said to him, Doc, if you was on one side of the Atlantic and I was on the other and I had to git to you and you only held out a straw, I'd grab for it. Go ahead and try to take them out.

We didn't have no idea who wouldda done such a thing, but the last person in the world Mabel or me wouldda thought of was Perry, and the doc kept picking out them slivers of bone all night and half the next day and then he tells Mabel, I think they're all out but there's no way of knowin'. I don't know how but he's still breathin'. The first time I went in I thought sure I'd kill him, but he kept on goin'. And then he told Mabel, He can't live. You best tell the children so as to prepare them. Ain't no reason to hold out false hope, so Mabel she gets Miranda and Albert together and she says, Your Pa's dyin', and she says she never saw two kids act better nor be braver than they was. But I didn't die. I went right on breathin', rattlin' hat awful way with all that blood in my lungs. The fifth day it begun to come up in hard clots, and I woke up once and said, *Whot happened?* and then I fell back into that half-live, half-dead state I been in since I was hit, but gradual-like I begin to come back and I'm almost good as new. I've got this indent in my head—don't mind if you feel it—not a bump nor a knot nor anythin' what you'd expect, but this kind of sunk-in spot where that hinge of bone never growed back and I git terrible headaches if I go in the cart far. I got to hold my head in place to keep it from rollin', but the thing I kin never understand is what made him do it. All he ever said by way of explainin' after he was tracked down was, I seen you standin' there and I felt like hittin' you so I got the hoe and hit you.

Mason Raymond, grateful to see anyone who might talk to him, an admirer of Hart's hunting stories and his encyclopedic knowledge about dogs, his good will toward everyone, even an awkward, gangling boy, called out he could help, he was stronger than he looked.

Hart never raised his head. "Your uncle said I might find you here in town," he said, hefting the sack of produce against the wall. "He said as how it might be a good idear for me to look around for you long as I was down this way. He's fixin' on goin' huntin' sometime this week and he said you wanted to go." Hart hitched his britches. "Saw him up at the farm yestiddy—went up to take him a pup of Brownie's, promised him one last summer and it's been ready to go a couple of months, but time flies faster than me—most full-growed before I got it up. Good a pup as I ever got out of her, treed on her own last week like she'd been doin' it all her life. I didn't git her up there before, but mabbee jest as well. Those young pups of your uncle's mightta spoiled her. Never saw such boys for ruinin' good dogs. Spoil them, they do. Treat 'em like they was human."

He wondered what Hart said about him. He wasn't good for anything he could see, not even school. He was a day-dreamer, one who brought down the scorn of firm teachers and was the despair of the lackadaisical ones. Fat old Morphis would look at him, puzzled. "What do you think about all the time, staring out into space."

"Oh, just things."

"What kind of things?"

How could he say: I think about where things come from. Where they go. Why.

Now he drew a deep breath and gave away one of his inmost secrets. "I'd sure like one of those dogs myself one day —oh, not from Brownie, I know she's the best you got—but any one of your dogs. Everyone knows you have the best dogs around— . . ."

"I thought, you know, you was bent more on books than runnin' out wild the way some of us do."

"Can't you do both?"

Hart considered a moment. "Never thought of it that way, always thought of it as either/or, not both/and. I always thought of them two things as fightin' one another."

Mason Raymond took Worth's statement to be a summation of all that was wrong with him: everything about him was in conflict, the Buttes part of him versus the Raymond, his intro-spective side against that part of him that longed to be at home in rough nature; he wanted to be both tough and tender, and now his world of books was being opposed to the world of the woods. He looked away from Hart across the vast, ice-capped waters of Federation Lake trying to make out where his uncle's house was. Cobus Buttes seemed to him a man who had been able to reconcile opposites. He had been to war and killed, but he was the most quiet, peaceable man Mason Raymond knew. No man messed with him; yet he deferred to the gentlest wish of his wife. Was it too much to hope that he, also related in blood and heart, might not in some mysterious, unknown way pass through rites that would purify him and make him such a man?

"You reckon," he asked, picking the country word *reckon* deliberately, "it's possible I could learn a lot of these things folks around here just automatically suppose I can't ever know?" He was watching Lite leave the store and advance toward them in that characteristic high-toed gait that made him look as if he were poised on the tip of his toes.

Hart chewed, spit, moved the plug of tobacco from one side of his mouth to the other; he was also watching Lite. Lite prided himself his dogs were better than any man's in the country, he didn't care whose. He had blueticks whereas Hart's were mostly blacks and tans.

But Lite had had bad luck; some strange bug had hit his newborn and killed them off. Whatever it was had hindered his bitches, too. They came into season, but they would not breed. Mason Raymond felt that Lite held Hart accountable that his dogs were not strong, prolific producers.

"O'nery bugger," Worth muttered and carried another sack over against Crane's blacksmith shop. He was repaying a shoeing job the only way he could—from the produce off his land. Fussing with the second sack, ignoring Lite lounging alongside the cart watching him, he said to Mason Raymond, "I've thunk on it a while and I can't see no reason why you can't have a dog. Any time your Ma says she'll put up with one of my hounds, I'll be glad to gift you with one of them. I like to see my best blood stay in the parts. With the right people."

"He gift you with one of them bear dogs, that'd be something," Lite said.

Worth snorted, shoving the sack of grain over further along the shed. Lite knew as well as anyone Hart didn't have a bear dog any more. Ain't many men come acrosst the honor of

] *21* [

"Feller I know says I should be careful how I bet with you this time. I ain't forget you hoodwinked me out of that sow last fall."

"I won that sow fair and square," Lite said hotly. "My dog treed first and you know it."

"I know a couple of other things as well."

"Like what?"

"Like mabbee your knowin' where that coon was gonna be. One of them boys of yourn wouldn't have turned a coon out around there, would he now?"

"You sayin' I planted a coon to win that bet?"

"I'm jest askin' politelike, Frank, how come your dog was like almost at that tree when—"

"You don't want to hunt with us, don't. You want to hunt, lose fair and square."

"That's what I aim to do—lose *fair* and square."

"You lost that sow fair and square. Nobody asked you to make that bet."

"That's a fact. But someone sure set me up. I'm much obliged to you for the confidence I could be had so easy. Ain't many men who'd have took a winter neither to figure it out. I'd call that downright dumb on my part to be took so easy and to take so long figurin' out how I got took, deserves some sort of forfeit. But, mind, I ain't dumb enough not to know what I'm up against twice in a row. I make any more wagers with you, someone else is gonna handle both our dogs, someone I know *I* kin trust."

"You want to go out or don't you?"

"I've a mind to. If it don't snow. My scalp don't take to rain and snow. Took me a whole winter to figure out one little trick, plain dumb, I guet. Don't build a man's confidence none to know he was on the short end of the stick when the brains was passed out. But I ain't never run neither when I shouldda stood still," he said, giving Lite a long, steady look. "I may be dumb, but I ain't no runner. I ain't afraid of what's at the end of the hunt like some I could mention if I had a mind to."

"And I suppose you'd like to run Old Cassius in Blackwood Hollow," Lite said sarcastically.

Three years before, a big, wise old coon had moved into the Hollow. Coons had always been plentiful there, and the spot, up back a mile or so of Crane's blacksmith shop, had been a popular place for dog men—until Old Cassius had moved in. He had been nicknamed by Doc Bronson, who had enough classical background to appreciate treachery and craftiness. Cassius was a big, vicious coon who took on dogs with ease. The first stories that came from hunters who had run into Cassius in the Hollow were overlooked as exaggerations to cover the ineffectiveness of backward dogs. Then the stories began coming from men whose dogs had been top hunters and had come out of the Hollow badly mauled or maimed. People began to believe.

Old Cassius was easily recognizable because of a deformed ear. He killed nine hounds before hunters quit taking their dogs up to the Hollow. The last one had been a bluetick Lite had been bragging up, dog by the name of Lick (Lite had a habit of naming all his dogs something that began with *L,* as if honoring them with his own initial), he'd carried on so about that Lick dog of his that Cob Buttes had finally called him on it and said, This Lick dog such a scrapper, you willin' to take him up to Blackwood Hollow and let him have a go at Old Cassius, and Lite, whose pride was bigger than his common sense, got mad and said, Goddam it, there ain't no coon nowhere this Lick dog can't take on.

That Lick dog ran in and caught Old Cassius off guard. Still, the coon hadn't run, just turned and reared back, and gave that powerful hissing sound an angry coon makes when he is warning enemies to let him be.

Lick ran in and caught him by the back of the neck and started to shake him up the way he'd maul a normal coon, but Old Cassius was no normal coon. He gave Lick a scratching before he broke free and then, spitting and snarling, grabbed hold of the dog's throat. Cobus Buttes and some of the others wanted to go in and save the dog, but Lite waved them away, furious. "He ain't *worth* savin'," he said. "Let him fight 'nd save hisself, or let him git what he deserves."

The dog staggered and fell, the coon dangling from his throat. He tried rolling the coon off, but Old Cassius clung determinedly; then that Lick dog tried to leap up in the air and swing the coon free, he tried to shake and paw it loose. Lite didn't even wait to see the finish. When he saw the dog's throat bleeding its life away, he turned and walked away. Cobus Buttes shot and buried the dog. Lite's prestige had risen in the manner of a man who has committed a terrible and cowardly act and shows no remorse for his cravenness; a terrible kind of respect arises out of perfidy and treachery and cowardice, as if those who transgress in some large way gain recognition for the intensity of their acts rather than the quality. A man who could turn his back on his own damaged dog and walk away without looking back was a man to fear; he would perhaps have no more compunction about any of the other levels of life. After Lite's Lick dog went down, people began to resurrect an older story of the day Lite ran, how he'd been out with his Lucky dog over toward the Vermont side, hunting bear with Hart, Crane, and the other bear men, and Lite had come on a bear on the ground with dogs holding him at bay, the bear had charged the dogs, and instead of shooting, Lite had run. It was an old story but one hunters remembered and retold after Lite left his dog in the hollow. Now Hart stood looking at Lite and there was a kind of pity in his eyes, as if he could never understand how a man could run when he had a bear cornered, especially when his own dog was in the bear's path. Hart would have to be held back so that he wouldn't get mauled or killed trying to save his own dog and Frank Lite would turn tail and run; that was the difference between them.

The two men stood looking at one another, Lite smiling his peculiar dark smile; then he spit. "You an old, o'nery man," he said, and turned and walked back toward his general store, Hart watching him, shaking his head back and forth. "Makes you wonder why they put people like that on this earth, don't it?" he asked of nobody in particular, shaking his head. "People with such deep, mossy things inside."

The men began to gather at dusk. They stood with their dogs at the bottom of the Raymond property and waited, two or three men standing together surrounded by dogs, talking excitedly about where the tracks of the Union and Pacific Railroad were maybe going to get joined and a golden spike would be driven into place for the last tie that linked the Atlantic with the Pacific. They looked like grandiose warriors lost from some battle, standing around waiting for the chief to come and gather them together to begin the siege again. There was Crane, the new blacksmith: a big, dark man with a white scar that ran all the way down one cheek, a man whose wife was said to see into the future; the scar was the gift of a horse that reached up and kicked him after he'd let it down from the sling, and it had been standing patiently maybe ten or fifteen minutes while its owner gabbed with Crane. When Crane reached out for his money, the horse lifted his leg and let him have it. His wife had told him to be extra careful that day, but he hadn't listened. "I never put much store by her gift before," he said, "but I listen sharp now."

There was Old Eben Stuart, standing next to him, they had shared the same trade; and although his bad leg would make the going rough for him, his young wife, the old-timers said, would give him a coward's courage and a fool's recklessness. She is the prettiest thing you ever did see, they said, but her morals ain't too good. During the war, she'd liked soldiers. Now it was rumored her fancy turned to trappers. Big men, tall and rough, and full of no nonsense, she liked, but she'd married Stuart, he was a safe bet to give her full rein.

Hart was talking with his son Albert and his son-in-law Arthur, two men as alike as twins, though they hated anyone to say so. Married her own brother, people said of Hart's girl, making an awkward joke. As alike as two grains off the same ear of corn, her brother and her husband, look alike, work alike. Work an average man into the ground, too, both of them. Arthur ain't always mislaying something like Hart; he's a real particular man, his tools in place, his house shipshape, his wife looking sharp to keep in line. Miranda Hart looked sharp, too; she bullied her father and said, right in front of him, he couldn't hang onto anything that wasn't permanently attached to him.

Mason Raymond's uncle, Cobus Buttes, was talking to Lite, who stood with his big half-breed Walker and the redbone,

] 27 [

turning his foot in the mud. They both kept glancing up the road to see who else might be coming, saying, Can you beat that, a railroad gonna run all the way across the country in spite of Indians and mountains and country you hear tell is so awful men call places Hell-on-Wheels and Deadwood. Who'd want to go there? someone asked wonderingly, and Mason Raymond thought of how for most of the people here the world began and ended with Federation Lake and (maybe) the Falls, but that for some people, himself included, there was a long, wagon-rutted ribbon into the unknown and there was something in them that made them set out to follow it, and now in a way even that adventure would be over because there would be a train, a thing of metal and motor to carry where once walking went, and if he didn't hurry, most of the adventures were going to be over before he got big enough to take part in them. The war, for instance. Now the Trails, with their magic names—Oregon, Chisholm, Sante Fe, paths where men pushed into new lands and lived strange and often terrifying lives, while he stayed East and went to school and lived the kind of life everyone else did, unadventurous, hemmed in, happenstance.

Even the men gathering here, for instance, knew so much more about living, real living, than he did; though they might never venture West, hard tests of survival showed in their faces. When he looked at them, he felt weak and soft and no-account; perhaps nothing important would ever happen to him, not here, not anywhere; he'd never go to war or out West, never do anything worthwhile or exciting or memorable, so memorable that people talked about him in a certain awed tone of voice. They talked with that awe of his Uncle Cobus who had gone to war and come home a hero, as they still talked about his grandfather, Old Guthrie Buttes, who, when he was only a boy, had carried a man all mauled up by a bear out of the woods and had even sewed him up with strips from his leggings and made a pack to keep his chest closed up and carried him two days over some of the roughest country around; Guthrie Buttes had been a boy who had acted the way a man should, and men respected that in him, respected it then and talked about it so much that the story was passed on, people were still talking about it, would be maybe for a long time to come, because Guthrie Buttes was a special man, special and separate in a way Mason Raymond felt he would never be; he was the weak line in the family, the one on the Raymond side, the city people, the ones not to be trusted, rich as they were, because they were outsiders and rich and (most important) knew nothing about what it meant to hack a farm out of the mountains the way the first Buttes around here, Old Odder Buttes, had done, walked in all the way from Indiana or Illinois, one of those places way West, walked in all by himself over that old virgin land, big, mean, forest land no man in his right mind would go in alone, but he'd gone in and walked out on a mountain and said, This is going to be my farm, and my house is going here, and this is going to be my land. Buttes Landing was named for him, the first Buttes to come, way back fifty, sixty years before when there was nothing here but a scattering of trapper cabins, Indians maybe trying to figure out what to do in a white world, and a supply place. Buttes Landing wasn't even called Buttes Landing then. Mason Raymond couldn't remember what it had been called because to him the place was The Landing, but the truth was that the Landing had been named for his great-grandfather, Odder Buttes, a man whose wife had been taken in the birth of their first son, the one who grew up to walk out of the woods with that wounded man and who, when he was old, went back into those same woods to die because that was the way he wanted to go, out in the woods, to be a part of it dying the way he'd been a part of it living.

The Butteses all belonged, but he didn't belong. He was a Raymond, one of the Raymonds, that's what these men—Crane, Bronson, Stuart, Lite, maybe even Hart—said of him, He's one of the Raymonds. Doesn't even own a dog. All good woods men owned dogs. But Mason Raymond's mother kept cats, which was typical, he thought, just typical: in a world where men bred dogs, he and his mother kept cats.

You need to be recognized right to survive.

When the hunters first began to arrive, Mason Raymond's mother had come down to watch. She saw herself as hostess because the men were on her property, but she had no idea how to act with these rough men. With the first arrivals, she had gone directly up to them and asked them didn't they want to wait up at the house. No 'um, they said, looking down; it was obvious they thought she didn't know her place. Women belonged in the house, sewing and cooking and looking after children, doing the things women did. This was a man's world —guns, strong talk, dogs, killing. She didn't belong.

Only when his uncle went up to her and put his arm lightly on hers did her face brighten, and Mason Raymond felt a surge of relief. His uncle would do what was right.

Mason Raymond watched Lite untangle the lead of a dog, cuff the animal. It had done nothing Mason Raymond could see that was wrong; the blow appeared purely arbitrary, one Lite had given the dog for some tension inside Lite himself which was released only by violence.

Twenty yards away Hart was carefully going over a dog's paw, looking for bruises or cuts, small inconsequential injuries that would mean disablement, however, in a long run. He was moving the pads between his strong, calloused fingers and feeling for strangeness, speaking softly to the dog to reassure it.

All the dogs were excited because for most of them it was their first spring hunt. They had been kept tied all winter. If they were turned loose then, they would go off into the snow and hamstring deer. No decent dog man would let his dogs do that. Deer could not run in deep snow, but the dogs somehow managed; they would track and run a deer until it fell exhausted, then tear it apart. They did it not for food or fear but out of some kind of savage instinct, for pleasure, for the love of the hunt and the fulfillment of the killing. So they were kept chained during the bad winter months without being taken out. In summer they were chained, too, but they were hunted two, three, four times a week. Now, sensing that for the first time in months they were about to be free, they were impatient and edgy. The men would take them on restraints until they were well up in the woods, then turn them loose to run the spring-sluggish raccoons. Coons were destructive and costly to the farmers; come summer, they would take a cornfield apart, going down the rows, pulling an ear, stripping it, leaving it hardly gnawed while they went from row to row destroying. Like the dogs with the deer, the coons in the corn seemed to destroy for the sheer pleasure of it, not out of any real need.

Mason Raymond was impatient to be under way, but here the hunters lounged in the swiftly falling darkness, the murmur of their voices heavy on the cold spring air, the dogs whimpering to be off, impatient as he was to get going, but the hunters just stood there, lounging, laughing, loath, it seemed, to start off. Some of the older dogs had given up. They were lying down with their tongues hanging out, storing up their energy instead of running around senselessly like the younger, inexperienced ones.

It was suddenly black. Lanterns were ignited and in the narrow circle of men and dogs there was a flickering, eerie light that touched the faces of the men with strange shadows, making them look ruthless and dangerous.

"Lite ain't no better than the rest of us, no matter what airs he tries to put on," Hart was saying to Mason Raymond's uncle. "And there's many who say he ain't so good, and if facts prove anythin', they verify that. Because when that bear come out of the woods he run, that's what he done, he dropped his gun and run, and the dog had that critter cornered, wasn't nuthin' he couldda done to mark Lite, but he wasn't takin' no chances, he hightailed it over the hills and we never did catch sight of him 'til we brung the meat in and set up the fire. I always said it was only hunger brung him in at all."

Mason Raymond felt he would have been seized by the same blind panic as Lite, and now, standing next to Worth Hart and measuring himself against Worth's standards, he felt dread, for the thing a man could never know until the moment of trial and testing was whether he would stand or run. His uncle was always saying there were two kinds of men in this world, those who fought and those who fled, but Mason Raymond believed Cobus Buttes made this differentiation because of the war. There were other ways, at least he hoped there were, of separating and segregating men. And Cobus Buttes, Mason Raymond knew, never favored just fighting for no real

reason. Maybe there'd be good reasons for running sometimes; yes, of course there would be: there were always good
reasons for almost anything, even killing.

The older dogs were getting up, stretching; they sniffed
the air and looked up into their masters' faces expectantly,
but they did not shriek and bound; when the time came,
they would go. There was something comforting to Mason
Raymond in the fatalism of their feelings. Surely they had
seen enough of their own injured and dead to have some
sensation of premonition. Or didn't animals have enough insight to understand that the future always ended in death.
And did this inability to visualize an ultimate end give them
a peace of mind and a faith of heart that men lacked? Was it
possible that even though the dogs "knew" that other dogs
were maimed, eviscerated, torn apart, broken in the mouth
of the bear or tangled into shreds by the bobcat, quilled so
severely by the porcupine that some of them died, even
clawed and scarred by the coons, they could not "imagine"
as men could and thus could not envision such a thing happening to them? They would live forever and go scot free.
He supposed this was a "school" thought, but it was one
Morphis might even countenance if not "daydreamed." But
Mason Raymond didn't care about school or Morphis right
now—only the dogs, the night, and, he admitted, Maybe it's
selfish, but still, myself.

The lanterns that made the circle a magic ring of light, of
safety, gave the dogs' faces that same look of timelessness that
the hunters' faces had, of belonging to a savage, long-ago
time, creatures from a primitive world he knew nothing about.
The sputtering lanterns, the growling or restless dogs, the
hard-faced hunters—an old man, wise in face, bent over in the
road drawing a map, pointing, assigning positions, deciding
which dogs should run where, who would go with whom—
made Mason Raymond think of war councils long ago,
of ancient chieftains partitioning off groups of men to go
into battle. He pictured fat Morphis at his cluttered desk,
leaning forward. "That was a strange set of lines you
chose to examine," he had said, referring to a composition
he assigned: to choose some lines from *The Iliad* and

examine them in terms of the whole epic.

The lines Mason Raymond had picked were,

> *Then Jove again the Trojan courage fir'd,*
> *And backward to the ditch they forc'd the Greeks.*
> *Proud of his prowess, Hector led them on . . .*

Haltingly Mason Raymond had explained: the terrible delusion and violence of the story; the struggle was not physical so much as spiritual, in Achilles' soul, in Hector's, Hector the Hero, who *knew* he could not win because of that primal law his brother had broken, the fundamental law of hospitality which must be avenged and which doomed the Trojans to defeat, but who fought on because he was Hector, Hector the Hero; it was Hector people loved, not Achilles, and Hector had to die . . . and yet there he was, *proud* in his strength; the essence of all that was wrong with war and men and all that was right in the whole Greek understanding of pride and excessive arrogance, *hubris,* was in that line . . . and still, Mason Raymond saw from the expression on Morphis' face, he hadn't explained how he felt well enough so that Morphis could grasp that he was saying that Hector, who was better than Achilles, was doomed, but that for a moment he had had his golden hour. Maybe that was the way it was with all men, doomed but for an hour, and that was the essence of tragedy as he saw it, just as at this moment he was certain that no number of words could convey to anyone what he saw as he looked down into the lamplight at the old man bent forward scrabbling with a stick in the dust: the tendons of both feet, Hector's feet, were in those hastily scribbled lines, and in his mind Mason Raymond saw Achilles dragging the body behind his chariot and the dogs following, ready to lick the blood from the mangled body.

He stood on the periphery of the group of hunters and waited to hear his name called. He was pretty sure he would not be assigned to his uncle; kith and kin couldn't teach one another the way strangers could. He had heard that saying all his life, beginning with his great-grandfather, Old Mason Mowatt Raymond, trying to teach him to ride a horse and finally

giving up in exasperation, getting Cobus Buttes to come down
and give a hand, and Cobus Buttes hadn't had any success
either. He'd said, "Kith and kin don't teach their own." His
great-grandfather had pursed his lips, nodding. "Man forgets
sometimes—in his eagerness."

"You git an outsider in, he's gotta pay attention and mind,
but with family there's always an argument. Boys don't usually
lissen to their old man, don't think he knows nuthin'."

Later, when he was older, he'd asked his mother why John
Buttes could get on so well learning from his father if kith and
kin couldn't teach their own. "Cobus sent him down to Worth
for the fundamentals," she said cryptically, "and after he was
grounded, he was willing to listen to some sense."

Mason Raymond just hoped he would be sent with Worth
and not Lite; it wasn't just that he disliked Lite, that he didn't
trust him—it was even more that he felt luck was on the side
of Hart. Any man who could be struck down with a hoe that
way and get through it had to have luck.

He would not carry a gun. He might hold cartridges and
possibly a lantern at the moment of the kill, and along the way
he would help keep track of the dogs, one of those who circled
to keep them within earshot, but his time to shoot and be in
on the kill would come later. He had first to learn the different
sounds of the dogs' baying—when they were on the scent,
when they were on the trail, and finally when they treed. Each
part of the chase called for a different sound in the dogs'
voices, and a good hunter could distinguish each easily. He
had to know, too, when the dogs had treed a coon and
when they had got a cat. The bob would rest and then take
off and run again. It was a powerful runner for a mile, but
it winded fast because it had small lungs; then it would
climb and rest and as soon as its lungs were cleared it would
jump and change trees, fly down and begin to run again.
An experienced cat could run the hounds all night and
they would never catch it. They would come home spent
and shamed; it was bad for a good dog to feel that way. It
took the fiber out of him, Hart said. Mason Raymond had
heard this said before, as a "summer boy," too young and

too much a Raymond to be invited then to hunt.

The young dogs—the ones who were on their first hunt—needed a baptism of blood, Hart said; when they tasted blood and were given a sense of triumph in the chase, the catch, and the kill, they would make good dogs; but if something went wrong—if they never saw the connection between the chase, the treeing, and the coon, if the men took all the coons and didn't give any to the dogs, for instance—then they lost interest, there was nothing in it for them. Or if they chased too many cats and got discouraged too soon, they would give up because they couldn't feel the sense of all that running and no reward. Too much effort without reward exhausted them and too little robbed them of a feeling of satisfaction; there had to be a careful balance of effort expended and reward received.

So it was important for the young dogs to get the proper initiation. When they were older and more experienced, they would become leaders; that is, if they showed a gift for their calling. Similarly, if he were able to pass his tests with courage and skill, he would one day be a respected hunter like Worth, like his uncle; he would carry a gun and kill.

Nobody really, he knew, expected much of him. The Raymonds were money people, buyers and sellers; and his father, though a Buttes, was not one like his own father and grandfather, Guthrie and Odder, had done that thing that no real woods man would ever do. The hunters would be watching him out of the corners of their eyes for defects, for fear, for laziness, for cowardice. To prove himself the same as everyone else he would have to be better than all.

He had not been brought up with the easy familiarity with brutal or even senseless violence of these men. He had been with his mother first and then at the Academy in Albany with Morphis who, if anything, was gentler even than his mother, a man whose body had not been fashioned for hard use; its soft flesh belonged to blackboards and books . . .

Of man's First Disobedience, and the Fruit
Of that Forbidden Tree, whose mortal taste
Brought Death into the World, and all our woe,

he had forgotten a line—or lines—but he remembered quite clearly,

Sing Heav'nly Muse . . .

Morphis' voice singing, the whole class, Mason Raymond too, embarrassed over the intensity of his emotion; and yet some of that intensity must have registered, for now he unaccountably remembered those lines here in the wild lantern light of the wilderness and thought of Morphis and recognized, too, the tremendous debt he owed Morphis, whose patience and skill in nudging Mason Raymond's brain toward intelligence had been careful, crafty, and caring. Many of Morphis' words, his thoughts, his hopes and despairs, were engraved on Mason Raymond's mind. He respected Morphis, looked up to him— but he didn't want to be like him: just as he loved his mother, but could resent her at the same time; she was put together lopsided in some way he couldn't put his finger on, and that imbalance had ruined her whole life.

His mother—who was able to stand straight as a ramrod in front of his father's casket—covered her ears at stories like Worth Hart's being hit over the head with a hoe by a backward boy he'd tried to help, she shut her eyes to the fact that there wasn't a year that went by that some small, defective skeleton wasn't dug up in the woods around the Landing, a newly born child that had not been quite right and whose parents had taken it out, like primitive people of ancient times, to let it die because it would never be able to live a normal life. Was there some kind of distinction between mercy and murder in leaving an infant exposed instead of killing it yourself? But whatever it was, why couldn't his mother face its existence? Things you didn't want to exist in the world didn't go away just because you refused to accept their existence.

The Landing had churches now, and schools, and a few big, fancy houses; there were proper marriages and baptisms and all the rest of the ceremonies of a civilized people, but still it was a place where roots went deep into the native soil and where the original settlers counted their inheritance out of the woods and the earth rather than from the cash register.

Mason Raymond knew Landing people talked about his mother and him, using the worst of all possible gibes they could muster—"summer people." No one, he was certain, ever said of him, "He's a Buttes, you know." Marriage had made his father a Raymond; it had made him a Raymond too —perhaps because his father had never been a true Buttes, not the way his Uncle Cobus was. Families threw out opposites all the time, and here was a distinction, a separation in men Mason Raymond made for himself: the courageous ones and the cowards. He belonged to the soft side of a strong family; there it was, an isolating element in his life, and he stood isolated, watching the men gather together dogs, guns, lanterns, gun powder, fresh wicks, water. On the long chase throats closed up. A man wanted water more than anything else in the world, his uncle had said, so you be sure and bring you that fancy canteen your Ma's got. His uncle carried one he had had in the war. A lot of the men did. The Landing had been very patriotic; there were a lot of crosses next to the names that the town had put up on the War Memorial they had just got around to having constructed, though it was nearly five years since the end of the war and life had settled back to normal. Them days, his aunt said, we made do with blue milk and Indian meal.

"You go with Worth," his uncle said. Somehow his uncle understood his longings, his shyness, his inadequacies, and forgave him what he wouldn't have forgiven in his own three sons. Because of my background, Mason Raymond thought. He thinks I can't help how I am.

He asked Worth if he could carry his gun. It was an offer of true service as well as a symbolic acceptance of his role as vassal; Hart was famous for his absent-mindedness. On the hunt he would get hot and discard his shirt on a tree; there it would hang until it rotted and fell away; his lost lanterns were said to be capable of lighting the way from the Landing to the Vermont border; he counted four guns strayed somewhere in the hills, and countless scarves, bolts of rope, sweaters, hats, shells, penknives, even a hatchet and a pair of eyeglasses. The glasses had fallen into a snowbank when Hart, on a chase, had slipped and risen and run on, too bent on catching up to stop and paw around for his spectacles. I bought me another pair off one of them travelin' men, and they're better than the ones the doc down to the Falls made up special. Worth wore these on bailing twine around his neck so that he could keep count of them. He lost dogs and he even got himself lost once in a while, but there was no one more single-minded about what he wanted: he just wanted to hunt, with the best dogs in the county, all kinds of hunting. Ain't nuthin' smarter than a coon, he would say, shaking his head in admiration, and ain't nuthin' stronger than bear. You need *real* dogs to hunt them two.

I can trace my dogs back twenty generations, Worth would say. My Daddy and Granddaddy was as keen on the breedin' as I am and they kept records the same as I do. Ain't a dog on my place I can't tell you back twenty generations where he come from and how he's like to do. Ain't many men kin say that.

And ain't many men, his wife Mabel would say, can say they neglected everythin' else to devote their *whole* lives to dogs.

Yet they never quarreled, Hart and his beautiful wife who still looked like a young girl in the face, though her body was strong and stout as a man's. Worth had set eyes on her when she was thirteen. I wanted her even more than I ever wanted me a dog, he would say, don't know what that woman ever done to deserve me. The things she's put up with . . .

"You carry some of these, too, boy," Hart said, holding out a handful of homemade cases for shells.

The first hunters were already moving across the cornfield, heading for the woods where the brush grew seven, eight feet high and made a forest of thick stalks and spiny leaves under the vast trees overhead. Hart's dogs were circling him excitedly, but he wasn't paying attention to them; he was looking for something. Mason Raymond waited impatiently, looking at the procession of men and dogs moving out, swallowed up by darkness, the dogs circling and looking for scent. As he stood there, Hart fumbling in his overall pockets, the first trail cry went up, a lone, frantic yipping; a howl followed; the chase had started and Mason Raymond was still standing, stranded, waiting.

"Don't git excited," Hart said, emptying out his pockets.

"We got plenty of time. Go on, Drum, go, girl. By the time they find that coon Brownie'll be right with them. Go on, Brownie, go on, Drum. And you and me'll be there, too. Dang it anyway, where's that tobaccy?"

It was a missing item Mason Raymond couldn't supply. He wanted to suggest that Worth borrow some later on. He and Hart were the only ones left, but it wasn't his place to make such a suggestion. He stood, impatient and irritated, while the old hunter carefully and precisely laid out the contents of his pockets and went over them, searching for his missing plug. "Maybe it was in my coat," he said and went back toward the tree where he'd hung his jacket. "Here it is," he cried triumphantly, "Come on, son, let's git goin'," and he began to run across the mud flats, Mason Raymond trying to keep up with him, the double-barreled shotgun awkward in his hands and, without a lantern, the muddy field slippery and uncertain. Worth, ahead of him with a lantern, was sprinting, his overalls flapping as he galloped into the darkness; finally his light vanished; Mason Raymond was left running in blackness, the gun banging his ribs, the sound of the hysterical dogs in his ears, the world swallowed up in darkness—it was too early for moonlight—a sense of futility flooding through him. He would never catch Hart. The hunt would go on without him; at daybreak when the thin line of men and dogs straggled back he would be waiting, a sorry-looking figure of fun lolling in the same mudfield in which the run had begun. After such a performance, Hart and his uncle Cobus would wash their hands of him.

The prospect of another year at the (at this moment) effete academy in Albany where he suffered through a matriculation that seemed (again at this moment) geared to finishing off girls in needlepoint and piano, instead of preparing a boy for hunting in the woods, agonized him. He had this term off because of his father's death; his father's death, terrible as it had been, had at least given him a respite from the frustration he felt in the conflict between wanting to find out about life on his own and knowing there had been others who had gone beyond what he'd ever experience and who had come back from those distances to record what they'd felt. In books you lived with an intensity you often lacked in life. But it was second-hand living. At fifteen Mason Raymond wanted to do his own living; he didn't want to *read* about life.

He plunged on, stumbling through the darkness, tripping, but determined, God help him, to catch up. Suddenly he emerged into a small, open field. Hart was standing with the lantern, laughing. "Like a regular cow in corn," he said. "Couldda heared you for miles. They over this way, son."

Mason Raymond heard the hounds thrashing and jumping. Their baying was like a loud bellows, in out, in out; he began to babble in his excitement, but Worth was paying no attention, the lantern swinging back and forth; "We're comin', Brownie, hold 'er, girl, we're comin'."

Mason Raymond wanted to weep with gratitude when he saw the first dog, he was that happy. "Well, boys, we got ourselves one. Good girl, Brownie, good girl. Where the tarn'tion's Drum? Jest runnin' hisself ragged lookin' for rabbits," Hart said disgustedly. "Do it every time. Brownie here run rabbits her first year like to kill a normal dog. Run 'em day and night, never seen anythin' like it. Terrible, jest terrible, but when she treed her first coon, she weren't never the fool again. She never even glanced at rabbits no more. Them young dogs git in on a kill, it has a serious effect on their outlook."

Shots were going off during this recitation, men firing pell-mell into the huge pine in hope of hitting the coon, perhaps for the pure joy of firing. Worth was already hitching up his overalls; climbing was one of his specialities; he would never have let it be noised about that he was acting old and tuckered-out at a mere sixty-one.

Mason Raymond hung onto the gun; it had to be held tightly because, like everything else Hart owned, it had a tendency to come apart. Old, worn-out, make-shift, or lost. That old coot's two-thirds dog, Mason Raymond's uncle said, but I'm one-half horse, so we git on good.

Only the feet—hugging bark, scurrying up as if they had a life of their own—remained vaguely in view, the blurry essence of pine and the trembling motions of a man moving, indistinct in the patchy night. The darkness, Mason Raymond saw, came in bits and pieces, black here, gray there, a rustle of brown and glistening eyes where the dogs were caught momentarily leaping, a slant of lantern light off a white face, the burnished, metallic stock of a gun. It was foolish to talk of darkness; the night was made up of many colors and textures and he trembled at the recognition that he might one day learn his way, half-blind, through such patterns of blackness.

"I've spotted him, boys, I've spotted him. And, oh my lord, he's a big 'un, a big granddaddy of a coon, must weigh a quarter of a hundred, oh you mother . . . would you were that old bugger Cassius down in the Hollow . . ."

"Here he comes, boys, I'm shakin' him out . . ."

The dogs were panting and yelping. They knew what that vibration in the tree signified. A moment later the limbs gave an awful groan as the coon let go of his hold and came crashing down. There was a thud. Something ran across Mason Raymond's leg; then the dogs toppled him.

He lay winded, unable to rise, a ribbon of laughter unwinding out of the darkness and entangling him so that he felt chained to the earth, but even if he had been able to get up, shame would have held him tied down. Lite was laughing so hard that he was sputtering. "If that don't beat anythin' I ever seen," he kept saying over and over, slapping his thigh, clutching at his stomach, laughing himself gut-sick. "Coon run right over him and he never even knowed what took him."

Mason Raymond took the hand held out to him—his uncle's —and tried to pull himself up, smiling, as if he, too, appreciated the joke on the greenhorn. "You been 'nitiated sure enough," his uncle said, hitting him on the back. "Hart," he shouted up into the parting branches where Worth was backing down, cussing his run of luck, "you stick close to this boy, you ain't gonna have no trouble trackin' coons."

"Smartest critters there is," Hart said disgustedly. "If they ain't doublin' back on their tracks, they's disappearin' in hollow holes or givin' us the slip some fool way. My gun in one piece?"

Mason Raymond didn't even *have* his gun.

They didn't get the second coon—it holed—or the third, which went to water and lost the dogs. Mason Raymond was beginning to breathe a little more easily: the kill had been the one part of the hunt he was dreading, nothing in him able to conceive of any moment he would ever want the raccoon torn apart by the dogs or laid open by the bullets from the hunters' guns—there was something too human about a coon, something too close to himself in the clever hands and curious, alert eyes—but as one after another of the raccoons on the hunt began to give them the slip, Mason Raymond found his feelings beginning to alter. He began to wish they would get one. Apparently the urge to kill existed, even in the soft, city body of a boy who read *The Iliad* and *The Odyssey* by candlelight down at the Academy, hidden behind a closet door, experiencing his hardships and tests of courage in the exploits of others, and that urge to kill the wild creatures of the woods, the urge (perhaps, who was to know?) to stalk the human enemy and bring him down stealthily, secretly, tortuously, away from the eyes of others so that he was completely at his mercy; the urge to kill the oppressor (those who scorned him behind his back—Lite, yes, especially Lite, whom he saw clearly in his mind's eye bent double with laughter, saying, "If that don't beat . . ."), and his cousin, Young John Buttes (it was funny how many epithets people at the Landing carried, *Old* Eben Stuart, people always said, and *Young* John Buttes, and Cobus, Who Went to War; he wondered what they called him behind his back; yes, he knew; "summer boy"), his cousin standing always, as he had tonight, with the men, though he was three years younger than Mason Raymond, standing, smiling arrogantly, as if to say, "You ain't nuthin' more than a baby"—the desire for death always there, inside every single human being, not supplicating his own death of course, but someone else's, waiting there in the secret center of the heart, confident in the waiting, that after the tenderness and gentleness and mercy there would come the triumphant, primitive moment of the kill, when the blood raged; and no matter how anyone, even he, Mason Raymond Buttes, fought against this urge, this need for maiming and mutilating and killing, this insatiable burning for blood, fought and suppressed and denied, it had to surface because there was almost something fundamental in killing, in death, in violence; and to be a man, Mason Raymond thought, maybe a boy had to learn to kill, and he wasn't sure he could do it, but who knew? because at this moment he was feeling something he would have never believed himself capable of experiencing: willing death on something defenseless, a feeling hot, buoyant with passion, a sense of the coming purification of his first bloodletting.

He was at one with Hart muttering that the young dogs would be put off, *ruined,* if they didn't get a taste of coon soon; he seconded his uncle's view, expressed a moment before, that they weren't traipsing around the woods to let a lot of coons git away; he sympathized with the impatient men peeling away from the pack (including his young cousin, John, calling over to his father this was a waste of time, he was going on back), men trudging back home empty-handed after the first hunt of the season; but he did not hold with Lite, cursing breathily, that the whole thing was Hart's fault—he had shook that first coon in the wrong direction and got the whole hunt off on the wrong start and any fool knew once a hunt went bad it had only one way to go from then on, downhill. Lettin' boys in, Lite said disgustedly, but Mason Raymond noted he stayed clear of his uncle or Hart as he muttered. It was only he who was supposed to hear—*he* couldn't do anything.

Now only a small score of the original pack of hunters remained, though Lite's dogs kept with them, especially his lead dog, Lead, the big redbone, padding after Mason Raymond disconsolately while its owner muttered under his breath he wasn't gonna hunt with no beginners agin, it was jest this kind of foolishness you could expect out of city people.

Hart pulled up short. "Lissen!" he commanded.

They stopped, scarcely breathing. Far away, the voices of dogs sounded.

"They got one treed."

The remaining men began to fan out, though the going was rougher than it had been all night, a swamp and slips of stones underfoot and the fetid stench of dead and dying things in the air: all around the sense of earth oozing, the life being sucked under, going down, gasping, the skeletons of trapped life under their feet as they slipped off stones and sank in the soft, sucking mud; yet neither Hart nor his uncle took any notice; they had cut off from the main group and were traveling like men possessed, they even looked diabolical in splatters of lantern light, their faces blackened, eyes red-rimmed, most of all that passionate, intent look on their faces that blocked out everything else except the one instinct to trap and kill; the moaning of the dogs in the distance echoed in the rasping breath of the men, in the crunch and crackle of bushes and trees being parted and broken, in the slip-slap sounds of feet as they slid from the rocks into the mud, until suddenly in that maddened tracking Hart stopped abruptly. "They've doubled back. That ain't no coon they's on, it's cat."

A shiver went up Mason Raymond's spine. He didn't know why—bobcats weren't that dangerous; for a fact, they were far more afraid of a man than he was of them—but he was remembering an incident years before when he was eight or nine and had been out berrying in the patch in back of the house and a slight rustle had sounded to one side of him. He had thought nothing of it, assuming it came from one of his mother's fancy Persians playing in the long grass. If his mother didn't like dogs, there wasn't much she wouldn't do for a cat.

Mason Raymond had gone on filling his pail—only half-filling it, he had been busier popping berries into his own mouth than the mouth of the pail—when the grass parted and bright, gleaming, yellow eyes caught his. The two of them, boy and bobcat, had stood motionless for what seemed to Mason Raymond a moment stilled out of all time; then the bobcat had made a funny noise in its throat, not its cry, which was said to be like a woman's scream; not a growl, which Mason Raymond would have immediately identified; just this small warning, low and muted, as if it were a sound the animal had conjured up specifically for Mason Raymond, a warning of some terrible moment waiting for him in the future when the woods would claim him because he was an ignorant, un-trained boy who presumed to trespass where he had no busi-ness—even if his family had a big house up here—no business at all because he was a weakling come tramping into territory that didn't want him and wouldn't have him and if he insisted on coming would see to it that he was punished; you didn't transgress where you weren't wanted unless you were strong, and if ever, those yellow eyes seemed to say, there was a boy who was weak and worthless, here is one. All this, in a flash, in scarcely one beating of his heart, Mason Raymond remem-bered when Hart cried out, "It's cat."

"Dad rat it. That cat'll run them damn dogs all night long, won't git off its tail one minute and won't never git it neither, that's the end of our hunt."

Mason Raymond's uncle said nothing. He was leaning against a fallen tree whistling softly, low in the throat, like a man who has nothing to do except pleasure himself on a hot, sunny afternoon, standing there looking over his fields, sur-veying all that was his and pleased; yes, it was fine fields stretched in front of him, and here they stood in the midst of this stinking swamp, in patched blackness, a lantern smoking and hissing, the glint of guns and the feel of fatigue like some kind of sentence on fools who went out to track down the woods' own. "Where you reckon we at?" he said to Hart.

Hart, cursing, didn't bother to answer; he was making an-gry, jerking movements with his hands against his suspenders, punishing the suspenders for the dogs' foolishness. When he had worked out his anger, he said, "Coswell Swamp some-where."

"Yes, but where?"

"Up back. Jest where, I couldn't say. Been followin' those damn fool dogs so long I didn't keep track."

"We wouldn't want to go east."

"No, we wouldn't want to do that for sure."

Something in their tone—*why* wouldn't they want to go east?

"Best mabbe not to backtrack neither."

Hart, nodding in the lantern light, looked worried. "No, wouldn't want to do that for certain." He saw Mason Raymond watching him. "This here swamp's like my thumb," he said, holding up one scarred thumb, sideways, so that Mason Raymond saw the cracked, blackened nail, "the Coswell woods is horseshoe shaped, you come off one edge of the horseshoe, you come into swamp, and you come off the other edge, you come into swamp, and the thin' is that swamp is more like bog, bad bog, while the part we jest went through is, well, jest swamp, but the rest is somethin' you want to stay away from. Reckon we ought to wait out until light, Cob?" he asked.

"Ain't the best place in the world to lie out."

"No, but it ain't the best place to walk 'round in the dark neither. You got the same thirst I do? Feel like my mouth's fell out. Can't drink none of this water though, that's for sure. What you reckon we oughtta do?"

"If we was to find the creek," his uncle mused, "and follow that south we could walk our way out easy."

"Ain't easy to come on in the dark though."

"I got my canteen," Mason Raymond said. He felt proud, like a savior of sorts.

The two men laughed, then set to drinking.

"I won't badger your Ma no more about her fancy gadgets," Mason Raymond's uncle said. "And that's a promise."

The sound of the dogs was growing weaker and weaker; the three stood in the midst of the swamp gazing into the darkness without speaking. Mason Raymond was so tired that he didn't care what they decided to do; he would curl up and sleep (easy) or he would walk (numbly) on. He didn't even want a drink of water. It seemed to him crazy that a couple of woodsmen could go and get themselves lost. Hart said apologetically, "Jest wasn't watchin', got to runnin' without thinkin'."

His uncle laughed. "Wouldn't be the first time—for neither of us."

"You want to walk on, Cob?"

"I do and I don't." He took out a braid of tobacco and handed it across to Worth who, grunting thanks, took it and pulled out a twist with his mouth. After a second's hesitation, he passed it to Mason Raymond. Mason Raymond had never chewed tobacco in his life, but up until this night there were a lot of things he had never done—including getting lost in the woods; he took one braid of tobacco and yanked off the end. The taste was sharp and acrid, like something bad had happened to his mouth; but presently his numbness began to lift a little, as if the tobacco were some kind of strange agent that worked in his blood giving it energy and confidence. "Why not walk on?" he heard himself asking.

"You go down in that bog—" Hart left the sentence unfinished; there was no need to finish it.

"Still, we can't have missed the creek by much," his uncle said. "Don't seem right to lay out while everyone else goes back."

"Too much pride undo-es many a man."

"Takes one to know one." The two men began to laugh. They sat down. The decision had been made.

The ground was wet with rotten leaves and the smell in the darkness was of rancid, decaying leaves. These had been a long time dying and they would be a lot longer decaying; now they were smelling their worst. Mason Raymond sat cross-legged with the plug of tobacco stored in his cheek and tried to sleep, Indian fashion, sitting the way his uncle did. His uncle was one-quarter Indian, but he looked pure Iroquois, sitting humped up like that. He had a deep brown face, not tanned the way the sun turned the skin dark, but built-in brown, Indian brown, and he had black hair and black eyes, almost expressionless, but they could change color. When he got angry, for instance, they went milky, almost white, as if the color had drained out of them. (*Zeus vouchsafed him glory,* Mason Raymond heard Morphis reading inside his head. If Morphis could only see him now—)

He shifted his weight, trying to find a place where his bones wouldn't have such a hard time of it. The ground gave a groan, sucking with a thousand lips of mud that wanted to take him in; he was suddenly frightened, knowing now why his uncle and Hart had a healthy respect for the swamp; it was the kind of mud that swallowed big things, bogs that took in and buried that part of the world that dared venture into them. To stumble into a place like that would be fatal, and as well as his uncle and Hart knew the woods there was enough margin of error to make plodding on dangerous. Possibly if they had been alone they might have attempted it, but with a young boy —it even came down, he thought, to more than kin and kindness, it was a matter of responsibility, the responsibility of the old to the young. If you were lost and you had done something foolish, you tried to correct it in the wisest manner possible, even if that meant showing up your own foolishness. That was what they had been bantering about when they had said *Too much pride undo-es a man* and *Takes one to know one.*

He was bitterly cold, the last damp, seeping cold of winter coming up out of the April ground and moving itself into his bones. His teeth banged together, he shivered, his throat felt raw. He glanced across at his uncle, curled into a ball. Worth was stamping about trying, he said, to raise the sugar in his blood, an odd concept, but no odder, Mason Raymond considered after a moment, than some of the other ideas Worth held. He decided to try it himself; nothing could be worse than squatting numb and feckless on this frigid ground.

His clothes gave off steam as he rose; a white plume of frost escaped his mouth. How long would it be before light? Hours, he figured, hours of freezing. He and Worth were slamming about, going back and forth past his uncle, who ignored them, head tucked down into his arms (like a bird or an animal, Mason Raymond thought), his body crouched in on itself. Presently he snored. How can he *sleep?* Mason Raymond asked himself.

Out there within a few feet of them lay a strange, perilous world. He knew nothing, nothing—he was less than no help; he was a hindrance. It was he who in his excitement had left Hart's gun somewhere in the woods and only blind luck had given it back, a hunter stumbling over the barrel in the dark, exclaiming, "What the—," flashing his lantern and crying out, "For God's sake, here's someone's *gun.*"

Hart had gone and got it as if its loss were another proof of *his* absent-mindedness. He had not reproached Mason Raymond for his carelessness nor commented on it; more than that, he had concealed it from the others. Shame (always shame, Mason Raymond thought) had kept Mason Raymond quiet; now he turned to Hart and said, "You didn't say anything about the gun."

"Can't have the kettle callin' the pot black. Give half my belongin's to these woods one time or another."

"But it was such a dumb thing to do."

"Excitement gits you, you don't always think too far ahead. Look at the predicament I got us in here runnin' loose in my excitement."

He glanced over at Hart now, hands crisscrossed and tucked into his armpits for warmth, famous for his failures, his forgetfulness, his crazy obsession for keeping things and his crackpot schemes for making money. Yet he was respected. He met life head-on; long ago he had come to terms with what he was, even the worst and weakest of it, acknowledged and accepted and stopped bothering over the inadequacies. How had he done that?

Nor was Hart's respect the kind given his uncle, hunched in Indian fashion, solid as stone, oblivious to discomfort, a man who ignored as much as possible gross physical intrusions on his life—hard from years in the woods lumbering, tough from fighting in the war, yes, that was true; but what was truer was that he had been born with a sternness and discipline and strength his own twin, Mason Raymond's father, lacked: some people seemingly were born with iron in them, some not. He doesn't ask about himself, Mason Raymond thought, he sees his life as a series of duties, not rights. Both he and Worth—do what you should, no matter how difficult, no matter how dislocating, do it—because you should—while I keep thinking about what I want, what rights I ought to have, about prerogatives instead of obligations.

He stopped, pondering that basic division between the two older men and himself; the distinction, however, did not rest in age but point of view; they believed in imperatives he had not yet acknowledged.

I am a kid, he thought, disgusted. Nothing but a goddam kid leaves guns out in the middle of nowhere, so green even the coons can tell it, so cold he could hardly move his feet.

"You put out with yourself for jest misplacin' a gun?" Hart asked.

"It's more than that. It's—oh, hell, I don't know *what* it is."

"You take everythin' to heart. You take me, I'm an easy-goin' cuss, I guess. I come up on a farm with a big family. My Ma passed on afore I really knowed her, and my Pa, he went down and brought Laura back. She was a young, pretty thing, didn't even know how to milk and egg. Walk, boy, walk. That'll keep you warm."

They commenced tramping, Hart talking right on. "She used to cry all the time. My Pa set a lot of store by her and he got us young 'uns out helpin', even the ones could barely toddle done somethin'. The littlest could spy out eggs. We was all so busy we never had time to ponder much. I growed workin' and gittin' praised from Laura for what I done right and when what I done wasn't right she didn't say nuthin' 'cause I 'spect she knew she couldn't adone it no better herself. That way I grew up easy with myself, and I ain't never changed.

"The way I figure, you got one time 'round, one and one only, you ain't put here to make mistakes the first time and alter them to profit the second. It's like a good dog. He runs to git the game. Sometimes he gits off the track and sometimes he does dang fool things like run the wrong critter, but the point is he's runnin', he's tryin'. If you keep at him all the time scoldin' him over the faults, he's gonna git discouraged and give up. But if you praise him when he's done good, he's likely gonna try harder. Trainin' a boy ain't much different than trainin' a dog, in principle leastwise. Dogs cost less, a point in their favor, but boys last longer—if they don't freeze to death on some damn fool expedition like this.

"Ain't your uncle a specimen though, sleep right out in the open like this and think nuthin' of it. Don't think about the cold, boy, jest keep movin'; don't let it settle down on you . . . You take me, I'm jest the opposite of Cob Buttes. Without my dogs I wouldn't git up in the mornin'. What'dda be the use? Jest scrapin' out a livin' workin' yourself to the bone every day at the same old wearyin' thin's, all the thin's that go wrong, who'd want to face all them day after day? But when I git to feelin' down and lie around and don't put myself out none, Mabel, she says, 'Worth, Worth, it's time to git yourself up,' and I don't take to the idea none, but I say to myself, 'Git goin', old man, there's still time for you to git yourself down to Carolina and git yourself another one of them bear dogs.' Then I git on my feet and go trampin' out to the barn and tell myself, 'Might as well git two as one this time in case somethin' happens the way it did last time, I got me a replacement.' You take me, I don't do nuthin' unless it's to *git* somethin' I think I'm gonna need. But that's wrong, because you don't never know what you're gonna need in the future.''

Mason Raymond stumbled, righted himself; his frozen feet clanked against the ground as he forced them forward.

''I was dead set against schoolin' and it's only now I realize how much there is to it. I don't write too good because I didn't apply myself when I shouldda, but I'm glad I got what little I did, even if it was by force, because I wouldn't be able to keep no papers, no records, if I hadn't been force-fed the learnin' I got. And now I see: that's what everythin's about, writin' and re-viewin' thin's.''

Mason thought, but didn't want to break into Hart's reminiscing, that if Hart was right, then some force must go into raising a boy, not just the praise Hart's Pa and Laura had used. Force came into it, too.

''One way or t'other people never disciplines theirselves the way they ought. Oh my God, we can't all huddle up all our lives, like your uncle's huddled up there and shrunk down inside. Git up, Cob,'' he shouted. ''You may be part Indian and can hold off this cold, but this boy and I are perishin'. We got to move on before we git to the point we can't. Cob—Cob, you gotta git up. This boy ain't walkin' straight.''

Mason Raymond's uncle lifted his head.

''Cob, this here boy's stumblin' and fallin'. He's freezin'. I been tryin' to *talk* him straight, but it ain't no use. He's freezin' hisself right to the bone.''

Mason Raymond's uncle began to unbend. He rose slowly,

swaying a little, searching Mason Raymond out in the dark. Stars and a sliver moon were not light; yet for Mason Raymond, becoming accustomed to what dark meant, the night was no longer black, but a purplish glow through which, murkily, the shapes of trees, the figures of Hart and his uncle, stood out clearly.

"We could roll up together."

"Cob, we got to move."

"Out into that swamp?"

"Out into swamp."

Stay put and freeze or go out in that swamp and maybe be sucked up: he felt the despair of a man given two alternatives, neither of which he wants, a man with two wolves as pets who fears the fangs but cannot turn them loose in the wild because he cares about them.

His uncle put his arms around him and clasped him close. "You git on the other side, Worth, and we'll try and warm him a little between us. You're froze right through, Ray, ain't you?"

His uncle seldom used that nickname. The situation must be serious. He took inventory of his numbness, his pains. He was more numbness than sensation—frozen, he thought with horror, frost-bite and worse, frozen; but I don't feel sleepy, they say you feel sleepy and then you don't feel anything at all, you just lie down and go to sleep.

Between the two men he shook and trembled, his legs weak, his head light, a sudden vertigo that would have sent him sprawling had he not been propped up. He heard himself groan, he heard their concerned voices, though he could not make out their words; then he felt himself sinking; for a moment he thought he was being sucked up by the mud, was going down, down in darkness, the air sucked out of his lungs, in black, oozing earth; and then—brightly, with a sense of light at the far end of a tunnel, he heard voices, hands seemed to be clutching him, he felt those hands pulling him back from the blackness and out of the wood, and he tried to cry out, to say they were pulling him free, in just a minute he'd be all right, he was conscious again, and his first thought, quite lucid was, You fainted, you darn fool.

The flow was warm for a moment, then began to freeze. His crotch clothes clung to him, stiffening with cold. Had he the ability, he would have wept with humiliation; but he was too tired and spent to do more than balance slackly between the two men.

He was weak and tired and wet and cold, but what he wanted to tell them was that he hadn't given up.

They were searching for the creek (like all the Landing people, Hart called it crick). It lay, according to Hart's calculations, somewhere to the left of them, on the outer corner of the swamp, and when they found it (presuming they did) they could follow it downstream to the edge of the Raymond property, over by Old Guthrie's mill. This small swamp stream started as a trickle up in the hills and worked itself up to a size large enough to turn grindstones and mill grain, miracle enough in itself when Mason Raymond considered the muck they were thrashing about in, but truly inspiring if, as Hart promised, this thin stream could pilot them to safety.

In the meantime, having roused himself and been slapped about by the men, his circulation had again taken up functioning (if weakly) and he was able to walk (stumble would have been more accurate); down over a fall and through boggy ferns they plunged, *singing* (raised the spirit, Hart insisted), slipping, stumbling, sometimes flattened, their voices rusty but resplendent underneath the stars——

> . . . *Give your heart to Je—sus;*
> *Do not lin—ger, do not wait;*
> *Yon—der stands the o—pen gate;*
> *Enter ere it be too late;*
> *Give your heart to Je—sus.*

They sang "When the King Shall Come," "What a Friend Thou Art to Me," and "I Am the Light" before they came to a dead standstill on the edge of the great swamp. Fighting their way back over the trail they had just broken through, they tried "Make Me Willing" (unsuccessful because not even Hart could remember the words, he confessed he was no regular church-attender, a confession neither Mason Raymond nor his uncle disputed), "I Am Redeemed," and "Let the Sunshine In," repeating "Give Your Heart to Je—sus" when they cut off through a small, frozen blackberry patch (no hindrance now, winter-blighted and broken-down from the snows) and trudged up a small incline bellowing "Open Wide the Door." Then they rested.

This was appropriate, Hart theorized, because they ought to give the Lord a chance to size up how things were going with them and send down some signal to show He was on their side. Mason Raymond felt Hart's approach was perhaps a little irregular—calling the Lord "The Old Man," for instance, but he hadn't been raised on religion, or in these hills, so he left the formalities to those more familiar with them—and what Hart might have lacked in etiquette, he made up in enthusiasm. He stood on the top of the knoll and hollered that he hadn't asked that his clothes and lanterns and guns and coats be given back by the woods, but he was of a mind to be delivered up himself, he didn't want to end up hanging off the limb of some tree, forgotten out in these woods, he had that dog to git yet down in Carolina, The Old Man best not disremember.

They went down the hill on "Praise God From Whom All Blessings Flow," and kept working their way, wetly, west, Hart somewhat discouraged now and songless, Mason Raymond's uncle out ahead making trail. The singing and hiking had raised the boy's blood and, though he was light-headed, he was happy; a premonition that somehow all this would end well, good things would flow from this night, sustaining him, a presentiment confirmed an instant later by Hart, swearing instead of singing, suddenly bawling, "If I ever git out of this son-of-a-bitchin' swamp, I'm gonna git myself down to Carolina before this summer's closed, I don't care if I have to git shut of house and wife to do it. A man's got to learn all over again, it seems like, when to put first things first."

His uncle laughed. "Mabel'll have a thing or two to say about that."

Hart reassured him. "She don't care where she is so long as she's got a can big enough to cover her young pullets.

Never seen a woman so keen on chickens in my life. She'd go live in a cave if you told her it was all right to bring her hens."

"Listen," Cobus Buttes said.

Mason Raymond strained his ears. He could hear nothing but the normal night noises—wind, small animal sounds, the mud oozing—then, ever so faintly, he thought he heard a dog baying. He wasn't sure, but he was almost sure. He listened, concentrating all his power into the hearing bones in his ears, and the wind cooed, the branches cracked, a tree groaned, and then he thought (but he couldn't be sure) he heard a hound again.

"Treed, by Gawd," Hart bellowed triumphantly. "It's Brownie and she's treed and she's waitin' for us to come shake that coon loose for her. No dog's goin' in the big swamp, no dog of mine, leastwise. Lite's dog might sink in one—you can't expect an animal to have more sense than its master—but none of mine will go near bog. They *know.* We follow that voice, old Brownie'll cry us right out of this here wilderness home." He began to beat jubilantly on his thighs.

Mason Raymond watched him, awed. So far as Hart was concerned the hunt had only begun. They had done a fair job on the chase, considering how they'd gone and got lost and all, but that was only a parcel of it; you couldn't call it a proper night unless you shook out a coon for the young dogs and gave them a taste of meat. The kill was the end of it; they still had that ahead.

The swamp belonged now to memory; for a quarter of an hour they had been climbing. Hart's boots walloped the hill, punishing it for holding him back; ahead the long, beautiful bawl of his dog sounded high and clear on the cold April air.

Dawn was breaking. The great woods rose all around Mason Raymond, larger than life, larger, it seemed to him, than anything he had ever known, linked limbs and landscape in a giant nether world that would rustle and glow long after he and his had fled underground; though it seemed possible that Hart, crashing bull-like through brush, swearing and stomping and hollering, would never be driven from this place, even by death, chasing his hound and blaspheming and screaming into the rising blackness, "Jest wait, Brownie, I'm comin', it's that ding-busted swamp held me up."

"Git out of my way," he hollered at the trees, giving them belligerent blows as he thrashed past. He doesn't see this the way I do, Mason Raymond thought. To him it's something familiar, easy to get along with, as natural as his own home; it *is* his home; but to me the woods . . .

With a whoop Hart sprang out of the forest and into a clearing; a hundred yards ahead Lite and two or three men were strapping their dogs to leashes; only Hart's hounds ran free, circling, noses to the ground, looking for fresh scent. Hart had come too late; the men had taken the coon while Hart and Mason Raymond and his uncle beat their way out of the swamp.

Lite, face pearl-pale in the early morning light, a dark stubble on cheeks and chin, smiled as he hailed them, standing with his dogs straining against their ropes, bent gracefully toward Worth, stroking his chin, perched lightly on his toes, forceful and easy, smiling, smiling, "Where you been, Worth? We been treein' all night—got ourselves two fine coon, give 'em to the dogs, but your dog, she wouldn't come near. Tried to git her for you—wouldn't want her lost out here in the woods, maybe git into that swamp—" grinning, happy over misfortune, joyous in the face of others' pain.

"We miscalculated some," Hart said.

"You got stuck in the swamp, Hart?" Old Eben Stuart asked in disbelief.

"Some," Hart conceded, bending over and grasping Brownie's collar.

"Lost in the swamp, Worth Hart lost in the swamp?"

"It wasn't him, it was me," Mason Raymond blurted, wanting to take the blame, wanting to even things out. Had Hart not kept silent about the gun? Now it was his turn to do something of the same. "I'm the one. I ran on and on and then the first thing I knew I was in trouble. They—they come in to get me." It would have been a better speech if he could have remembered to say *git*.

Hart, looking up in astonishment, let the dog go. "Oh, tarn'tion," scrambling after, tripping, grabbing for the collar, missing, Mason Raymond's uncle falling on top of her, man and dog going down in the weak dawn light, a flash of fur and heavy coat in the dishwater light.

"I got her, I got her," his uncle kept saying. "I got her, I got her," but the dog was determined. She rolled over, Cobus Buttes hanging onto her, Brownie pawing in the leaves and dirt, Hart hollering, the other men laughing and slapping their sides, and suspended on the slim elegant pillar of his body, Lite, smiling, smiling.

"I reckon," he said, "this is gonna be one good year of bettin', that's what I reckon."

Hart hauled up on his dog, snapped the chain. "You always did count your blessin's afore they come in."

"You goin' to lug an ignorant boy 'round all season—"

"Leave him out of it. He ain't none of your concern. For a fact I'd ruther have him, green as he is, than some I knows, experienced though they might claim to be. There's one thing I'd swear on a stack to and that's that he wouldn't never turn tail and skedaddle when the situation tightens up. He's got *stuff* in him."

"It wasn't your dog, Hart, no need for me to expose myself for *my* dog if I don't want to."

"No, no need atall, but most men would have stuck by to see if they couldda helped; most men wouldn't have turned tail and run, scairt to death like—"

"If that dog was fool enough to go in by itself—"

"You ain't the only man in a hunt ever had a dog could go in by itself. But the point you missed, the one that's important is that a dog like that, that would go in all by itself on a bear, most men would give their lives for a dog like that. Your dog'd be alive today if you'd stood ground and fired 'stead of turnin' tail and runnin'. But you run and that blood's gone and it's as much all our loss as yours. You jest too darned thick to see that. Ain't a man 'round here wouldn't welcome the opportunity to give you what you want for a pup outta a dog like that."

Lite almost bent double laughing.

"I wouldda, too, but that's the kind of competin' and sharin' you can't understand. A man don't jest want to win, he wants

] 57 [

to win worthwhile. We couldda had the best breedin' in the whole county, maybe three, four counties, if you hadn't turned tail and run and I hadn't been hit by pride and run a dog I shouldda kept home. But it ain't no use discussin' what mightta been. You lit out, and that's that. And I lost my dog, and that's that. And what's more, I been in the swamp, and *that's* that."

"Jawin', always jawin'," Lite said, turning, yanking his dogs. "Never knew a man couldn't control his mouth the way you can't."

Hart clomped down on a log and pulled out his chewing tobacco. "And I never in all my born days seen a man with sech a square smile."

II

"*Oh, I've just been worried sick,*" his mother said, standing in the weak-tea early morning light wringing her hands, wobbling dramatically against the door jamb as if she were going under in grief and would never rise again, but just before she sank she wanted to be sure one last, dying message got through, "just worried sick, half out of my mind with worry—where *have* you been?"

"Now, Ardis," his uncle said, logical, unperturbed; a small thing like a hysterical woman wasn't going to upset *him*. "You know hunts run late."

"But it's *seven o'clock* in the morning," Mason Raymond's mother cried out to those heartless male betrayers before her who gave not a fig in fate for female sensitivity.

"You're lucky we got in this early." His uncle plopped down on the porch pulling at his boots. "It's been some night."

"Mornin', M'am," Hart said deferentially. Mabel had put fear of the female in him. Mason Raymond saw in Hart's face the same look of awe that it had held when Hart, his famous thirty-six coonskin cap turning in his hands, stood in front of his father's coffin. Hart had made none of the usual comments about how natural the body looked or how artistic the face was done up. Standing in front of the coffin, shaking his head (as his mother standing in front of him at this moment was shaking hers, bewildered, unhappy, suddenly plunged into a world not going according to the proper timetable), Hart had seen into a universe where nothing goes according to a timetable. "All of us git lost one time or another," he said now as he might have said then. Death was for Hart "getting lost." Well, why not?

"It's *seven o'clock in the morning*," Mason Raymond's mother repeated as if there were cosmic significance to that hour; she was prepared for the earth to stop turning on its axis.

Mason Raymond looked at her—a small, frail capsule which encased iron. The properties of iron were strength, hardness, rigidity. It also rusted easily in moist air and was readily attracted by a magnet. That defined his mother with exactitude, if you made him the magnet. "Rivers," she had called on Christmas Eve, *"Rivers!"* The coachman must have heard the controlled anger and outrage in her voice, probably thought he had done something to incur her wrath because he had come running, then stopped dead, staring up in horror at the swinging body. "You must cut him down," she had said imperiously, "right now. Turn away, *turn away*," she cried out to Mason Raymond. "Don't look!"

Love was an iron gate that swung shut. She was always trying to protect him, always trying to hold him back from pain: and love was the name she gave the prison she had put him in. In a minute, she'd throw her arms around his neck and *in front of Hart and his uncle*, she'd say, "Oh, you don't know how much I love you, baby. You don't know. Never leave me, promise me you'll never leave me."

His father's death, Mason Raymond realized, had made her a grasper again. She was hanging on his arm right now, clinging, asserting her right to make him miserable because she had been through so much these past weeks and because he was all she had.

"You could vittle us, Ardis," his uncle said, banging his boots against the side of the porch, making mud fly this way and that. "I'm plain tuckered out. Been walkin' most of my life. The war don't teach damn fools like me one thing. Trampin' around a swamp all night. More brawn than brains."

"Oh, Cobus, you weren't in the big swamp, were you? Not the Coswell Swamp?"

"That canteen sure come in handy, Ardis. I won't never talk against your fancy gadgets again. 'Bout saved our lives, we was perished with parchedness."

"Dadrat it, I've misplaced the tobaccy agin."

His mother had put in a whole supply at Christmas in anticipation of his father's coming; he was such a heavy smoker that he coughed constantly in the morning and he used camphor on his lips because they burned. Now she told Hart matter-of-factly, "There's some inside, on the mantel. We had it for my husband."

Nothing wasted, nothing wanted. She had expertly dispensed what she didn't want and kept what might come in handy. Rivers had carried a whole cartful of things up to his uncle—suits, men's linen, shoes, anything his father had had that Cobus, his twin, might make serve. Though they had not looked alike, the twins had been more or less the same size. No, not the same size—size meant more than shape; size had to do with breadth.

Though I wander through the valley of the shadow of death, I will fear no evil. But Mason Raymond feared all the large efforts to entrap him—love and pride and cowardice. He feared most of all ineffectiveness.

"Who's that?" his mother demanded in a voice that plainly said, I will not put up with one more thing.

That was Lite, waving something in his hand—a gun. Oh God, he'd gone and forgotten Hart's gun again.

"Oh, do have some more, Mr. Lite, please do. I'll feel insulted if you don't."

She had begun acting nice, hostessy, the minute Lite got up close, not because she was being polite, but because she liked Lite's looks (she was to say later at least ten or twelve times he was a *handsome* man, making the word *handsome* sound like the best thing you could be), and though Mason Raymond had had little experience with women, one thing he had observed:

women started acting silly and unnatural around *handsome* men. The handsome men noticed of course and then something got into them and they started acting silly and unnatural and puffy back. In a short time the whole atmosphere was charged with people acting like they were putting on performances and having trouble with their lines; he had seen the same kind of fatuous prancing down at the Academy when Morphis had taken it into his head to put on *Two Gentlemen of Verona.* A disaster of the first order. It was a crazy play to begin with to Mason Raymond's way of thinking, and God knew the Academy actors hadn't added any luster to it, nor had those sisters of students Morphis had imported for the female leads; the girls had gone to pieces opening night and forgotten all their lines, and Morphis had carried on with their mothers, trying to comfort them, the way Lite was carrying on with his mother.

Mason Raymond looked across the table at Lite, smirking, vanity-stricken by his mother's flattering attention. As he had come up the walk, his mother had said, "Oh, it's that handsome Mr. Lite," and his uncle had said, "A well-made man" in a tone Mason Raymond wasn't quite able to identify. Somehow he was sure that compliment turned to vinegar in his uncle's mouth, but his uncle's face had remained impassive.

His mother had been too caught up in her pleasure at having the handsome, well-made man to pay attention to irony; she hadn't paid attention to anything except Lite since he had arrived; glumly Mason Raymond contemplated the two yellow eyes of his eggs, saying to himself, She thinks that well-made means all right. "No, I don't want any more biscuits," he said grumpily, even though she hadn't offered him any. Why couldn't she fall all over Hart that way instead of that square-smiling son of a bitch?

She smiled. She was happy. Women were always in a better mood when handsome, well-made men were about. How could his uncle chew so complacently and talk in such a normal tone of voice, as if he couldn't see the spectacle she was making of herself or—if he saw—didn't particularly care. "Crops'll be late agin this year, late and light," he was saying to Worth. "Another of these cold, put-off springs."

"Everythin's goin' to winter. It was the war done it, all that shootin' upset the balance of things. Man got no right to tamper with nature that way."

His mother had her elbows propped up on the table—a transgression he was never permitted, "it isn't po-lite to put your elbows on the table, honey," she always reminded him —and yet here she was now resting her elbows on the table, her head bent over and cupped in her hands, her whole attention focused on Lite's mouth as it chewed first up, then down. She was watching him eat as if that was the most beautiful act she had ever seen. She wasn't eating herself. She almost never did more than pick at her food any more. For the first time it struck him how fleshy she'd gotten and how odd that was when she never seemed to eat anything much at all now, she who had once been such a big eater.

"No," she was saying, "I don't miss Albany too much—just the company and conversation sometimes. You know how it is around here," she looked at his uncle, frowning, "just crops and 'coons, that's all you ever hear." She wrinkled her nose which meant she wasn't really reproving Cobus Buttes, just making some kind of adult joke Mason Raymond couldn't find in the least funny. Anyway, he knew she'd never say anything really strong to his uncle, even to impress Lite; she set too much store by Cobus Buttes's opinion. She always had; Cobus Buttes had the strength of character Clyde Buttes had lacked. Women needed strong men to lean on, Mason Raymond supposed.

His uncle looked up from buttering his own biscuit and said, his eyes almost translucent, "Crops and coons: better'n goin' into what's goin' on out West or down South, war tore everythin' up and nuthin' bein' put back together proper and railroads ruinin' good land, crazy Congress ruinin' good men. Some thin's a man don't want to talk about, he deliberately sets his mind against thinkin' about them because he knows all the thinkin' and talkin' in the world won't change them. I done my time out in the world. Now I come back home I don't want to think about nuthin' but crops 'nd coons."

"Oh, Cobus, you're too much." She turned her eyes again on Lite, looking at him, Mason Raymond thought, as if she were saying inside her mind, Yes, he *is* a real well-turned-out man. "Tell me, Mr. Lite, is that how you see things, too?"

Lite blotted at his mouth with a napkin, raised a glass of water and sucked some in. "Those Southerners ain't goin' to give up nuthin' to their niggers unless they're made to—with the butt of a gun. The war never learn'd them nuthin'. And I can't blame them none. Niggers ain't like whites, and that's a fact."

"Well . . ." his mother said falteringly. In spite of her protestations about missing "good conversation," she became acutely uncomfortable in the face of controversy and Reconstruction was one of those subjects bound to unleash tempers. She looked helplessly at Cobus Buttes, trying to head off what she sensed was coming. Mason Raymond's uncle had passionate, unpopular views on the subject; a heated argument was coming. "He's a crank on the subject," Mason Raymond's mother often said about Cobus Buttes' views on Reconstruction, hence dismissing the validity of his arguments from her mind. Now she saw her lovely breakfast party being ruined. "But you know, Cobus, even Lincoln didn't mean for them to *vote,* and there's no sense in making such a fuss here. We don't have to worry, we don't have all those darkies, thank goodness —not that I have anything against niggers, why William, who used to work for my grandfather, was just like one of the family; but—but—well, I mean, everyone knows they're not the same." His mother was getting flushed—and also defiant. "If you lived down South, Cobus, and had those uppity niggers pushing you off the sidewalks and—"

"You don't know whether those stories are true or not, Ardis."

"What can you do with him?" she said, throwing up her hands in defeat.

Lite, seeing the situation, tried to act the man of the world. Showing off, the same as she's been doing, Mason Raymond thought. What is there makes men and women act so unnatural around one another? "Reckon there's a lot to be said on both sides. But you're certainly right, M'am, when you say we're lucky we don't have the problem up here. There's people, I bet you, make fun of places like the Landing, but we got a good life up here, it's a good, decent place to bring up young 'uns right. There's *decency* here," he repeated, laying his napkin down for emphasis and looking around. "You can't take away neither what's the backbone of this country, and that's white folk, not black."

"A lot of the backbone of this nation came from black sweat," Cobus said quietly.

Suddenly Hart started to laugh. It was so unexpected and out of place that all of them turned and stared. "You sure can't win no argument where you don't think alike," he said. "And I can't think of two people think *less* alike than Frank Lite and Cobus Buttes."

Ardis Raymond Buttes tried valiantly to pull things back together. "You must have a little more of this smoked fish," she pleaded at Lite. "It's really a specialty of the house, an old recipe that's secret," she said, smiling brightly. "We won't give it away no matter who pleads." So much for Reconstruction.

Lite took the dish and spooned a large glob of the smoked, creamed fish onto his plate. Mason Raymond hated with a blind, unreasoning hatred which burned in his chest and throat and even in his head. And when Lite said, "That's a mighty fine boy you got there, you should have seen him out there in the woods—" he glared savagely, feeling the heat of hate rising right up from his belly into his throat, sickening him. Couldn't his mother see what a square-smiling two-faced son of a bitch he was? No, of course she couldn't. Looks were everything to her, just like all women. He wouldn't have been born a woman for anything in the world.

"Yes, you've got a fine boy there, Missus Raymond," Lite said pontifically, as if what he said went on record. "Accredited hisself real well today." Lite even had the unmitigated gall to smile at Mason Raymond. "Not often someone who isn't —well, you know—brung up in these parts, can accommodate hisself so well to the woods."

"He's a real heartbreaker," Hart choked into his hand.

Slowly, oh so slowly, Cobus Buttes put down his napkin. It lay mortally wounded at the side of his plate. "I jest wish for once you'd put your money where your mouth is," he said.

"Cobus!"

"It's all right, Ardis, don't worry none, we ain't goin' to do nuthin' to upset you bad, jest that I like to see a man kind of consistent. Riles me when I have to come to terms with opposite sentiments in the same day from the same man. You weren't so full of paradises of praise a couple of hours back, you found plenty to find fault with then, it seems to me, if I recollect right, Frank Lite."

"I'm afraid I don't follow you, Cob—"

Almost no one besides Hart called Mason Raymond's uncle Cob. It was a privilege name, the one he had from his logging days years before. He went into the woods when he was the same age as I am now, Mason Raymond thought, he spent years in the woods hardening himself, learning things I'll never know; right from the beginning he set out to make himself strong and invulnerable, something I'll never be. I wouldn't even know what to do in the woods.

Lite had made an error when he tried to be familiar with his uncle, putting on airs, acting as if he were close to Cobus Buttes. "I don't know as anyone but family got a right to call me Cob," Cobus Buttes said.

"No offense meant," Lite said quickly, uncomfortably.

"If you're such an admirer of this here boy, you should be willin' to back them feelin's with a little hard cash," his uncle said.

Lite fidgeted with the heavy silverware.

"If Frank here got so much confidence in Mason Raymond's abilities, Ardis, then maybe he'd like to make a little bet on the boy—"

"Oh, Cobus, I don't want Mason involved in something like that, he isn't—"

"We won't put him up against anythin' unfair, nuthin' we don't all agree on—How'd you like to run a couple of boys on a hunt, Frank, first one that trees and brings in a coon wins the bet?"

"What kind of boys?"

"Well, this here boy," Cobus Buttes said, indicating Mason Raymond with a nod of his head. "And another boy, one maybe I chose, say my John. He's three years younger—"

"Why, he's one of the best hunters, man or boy, around!"

"Oh, I wasn't thinkin' of them runnin' right off. This boy here, he'll need a little time to git ready some. A month, say. You think his potential is so great, Frank, in a month or so he ought to be an absolute genius."

What Mason Raymond couldn't understand was why his uncle would want to set him up like this. His anger's got away from him, he thought. He isn't thinking, he's just reacting.

A gleam had come into Lite's eyes. "You sure set me up, didn't you?"

Hart leaned forward. Sparks flew out of his bright blue eyes; even his hair seemed to rise and applaud. "You always was a runnin' man," he said.

Lite gave a small exhalation, as if he were owning up that this time he would have to stand and abide. "Don't take me for no fool," Lite said angrily. "You know your boy got the best trainin' there is to git. This boy'd have no chance at all."

"Then I'll tell you what," Mason Raymond's uncle said, leaning across the table, his eyes glowing white. "We'll switch. I'll take him—" pointing at Mason Raymond—"and you take Young John. One hundred dollars says in a month this boy'll beat mine."

Hart was slapping his thigh in glee. "If you ain't the beatin'-est," he said, "if you ain't the beatin'est man alive."

Mason Raymond looked at his uncle. Money was scarce, hard cash money. Or—granted the miracle, the absolute impossibility, that maybe some crazy things happened and Mason Raymond did win—how could his uncle want to see his own son bested?

Yet his uncle, rising, putting a hand across the table to strike the wager, was a man whose face said he had had a memorably fine day to chalk up in his mind.

"No, 'course you don't see," he said later, standing on the front porch, looking down over the lake toward the Landing where smoke and bustle and noise drifted up. "And maybe John won't neither, but I'm hopin' he will. Who wins don't matter. It's a pile of money, but what it's goin' to git is worth every penny of it. You or John, it don't matter—what both of you'll git out of it can't be put down in terms of dollars and

] 67 [

cents." He went off with that, an explanation that wasn't really an explanation at all. How could he possibly believe John might not win? John was the kind that always won.

Hart, badgering his gun back together and trying to wire it up, chewing energetically on the big plug of tobacco that made a bulge in his cheek, chuckling and worrying with his gun as if there weren't a luckier man in the Landing than Worth Hart who owed his soul to the bank and his life to a place that was falling down around his ears, stopped fussing with the gun and tried to clarify. "Little John's britches has got pretty big on him this past year. He's got confidence plumb bustin' out of them. Your uncle, he don't take to that, and he don't take neither to the way you go 'round puttin' yourself down. One of you's got too much feelin' for hisself 'nd the other don't have enough. I think what he's got in mind is equalizin' those two out."

"But I can't ever learn enough in a month to beat John. You know how good he is. He doesn't even hunt with the men much any more. He's so good he goes out on his own." Mason Raymond sank down on the porch steps in despair. "He's got a reputation all over these parts. They didn't even *say* John in the store the other day when they were talkin' about all the coons 'the Buttes boy' got."

Hart didn't argue. "I can't beat John," Mason Raymond said.

"You kin try."

"Trying only takes you so far."

"Well, one thin' you kin say for sure."

"What's that?"

"You'll be farther than you are now." He looked at Mason Raymond curiously. "Tell me somethin'. You git up in the mornin' and ask yourself, Well, what you gonna do wrong today, you no-good son of a bitch?"

"Something like that," Mason Raymond said morosely.

"That's a self-respectin' way to start the day."

"I'm not equipped for this life. It's not that I don't want to be or don't try, it's just that it isn't natural to me, it isn't in the blood."

"Nuthin's in the blood. It has to be put there. You take a

young'un, he's like a slate, jest ready to be writ on and what's writ there is how he sees hisself when he reads back over it. But you done forgot there's sech a thing as eras-ers. Some thin's can be wiped out—oh, not all, I don't say all, but some. And another thin' you plumb forgot, maybe the most important thin', is that the kind of blackboard this is, it's always got more space to be writ on. You ain't *experienced,*" Hart agreed, "but you ain't unfeelin' neither."

"What's that got to do with it?"

"You got the spirit if you're showed."

Mason Raymond shook his head. "I'll try until I can't try any more, but trying doesn't mean I'm going to succeed."

"There are all kinds of succeedin'. You 'member you spoke as how you had a hankerin' for a dog?"

"I do, but my mother, she isn't very particular on dogs. Cats are all right, but dogs—"

"You could keep it up to my place. You gonna go in the woods and try and beat Young John Buttes, you gotta have a dog you can depend on, one you know as well, maybe better, than you know yourself. A dog don't git mixed up about what he wants. He's got a straight line of reasonin'. You git a good huntin' animal and you vittle him well, you treat him good, you keep him up, the only thin' he'll have on his mind is huntin' and pleasin' you. You got to match yourself to a dog. Don't do no good if you and the dog don't take to one another. Don't matter how good the dog or how good the hunter if they don't take to one another. But a man and a dog that take to one another, that's a story all in itself. You tell your Ma we'll put you up a coupla days while we're orientin' you. On second thought, I'll tell her. She'll take it better comin' from an outsider."

Mabel Hart was bent down, kneeling in front of an overturned sap pot, making clucking noises in her throat and beating the side of the big vat with one hand. "Git out of there, you blamed pests, come on out." When she saw Mason Raymond, she stopped banging and stood up. "Worth said you was comin', but I didn't expect you so soon. Ain't you tired from all that traipsin' 'round in the woods last night? He's out in the barn messin' with those cussed pigs of his agin. They're physicked, and he's afraid he's goin' to lose them. Sets a terrible store by them pigs, he does, because they're streaked. A pig's a pig, streaked or not. Lecherous animals," she said. "You growed agin," she said, examining him. "You're goin' to be well-made."

He did not like the wording, but he supposed she meant well. After all, she had no knowledge of the background of the remark. He didn't know how to deal with her, she was so different from his mother. But shyness didn't make her uneasy; she was getting ready to forget him and go back to her chores. "Leave your gear up to the house and go tell the old man his pigs are a wonder. It don't cost nuthin' to say so, and it'll pleasure him all day. Here, chick-a-chick-a-chick, come on chickies, git back with your mama."

Mason Raymond trudged up to the shutter-flapping house, stumbling over an old upturned rake hidden in the high grass. Hart's dogs were making a terrible commotion; cats peered from under the porch and out from half-dismantled carts, broken-springed buggies, piles of boards and old machinery that had gone to rust. Hens and roosters were running every which way. An old goat poked around in the rubbish with an air of no hope.

He crossed the yard and stood in front of the stairs where years before the half-witted boy had seen Hart painting and had had the urge to hit Hart with the hoe and had gone and done it; he saw for an instant, trembling inside his mind, the beating pulse of Hart's brain, let loose from between the two ridges of bone, and the image of the beating brain made him immediately think of Rivers, with his big, bloated, beating stomach; maybe also it was seeing the stairs that reminded him of Rivers . . .

He could not use the front stairs, Mason Raymond. His mother unconcernedly went up and down those stairs a dozen times a day; she seemed to think no more of passing under the place where his father's body had swung than she did of cleaning up any mess (often she stopped at the very spot where they'd found his father and bent down picking up a thread, a scrap of paper, or dirt, something someone had carried in on a boot or shoe). Mason Raymond lacked her nonchalance. He used the back stairs, what his mother always referred to as the servants' stairs because the narrow, steep passageway lead to the long hall off which the "girls" and Rivers had rooms. Rivers' room was the largest—by necessity, since he was always hauling a saddle up there to mend or polish and he had to keep the brass and leather for the carriage harnesses in condition. He was considered trustworthy because he had never gotten a girl in trouble. Mason Raymond thought his virtue came not so much from abstinence as from ugliness. He was a dull, silent man who seemed to have no interests at all except eating. He had started out, Mason Raymond supposed, with a normal enough constitution, but years of gluttony had warped his frame, the central part of his body had swelled up into a huge, bloated blob while his thin, hairy, spidery arms and legs had put on no weight at all. When Rivers sat, his stomach protruded and breathed. Mason Raymond watched, fascinated, while it heaved up, straining at the shirt, the belt, the trousers, then fell back, heaved up again, threatening to burst through its restraints. Rivers' skinny little arms, hirsute and warty, were revealed by rolled-up sleeves; his hands were bubbling globs of gray from the harness polish. A silent man, he neither smoked nor chewed to alleviate boredom; yet somewhere within that bulbous center that was expanding at such a prodigious rate there beat the pulse of superiority: *that* was easy enough to trace in Rivers' smile which seemed to say, I'm just as good, maybe better, than you even if I was born lower down the ladder.

What made him seek out Rivers? For he did—three, four times a day. Not loneliness. He wasn't really lonely. No one was lonely who had learned to live with books. No, it was something else, a fascination with ugliness maybe. He would climb the back stairs and knock at Rivers' door and the coachman would grumble and tell him to come in, but close the door, he didn't like no drafts. Mason Raymond would sit and watch him polish or mend or repair. He watched the stomach move up and down, up and down, a hypnotic kind of effect that made him drowsy and peaceful. They didn't talk much, a word or two here and there, nothing at all of any consequence, but Mason Raymond went back again and again. He had knocked at Rivers' door one day and got no answer. Rivers was probably out in the barn. Mason Raymond turned, started down the hall, stopped. He fought with himself a moment, lost, turned back, pausing only an instant with his hand on the doorknob before he let himself in. Even silent, secret Rivers had to have strange mysteries working inside him; everyone did.

The room seemed larger than it actually was because there was nothing in it to suggest occupancy. The bed had obviously been made by demanding, disciplined hands, not a wrinkle or ridge; no clothes had been thrown across the single chair; the dresser was bare, not even a comb or brush lay on the expanse of its dark wood; even the sawhorse where Rivers worked on the saddles was empty.

Mason Raymond closed the door and went quickly to the dresser and slid out the top drawer: a pile of undershirts and long underwear, some neckwear, a carefully wedged-in pile of scarves. He lifted socks. Nothing. He lifted the undervests: nothing. Nothing either under the mound of bandanas. He was ready to close the drawer when something made him pause and reconsider. There was something not quite right. He didn't know why, he just felt something was off. He looked hard at each neat pile, his glance resting on the bandanas. He lifted the scarves carefully again and examined them, letting them ripple through his hands as if they were a deck of cards. And then he found the mystery for which he had been searching: one of his mother's white lace handkerchiefs.

Worth's porch stairs were rickety, one of them completely loose from its nails; slanting crazily, it creaked and wobbled as Mason Raymond's foot came down on it. What had prompted him to pry into Rivers' secret life that way, systematically searching through all the other drawers (futilely) for some other evidence of Rivers' private dreams? There was nothing but that white scrap of linen and lace to give Rivers away. Mason Raymond, re-examining it, seeing and smelling so clearly even in such a small square the presence of his mother, had been enveloped with gloom. What good could

] 72 [

come of his knowing Rivers hid secretly a handkerchief of his mother's over which to weave fantasies and summon up dreams?

The porch was a collection of unidentifiable objects—piled, jammed, wedged, crammed, boxed together. Everything was defective in one way or another but still usable—or at least one day might be so far as Hart was concerned. "What you finally throw away, you want the next day," Hart was always saying.

Mason Raymond had to work with the door to get it open; it was off-balance and wedged in one corner. He forced it, hoping it wouldn't spring its rusted hinges; the cat curled up near the door roused itself at the racket, arched, stretched, yawned, and sprang up on a three-legged chair propped against the wall. The animals looked at him with slitted green eyes. Like the bobcat, the cat's eyes were saying to him, You come of a family whose past consumes its future.

He pushed open the half-shut door, lurched against a sack, and knocked over a pail of cream. The silver pool looked to him like the silver-capped lake when moonlight flowed over it and made it seem some exotic, far-away token that had, for a moment, been laid down against the hills to bewitch him. In the morning it was always gone, that magical body of water, and in its place was the common, ordinary, everyday lake he knew, but at night, in moonlight, it was something faraway and unknown. He felt this, but nothing, even torture and the promise of death, could have wrested this secret from him, a confession, he felt, of the fact that he was so different from everyone else. He imagined that in town when people spoke of him they said he had a weak character whereas when they talked of his cousin John Buttes they said, There's a real strong boy. Brown, thick, arrogant John swaggered through the streets as if daring anyone to question his right to kingship. "That boy's Buttes all the way through," people said. "He's his daddy all over again, before his daddy went to war."

Mason Raymond thought of the time John was three and ran off the end of the Landing dock and sank. Sank like a stone, lay on the bottom of the lake with his black eyes open, waiting for someone to jump in and get him. Sure he would be saved.

He was always sure he would be saved. That was their difference, his and Mason Raymond's. Mason Raymond never felt
he was going to be saved.

To come, just arrive, and spill their good cream all over the
floor. Hopeless, just hopeless. Everything about him was
hopeless.

John was only twelve, but he was like a man. He'd always
been that way. Swing down the path with a man's thrust, sure
of himself. When he said Mason Raymond, he said May—son
Ray—mond as if the name itself said *sissy, sissy—baby.* Mason
Raymond's politeness, school-learned, drawing room tried-
and-true, failed him; his sturdy cousin, brown and dirt-stained
thumbs hitched to his pants, grunting, looking at him, sizing
him up, a city kid, *soft,* hopeless, hopeless. "Hello, John"—
John not even bothering to answer, jogging up the path,
grunting, breathing hard, shaking his head—he wasn't going
to waste time on no baby, never mind Mason Raymond was
three years older and knew who Patroclus and Priam, An-
tayanax and Andromache were. Who cared about what happened thousands of years ago in some *Greek* place? John was
obviously a man of the future; *his* past hadn't put an indemnity
against *his* future.

"I got me this knife and I killed me this bobcat and I cut
him up in *pieces.*" Never mind all this was a lie, John made it
sound like the truth: it might have happened.

Some people radiated confidence. "You can't even make
him cry," John's father, Cobus Buttes, said. "Take a stick to
him, crack him good, he jest stands and takes it, don't even
whimper, turns and looks at you when it's over and walks
away. Jest no way to punish that boy."

John in the tree, way up, swinging. The height in itself made
Mason Raymond dizzy, the notion of climbing up there and
swinging (the branch might snap, he might slip, *something*
might happen; imagination had always been his undoing) sick-
ened him. John swung. Happy. Knowing *he'd* never fall. He
began to taunt, taunt Mason Raymond, taunt his brothers,
taunt the whole wide world. "Ain't nobody but *me* gonna
come up here and swing."

None of them denied it, certainly not Mason Raymond,

hardly Lyman or Sarton gazing worshipfully up into the green, swinging, leafy world where their brother John's brown body arched back and forth, back and forth. Small tree limbs crashed down. Leaves fell in a green rain. The swishing sound of swinging stung the air. Mason Raymond's heart leapt and bounded with every arc John's body made. No, it would never happen to him, no matter how hard he tried or how much he yearned: he would never swing high and clear and clean; he was destined to be one of life's grounded.

The Landing people thought the Butteses had a crazy streak in them anyway because Old Odder Buttes had insisted on setting up his place where no man in his right mind would, across the lake, in the mountains, a man who had determined to do what no other man had done; and he had wanted, that Old Odder Buttes, to do it because it was difficult and different, and basically wasn't that really what all men wanted, to be different, to do something different? But wasn't that a definition of pride, too?

Stubborn, proud folk, that's how it went about the Butteses in town. First Odder Buttes, (well-named, they said; he was odd) carving his farm off the side of a mountain, settling down on the side of the lake no one wanted, got so peculiar after his woman went, died in childbirth, you know; it's her tree they talk about when they say Emily's larch, and her and hisn's boy, why that was Old Guthrie Buttes, the one carried the bear-mauled man out of the woods—he was brung up more Indian than white; oh, they're a private people, those Butteses, and it tells, it tells. He went and married Indian, you know, Old Guthrie did—leastwise she was halfway Indian, her ma was full Onondowa, lazy as they come. She give Guthrie a pile of trouble, you can bank on that. Don't *nuthin'* good come of mixin' blood, but you can't never tell those Butteses nuthin'. Pride-heavy bunch, full of theirselves. Don't *mix,* like to stay standoffish by theirselves over on that side of the lake, well, let 'em. Never was one you really *knew.* Quiet and shut in on theirselves and standoffish.

Mason Raymond went to the door and tried to coax the wary cat into the kitchen; it backed away from him, inching slowly over fallen furniture, around a cluttered corner, its eyes almost translucent, eyes like his uncle's eyes. Cobus Buttes was a stubborn man, too ("A black's as good as a white, and don't try to tell me different!"). Atop some boxes piled high in the corner the cat tucked its paws in and settled down; cream could not cajole it away from independence. "Oh, blame it," Mason Raymond said loudly, trying to sound like a man. He tramped back into the kitchen and looked around for papers to blot up the mess, hearing footsteps sounding on the porch stairs, standing in front of the spilled cream realizing he was going to be caught before he had cleaned up.

"Lord have mercy," Mabel said, "what's been going on here? *I told* Worth not to leave the vessel there, *told* him one of them dogs'd git to it, or someone'd come tearin' through the door in a storm—like as not hisself—and turn it over, but he was so blessed agitated over them pigs he don't hear nuthin' but the sound of squeals. Don't take on over it, won't do no good now. I'll git some of them pups to come in, clean it up in no time flat." She began screaming names out the porch door.

Mason Raymond watched the young hounds tumbling over one another to get at the sweet, thick cream, squealing, snapping, snarling, groaning with pleasure, their pink tongues like miniature mops cleaning up the floor. He felt tired to the bone, sitting there with his rucksack between his legs trying to think of something to say to Mabel Hart. She was bustling about in one of those female fits of energy so exasperating to men, touching plates, slamming drawers, moving things from place to place, picking up and sorting, carrying on a low hum of directions to herself—"Where'd I put that blamed—oh, there it is. Now, got to remember to git that milk goin' for the cheese—where's that cheese crock?"—paying no more attention to Mason Raymond than if he had been one of the pups licking up cream underfoot, a woman in a world all her own so that when she suddenly turned and saw Mason Raymond humped up in his chair, she said in surprise, "How come you ain't out to the barn praisin' them streaked pigs of Worth's?"

He pictured his mother in one of her "morning" gowns lying upstairs on the long, low lounge opening her mail with a thin, silver letter opener, one pudgy hand occasionally lifting from the table beside her a perfumed handkerchief to press to her nose, her eyes, her forehead. She complained she was thirsty all the time, no matter how much she drank, and that her legs were giving her trouble.

Mabel Hart worked hard as a man; his Aunt Kam up at what was always called the New House, though it was older than his Uncle Cobus, went into the fields when they were short-handed and hayed beside the men. But his mother somehow had a dispensation from such chores. Money made all kinds of dispensations—if you wanted to take them. Well, he didn't.

There were several barns, and Worth and his prize pigs might be in any one of them. He was always moving things, throwing young pigs and cows and sheep into a panic as he routed them out of familiar quarters and drove them to some new spot where he thought they'd thrive better. Mason Raymond called, waited, called again.

An answer came from one of the buildings, Mason Raymond wasn't sure which; and while he stood there puzzling it out, he heard the horse and then saw Rivers and thought, it's some babying errand *she's* sent him down on, why can't she just leave me be? He held up his hand, waving, hoping Rivers wouldn't shout and bring the Harts out to witness his newest humiliation.

Rivers reined the horse in and climbed down, leaning his queer, toadlike body lumpily against the horse's flank, though it surprised Mason Raymond to discover the man had really (if you looked) quite a nice face, good eyes, a clean, straight mouth, big white teeth. "You forgot your warm coat, and your Ma was afraid you might take cold without it."

Mason Raymond had visions of her posting Rivers down here two, three times a day with scarves, handkerchiefs, tonics, fresh shirts, clean underwear, better socks, God knew what else she could find to fuss about. He accepted the coat sullenly. He never knew what to say to Rivers now that he had uncovered his secret. Rivers, having discharged his obligation, was hoisting his bloated body back up in the saddle and getting ready to ride back where he was needed—and, hopefully, wanted. He leaned down and said, friendly enough but basically really not interested, "She said for you to *be careful.*"

"What does that mean?"

"Why, not to go and git yourself hurt."

"I'm only working with a dog."

"She's worried about guns, and she ain't been too fit lately, short of breath, weak in her legs, dizzy some. She don't need no more worryin' right in through here."

"I'm not using Hart's gun. I'm not even using any gun, I'm just working with dogs. You can tell her to stop worrying, I'm not even around guns."

"Yes, sir, Mr. Raymond, I'll tell her—but I don't think that's going to stop her worryin' none."

"She *wants* to worry."

"She loves you," Rivers said in a reproving voice, that act of love no doubt the most wondrous one he could imagine and Mason Raymond's desire to reject it, the most mysterious and ungrateful. Well, Mason Raymond wanted to tell him, there are different levels of love. They aren't all as hot as you think.

He hung his head and looked at his feet. His feet were small and narrow. All *men* had big, lumpy, awkward feet. He just couldn't do or grow anything right. He didn't even have hair under his arms and he was fifteen. Fifteen-year-old boys around here not only had hair on all the right parts of them, but they also did things to girls.

The idea was dizzying. He would never, never use himself in that way; it was—there was no word for what it was. But if Rivers hid his mother's handkerchief that meant he wanted to do that to her. He looked at Rivers: that toadlike little man and *his mother.*

Rivers was gazing over his head. "Mr. Worth, sir," he said.

Mason Raymond died.

"You ever see a striped pig, Rivers? I got *three* of them out in that barn."

Rivers' face registered not a single sign of astonishment, and Worth, seeing Rivers hadn't comprehended the significance of what he was saying, repeated, *"Three striped pigs."*

Rivers panted himself back off the horse and onto the ground; his whole posture seemed to say, In my position in life, you're always having to humor somebody. He straightened himself up, martyred, and prepared to go see the pigs.

In Mason Raymond's view the pigs weren't all that sensational. Mabel had said they were physicked, a country way of explaining they had diarrhea, and now the whole litter, some ten or twelve of them, lay weakly in the straw, tumbled in on one another so that it was hard at first to find the striped ones, the big, milk-heavy sow on her side, too, grunting and complaining, looking at them from sour eyes rimmed by long, coarse tufts of hair, an ugly old thing and the sick pigs weren't much better, but Hart was carrying on about them as if they were one of the recorded wonders of the world. "People say there ain't no such thin' as streaked pigs, but there you see some with your own eyes. I been breedin' for them all my life —but I've had an awful run of bad luck with them. I can born them, but I jest can't seem to raise 'em. One thing or another, they're always dyin' off on me."

Rivers said something about being sorry Hart had had so much trouble with his pigs; Mason Raymond said something along the same line, looking at a tan hound tied to one side of the barn, a big, muscled dog staring at him not as the cat had, in mistrust or disdain, but with an expression which seemed to say, I'm an outsider, too, good for nothing but trouble and ticks.

Solid-colored hunting dogs were considered bad luck, and for some reason Mason Raymond had never understood, tans were supposed to be the worst luck. Most dog men drowned or brained the tans in a litter, but Worth, with his soft heart, had apparently been unable to bring himself to do so. That's why, Mason Raymond supposed, the dog was tied up out of sight here in the barn; no one would see the evidence of Hart's weakness.

He went over toward the dog slowly, not wanting to make it nervous by being hasty and clumsy; in back of him Hart was raving on about his pigs, Rivers mumbling now and again some conscience-stricken token of admiration; in front of Mason Raymond the dog watched him happily, wagging its tail which, now that Mason Raymond was up close and could see more clearly, had a black spot at its tip—maybe that was why Hart hadn't put the dog away, he wasn't all tan, but he was about as close as you could come—a big, tan dog with a little tailtipped black, straining at his tie-up, looking eagerly at Mason Raymond with bright, begging eyes.

Mason Raymond dropped to his knees and began to fondle the dog. Every single thing he did in the world was wrong. No hunter in his right mind would have chosen a tan hound, but he couldn't help it, this was his dog; hadn't Hart himself said there was no point in matching a good dog, even a great dog, to a man who just didn't have a feel for him?

"That the dog he picked out?" his uncle asked.

"That's the one," Hart said.

The two men were struggling not to give any emotional connotation to their words, but John Buttes, big and brown and burly beside his father, let out a hoot.

Mason Raymond didn't know what to say. He couldn't defend a dog he'd never seen hunt; he couldn't rationalize the color, and then, on top of everything, there was the business about the dog's name. Hart had pointed out that it was bad luck to change an animal's name; but Hart hadn't really argued much because the dog's name was Tip (on account of that small black tip at the end of his tail) and Hart could most certainly see Mason Raymond couldn't have a dog named Tip. Tip had been his father's childhood nickname. Clyde Buttes had been Tip once.

He told Hart he was going to call the dog Hector. "Hector," Hart said, kneeling down and scratching Hector behind the ears. "Hector. Here, Hector," he said, still unconvinced. "Here, boy."

The dog lay down, plopping his head on his paws. Hart looked at Mason Raymond and shrugged his shoulders. "He don't answer to the name," he said.

Mason Raymond bent down, clapping his hands. "Hector," he said. "Here, boy, Come on, Hector."

The dog closed his eyes.

"Up, Hector, up. Come on, boy." Mason Raymond seized the dog by the collar and jerked him to his feet. He could never remember being so tough with an animal, but then his experience with anything but cats was limited—big, feminine, ugly-tempered Persians running around the house shedding and clawing the furniture.

The dog began that dog-fawning that Mason Raymond couldn't cope with. He tried to calm him by petting him and giving him inadequate advice like "Now, now; now, now" while Hart shook his head. "No way to treat a huntin' dog," he said.

Young John Buttes kept saying, "He ain't even got con—for—ma—tion."

This, too, was true. The dog was put together all wrong, long in the leg, huge in the shoulders, smallish in the middle, enormous muscles in the hindquarters, a big head, and almost no neck. "He'll run," Cobus Buttes said. Mason Raymond picked up something in his uncle's voice. "Git him up," he said after a moment, "so he stands instead of kind of leaning over like that. I want to see him standin'."

"Up, Hector, *up!*"

Miraculously the dog rose.

"Hector?" his uncle said, turning to Hart. "Where'd he get a name like that?"

"Him," Hart said, nodding his head toward Mason Raymond.

"You changed his name?"

"It's kinda complicated, Cob," Hart said.

Cobus Buttes took his time examining the dog. "You're gonna have one hell of a way to go to beat him, John. He's built to run and that 'culiar way he's strung together means he's got stayin' power. Only trouble with him," he said to Mason Raymond, "is he's soft, all fat, no muscle. You want to start workin' that right off. You ain't got a whole lot of time. I figure maybe he'll git in shape if you work him every day, but I wouldn't count on it."

"Yes, sir, I'm aimin' to start right away. You really think he's all right? You really think he'll make a good hunter?"

Mason Raymond could feel the pride taking hold of him and that feeling of pride gave him such a feeling of pleasure that he could hardly stand it. There was something in John Buttes's face that encouraged just such a sense of superiority, too, a sullen stubbornness that wouldn't allow him to concede that the big tan dog might maybe be better than he wanted to believe. But a month wasn't very long—

He had longer than that in the end because of the weather. "Worst weather I ever been subjected to," Hart grumbled. "Can't take dogs out in *this.*" It had rained every day but two; on those it had snowed. April came and went without a vestige of spring; sullen, stubborn winds blew over the sodden ground; farmers worried about planting, no way to plough in weather like this and if you did the seeds would rot in the ground, those the blackbirds didn't get; farmers, with all that free time on their hands, stood around passing the time of day by cursing the wet weather, complaining about not getting seed in, and talking about Grant being inaugurated and about the Union and Central Pacifics meeting soon somewhere out West, the first railroad to go all the way cross-country. They talked about faraway things mostly when near-at-hand things were out of kilter. Indians were settling down, too, with the Treaty of '68; things looked good for the West, for the whole country, if only the all-fired rain would stop.

There was a lot of talk about the bet having to be postponed, too. The weather was so poor that the dogs couldn't pick up any trails. Mason Raymond, half crazy to get on with his training, waited up at his house and waited and still the sun wouldn't spring through and the ground stop oozing mud and moisture. The run was postponed until the middle of May, Lite finally agreeing (reluctantly) that it would be only fair to give "the Summer Boy," Mason Raymond, a little time to bone up.

Young John Buttes said he didn't give a damn when it was or how much Mason Raymond worked. When the time came, he'd win. John being John, not even his mother, Mason Raymond's Aunt Kam, called into question either his language or the likelihood of his being inaccurate. Still, his father said, those who count their chickens at night aren't up on foxes. He and Hart were about the only ones who had even the mildest confidence in Mason Raymond, and Hart had moments of desperation, going out with Mason Raymond to give the initial pointers, trotting along with Brownie and Drum leashed, and a lantern, managing to hang onto that though the dogs pulled and tugged and leapt about his legs, constantly on the verge of upsetting him, Mason Raymond, with an utterly indifferent Hector, loping along beside him. From Hector's behavior any sensible person would have assumed the dog was just out for a friendly little amble after dark while those two crazy hounds ahead, thrashing and barking and straining, were out of their heads with the heat of the hunt even though it was a good night for May—you could get anything in May, eighties or thirties, snow or summer, mountain weather—, one of those sudden, soft nights, muggy after the rain, but the bugs just awful. Insects swarmed from every direction; they were devouring Mason Raymond, who swatted and swore (feeling quite manly to know such words), but Hart didn't even seem bothered, trudging along with his half-crazed dogs and his lantern, humming a little, "We Are on the Road to Je—sus," and spitting now and again the dregs of the chewing tobacco he'd plugged into the side of his cheek just before they'd set out, a happy man even if he was being eaten alive. He was in the woods, wasn't he?

Hart had already unpeeled his jacket and left it back aways —"You make note of where I left that, boy"—and now he was struggling with his thick wool winter shirt, stripping away one layer after another as he bounded along, humming, hawking tobacco juice, losing his clothes. Mason Raymond supposed he would have to try to locate them when the hunt was over. Hart stood for a moment getting out of the shirt, hung it on a tree knob, hardly paying attention to what he was doing; then he perked up, gave a whoop of joy, and bent down and set Brownie and Drum free. "Let 'im go, boy," he shouted to Mason Raymond, who bent down and fumbled with the snap on Hector's collar.

Brownie and Drum had disappeared at a high run into the woods ahead, but he couldn't get his fingers to release the catch, jiggling and twisting and working the collar this way and that, until Hart reached over and undid the dog and shouted, "Go, boy, go! Go on, Hector!" while Hector looked up at him, tongue lolling, it was awfully hot and there were so many bugs, who'd want to run?

"Oh, my God," Mason Raymond said in despair. "Get up. Up, Hector, up. Oh, for God's sake," he cried in absolute despair, "he won't even get up."

"He ain't ready yet, I guess," Hart said after a time.

Mason Raymond was beside himself. "This isn't any time for jokes. The damn dog won't even get up, let alone run!"

"Well, tie him up again and bring him along a bit and maybe he'll git the idea."

"It's hopeless, just hopeless. Look at him, just look at him, he's not even interested."

The dog looked happy and relaxed, as if the last thing on his mind was running on such a damp, buggy night. Let the unhinged like Hart do that.

Mason Raymond snapped the lead back on the dog and hauled him up, dragging him along. The dog didn't fight him, but on the other hand he didn't help either. Hector was a big dog, the terrain was rough; Mason Raymond found it hard work hauling a sixty- to seventy-pound dog uphill. Finally, winded, he had to call out to Hart to stop, he was pooped. In the distance a disturbance said Hart's dogs were treeing. It wasn't the excited, disruptive enthusiasm of finding a scent and tracking; these voices were steady and sure. Hart, dancing about wildly, tried to get Hector going, but the dog had fallen over on its side, hot and heaving; he showed no enthusiasm for getting up and running.

"Tell you what," Hart said excitedly. "You wait here and I'll go ahead and flush out what Brownie 'nd Drum got treed. We git ourselves a coon, show it to this dog, give him the idea—"

Mason Raymond had no confidence, but he said Hart had a good idea, "You go on. You go ahead," but already the light of Hart's lantern was diminishing; a second later it was extinguished by woods.

Mason Raymond looked at the dog. He'd be damned if he was going to drag a sixty- or seventy-pound dog around the woods all night. Let him lie there, let the bugs get him, to hell with it. He undid the lead and started tramping on toward where Hart's dogs were carrying on, proud hunters who had brought their prey to bay. Their chops were steady; that meant

Hart hadn't reached them yet. When he got to the tree, the dogs always quieted a lot. They had confidence in him.

Mason Raymond looked back once and couldn't see Hector; the moon hadn't come out; it was pretty dark, dark and damp and awfully buggy. Maybe hunting wasn't all that wonderful.

He went into thick woods listening for Hart's dogs. They had stopped their yelping, except for an occasional outburst, and Mason Raymond couldn't find any openings in the brush where either Hart or the dogs had crashed through. He came upon a little rocky declivity with running water—a spring freshet that would be dry in another couple of weeks—and he stumbled along that. He heard a dog ahead—at least the sound seemed to come to him from somewhere up ahead—and he picked up his pace, breathing heavily; he was as out of shape as his dog. Thinking about that lazy, good-for-nothing dog made him push himself harder; someone in the family had to show some initiative; listening for Hart's dogs and their bays, trying to identify direction, plunging on, then pulling up short, listening. He must have come too far. He was pretty sure he heard dogs over to his left and downhill. He broke away from the stream and plunged into brush. It was tangled and prickly—blackberries, raspberries probably—but not as thick as it would have been in summer, all in all manageable, even the bugs seemed better. He called once, but got no answer. It seemed to him Hart's dogs had been quiet for an awfully long time. Maybe Hart already had the coon and had gone back to where Hector was and—no, Hart hadn't had that much time. The best thing was to keep going, pick up speed, keep calling. He pushed on.

The ground went up—a steep hill—and was slippery after all the recent rains; Mason Raymond kept tripping and sliding. He kept calling, too, but he got no answer, heard nothing—not even a dog trailing.

At the top of the hill he had a moment of real uncertainty. He looked out and all he could see were woods and hills. He ought, he thought, to have been able to locate at least a slice of the lake, but it had apparently sunk behind a hill somewhere —not a good sign at all because if he'd had the lake as a guide he would have been all right; all he would have had to do was keep walking toward it; but with nothing to use for bearings, he suddenly realized how much alike all these hills looked, there was no distinguishing one from the other.

The thing to do was walk back, try to retrace his steps, get back down and try to hear a dog or find the field where he'd left Hector, maybe even stumble on one of Hart's shirts; it shouldn't be too hard to find some sign to help him back to one of the old logging roads. He wished there was a moon and he wished the bugs, which were congregating again, would leave off, but all in all things could have been worse.

He started back, trying to discern where he'd broken through brush, but the brush all seemed to have closed back together or else he'd taken a wrong turn some place; he didn't see any broken tracks, didn't recognize anything. Well, he was all right so long as he kept working back down in the same general direction he'd come. He might be a little off one way or the other, but generally he'd end up back where he wanted to be.

He was halted by a tangle of fallen trees and high brush and big rocks that forced him to go right. He kept moving further and further away from what he felt was his original course, but he kept reassuring himself that when he got to the end of the bad part here, he would backtrack, try to find where he'd probably been headed, and he'd be near where he'd left the dog.

He probably shouldn't be going right at all; he ought maybe to backtrack right now and try to get around the bad part on the left instead of heading right, but at all costs he must try to keep out of the windfall Hart said was one of the worst he'd ever been in. "Got in it once," he had told Mason Raymond, "and like never to have got out. We want to stick clear of that."

Still, he could maybe just cut through a little of it, working his way back, saving time by going on a diagonal instead of straight. He tried working around the first fallen trees, through the heavy brush, but finally decided he was losing more time fighting the thicket than going the longer way around. He was pretty tired anyway. He thought maybe he ought to rest before he cut back up through the thicket, but then it seemed like a better idea to get back up into easier land and then rest. He kept scrambling up over massive fallen trunks, coming down into bracken and brush and thorns that were sometimes shoulder high; he was hot and thirsty and bitten. His legs started to get terribly tired from all the unaccustomed punishment they were taking, but he was pretty sure in a few minutes he'd be out of all this really bad woods; only he wished now he'd stayed in a straight line, hadn't tried to save time; he kept on, his breath raspy, his throat raw with thirst, his legs trembling. Then he stumbled, lay for a moment with a bursting sensation inside his head.

He wasn't out. At least he didn't think he was unconscious because he was aware of a lot that was happening to him—all the bugs swarming all over him, for instance—but he just couldn't get up. He must have been down this way for a long time because when he got up there was a big half moon hanging high overhead and when he'd fallen there had been no moon. In between when he'd gone down and now, the moon had had time to rise and work its way halfway across the sky.

Nothing broken, or even strained. Just that blow from something (probably a branch) on the head stunning him and of course he was tired, but he wasn't really worried. All he had to do was work left and down, and he'd be all right. It wasn't as if he were lost.

It was silly (bad woodsmanship) to push himself to the point of an accident the way he had. The thing to do was to keep his head, go slowly, calmly, no matter how long it took. He found he didn't have any choice about his pace, he was tired out. Finally he sat down and rested, then made himself get right up again. The minute he'd stopped it was like he never wanted to get up again.

He leaned against a big rock and looked around. The moonlight wasn't bright, but it gave enough light—if there was any cleared area—to see somewhat ahead. Mason Raymond's trouble was that there wasn't anything but boulders, stumps, downed trees, high brush, all around. The way he figured it, he should be nearly clear of the windfall. The thing to do was to take a long rest, and then push on. The windfall couldn't last much longer and once he was free of climbing and stumbling, going around and breaking through, the worst would be over, he'd be out in the open. Nothing to it then. All he had to do was get out of the windfall.

An hour later he tripped and went down on his knees, gashing both on a long, sharply ridged rock. His pants were torn and wet—his knees were bleeding. He sprawled down on the damp, rough earth and waited for the pain and bleeding to subside. He was lost, lost probably in the midst of that windfall Hart had said any fool would keep clear of.

He didn't have a gun—not even a knife, no string—he didn't have any way to make a fire.

While he lay waiting for the smarting in his knees to stop, he thought of his uncle curling up in a ball to keep warm while he was sleeping. Mason Raymond was sure he couldn't manage that position with his bad knees. He remembered Hart once saying a porcupine was a lost woodsman's last hope for food. Porcupines moved so slowly that a man could run up on them and club them to death. What Mason Raymond couldn't remember was what—if anything—Hart had advised about getting the quills out and the meat loose enough to eat. If you could eat it. Some people (poor) at the Landing ate porcupine. Occasionally. But even after it had been boiled for hours it was supposed to be tough and tasteless. The idea of even coming on a porcupine, let alone battering it to death with a rock, seemed pretty unlikely, but even given a dead porcupine, eating it was out of the question. *Raw* meat?

He got to his feet. One knee was really in bad shape. He didn't want to make too much of it; it was better to keep going, no matter how slowly. If you kept going, at least you were making some progress. Well, maybe not progress, but at least you were trying, you hadn't just given up.

He limped a little and stopped. Ahead lay such a thick tangle of briars and bushes he wouldn't be able to get through without an axe. Going back was pointless and he couldn't go ahead; he moved off downhill, a little to the left, so confused at this point that he had to admit maybe he only thought he was going left, maybe it wasn't left at all.

Both knees were stiffening. He wasn't sure how long he'd be able to keep going. He was tired and light-headed—maybe that was why he wasn't discouraged—because he didn't feel in any way defeated, just different. Just how would have been hard to say, but different, somehow changed; yes, that was it —changed and different; he wasn't the same and he didn't know what had altered, he just knew something was different. The light-headedness had something to do with this, as if he were beginning to separate worlds; there were two of them, this one and the one behind this one. The one behind this one wasn't another world, it was just a different view of this one, just as he himself was different; there were maybe two of him, the outside one and the one that was hidden inside, and he had to plunge through the outside one to get to the real one inside; and all this painful stumbling and falling and pushing was in some way related to getting through the outer world into the real world there inside his head.

He tripped again and reopened both knees. The pain was so intense that he cried out, not once, but again and again (What was the difference? Who was there to hear him?), and then he lay broken (that was the vision inside his head, that he had been broken, the outer shell of him cracked open) and he saw this other world inside his head and it was spilling out so that as he lay there he could see himself quite clearly and the world behind himself breaking through, taking shape. And maybe (he was never quite sure of time, but he wanted it to be at this moment so he made it happen at this moment when he went back over the events in his mind) then it was that he heard the slight rustle, the sound of something moving in the woods, and he lay still and let it come to him, lying there waiting, the woods parting as the sound increased and for one moment, lying there looking up, he saw eyes looking down at him.

The eyes never wavered. Mason Raymond lay, unmoving, and looked back, and then nothing moved, nothing sounded, the world was just for that instant nothing but his eyes and those eyes, and then he felt, (and there was nothing else but this knowledge) that there at the heart of life was an eye, all-seeing, looking out, calm, beyond him, into the unknown of the universe: that's what the world was, an eye.

He wasn't going to get up because he couldn't; his immobility had something to do with his knees, but not all; more came from the images flowing in and out of his mind, a feeling of acceptance, as if after all what he did did not matter because he did not matter; he was insignificant and meaningless in all that the eye took in, he had only to realize his insignificance in the face of the immensity of all that was outside himself to resign himself to the unblinking eye and all that it beheld.

He heard the forest parting again, this time louder, more confident, the bobcat—he knew it was a cat—coming arrogantly to claim him, and he waited, not quite sure what was ahead, but convinced that when the cat came closer and he saw the eyes and heard—saw—the animal lunge, another part of him would come into view as well, that part of him that was as secret and hidden and mysterious as the white lace linen handkerchief tucked away from the world in Rivers' drawer.

The huge body hesitated a brief instant in space and then came down in a crash in what seemed all tongue and tail; it took Mason Raymond a moment to realize it wasn't the cat at all this time but a dog, his dog, Hector, who had somehow come out of the woods to claim him and bring him back to himself.

III

The dog knocked Mason Raymond about affectionately, jumping all over him, his hot, moist breath on Mason Raymond's face, the dog's paws pushing and shoving and scratching, so excited he couldn't be controlled, scrambling this way and that, hunched down, then leaping, running, barking, hunching down again, as if waiting for Mason Raymond to get up and play with him; finally when Hector wore himself out with happiness, he lay down and curled up beside Mason Raymond, giving off a hot, furry warmth. Mason Raymond was grateful for this because now cold was coming on and because the wide, dark, alien woods had given him a sense of great isolation. That moment when he had become a part of the eye of the earth was gone, and from the eye of light he had plunged back into the small, whole center of self, a lonely place to inhabit under the tall trees and distant, dark sky.

Still, he was not alone.

Beside him the dog lay snoring, noisy enough to be accused (on top of all his other faults) of having asthma, but Mason Raymond did not want to sleep, staring up at the sweaty, lightening sky in which the moon mellowed from saffron to gold, light streaking over the trees, the early morning birds beginning their incessant complaints about food. In the cold, sticky dawn the dog was warmth and security (who could sleep so soundly and snore so complacently without giving off an aura of confidence?).

Both his knees were badly swollen, his whole body felt stiff and rusty, he had been half-eaten by bugs, had had nothing to eat and drink: but if the dog had found him, it was possible others could, too.

Blood tells, Lite had said in the sure, confident voice of one who knows. Mason Raymond just wished Lite could see him now. Part Indian from his grandmother, Old Guthrie Buttes's half-Indian wife, (granted he didn't look it) lying out in the woods as pure and dumb as any full-bred white could ever hope to be. He'd like to have hollered triumphantly at Lite, How's that for blood, Lite; how's that for blood telling? Shouldn't the old Indian blood begin working pretty soon? Shouldn't the old brute Indian blood get me out of this mess?

In other circumstances the notion would have been comic, was, anyway—wasn't he smiling into the wet, sticky, buff light coming in over the treetops? He snuggled next to the dog and began to laugh. He couldn't help himself, the whole damn thing was so absurd, he, Mason Raymond Buttes, laying out God knew where in the woods with this no-good, tan, hunting, name-changed hound who couldn't work up any interest in hunting down what he was bred to kill but (in boredom? or interest? curiosity or distress? who knew) had tracked down Mason Raymond and now lay nasally noisy by his side, pleased as Punch with himself. They were a great pair all right. Mason Raymond could just imagine the kind of shenanigans they would get into turned loose to hunt on their own. Young John Buttes would be back with his coon before they even got themselves untangled and out of the first cornfield and into the woods—which was just as well. It wasn't safe to turn such a dumb kid and such a dumb dog loose on the world. "You dumb dog," Mason Raymond said. "You dumb dog. No wonder I picked you. If ever two losers deserved one another, it's us two."

It began to rain. Huge, cold drops splashed raucously

against the tree tops before he actually felt them. Though he had made a covering of leaves to keep out the cold because exposure could kill you even when the weather wasn't down to freezing, and though he was chilled, he wasn't bone-cold, just cold enough to be careful; men had died of exposure when the temperature didn't get any lower than the forties, it was rudimentary; he would have to do better than this now that a storm had hit. Already his clothes felt damp, moisture was forming on his face and head, all over the dog; beads of rain clung to the trees, a wet, numbing, all-day kind of rain. The pines looked menacing dripping dew and rain, flashing beads of moisture, holding up cold, black shoulders against the light. It's going to rain, he thought, *now it's going to rain.*

Lite, he thought, Lite's lounging in his store, leaning over the counter, saying, "Hart's done lost everythin' in the woods one time or another; now, I reckon, even a boy," and all those rheumy-eyed men'd hit their thighs, laugh, oh how they'd laugh. I mean, he thought, like the mountain doesn't come to Mohammed, Mohammed has finally got to say to himself, You better get up and start goin' to that mountain yourself because that mountain ain't *never* gonna move toward you. Light-headed, giddy, laughing (Mason Raymond Buttes as Mohammed, didn't Lite wish he knew *that),* he rose and tried to start trail, but his knees weren't going to do their share; they had stopped cooperating somewhere along the way. You could endure for a long time without food (so much for the porcupine) but you had to have water. There was water near because twice in the past couple of hours the dog had gotten up and, panting, looked expectantly at Mason Raymond, waited a moment, then finally run off on his own and come back, looking refreshed. Mason Raymond took this to mean the dog had gone and got himself a drink. He recalled the stream from earlier in his wandering; possibly it was nearby. He had to explore, which meant walking; ergo, his knees had to function, whether they chose to or not.

He looked around until he spied a long, thick branch lying about a hundred yards away, one which would make a good prop. Groping his way painfully from stump to rock to tree trunk, he finally managed to reach the branch; he was sweating furiously, the drops running off his face, down his armpits, soaking his back and chest, though maybe part of this was rain; it was difficult to tell what was rain and what was sweat, he just knew he was sticky all over. His knees were centers from which long needles of pain pierced his legs and thighs. Even his groin, wet with sweat, ached with effort—again something different in him, a sensation (heavy, pulsing, threatening) which he'd never experienced before—no, that wasn't quite true either, for wasn't this the same or similar to a sensation he'd felt at the moment he yearned for the kill, willing the blood-letting out there in the woods where he'd felt his heart heavy with guilt and pleasure and shame, a sensation too of grief and loss, a memory fed by guilt and despair when he heard the "developed" boys at the Academy talk about what they did to women, even though this was lying and boasting; he had felt then, this same peculiar, heavy swelling in himself, a stirring he couldn't control, a weight so deep it was a terrible burden to a boy to whom Morphis had taught the principles of purity and truth.

Leaning caved-in against a tree, he fought for breath, fought against pain, tried to make his pores dry the sweat (by force of will) before he got that bone-frozen feeling from which it was almost impossible to recover, leaning heavily against the tree (he was so dumb he didn't even know what kind of tree it was, he couldn't tell one damn tree from another, could name all or most all of the participants at Patroclus' funeral games, but couldn't tell an elm from an oak), his breath coming in gasps, his knees refusing to hold him up, rained on, drenched, *soaked,* he then came crashing down against the forest debris, all the heart gone out of him (where was any of his brave, hysterical pride and laughter now?). He began to sob uncontrollably into the earth, the earth who cared nothing for him or his, all this emotion wasted, utterly wasted, and yet he couldn't help it, he was heart-broken with helplessness; the dog uncontrollable at Mason Raymond's grief, leaping all over him, whining, pawing, licking Mason Raymond furiously, and Mason Raymond screaming, "Get away, get away, you dumb dog," cuffing at him, all his efforts useless, the dog paying no attention, Mason Raymond unable to drive or scream him off, until, just plain giving up, Mason Raymond lay spent and sore upon the ground so thirsty with the salt of his tears burning his mouth that he wanted to start weeping all over again. Everything was just hopeless.

After a time he hoisted himself up. He had the branch (awkward but usable) and the dog. He had also the picture inside his mind of Young John Buttes swaggering down the lane saying May-son Ray-mond, and a rage so great it brought bile up into his throat consumed him, and he said, "I don't care what that son of a bitch thinks."

Hector watched him struggling along the path. Finally he loped over and kept on one side of him; Mason Raymond could support himself on the dog when he had to, the dog seeming to sense he was needed and carefully gauging his pace so that he didn't get ahead of Mason Raymond, stopping when Mason Raymond stopped, looking up, his tongue hanging out unhappily as if he were dismayed at the way Mason Raymond was moving so slowly, but as if he were trying to tell him that it was all right, keep going, water was ahead.

Light—Lite, Mason Raymond thought, would have loved a picture of the boy and dog stumbling along together here in the midst of nowhere—light was going dim (or maybe something was happening again inside his head, there was no way to know, all he knew was that everything was going gray as if light was being swept away) and (of this he was absolutely certain) a thick, chill wind was settling in, boiling black clouds colliding overhead, the breeze beginning as a small stirring in the brush, then rising, gaining, until it grew angry and wild, whipping and lashing through the windfall so that branches and leaves were blown about, knocking into each other, crashing against the few sentinel trees, banging Mason Raymond about, bringing that whole cold, sodden world alive. *Now it's going to BLOW*, Mason Raymond thought.

He crouched, cold, against a fallen tree, shivering, the dog huddled up next to him, whining (what the hell did *he* have to whine about, he had fur), the rain blowing over them, wind whipping up the landscape all around. He had to keep going, and he couldn't. He lay against the tree and gave up.

But the dog was not about to lie down and quit. He commenced that crazy jumping about, barking and groaning, pawing and licking, driving Mason Raymond nuts. "Get away. Go leave me alone, for God's sake." All he wanted to do was lie down and die and this dumb dog wouldn't even let him do that.

The dog was furious, absolutely enraged. He was biting and pulling, snapping and barking; it was all so hopeless Mason Raymond didn't see that it much mattered whether he died on his feet or leaning against a tree; on his feet at least the dog would leave off pestering him, he could die in peace.

He stumbled on, falling, the dog all over him. He got up and stumbled forward and fell again. The dog wouldn't let him stay down. Once he even tried to *drag* Mason Raymond. Mason Raymond's clothes were torn; his knees were stiff and swollen; he had bruised his hands in falling, his face was scratched and bitten. He couldn't walk and he couldn't lie down and give up and die, the dog wouldn't let him. He wondered if there was any way on God's awful earth to be more miserable. He began to weep again in the tearing wind; then he realized he was beyond weeping, the wet on his face was rain. He lunged forward and fell on a pile of rocks and broken branches and old animal droppings.

Ahead he heard a crackling, running sound that had to be water. Forcing himself to his knees, he crawled over the mound on which he had fallen. Ahead was a trickle of water, no more than the beginnings of a spring freshet, but water. He pushed himself upright and the last few yards to the bank he floundered, plummeting down and washing his face in water, gulping (never mind it was shallow and he had shaken up mud, it was water), feeling as if he could never drink enough, he was an empty well of thirst, the dog beside him lapping furiously, the two of them sprawled side by side in the wind and cold of coming night drinking their insides out.

He had found water. Really a great triumph when you thought about it. Water was life. So was food, but water was more important; in a moment warmth was going to be a necessity, too, because the wind was making the temperature plummet at an alarming rate; it was getting terribly cold, as cold as it had been that night he and Hart and his uncle had been swallowed up in the swamp. There was no question of the dog and he just huddling together in some leaves for warmth; this night was going to be much too cold for that. Hector could probably get along; after all, these dogs were bred for hardship (blood tells, he said sardonically to the dog), but Mason Raymond was absolutely sure he had to have some kind of decent shelter—one not too far from this water because he couldn't do much more moving about, his knees were that bad, bad enough in fact that when he examined them he realized they needed attention that he couldn't give them, they couldn't be let go much longer, they were in really bad shape—so many decisions, he couldn't keep up with all that had to be attended to—find food, do something about his knees, get some sort of shelter, maybe construct one—and he was so tired, so blamed tired from the journey they'd made to the creek, a part of Indian Creek probably, a thin tracery of water that ran down from the Indian Hills behind his house and cascaded downhill until it emptied into the lake. Nobody swam where that outlet was, the water was so icy—colder even than those spots in the lake where when you were paddling along, you ran across one of the subterranean springs that fed the lake and you felt a shock all over you; but swimming in the lake that way, when you came upon a spring you could swim out of the cold, whereas here you couldn't escape it, the cold held you down and pressed against you—*Exposure,* men in the Landing said of men they came across dead and decaying who had been caught unprepared out in the woods in bad weather and hadn't been able to insulate themselves against the plummeting temperature, *he died of exposure.* So maybe water wasn't as important as warmth. Why one over the other? He had to have both.

Indians (where had he come across this? read it? heard it, not from Morphis certainly? maybe even only in some strange way imagined it? perhaps it *was* in his blood), Indians, caught out in the open, burrowed holes and nestled down in them, lined them with leaves to keep the ground cold out, covered them over with brush to preserve their body heat within the small, scooped-out holes. If he were caught out here (who knew how long?) he would need a hole against the rain and wind as well as the cold. Not just a hole, he thought, starting that crazy, inexplicable laughter again which he couldn't help since everything, the whole world, had started to strike him as absurd, not just any old hole, but a good hole, a superb hole, a hole in which any man would be proud to lie down in, maybe die in.

Perhaps a hundred yards upstream an enormous old tree (what kind? for peace of mind he decided to call it an oak; all right, an enormous old oak) lay felled on its side, the massive trunk maybe six or eight inches above the ground. If he dug under this, it would make an ideal shield, and for extra warmth he could strip off some branches (already he was getting prepared to press his legs into services they didn't want to perform), ideal, just ideal, but of course the problem was how to *dig* such an absolutely ideal hole. I mean, he thought, it's not like you just go out and start with a shovel.

A day had passed. It had been night when he lost himself in the windfall and now darkness was coming on again; this was going to be one hell of a cold night. He hobbled, leaning against his homemade staff, heading upstream, thinking through a number of things he might use as a gouge (primitive men after all had not had shovels). Primitive man shaped tools —crude perhaps, but effective—a pointed stick, Mason Raymond thought. But with darkness coming on, he had little time to fashion a tool. He examined the end of his staff—with some minor moderations it might do. He thanked heaven for the spring rains these past weeks (though not for the May rain pelting him now or the wind; he could hardly bring himself to be thankful for those) because those rains had made the ground wet and hence easier to work. He would not have been able to drive the stick into summer-dry, packed earth, move it back and forth, dislodge enough earth to scoop out any appreciable amount. Making such an opening to fit himself into would take hours, but, after all, what pressing engagement did he have—better occupied with work (hard work which would keep him warm) than moping (freezing) about trying to keep his spirits up. But the odd thing was that his spirits *were* up, maybe because of the challenge that had been given him, he didn't know, he only knew he felt a sense of elation, a running pleasure that answered the voice of Young John Buttes inside his head saying *He can't never make it* with *Yes, I can.*

He shivered. The wind was really terrible, a real blow, as Hart would have said. He leaned against the fallen tree and drove his walking stick into the ground, barely disturbing the forest debris. Best to clean that out first. He bent down creakily on his stiff knees and began digging away brush and leaves with his hands.

The dog was watching curiously, head cocked to one side, eyes alert; then he bounced up and began jumping about, barking excitedly. "Oh, shut up, you dumb dog," Mason Raymond said, rooting in the leaves. But the dog would not leave off, barking and bouncing around as if he were having the time of his life. "Crazy dog," Mason Raymond muttered, losing patience. He had important things to do, he didn't have time to mess around with a dumb dog.

Hector, dancing about, diving in and out among the brush, suddenly stopped, hunched down, barking, wiggling with affection; then he raced over to Mason Raymond, hunched down, and began to dig. The ground flew on either side of him. "Good boy, good boy, that's the way, good boy." The dog stopped digging. "Oh, my God," Mason Raymond said in despair. He doubled over stiffly and started digging again and Hector, imitating, went back to scratching with his paws. They went on scooping out dirt side by side for what must have been well over an hour; at the end of that time they had made a really quite professional, homelike hole. Mason Raymond gathered the leaves that were driest, those in the middle between the wet ones on top and some stiff, frozen ones on the bottom, lined the hole and then lay down, proud, under the wind. The rain had stopped, but there was a gale working up the woods. The whole top of the earth was coming away and from overhead limbs and branches crashed down.

Toward morning it began to rain again. As the angry, dark clouds bumped about, the sky became black; big black-white drops poured out of the heavens, grew larger and larger; they struck against things with the sound of falling stones. The skies were bombarding them; even the thick oak (or whatever it was) couldn't stop the deluge. "That's all we need," Mason cried to the skies, *"hail!"*

The skies paid no attention. For a good twenty minutes big diamond shards of ice fell. The ground turned a mica-brilliant gloss of white and gold; the whole forest seemed to be falling apart, leaves and branches and limbs of trees flying about, and the dog, the dog went crazy with barking and jumping, trying to catch the hail in his mouth, leaping up in the air, snapping, yelping, chasing hail this way and that.

Finally the hail stopped and was replaced by a steady dripping, a drizzle, with the skies lightening a little. Then big, thunderous cloudheads blew about overhead, converging; once more rain came in torrents, the water ran over the ground so fast that it turned the tricklet of stream into a raging creek, ran so fast that it poured into the hole and began to fill it up, ran so fast and furiously that the whole top of the forest floor began to catch pools of water. Mason Raymond lifted up the brush covering the hole and using his hands as scoops tried to throw the muddy water out. It leaked through his fingers and soaked his clothes. Rain poured down on either side of the fallen tree and ran into the hole. Riverlets of water tunneled miniature river paths into the hole.

In the hole Mason Raymond and Hector, under the shield of the big fallen—oak, was it?—crouched together. Mason Raymond had given up scooping. They were soaked, at least Mason Raymond was. His legs were troubling him, but things might have been worse—and though he wasn't sure why—he had an unreasonable faith in his feeling that, all things considered, he was acquitting himself if not masterfully at least competently. He had—this time—neither screamed at the sky nor broken down weeping on the earth. That in itself was something. Could John Buttes have done better? Yes, probably he could, but for a soft, summer, school boy he felt he had reason to be proud; he *was* proud, though that second, inner voice of examination inside him could not be stilled, kept saying to him, pride is the root of all the sins, a sentence he was sure was a bequest from Morphis whose obsession it suggested. His mind offered up two contrasting images, his young strong cousin John and the fat, flabby schoolmaster Morphis, as if they existed in two worlds poles apart, like two ruptured beliefs about worlds that could never be united, and he, Mason Raymond Buttes, straddled each, one foot in one, one foot in the other, swaying, close to toppling, trying to achieve a precarious balance that no man could ever accomplish. Cobus Buttes owned no books except the big old Buttes Bible and possibly (Mason Raymond wasn't sure) the farmer's almanac. Worth Hart had his own bible of dog records, his list of debts; but books, real reading books, no, he wasn't involved with these. In Morphis' dark room all the tables, the bureau, the bookcases were piled high with the tattered volumes of Morphis' beliefs; he was a reservoir of many men's ideas, and he revealed in his hard-won knowledge his right to be called scholar.

Which world was the right one and how could he ever be sure? The Achaeans whom Morphis admired so much and wanted so much to emulate had in many ways already out-civilized themselves for an age of heroism. Violence, destruction and death: that was the true message of *The Iliad,* and all the stories of their homecomings from Troy testified to blood ending in blood. In the doomed Hector's heart struggled sentiments the doomed Achilles never dreamed of. Yet Hector was more doomed than Achilles; his family perished as well, the young son dashed from the wall, the tender wife dragged into captivity. They were all doomed—that was the final message—the brute battler and the susceptible book-reader, he who was brutal, she who was loving. Nowhere was there the transcendent virtue of compassion, of forgiveness. *It's a hard world:* Hart said it, but never really accepted it. Well it is, Mason Raymond could tell him, and mean it.

I mean, he thought, crouched next to Hector who was once again snoring—he was the snoringest dog Mason Raymond had ever come across—I mean when Hart and Uncle Cob (he had pre-empted the right to that shortened version of his uncle's name by the right of his trials), when they got lost, they didn't do much better than I've been doing for all their years out in swamps and windfalls and woods. Of course it was also true his uncle and Hart and he had been involved in what you might call a short-term lostness whereas there was no telling how long this one might go on. He put the word *permanent* from his mind; nothing was ever permanent, not even maybe death—who really knew? and death was a long way off, he thought, because maybe it was a state of mind as well as a physical fact. When he thought about it, his father had really been dying a long time, starting back three, four years before when some scandal (with a woman, the problems with his father almost always revolved around women or cards) had tarnished his reputation badly enough so that it couldn't easily be refurbished. His father's not going to war went against him with a lot of people, too. Why hadn't he gone? His twin brother Cobus had gone, had been in some of the worst fighting, had come home an almost Achaean hero; but Mason Raymond's father had stayed in Albany giving his parties, gambling with his cronies, going off with his women, angling to get himself elected to office, his eye on the governor's chair, his life unchanged although the whole country around him had been caught up in the maelstrom. Women and poker had been more important to him than the issue of union. Maybe that was also one of the reasons he had lost his political weight.

Maybe when his father had denied his unwhite blood—easy to do since he didn't look Indian—had married into the rich Raymond family, conducting himself in what most people would have considered a very un-Indian fashion, his father had been (he saw in this moment which was so basic in terms of life and death, of the elements and himself) weak in the worst way. A weak character, people said in the Landing about men who didn't have self-discipline, who couldn't postpone pleasures of the moment for rewards of the future.

You had to keep your mind disciplined just the way you had to keep a good horse disciplined. His father's mind had gotten heavy and dull and resentful of discipline after all those years of indulgence, and maybe his father had realized this (Mason Raymond would like to think he had) and this was why Clyde Buttes had decided, in a kind of desperate decision, that he had to get in condition—but it was too late. Too much time had passed, he had been out to pasture too long; he had foundered. His father's hope to go back and redirect his life had come too late; he was a diseased and dying man who had let his life slip away in unessentials. Mason Raymond wanted to believe that his father had had the vision to see he had to try to get back and that was why he had wanted to come to the Landing once more, to get back to basic things. But it was too late and his father had seen that—he was Clyde Buttes, he could never be Cobus—and that's why he had pinned that psalm to his breast, asking forgiveness maybe, but more, saying he wasn't afraid, he faced the fact he had misused his small strengths in perverse ways. There was no going back, or ahead. His father had balked too long at the curbing of his freedom. But what his father called freedom others could just as readily define as laxity. His mother was growing lax too, putting on so much weight, lying around complaining and fussing that she didn't have anything to *do*. When they'd first come up from Albany, she had been thin and peaked, and it was right she should fill out and color up; but it wasn't good to get fat and (there was no other way to describe it) careless.

What did she do with all her time? She didn't read, either. Oh, she'd flip through a book looking at a page here and there, but that wasn't reading. And the kind of books she flipped through weren't what you'd call real books anyway. Reading to Mason Raymond meant making a discovery you'd never made before one that opened further the incredible mysteries of life.

She didn't read, didn't sew, didn't ride at all any more, didn't even do much visiting. What did she do? He'd be damned if he knew. She was rusting out the way his father had rusted out. Dying a little, day by day. And he loved her and this self-indulgence on her part made him angry because there was no need for it. What was there in people that as they grew older they became more and more involved with the physical sides of themselves? Old people were always, Mason Raymond's grandfather had shown him, doing a lot of internal listening, checking on their plumbing and breathing, trying to measure heartbeats and digestive action, obsessed by the vital functions the young took for granted, as if they were afraid something inside they'd never paid enough attention to would break down and give up.

His grandfather, Old Guthrie Buttes, had been that way at the end, turned inward listening to his vital signs to see if they faltered or failed, a frail garrulous old man brought out in a chair to sun on the front porch of the New House, a blanket over his arthritic legs, his liver-spotted, blue-veined hands trembling with age and breakdown, but his eyes bright, looking down on *his* lake, those bright eyes the legacy of his heroic past.

Guthrie Buttes was in Young John Buttes, people said. He's a regular throw-back to his grandfather, that John, looks like him, too, jest like o'nery old Guthrie. Got his cussedness, too. He was my grandfather, too, Mason Raymond thought. There's as much of his blood in me as there is in John.

Once, sun-dozing, his grandfather had jerked awake with a start, as if he were rousing himself from a bad dream. "Afore we had the war, this was a peaceful place. Now look at it— can't hear yourself think over to the Landin' no more so much *junk* goin'. War ain't good for nuthin' but machines. The machines done took over, and that's the fault of the war. We was a country proud of the land until this fight come and now all you ever hear talk of is machines and cities and big money. We'dda been better off stayin' with what we had. Can't never do that though. Things is always changin'."

He looked at Mason Raymond. "You take two people, they start out gittin' to know one another and they git on well together, they got a good feelin' about one another. But if that bond's gonna stick, they got to keep workin' at it—changin'. They got to keep movin', deepenin'. You can't never stay at A in anythin', you gotta move from A to B and then from B to C and you gotta keep goin'. If you stop and git hung up at B or C or any place, thin's don't keep movin' on, and stoppin's not movin' and not movin's not gittin' anywhere."

Mason Raymond understood his grandfather wasn't just talking about the country, he was also describing how he felt about people, and Mason Raymond suddenly realized why his grandfather had married a half-Indian. He was getting from A to B or from B to C; he was moving from one step to the next, something to do with his Indian upbringing. Another Indian woman had helped raise his grandfather when his own mother had died. Her Indian kin had taught him Indian skills. Very few white people went across the lake to the Buttes place, but these Indians did. Old Guthrie Buttes had been Indian-linked and he was repaying his debt.

Indian blood in me, in John, Mason Raymond thought. His grandfather acknowledged his accountability; there would be a day when he, too, would have to get from A to B, B to C.

"Tell me about the time you brought that man out of the woods," he'd plead and his grandfather, caught midsentence, would look up, surprised. "Oh, that was a long time ago," he'd say. "And not too much to it."

"Tell me anyway, I want to hear."

"Oh, Clyde Burroughs, he got strung out some by a b'ar and I brung him home. That's about all there was to it."

Exasperated, Mason Raymond would badger him for details, but the old man was more intent on checking his inner system for breakdowns and refusals. Presently he would doze, his head gently nodding back and forth. In one of these naps his heart, to which at the moment he had been paying little attention and was thus himself unwarned, ceased; the head became still, the hands opened, closed, stayed closed. "A wonderful way to go," people said. "I hope I go that way. Not one of those long sicknesses where you don't know yourself and are such a burden to the family."

It was a family funeral, not many people from the Landing, with the burial up back in the Buttes family cemetery where many of the Raymonds were also buried—his grandfather Buttes and his great-grandfather Raymond were up there. His father was there. You go to one spot where all your ancestors are, you're happier knowing they all lie together, someone had said. One day he would be there, under maybe what everyone called Emily's larch. A woman he had never known, but of whom wondrous stories were still told. She was a witch with animals. She *talked* to them, people still remembered. Too tall for a woman, the very, very old recalled. A real strong woman, they said still, who got her way. She must have been very strong to be remembered. Most women bring men into the world and see them out and no one remembers. But people remembered Emily and they remembered her son,

Guthrie, whose coming into the world had killed her. A hundred years from now they would be asking, Who was Mason Raymond Buttes? Another distinction: those remembered and those forgotten.

He hugged the snoring dog and it yelped, opened its eyes, startled, and then snuggled up to him.

A day and a half passed and he had nothing to eat; hunger pangs hammered at his stomach, his head was woozy; he kept re-experiencing that sensation where he was breaking through the outer shell of himself into the center of light, where airy and free he floated in hallucinatory hesitation, feeling wisdom in a way words couldn't define, images and shapes and dark parcels of his soul opened so that he saw himself as a swinger through trees.

There was no point in hunching endlessly in the hole letting his legs stiffen up. He had soon to look for food (not much in May, late summer or fall would have been better, but in such matters one is not the chooser, B to C). And he had to do something about his bites. He was so badly bitten that every inch of his body itched and smarted. He hoped that rubbing himself with mud might help. He had looked at the big mudholes all around and suddenly bent over and packed some mud to his face and it felt good, sticky at first, but cool and soothing. After he shucked all his clothes, he plastered himself with mud and clay and there was an immediate sense of relief in his hurt knees.

He could hear his grandfather, Old Guthrie Buttes, telling him, You git off course, you hunt yourself up water and follow it downstream, you'll end up all right, can't go wrong followin' a river downstream.

Well, he had the river; the only problem was being able to make his way on bad knees. Give them a day or two to heal up with this mud and maybe he'd be ready to go, be fit as a fiddle, as his grandfather would have said, but in the meantime he had to make accommodations to his stomach.

Hector was watching him, head cocked to one side. Hector was supposed to be a hunter, another entry to be made in the long list of Hector's failures. "Aren't you hungry?" Mason

Raymond asked, but the dog only looked pleased at the attention he was getting, a happy, happy dog with not a hungry problem in the world.

Disgusted, Mason Raymond turned—but the dog bounded up, nearly knocking him over, and began circling and barking. "Why don't you go do something useful, like finding a rabbit or something?" though what he would do with a raw rabbit . . . he wasn't *that* hungry. (Hunger is a powerful force, Old Guthrie Buttes said inside Mason Raymond's head. Makes men do lots they never dreamed they'd do. You can't talk principles to a starving man.) Well, he wasn't ready to tackle raw rabbit yet. He looked around, the dog keeping up his incessant yammering. Too dumb to know what roots he could eat (and too tired to do much digging); nuts all gone this time of year (except the rejects); frogs and maybe nesting fish (if they nested now, too dumb to know when fish nested, it was spring though, that much he knew, and fish sat on top of their eggs, you lay down and tickled their stomachs with one hand and grabbed them with the other), but *raw?*

God, it had gotten cold. No sun, the air yeasty, it was so wet. Getting ready to rain or hail again. Always something. He limped to the stream bank and lay down, gazing into the water; it was beautifully clear, running over stones and racing God knew where—to some town downstream where probably no one even knew he was up here lost in the woods.

"Oh my God, he's out in those woods *all by himself!*" he could hear his mother crying, Rivers moving anxiously toward her, but Rivers couldn't touch her, he was a man, a strong man with sure, steady hands that could handle spirited horses, but he couldn't comfort her because he worked for her, she was the master and he the servant. "You let him get lost in the woods, Cobus? How could you?" and in this drama Worth stepped up and took the blame and his mother calmed. She couldn't carry on with a stranger the way she could with family. But frantic she would of course remain—shredding a handkerchief between her never-still fingers, putting things in her mouth (the handkerchief, candy, nuts, whatever was at hand, comforting her fears with sucking the way a child reassures himself by putting his finger or thumb or blanket in his mouth), abusing her eyes by endless weeping (crying made her eyes redden and her lids puff and swell), finally bedded down by one of those blinding headaches to which she fell victim so often, flattened with pain, a wet cloth over her eyes, complaining of thirst and nausea, pains in the stomach, shortness of breath; with that strange fruit odor to her breath which he had only noticed in the past few months, but which seemed to become more pronounced the more flushed, excited, parched, and breathy she became.

Old Doc Bronson (whose town epithet was "cemetery filler") would be sent for, even though the town joke was that the family started getting out the crepe when he came up the drive. He had a drinking problem or he'd have had a practice in some decent place like the Falls. Confused—his breath as strong, stronger, than Mason Raymond's mother's—he would send for his son and the two of them would prescribe some medicine or other, most likely those same old white pills which would bring his mother nothing but a bill, while his uncle tried to calm her and she wouldn't be calmed, loving his uncle's ministrations more than she hated the pains, until, working herself up until she was really sick, she would lapse into semiconsciousness and sleep, her breath so short and shallow the whole house was alarmed, Rivers fidgeting outside the closed door waiting to see if he should take the horses to the Falls for the "real" doctor; meanwhile the search parties had been organized and sent out, fanning over the countryside with lanterns and dogs and guns, (he had been listening for the guns unconsciously all this time without realizing it, knowing that there would be intermittent shots to alert him they were looking for him, the men breaking brush ten, fifteen feet apart, tracking more worried as each hour passed); it was bad weather to be out in, rendez-vousing back under the big Raymond porch, the piazza his mother called it, swinging their lanterns and shuffling their big, muddy boots, no, they hadn't come on a thing, funny how a boy could jest be swallowed up in the woods that way, leave no trace at all.

They would begin to remember other cases, recalling how a man or boy had disappeared into the scrub never to be seen again, not one single trace of him ever come upon or, maybe, some bits of cloth and bone turned up a year or two later, telling these tales even though all of them were familiar with the stories, because the telling had a purpose: it was meant to signify the waning of hope, the recognition that if some evidence didn't turn up in a day or two, the searching was hopeless.

His mother wouldn't hear any of this of course, but she'd know. Every hour that passed without any trace of him was a signal for new hysteria. Her fears, formless at first, would begin to become specific and final; she would grow frantic, his uncle would send word up to the New House for his wife, Mason Raymond's Aunt Kam, to come, though (for some reason Mason Raymond had never understood) his mother was cold to Kam Buttes, fault-finding and uncharitable; but Katherine Ann Morgan Buttes was competent, she was strong. No nonsense went on when she was around. Though Mason Raymond's mother might not like her, she was afraid of her; order of a sort would be restored when his aunt arrived. The house would become quiet; that ominous absence of sound which disaster so often brought with it would imprison the rooms. The servants would whisper, all save Rivers. Mason Raymond imagined him speechless with anguish, stationary and helpless by the door through which only women were allowed to pass; men gathering quietly in front of the house waiting for one weary searching party to come in so that they could go out, relieving them, the news bad—worse than the day before because the more time that passed the less chance there was for survival, witnessing the rain, the wind, the hail with apprehension, thinking, No one can survive out in weather like that, especially a city boy, thinking it first and then finally saying it, gathering in groups to fortify one another's decision that it was time to give up, there wasn't any more chance for hope, the boy was gone for good.

Well, let them give up. He'd show them. He didn't care how long it took or how bad things got, he wasn't going to go under. There had to be ways to survive in the woods, even in weather like this. Other men had done it. He could do it.

The main thing was not to lose courage, not to give into despair, not to—

Snow began to fall. *Snow?*

Hector kept hogging the leaves. He would shift himself around, wiggling this way and that until he got most of the leaves under him, and then, grunting, he'd settle down and start snoring. There was no way to budge him. Shoving and swearing, Mason Raymond would try to inch him over, but the dog was dead, determined weight. Coaxing worked no wonders; he had turned out to be a pretty selfish dog, Mason Raymond concluded, but his selfishness had one advantage: Hector's fur had soaked up most of the water that had accumulated in the bottom of the hole. Better him than me, Mason Raymond thought, shoving leaves under the dog and trying to nest the hole.

The snow fell in a blizzard-like drive that gathered an inch of white on the ground before much more than a half hour had passed, Mason Raymond limping around under the downfall raking up new leaves and trying to do something about his clothes. They had frozen stiff.

He was cold, bad cold, and worse, leaves weren't the answer. He needed the protection of cloth. Finally he saw that the dog's selfishness might be another asset; he stuffed all his things under Hector and, hoping the dog's body heat would thaw them, kept his own heat up, pushing himself to gather more insulation for the hole, hobbling at an even pace though, careful not to work up a sweat, because sweat would chill on him and that chill was to be avoided at all cost. One thing he knew, the essential one: panic had killed more men than cold. Men beset by fear started running around crazily, exhausting themselves, working up a heavy sweat that, when the wind hit, froze them to the bone. The trick was to keep the body going at a steady enough pace to keep up heat but not so fast as to raise a sweat.

You kept having so much bad luck, so many things go wrong, eventually the scales tipped, your turn came for some good luck. The only way to look at the snow then was in a positive light; maybe the snow, which was just about rock bottom, would be the turning point. Things couldn't go down forever, there had to be a bottom. He'd reached bottom; it was going to be up all the way from now on. The Fates said, That boy's done well, reward him.

All right, so it was snowing, he was cold, the dog was hogging the hole, he was lost in the woods and search parties wouldn't go out in weather like this and when they did the snow would have obliterated his tracks. All right, so his knees were in tough shape, he was hungry, his clothes were frozen stiff, the mud had dried and stiffened and made him feel as if he were encased in a cast, all right, so he had no idea what he was going to do next, except that goddam it he wasn't going to cry (at least not quite yet), goddam it, he wasn't going to give up; he wasn't asking to be saved, but he was willing to work for it, that wasn't asking; not afraid so much as inept, tremulous before the enormity of power of that sky overhead and this great forest around, but beginning to be determined of his own small worth as well, because the whole point (at least so it seemed to him) was that you had to be tested and tried, and then if you came through you had earned what you got; and for reasons he did not very well understand and over which he had no control, the balance of power lay in this moment here in the woods and that realization, not fear, was what caused the hammering in his heart, gave him the overwhelming sense of his standing at the crossroads of his life and choosing which way he would go. Move the damn dog over and get your clothes on and get warm; you aren't going get *any*where running around bareass naked in this weather. Go find yourself something to eat, I don't care *what*. You've gotta have something to eat to stay alive.

The snow fell all day. After a time the dog's warmth worked through the clothes and they thawed out—damp, but protective; he struggled into them, shivering, and huddled up next to the dog, but that didn't stop the shivering. Finally he stuffed leaves between his mud-caked skin and the cold cloth, and though they were wet, that was better; he curled up and slept, slept badly, dreaming dreams which frightened him back to consciousness, but when he started up, shuddering, he couldn't remember the dreams whole, just patches and flashes here and there, so that his shivering was made up as much of his nightmares as of the snow and cold and his predicament.

The dog, though totally engrossed in his own dreams, noisy and grumbling or yipping, scared, gave warmth and companionship, and in some strange way, encouragement. Without the dog his chances of survival would have been slim because survival depended upon attitude. He felt good about the world because of the dog. He hugged Hector and went back to sleep.

He slept most of the day. He would dream himself awake with the frightening images, lie open-eyed watching the snow fall, then gradually drift back to a state which was neither waking nor sleeping. He was conscious all the time of his knees, they hurt, hurt terribly, and inside there was the hurt he felt for all the people whose fears troubled him—his mother, his aunt and uncle, Hart—all part of his thoughts and dreams. His father came at one point and handed him a paper. Mason Raymond couldn't read what was on it, but when he broke consciousness he was pretty sure he knew what that paper said:

The Lord is my shepherd . . . I shall not want . . .

The snow cast a spell, falling rhythmically, sleepily, the endless flakes making a small vibration, almost a hum; he heard the snow song because there was no wind now, not a murmur anywhere, no stirring of air, just that quickly falling, humming snow inundating the world with white.

Sometime in the night the storm passed; Mason Raymond awoke to a sky full of stars. He shifted himself, feeling cramped and uncomfortable, his knees half scabby, half open, and the open parts full of pus; it took him a second to realize he had been able to move so freely because the dog was gone. He sat up in panic, shouting, his voice strange and unrecognizable.

There was no answer.

For a moment he couldn't think. The dog had come out of the woods; now he had gone back to the woods, gone home probably, fed up with being crowded in a skimpy little old hole, and who'd ever know he'd even been near Mason Raymond? Dogs could probably communicate, but men were too dumb to understand their signals.

After this snowfall no one would believe he was alive anyway. Probably this morning it would be his uncle Cobus' duty to go to his mother and say the men had decided to call off the search. There just wasn't any hope. She would go to pieces. Finding his father had hardly fazed her—because she had ceased believing in the efficacy of her love for him. But her belief in her love for Mason Raymond was the center of her existence; she had counted on it to carry her through the rest of her life. He pictured her shrieking, envisioned Rivers (in the hall) trembling, bolting toward the door, then pausing, hand on the door, hearing the cries of protest, unable to move; love did so many things, not the least of which was destroy. It had helped destroy his mother, maybe his father (in fact with his father he sort of hoped it *was* love); it was destroying Rivers; most of his life, Mason Raymond felt, it had also worked against him. Maybe love always destroys in the end, Mason Raymond thought. Maybe it's the most destructive force there is.

He half-rose, crouching on the edge of the hole, brushing aside snow. Quite clearly the dog's tracks showed where he had bounded through the snow; the path disappeared a hundred yards ahead into the brush. God knew where Hector was now. Someplace safe. Not that Mason Raymond blamed him.

The world looked lonely and white, silent and untouched. Made him feel cold to the soul. For the first time he felt defeated. He flopped back in the hole and buried his head in his arms, not crying—he was beyond crying—his was a dry, bottomless despair. Inside his head he saw Hart twisting his thirty-six coonskin hat in his hands, standing in that rusty green dress-up suit, looking responsible. "It's all *your* fault," his mother cried. "You're the one that lost him!"

But Mason Raymond didn't blame Hart. It wasn't his fault, only the failing of his enthusiasm: he had been so anxious to get to his dogs his mind hadn't been doing any long-range figuring. "He's two-thirds dog and I'm half horse," his uncle said inside his head. Suddenly Mason Raymond straightened up. If Hart were two-thirds dog, mightn't he be able to understand if Hector went back and tried to tell him where Mason Raymond was? Maybe the dog would understand that. Maybe he'd suddenly understood that and hightailed it for home to tell Hart. Maybe . . . The dog came flying toward him; his whole head was bristling with quills. "Oh, you dumb dog," Mason Raymond cried in anguish. "You're supposed to knock a porcupine on the head—" But at least the dog had been trying; you had to give him credit for that.

Mason Raymond tried to pull the quills by hand. A few came free, but most were so deeply imbedded that he couldn't get them out. The dog put up a terrible commotion, yipping, snarling, growling, yelping, snapping. It was no use. And yet he had to get the quills loose; otherwise Hector would die. There were quills embedded in his muzzle, neck, shoulder, near his eyes, in his ears, even in the upper part of his legs. If these were not extracted, the dog could neither eat nor drink. The quills would work their way in, fester, one might easily pierce his brain or come out through his heart.

Mason Raymond remembered Hart, laughing—though it was no laughing matter—telling how his young pups were always getting tangled up with porcupines. He had to tie their feet because being scratched was as bad as being bitten. Hart would make a noose around the dog's mouth and pull. If two or three dogs had got into quills, it would take him all day to get them clean. Somehow one of those quills had got into Hart himself and worked its way into his system and come out through the top of his head. "Felt somethin' funny in my scalp and Mabel she looked at it and she couldn't see nuthin' and then a day or two later I was dunkin' my head and I went to smooth down my hair and this thing pricked me and I yelled to Mabel and that woman of mine come and looked agin and said, 'Oh, my God, you got a quill comin' right out of your head. You're the worst man I ever seen for punishin' your head one way or the other.' "

Hart hitched up his overalls and ran his hand over his wild, furlike hair. "Got sick of extractin' them quills from them critters three, four times a week and I decided to learn them some sense. Got me a porky and put it in a cage and sicked them young dogs one at a time on it until they was all quilled up and then I tied 'em and pulled and sicked them on that porky agin and went to pullin' some more. Done that four or five times and they turned on me and tried to take me on rather than the quills and that was that. They never went near no porcupines agin. Do it with all my young stock regular as clockwork now and that's the end of that."

Mason Raymond wondered what else could go wrong. Something was bound to. It came to him a man could make a list of all the things that could go wrong and think he'd reached bottom and would start up again, but the truth was there was never any bottom, there were always more disasters to overtake a man than he could ever think of. There was always one more thing that could go wrong no matter how far down he had dropped.

Mason Raymond pulled quills until the dog got so ornery that he couldn't do anything with him; then he stopped and waited until Hector calmed down and started again. It got so that every time the dog saw him raise his hand he snarled, and there were maybe a hundred quills still left in him and Mason Raymond didn't see how he was ever going to get them out.

He was discouraged and cranky and hungry and cold, but since his knees weren't so bad as they had been, he started off to get a drink of water. The dog came with him but couldn't drink. He stood looking at Mason Raymond expectantly, and Mason Raymond went over the whole problem with him, explaining in detail how he was in rough shape and the quills had to come out, but the dog wasn't interested in rational explanations. When Mason Raymond bent down to try to take some more out, Hector backed up and bared his teeth. So much for that.

Mason Raymond limped back to the hole, realizing he'd made another error. He'd gotten his feet wet in the snow. If his feet froze, he'd never be able to move. He took off his boots and stuffed them with leaves, but when he put them back on they still felt cold and wet. The leaves were wet and soggy.

He had two paramount problems now, his wet feet and the

dog's quills. He sat in the hole and watched the sun struggling to get free from black clouds moving in with a wind and tried to think constructively. He couldn't go through snow even if his legs were well enough to carry him. In no time at all his boots would be soaked and then when darkness came and the temperature dropped, his boots would freeze his feet. He sat in the hole and watched the dripping pines and thought about roast beef, a big bowl of mashed potatoes, a steaming pitcher of hot cocoa.

The dog began to howl, a long, piercing baying that went on and on. It would have been difficult to decide who was more miserable, but in a case like this, Mason Raymond concluded, degree didn't make much difference: they were both two poor specimens, that much was sure.

Birds had begun to make a terrible racket. They were racing around the sky screaming their heads off, trying to tell Mason Raymond something he was too dumb to get. He sprawled in the hole, the dog hovering just out of range, wary of Mason Raymond's efforts to get at him and start pulling quills again. If he'd had a gun, even a bow and arrow, he could have killed one of those birds; but without a fire, how could he have eaten it? Raw, that's how, he told himself.

Damned dumb birds. Damned dumb dog. Damned dumb kid.

His feet *were* freezing. His stomach hollowly sent signals of protest. He was so confused with cold and hunger that he knew he was no longer thinking clearly, the inside of his head filled with visions of the cheeses and smoked meats in Lite's store, the bowls of eggs in Mabel Hart's kitchen, and the smell of one of her chickens simmering on the stove. He remembered the thick, rich cream he had spilled and groaned when he saw, inside his mind, *dogs* licking it up. He remembered Morphis at the Academy smacking his lips whenever hot rolls were sent out from the big school kitchen. Morphis would slit open a hot roll and stuff the inside with butter. As the butter melted and ran into a pool on his plate, Morphis broke an end from a roll and mopped up the shiny yellow pool with it. Grease gleamed on his mouth; his eyes shone with pleasure.

He chewed like one in a splendid, euphoric dream.

The sun was shining, then hiding. The trees dripped; bare patches of earth appeared where there were small openings under the trees. The air felt warmer. He was going to have to try to break out of this prison. His mind had just acknowledged the decision; now he was trying to get his heart to accept it. The three basic steps: awareness, acknowledgment, acceptance.

He could not go with snow. But the snow was melting. He could not go with infected knees. But his knees were much better. He could not go without food. But he would find something to eat along the way. But what had made his decision irrevocable was the dog's plight. He now knew in a way he could never have explained logically that the dog would never leave him and go back to where he could get help. He was responsible then for Hector. Those quills had to come out or Hector would die. If Hector died, it would be his fault.

He looked at the dog. He had never really been responsible for anything in his life, not any living thing. He looked at the dog, mournful, his muzzle abristle with quills; and Hector, sad-eyed, gazed back. "I'll get you through," Mason Raymond said to the dog. "You wait and see."

They stood in a clearing, he and the dog. There was still some snow on the ground, but it was melting fast; the ground that was uncovered was spongy; an immense ball of sun hung glittering overhead. Noon, Mason Raymond guessed. The birds were still carrying on, creating a terrific din all around, feasting on the thousands of bugs which seemed to have sprung up as soon as the sun won out over the clouds.

The air was moist and heavy, the perfect incubator for insects. Of everything, Mason Raymond dreaded the bugs most. He stripped and rolled his clothes into a ball and again plastered himself with a thick coating of mud. He was going to try to use it as an insulator against the insects. He must have been a sight, stark naked except for his socks and boots, plastered with mud stuck with leaves, a pin-cushion mutt of a dog by his side. He went over to the brook and put another layer of mud over his skin. It was the best protection he could think of against the rage of the insects. His eyelids were the worst, stinging and swollen with bites. In the ways of nature, might not these bugs pick his bones clean?

One against millions—no odds at all—and in the mysterious way of existence did not the bugs love their lives the same as he loved his? Standing in the midst of woods which were no longer hostile now that the sun was out, but not friendly either, just neutral, profoundly indifferent to his plight, something apart, yet with (it seemed to him) an existence of their own, he called silently to the spirit of the woods, wanting to shake its indifference, to move it to concern: to propitiate those gods whom he knew nothing of but whose strength might crush the fragile spirit he called his own, as he thoughtlessly, yet violently, crushed the bugs.

His uncle said the Indians asked pardon of the spirits of the animals they had to kill on the hunt, that they never killed in sport (as, suddenly, it occurred to him, most men did, his uncle and Lite included, and remembering too the surge of his own instinct for the kill). He would never carelessly shed woodland blood again; that was the vow he made to the forest in exchange for his life. He would hunt, yes, because he admired the instincts and skills of the dogs, but he would not kill.

I will never own or carry a gun, he said to the woods. I will neither shoot nor trap and if the time comes when one life depends upon my taking another, I will, like the Indians, bless first the spirit of he whom it is necessary to take. Before I leave these woods I may have to destroy in order to survive, he conceded. I must take the plant from the ground or snare the bird or animal from its nest. *But only in need.* And only with my hands. I will never carry a man-made gun and kill for pleasure or gain.

He bent and touched his hand to the thick riverbank mud, then anointed his forehead, chest, left and right shoulder, with it. He was ready to start.

The creek was fuller than it would be any other time of the year because of the spring snow freshets that had flooded it. Water raged downhill, lumping rocks and stones along in its path as it careened furiously through the thick bracken path it had worn in the woods. In some places erosion had made gulleys three or four feet deep; in others a sudden drop over rocks left Mason Raymond and the dog stranded on a bluff looking down on a cliff too steep, with his hurt knees, to descend.

Progress was much slower than Mason Raymond had anticipated. The dog slouched along beside him, moping over its own problems. The terrain was rough, especially when two or three fallen trees seemed to have collided, but worst of all were the bugs. They formed a shroud around Mason Raymond's body, a halo around his head, veiled his vision: he saw everything through a haze of hovering insects. They whirled and danced and dived and bit him inside the ears, where he had no mud, on the eyelids, inside the tender area of his mouth that was exposed when he briefly breathed deeply. They burrowed down inside his hair and fed on his scalp, worked their way into the exposed areas under his arms, between his fingers and legs where friction had worked the mud away. His private parts they tormented so incessantly that he finally put on his underwear over the mud, but they penetrated openings on his thighs that were made as he strode in and out, moving the cloth away.

The dog went mad occasionally, running around and around trying to catch himself, his quilled mouth snapping furiously, emptily, in a frantic effort to stop the itching and smarting and pointed jabbing. They plowed on, driven and bitten, crashing through brush and bracken, trying to follow the water downstream.

Mason Raymond had no way of knowing how far he was from people. He would have said not too far if he hadn't enough insight to realize that in fumbling about in the windfall there was no knowing really how confused he had become or in which direction he was moving. He assumed he would come out at the lake, but there was no guarantee of this; it just seemed logical, but then many things that seemed logical turned out not to obey the rules but ran to strange laws of their own.

A flushed bird fluttered up against the tangle of growth

] *119* [

ahead, hung suspended for a moment in mid-air, then dropped back to earth, flopping about in the brush. "Come on, Heck," Mason Raymond shouted, flailing forward in a wild attempt to try to trap food. Forgive me, he said silently, but this is necessary.

The bird—brownish, almost as large as a chicken, handsome—whose bright, frightened eyes Mason Raymond glimpsed for an instant, flopped over, then rose awkwardly, trailing a wing, and lunged a few yards ahead. It turned its frantic eyes for an instant on Mason Raymond, then tried to fly, fell back, dragging its injured wing, rose again and staggered ten or fifteen yards forward and fell to the ground again. Mason Raymond and the dog plunged after.

The bird rose and bumbled on, flapped, flopped down, rose briefly and struggled on. Sweat began to blind Mason Raymond as he thrashed on, but he ignored it, seeing in that wounded wing the means to nourishment, the promise of strength and a way home.

They were not, for some reason, gaining on the bird. For a fact, it seemed to Mason Raymond to be outdistancing them, and yet if it had a broken wing, as it certainly seemed to have, all that effort toward flying ought to have exhausted it; they should be steadily gaining, should have overtaken it by this time; but the bird was not tiring. Its efforts were more agitated and energetic than when they'd first surprised it, as if it were gaining strength as it went along instead of losing it.

How was that possible?

A bird as big as that with a broken wing struggling to fly ought to be grounded by now, lie feebly flopping from side to side with its frightened heart pounding so violently that its breast beat a visible tattoo of terror.

Scratched and bleeding, Mason Raymond forgot his knees and vaulted over the short brush, tore against the larger, more formidable shrubs. The bird, a whir of white and brown, rose in flight and disappeared in a sprint of speed over the next rise. "There's nothing the matter with that bird, nothing at all," Mason Raymond said.

The dog made no reply. As soon as Mason Raymond pulled up, Hector flopped down, panting, to rest. Besides its snoring, it was the restingest dog Mason Raymond had ever seen. If it hadn't been for its resting, neither of them would have been in this predicament. Still those quills must be bothering him terribly. All that crashing through this miserable tangle of trees and ferns and berry bushes must have raised a powerful thirst in Hector, but of course he couldn't drink with a mouth bristling with quills.

"Why would that dumb bird act hurt?" Mason Raymond asked the dog. Quilled muzzle between his legs, Hector looked at Mason Raymond with sad, reproachful eyes. Thrashing around hopelessly was Mason Raymond's fault, and what had it got them?

"Why would a bird *act* hurt?" Mason Raymond repeated, standing trying to puzzle it out.

Why did anything act hurt? He thought of his mother's complaints about her head pounding, about how thirsty she was and couldn't seem to get rid of that thirst, no matter how much water she drank. She wants attention, he would think to himself, that's her way of getting attention. But a bird wasn't a woman; why should it want Mason Raymond's attention?

To get me away from something, he realized. That bird had a nest back there! He turned, stumbling back through the clearly marked path they'd made as they broke through at a run, retracing his way between the fallen and broken limbs and brush, thinking, I hope it's eggs and not young.

He could picture himself sucking eggs, but it was impossible for him to visualize eating tiny, fluffy young. He was raising another sweat: the excitement as well as the exertion. He forced himself to stop and rest. The dog flopped again, panting through his quills.

They commenced again, slower this time, Mason Raymond carefully pacing himself. At the original spot where he thought they had suddenly flushed the bird, the nest would be somewhere about. He would have to go carefully so as not to miss it, not to step on it inadvertently. He didn't know whether it would be in a tree or on the ground, but it seemed to him the larger birds made ground nests. He wasn't sure, but he was pretty sure.

He wasn't going to get himself all mixed up again. That much at least he was learning. He took a broken limb of birch and made a standing sign in the middle of the clearing. He would start in close, circling, moving in a wider and wider arc, until he had covered all the area around that central stick. He would go cautiously, looking underfoot, searching overhead.

Of course there was no controlling the dog (he wondered if there would ever be any controlling that dog); Hector might crash into the nest and ruin the eggs, and that would be that, but hunting dogs were supposed to have some sense about these things, weren't they? Most hunting dogs. But he wouldn't want to make any predictions about this namesake of the great warrior of Troy.

He doubled around the first circle. Nothing. On the second he moved even more warily, parting brown, winter-shriveled ferns and some new green spring shoots he didn't know the names of, feeling along the ground blindly, then pausing, carefully checking out the trees overhead. He was standing examining a tree (a beech, he thought, but of course didn't really know), letting his eyes travel slowly up and down each branch, when he felt a sharp stabbing at his back. He let out a yelp and automatically put his hand to the spot. Blood was running. A second later, in a whirl of wings, the bird came at him again, piercing him in the shoulder. Mason Raymond threw his hands over his head and dropped to the ground, shouting at Hector. The bird was whirling overhead getting ready to attack again. He marveled at the protectiveness of that pair of birds—one pretending to be wounded and leading the enemy away, the other attacking directly though the enemy was a hundred times his size.

He heard the dog crashing through the brush. "Damn bird came right at me," he marveled. "First the one pretending she was hurt and then this one coming right at me."

He peered up cautiously. Hector had driven the bird off, had disappeared himself. Probably resting somewhere after his efforts. The nest must be very close. On hands and knees Mason Raymond crawled along, letting his fingers do the searching. There was a rock ahead and a slight disturbance of the ground covering. He had found what the parent birds had tried so desperately to protect: ten buff eggs. To take what was so strongly and clearly someone else's must surely be a great sin.

Forgive me, he said to the woods. But this is truly necessary. And bless this food.

He reached over and picked up the first egg.

His hunger was not appeased, but aroused; the meager meal of eggs had reminded his stomach how abused it had been; it knotted and grumbled and gassed up on him. He was bent double with cramps, gasping with pain, then suddenly weak with a spasm that sent his bowels loose. For a time there was nothing to do but lie on the ground moaning, belching, making wind, the taste in his mouth so foul that he was ashamed to have it as a part of him.

The gray dimness of dusk, with its lonely exodus of light, alerted him to a new need. He could not be caught out in the open at night. There were fallen trees all about and he glanced quickly around for the best natural covering. His eyes were becoming practiced now. He could automatically select and reject, sort out possibilities. There were two or three promising places, but he selected as the best a fall of two trees, crisscrossing, that offered an almost ideal skeleton shelter. With a few branches as shields, some insulating leaves, he and the dog, returned from his victorious nest, should be covered sufficiently to keep out the worst of the cold. He began to assemble their shelter rapidly. The dog even cooperated by digging a little to give them some more space. It was as if Hector knew what was expected of him. Even the weather seemed to lend a hand. A warm wind came up, a late gray wind, and they slept for the first time, both of them, Mason Raymond knew, feeling somehow protected, watched over, and yet he had broken a vow he had made only a day before.

I couldn't help it, he kept saying to himself. I didn't do it because I wanted to, I did it because I had to. Even so, the best in him rebelled against necessity.

The next morning Mason Raymond and the dog plowed

through the windfall, stumbling and breathing heavily but
confidently, as if they had a premonition of the moment to
come midmorning, when the dog stopped and pricked up his
ears and a moment later Mason Raymond thought he heard
something ahead, voices—could it be voices?—and he began
floundering and shouting; it was voices, strong voices shouting, "Over here, he's over here!" and he crashed through the
brush into Hart's arms; there were tears—*tears*—on Hart's
face as he clasped Mason Raymond to him; he had on his
famous thirty-six coonskin hat ("For luck, boy," he said later,
"I never give up hope, even when the snow come") and he
was jumping up and down and shouting and weeping all at the
same time, unintelligible and incoherent, a madman dancing
and screaming with the pain of happiness, beating Mason
Raymond on the back, waving his coon cap, jumping and
sprinting and screaming; "You're a son to me, like a *real* son
to me," Hart hollered, embarrassed but emphatic—"as bumbling as I am, God bless you, Albert was always such a do-er,
runnin' around makin' thin's right while I stumbled behind
takin' 'em back apart. Never loses nuthin', my son Albert,
never mislays nuthin', never trips over or forgets nuthin'—he
took after some side of me got mislaid, I reckon. But you, boy,
you're the spittin' image of my forgetfulness, my o'neriness,
my awful awkwardness. I felt close to you right from the start
. . . nuthin' agin Albert, you understand, we gits our children
and parents, no choice to it and often no understandin', but
those we give presents from the heart we choose ourselves.
Oh, boy, you're saved—*saved!*" until finally he got out a sentence Mason Raymond could take in and understand, "How
are you, boy? How are YOU?"

Mason Raymond waited until he quieted down, maybe
three or four full minutes, savoring that wait because all the
time in the forest he had been preparing what he'd say if he
ever got out alive, and he had it perfect inside his head, but
he didn't want to go too fast and get it mixed up or have Hart
miss it, so he took his time and waited until Hart slowed up
and stopped romping around and hollering and asked again,
"How are you, boy? How was it out there in the woods?" and

Mason Raymond said very slowly and carefully,
"Well, first it rained,
And then it blew;
Then it hailed
And then it snew."

IV

"*You pretty low, ain't you, son?*"

Cobus Buttes kneeled down, squatting, sucking a piece of grass between his teeth. His eyes were brown, he had brown skin stretched over the Indian bone structure of his face, but his teeth were bright, white straight teeth. Mason Raymond could hear his mother say, He's not exactly a handsome man, but he's well-formed. Now she was fizzing about upstairs in her room in the froth that was all that was left of her brain.

Lying stretched out under Emily's larch, he regarded gray and green grass, a place he came to when he didn't want to be disturbed. Go away, he said, silent but determined, out of smoldering eyes. Why doesn't he go away?

"Ain't right to do somethin' so vital 'nd git no credit." Cobus Buttes collapsed on the grass, stretching out with a sigh. He's going to talk, Mason Raymond thought. Somebody—at least some adult—always wants to talk and set your world in order, figure you can't do it by yourself. Can't he see I don't want to talk. Nobody sees, Mason Raymond thought. I'm not like any of them, he thought, I'm not like anybody—father-loser, gun-loser, me-loser, mother-loser. *Go away,* he willed out of his frustration and impatience and anger at a world that refused to give him credit where credit was due, a world which kept presenting him with new, impossible challenges that asked him to restore order where chaos had taken over.

"Jest ain't right," his uncle muttered. "No way, no way atall. You done well out there in those woods, right well. Ain't no man couldda done better." In the green spring sun, the green spring song, he couldn't bear the notion of being patronized, especially by someone he loved. He sat up abruptly and cried out—his knees still gave him a lot of trouble. Home twelve hours, and the whole world crashing down on him and not one single soul—not one, not even Hart really—had said up to this point, You done well, boy. Of course he oughtn't to start parceling out blame. They had his mother to think about. He should be thinking about her too, should be up at the house—resolutely he closed his mind down on the duties that should be done. He had done the first duty, *kept alive,* and until now no one (except the possible babble of Hart when he stumbled forward in the woods and that wasn't *reasoned*) had said so much as a "done well," and now he was doing what he owed himself: he was sulking.

He stared moodily at the troubled face of his uncle, suddenly strange and mysterious in the harsh, burgeoning light, a man who'd been through all the worst maybe the world could hand a man and who'd come home and picked up where he'd left off and gone on and become what in the Landing they called a good, solid man. Envy closed Mason Raymond up tight as a vise. In the books he read reward followed hardship, but in the lessons of life this (like so many other things) turned out to be pretty untrue.

You should be up at the house, his censorious second self said to him. "All right, all right," Mason Raymond answered sulkily, "I know I should go up to the house." He rose, gasping, to his feet. His damned knees.

"There's time," his uncle said. "Five minutes more or less don't matter." He said that calmly when in fact just the opposite was true. Five minutes might mean the difference between life and death. How was it that in the space of such a short time so many final things could happen? Because the world didn't care, it didn't care about boys or women or wars or bad blood (Lite would be carrying on about Indians some way or other, Lite WAS the whole, damned, mixed-up world—Lite was evil and who could understand evil, either in the woods or in war or here at home?)—"I don't understand any of it," he said, wanting to be comforted and afraid of solace because it might make him a kid again and surely after his woods experience he had some claims on being a man. *Don't you believe it,* he told himself. In this world there are no claims on anything; just go ask your mother there upstairs.

Clumsily Cob Buttes's hand fell on his shoulder and Mason Raymond winced (he hated being touched, it made him feel so vulnerable) and his uncle, spitting out the battered grass, said, "I'm real proud of you, the way you handled yourself out there." They started downhill in a broken gait, Mason Raymond's knees acting mean on him and his uncle mumbling there was no accounting for how events would shape themselves, it was a cross-purposed world they lived in. Somewhere a bird (Christ, he didn't know the names of birds any more than he knew the names of trees) sang. Somewhere in the May sun it poured out its high-beating heart. Morphis had said birds lived at a tremendously accelerated speed in comparison to men; Mason Raymond just wished there was some way to tear out his own heart and post it down to Morphis and let him see *that* kind of acceleration.

What did birds say when they sang?

Maybe he ought to know, he had eaten the eggs, hadn't he?

He could hear her voice all the way downstairs, one word repeated over and over, "Please . . . please . . . please . . . please, please, please . . ." and then he heard other voices break in, trying to quiet her; there was a silence, then she began again, "Why . . . why . . . why . . ."

At the bottom of the stairs he paused. His father had hung here in milky December light, his bare feet with their horny heels almost head high as Mason Raymond and his mother stood at the bottom of the stairs gazing up, his mother looking into the heart of the gathering milk-white darkness, saying in her cold, dark-growing voice, "We should never have let him come up. He'd never have done it down in Albany."

Now that same voice had begun its litany. "Please . . . please
. . . *please* . . ." she was crying out in anguish, asking for
something that no one understood, relying on politeness to
re-open the gates of consciousness, but the word itself was not
the key. No one knew what she wanted. He trod the carpeted
stairs hearing her ask over and over, "Why . . . why . . . *why?*"
Why anything?

The Albany doctor—Murray? Murphy? something like that
—was standing alongside Young Doc Bronson, both of them
looking uncomfortable, Murray or Murphy or whatever his
name was fiddling with a thick, gold watch fob and Young
Doc Bronson was fingering his sideburns. A flash of recognition crossed Mason Raymond's mind; he saw quite clearly on
the slate where memory chalked its images, a portrait of hopeless, hapless Burnside, the failure at Fredericksburg, who took
his quarrel with Hooker straight to Lincoln and said, It's him
or me, and it turned out to be him. Hooker was always quarreling with someone. After Burnside, Halleck. Quit in a huff
and the gentle Meade replaced him. Lincoln looking for one
real general after another and not finding one until The
Butcher. Imagine being remembered for the way you wore
the whiskers on your face. Better than not being remembered
at all. He held out his hand to Young Doc Bronson, thinking
that just being back in this house had been a relinquishment
of the woods world; he was back to thinking in schoolboy
academic terms; he even acted them out, he noted disgustedly,
seeing his deference and shyness take over as he was re-intro-
duced to the Albany specialist whose name turned out to be
Morrow.

Mason Raymond noted the grip was tentative; there was
something overly fastidious about the imported Albany doctor. His mother began pleading again, "Please . . . please
. . . please . . ."

"She's just coming round," Morrow said. "She isn't really
in control—"

"But I thought my uncle said she'd come out of the coma
yesterday, that—"

"Well, yes, technically she came out of it yesterday, but it's

] *129* [

only today really there's been speech. You mustn't expect—
you must be prepared for quite a change." He spoke in a
clipped, disinterested voice which, behind the layers of professional phrases and objective scientific observations, conveyed
a distaste for the sick; there was something morally wrong
with people who let their cells break down and their organs
give way.

"Why . . . why . . . *why?*" Mason Raymond's mother began
to ask all over again.

There was no answer; there never was. He brushed past
Morrow, pausing a moment a step ahead of him. The question
in his mind was too terrible to ask; he put it aside and managed
one less final. "But she's better?" he asked.

"Oh, yes, she's better," their own doctor, nervous, fidgety,
said hastily. "Why, we never really expected her to pull out
of it, and even if she did—" He stopped abruptly. In the
silence, Mason Raymond framed the question. "And even if
she did?"

Clipped and calm, Morrow had no trouble getting the truth
out. "A living vegetable, the rest of her life," he said.

Mason Raymond identified him immediately: a sin-monger,
one of those who relished not clean, clear-cut fatalities, but
amputations, irreversible damage to vital organs, mental
black-outs and brain disintegration. He was the kind who
liked a long life of helplessness and misery to pay for the
sinfulness of living. He must go—today.

At the door, Mason Raymond hesitated; he knew how
debasing it would be for his mother to have him see her sick,
distraught, incontinent, worst of all, not "dressed." The wild
creature in front of him, however, was incapable of caring
about any distinctions, no matter how broad; she was an animal strapped into a chair whose only concern was to break
free. She fought the restraints round her arms and legs, straining with all her strength against the harness which locked her
against the chair, head thrown back, eyes translucent, as
though if Mason Raymond looked hard enough he could see
right through them to the broken brain inside her skull where
so little was going on, her mouth pushing out unrecognizable
sounds, spitting anger and helplessness out in mucous guttur-

als, her head bobbing, straining, rolling, and then finally out of that bared mouth a recognizable word, "Why . . . why . . . *why?*"

She saw him. For a moment her body tightened, almost as if she were going into another seizure; she rolled her tongue and bobbed her head and spit; her eyes went white, her tongue hung free, she began to drool, but she said one syllable quite clearly, "May —May —May."

She knew him.

He bent over her and took her writhing hands. They closed over his and kept closing; for such small hands they had enormous strength. He winced, but let her grip as hard as she needed; possibly she felt the only way to communicate was in force and pain. "It's all right," he said to her, "you're coming out of it and you're going to be all right."

The hands let go. Her head began to roll back and forth again, arms and legs thrashing against the restraints. "Why . . . why . . . why . . . why, why, why?"

The nurse could not hold her down. Maniacal strength like that was unpredictable; yet it was life, the strong, sure sign of life trying to hang on: which was worse, to be a living vegetable or a wild, inchoate being like this?

He could see Morphis writing on the board: LEARN BY SUFFERING. The supposition was of course that suffering was good. In those simplistic terms it was good because it was somehow purifying, you learned a depth from it that joy never gave. *This* suffering was good? This suffering served a purpose? Hart's being hit over the head *taught* him something, opened his heart in some new way?

He'd have liked to have Morphis here in this room watching that frantic woman struggling against the leather ties on her wrists and ankles, pulling futilely at the thick strap around her chest, babbling, "Please . . . please . . . please . . ." and he would like to grip Morphis by both wrists, imprison him the way *she* was imprisoned, make him stand hour after hour watching this helpless idiocy, and then he'd like to ask Morphis, "Do you still think you learn by suffering, that suffering is good?" You had to be careful not to live your life out of books.

And when I am forgotten, as I shall be,
And sleep in dull cold marble, where no mention
Of me more must be heard of, say, I taught thee . . .

And when I am forgotten . . . "Come on, boy, you can't do
anything more here." Mason Raymond looked into the Burnside face; the Bronsons were all doctors, this one's father had
taken the bone slivers out of Hart's brain; now he was the
drinker. In life everyone had labels. Dying destroyed the brief
epithets. Medicine, it seemed, like large estates, was passed
on; only the wealthy in both cases could afford so much conti-
nuity. People like Hart could never expect to be more than
the dumb beasts of burden of this earth, and yet clearly this
man was a fool and Hart was not. The wisest fool in Chris'en-
dom. He shook his arm loose.

"What is it you want, mother? What is it you're trying to
tell us?"

The wild eyes could not say; they could only plead.

He took her hands again and that terrible, yearning grinding commenced again. His fingers ached. "Listen," he said,
"listen!" The grinding ceased. "If you can understand me, just
press my hands." She nearly broke bones trying to show him
she could. "That's better, that's better, only not so hard,
you're hurting me. Can you understand?" This time the pressure was gentler, still crushing, but there was a noticeable
difference, which must mean that she could understand and
reason, that she still had some control. He pressured her hands
back. They sat locked together by their hands. She had
calmed; the nurse wiped her face and tried to put something
down her throat. One hand held the head up, rigid, while the
other poured from a cup into the gurgling, protesting mouth.

Mason Raymond let go of his mother's hands and jumped
up. "Stop that!" he said to the nurse. Like the specialist from
Albany, the nurse was treating his mother as if she were morally reprehensible for being sick. He grabbed the cup and said,
trying for control, but so furious he could have struck the
woman, "Don't do that! I can get it down her without having
to hurt her."

His mother had commenced her raving again. "Why . . . why . . . why . . ." He found himself in a rage with her as well as the nurse. "Listen, mother, just listen—stop, don't thrash around, that won't do any good—please, just listen—"

But he had lost her; she was beyond communication now, the eyes were the pale icy eyes of the lunatic, far away in a land of fears and forces over which he had no control. It would have been better if she had never come out of the coma, if she had come out of it to be like this. There is one thing you can do for an animal, he thought, that you can't do for a human being; you can put it out of its misery.

He set the cup down and went out of the room, standing in the hall looking into Morrow's questioning face, as if the doctor were asking *him* how it would go. They don't know any more than I do, Mason Raymond thought. They expect me to reassure *them.*

Young Doc Bronson was no better. Water weakens as it runs downhill, Hart said. The spring at the top tastes fresh and fair, but when its water runs downhill it picks up all kinds of 'taminations and abominations. Men ain't much different.

"She should have died," he said to both of them. "She'd be better off dead."

Out back Hart had the dog strapped up, Hector's back legs crisscrossed and roped securely together, his front ones snugly fitted together and wrapped with hemp, a line of cord through his mouth looped around the muzzle in and around quills, Hart astride the dog anchoring him to the ground, his short but powerful body, with his legs as aids, braced against the dog's resistance, one hand holding the head steady, the other working with a close-mouthed tool to extract the barbs. He had a cup half full, but Mason Raymond couldn't see he'd made much progress. The dog's eyes turned on him, accusing. "You didn't say she was so bad," Mason Raymond said. Hart's attention seemed totally involved with holding and pulling. "When you said she'd had a bad spell, I didn't think you meant —well—more than just being worried and upset about my getting myself lost—"

"You didn't git yourself lost. I done that."

Mason Raymond shook his head, but Hart refused to be let off the hook. "My fault all the way."

"No, it wasn't, I should never have—"

The dog let out a frantic yip and began to snarl. "Run off 'nd leave you like that—here, you, you cut that out." He gave the dog a gentle but firm cuff. "Leave you like that," he went on, "and run on, no sense at all, and me better'n sixty years old. Ain't fit for boys nor dogs."

"You can't blame yourself. It wasn't your fault."

"It was all my fault. Anythin' 'd happen'd to you, I'd never 've forgiven myself. Never," he said fervently.

In the incompatible silence the dog struggled, yelping and snapping. Hart waited him out. When he quieted down, he took his pliers and started pulling again. His hands were covered with blood and saliva.

"Won't never live it down. Lite won't let me. But that don't matter. What matters is I got no right to live it down. Go 'nd take you out 'nd don't even look after you proper."

"Never mind Lite, he's not worth worrying about."

Hart loosened the rope around the muzzle. "This dog's got to breathe some 'fore we go on." He rocked back and began searching through his pockets. "Know I had that plug on me this mornin' and now—" He rummaged, shaking his head in double disgust—lost the boy, lost the tobacco. A hopeless case.

Maybe Rivers had some—for the first time Mason Raymond realized he hadn't seen Rivers since his return, flanked by Hart and his uncle; his uncle had disappeared, too; it was all very odd. "Where's Rivers?"

"That boweevelly fella works for your Ma?" Hart's face took on further distress. "Gone to fetch help," he said uncertainly.

"Help?"

"He said you were gonna need help here."

"What kind of help?"

"Woman stuff, I imagine," he said after a time. "Cob, he didn't have no more idear than me your Ma was in the kind of shape she is. She was on her feet when we left ten o'clock, 'fore noon. The spell musta hit her right after we took off. She was fretted bad, but she wasn't flatten'd by it. Lost that plug prob'ly in the woods somewhere. Woods is always swallowin' up the good stuff, never the worthless. Why couldn't it reach out and reel in some empty critter like Lite instead of worth-while remnants?'' There was no answer for this and apparently Hart expected none. His face registered anguish, however, in the face of the unknowable. "I'm sorry you had to come home to this, young 'un.''

Young 'un. Mason Raymond wondered if Hart had any idea at all what had gone on in the woods. Probably (prob'ly, Hart would have said, shortening this as he did so many things, no time for lengthy examination of the apparent) prob'ly not. Having seen Mason Raymond was not too defunct, all he had said after that initial whoop of broken-worded astonishment was, "Didn't do much for your frame,'' referring to all the weight Mason Raymond had lost.

Mason Raymond had told no one about the plunder of the eggs. The woods knew. He knew. That was enough. There were many distinctions, he was learning, besides fleeing and fighting—in those divisions he would be accounted an eater-of-eggs, a despoiler of life.

A man's oath was only as good as the circumstance he was in, he might have said to Hart. I learned *that* in the woods. That and something about how to stay alive—"stay alive" was not the proper sense of what he meant. He ransacked his mind for the right perspective. Maybe "endure" was more like it. Not that anyone cares, he wanted to say—but of course that was untrue. Hart cared. His uncle cared. And since they were the only two men *he* cared about, he should be satisfied. But he wasn't. Like everyone else, the roots of his sins lay in self-justification, in an arrogant demand for acclaim, in the weak need for recognition. What was it he had thought? There is no identification without recognition—something like that.

Hart was wrapped up in his quill operation once more, the dog energetically resisting him, but the slivers were coming out regardless of how Hector struggled. All struggles were not meant to be equal. With his eyes riveted on the dog, Hart said, "Lite, he don't see what you been through. He don't want to see. He don't never want to give credit to nobody but hisself. It ain't likely he'll be willin' to call off that bet, even after your ordeal, leastwise he wasn't when we come on you, but now with your Ma hung up—" He looked up, bewildered by his own blunder. He had only been saying what jumped into his head, a country idiom; he hadn't meant any reference to Mason Raymond's father, but the inference was there.

Busy work saved Hart; he quilled furiously. But nothing could save Mason Raymond, standing there miserably accepting for the first time that he couldn't trust emotions in himself or others. Intellectual problems, yes, but not emotional ones. In a month no one at the Landing would remember how, miraculously, he had survived all alone through rain and snow and a gale, without anything to help him, not a knife or a piece of string, no gun or powder for fire, nothing but a scant slice of will which kept saying, You can. No, no one would remember. What people would remember would be the famous father—The Great Man—who'd humbled himself in the dust.

He turned away from Hart, conscious once more of how outside the ordinary world of give-and-take he felt. Others, it seemed to him, were able to live with themselves without this endless self-questioning. To survive (most of all inside the mind, that crucial test his father had failed) you had to harden yourself against endless self-evaluation and its consequent feeling of failure. *To accept simply, straightforwardly:* why couldn't he do that one basic and necessary thing?

"Goddam *people*," Mason Raymond said, furious, while Hart dropped his tweezerlike tool and looked up in astonishment. But what did Hart understand?

Should never have eaten the eggs, Mason Raymond thought. But he had, and that marked the difference between being a green boy and a guilty man. The woods—the eggs— were the turning point; once he had eaten the eggs there was no turning back. It shamed him even to remember how he had stripped off his clothes and gone naked except for mud and a few leaves.

Nothing existed on a straight plane. Everything was itself and something else. He longed, miserably, to be free of this knowledge, more so when he looked at Hart and surmised Hart knew none of these things. He was innocent. He wanted to shout at Hart, Beware of giving yourself too much. What Hart would say back, dismayed, was, Look at Mabel and me; and when Mason Raymond replied, People are different from one another, Hart wouldn't know what he meant and Mason Raymond couldn't explain. To Hart feeling was first: it formed. To Mason Raymond it deformed. It was as simple— and complicated—as that, whatever "that" meant.

Horses were coming down the old logging road; that meant most likely they were from the New House, his aunt and Rivers. Hart paused to look up, a smile on his face as if he were about to say, "Your aunt's come," meaning "Everythin's all right now," Katherine Ann Buttes could right any wrong. The dog took advantage of Hart's momentary inattention to struggle against the rope and free his back legs, Hart hollering at the dog as he made a break for freedom, grabbing and hanging on, Hector as caught as he, Mason Raymond Buttes, was; but Hector's captivity would end. In an hour or so he'd be shut of the quills, curled up in front of the fire, snoring and happy, with maybe only a distant dream of the woods, the quills, to disturb his sleep.

His aunt got down and embraced him. He was always surprised by how young her face seemed under the white hair. She wore it braided and coiled in a crown on top of her head, a big woman, all muscle and bone, heavy-set with the country power of hard work, the country mark of many trials and tribulations. People were afraid of her. Even Lite was afraid of her. When she came into his store for the few staples of flour, sugar, salt she made an infrequent trip across the lake to put in, he did not banter or make small talk. He got what she ordered, saying "Yes 'um," emphasizing the 'um, he knew a lady when he saw one. He never called Mason Raymond's mother 'um in that voice.

Mason Raymond's mother feared her, too—and disliked her, showing that distrust in small, petty ways. "Of course she's a *wonderful* woman," his mother was always saying, pausing a moment before she added, "It's a shame her mouth's so large. It spoils her whole face."

] *137* [

Her mouth had never seemed large to Mason Raymond until his mother had pointed out its size, but now every time he saw his aunt he couldn't help looking at her mouth, measuring it, just as now as she stepped back, her arms still lightly encircling him, the first thing he did was look at her mouth, doing it unconsciously and yet the moment he did it being conscious he was ashamed. There was no way he could help her mouth being spoiled for him. His mother had done that. Why?

Comfort flowed through her warm, strong arms. She held him close, not briefly or embarrassedly, but for a long time, recognizing need and ministering to it.

There was a famous story told of her: A celebration over Appomattox and everyone in the Landing drinking and singing and happy, drunk on themselves in a way no liquor could make them drunk, though there'd been plenty of liquor around, and someone had said, Let's go cross lake and get Cobus Buttes, he's the biggest hero we got out of the war; and though the trip took two, three hours, a parcel of men had put out, canoeing and swigging from jugs and singing their lungs out. When they got to the cove where the Buttes dock was, she was down to meet them, standing there with her hands on her hips and the words of scorn between her teeth: "What you celebratin'?" she demanded. "All those men dead on both sides?"

She was here to help. She was always found where help was needed. She had come down immediately the night his father had ended his life though it was Christmas Eve and she had young children, staying four days, right through the funeral, supplying the untiring hands and the unflagging strength that was essential to get through, with dignity, such an ordeal.

"I'm glad you're back and safe," she said now. She didn't say anything silly like "I knew you'd get through," because she hadn't known any such thing. She'd just—endured. It seemed to him she always would.

Rivers was standing beside her with a bag, his eyes red. He'd been drinking. The sick smell of a sour, liquored mouth was strong around him. Mason Raymond didn't feel contempt or anger for him. Maybe of all of them Rivers had the most right to grieve. He cared with a depth the others denied his mother. Mason Raymond knew this. Weren't the others, he wondered, able to see Rivers' feelings? They were so transparent.

Hart stayed working with the dog while Rivers put the horses up and his aunt flanked him up to the house. When they came through the back door, they could hear his mother asking, "Why . . . why . . . why?"

"You gotta keep that dog tied," Hart insisted.

He wouldn't like being chained all the time; why should the dog? "He won't run."

"He'll run all right. He was bred to run. All good huntin' dogs run if they ain't tied. If he runs he'll hunt on his own, he'll already have had a bellyful when you want him to run. Anyway, it ain't right to let a dog like that run loose, he'll bring down deer, hamstring 'em." He appeared not to be looking at Mason Raymond, seemingly scanning the lake but surreptitiously watching Mason Raymond out of the corner of his eye.

"He won't run," Mason Raymond repeated, stubborn. He hadn't seen Hart in almost a week and he knew Hart felt guilty about this, but Hart—like most people—was afraid of the sickroom. He had had to come to find out how Mason Raymond's mother was; he couldn't put it off any longer and he had not been able to disguise his uneasiness when Mason Raymond said, "About the same, some improvement, but not —well, back to normal."

"Suit yourself, but don't say I didn't warn you. Couple of people 'round here I can think of jest as soon see that dog didn't come home at all one of these nights, give him a good dose of buckshot and that'll be the end of him. Unpredictable critter like he is, never know what he'll do—fizz out complete one time, outrun and outtree every dog in the country next. There's a lot of money runnin' on that unpredictable dog. You 'liminate him, he's not so unpredictable any more."

Mason Raymond couldn't believe his ears. "You mean the bet's still on?"

It was Worth's turn to be startled. "Ain't been called off, I heered tell of. I told you that! Your knees are all patched up now, ain't they?"

Mason Raymond had been expecting Hart to say that naturally, under the circumstances, there would be some kind of postponement, but Hart just shrugged his shoulders and said fatalistically, "Jest have to do the best you kin in the time you got left."

"But my mother's—" The look on Hart's face plainly said, Why, yes, of course, she's bad took, but it ain't final. Naturally they would get on to the business at hand, a contest between (almost) men and dogs, never mind a woman might be dying, one of the participants had come about as close to death as you could and still struggled out to tell the story, the point was, nothing was final. Anyway the Landing regarded his survival as more miracle than merit. They didn't want him to succeed, all those people who lived hulked up in those little houses (little compared to his) in town. John Buttes belonged to them, even if he came from the other side of the lake, he was a Landing boy; Mason Raymond would never be one of their own. Diddle, diddle, my son John . . . went to bed with his stockings on . . .

"It's unfortunate," Hart conceded, "but I don't reckon they'll handicap any for it."

"No, I don't reckon they will," Mason Raymond said, but the irony was lost on Hart.

"Well, it's no use puttin' a face like that on it. It's unfortunate, I'm willin' to concede you that, but you gotta go by the rules—"

"*Rules?*"

"The way things is done. I recollect the time Abner Sutliff lost his best dog to poisonin'—always was somethin' off about that—and it was jest before the big hunt where he had made that wager on treein' first and bringin' in the first coon. His good Sadie-dog died and he had to go out with what he had, a green no-account dog I wouldn't have give the time of day to. Always said losin' that hunt was what put him out of business a couple of years later, but he'd give his word he was goin' to hunt and he never said with which dog. There was his fault. He should have been smart enough to specify, but he never thought, jest took it for granted, I guess, and so there you have it—it ain't jest so as your dog don't run deer, you want to keep him penned up, it's so you can keep an eye on him yourself."

Mason Raymond sat down on one of the iron benches his mother was so proud of. She had had a pair sent up from Albany and she had got Rivers to paint them white and set them out under what she called her "twin trees" (maples, he knew maples) overlooking the lake. She liked to come out here and sit and look out, the big white Persians weaving around her legs. The tranquillity of the sun-struck, calm waters in front of Mason Raymond now was in sharp contrast to the turbulent pounding of his heart. You couldn't live with two ways of seeing things at the same time, divided, confused, never knowing what was really right; but he could no more turn his back on Morphis, misty-eyed, reading that final scene from Troy

First quenched they with bright wine all the burning, so far as the fire's strength went, and then his brethren and comrades gathered his white bones lamenting, and big tears flowed down their cheeks. And the bones they took and laid in a golden urn, shrouding them in soft purple robes, and straightway laid the urn in a hollow grave and piled thereon great close-set stones, and heaped with speed a barrow, while watchers were set everywhere around, lest the well-greamed Achaeans should make onset before the time. And when they had heaped the barrow, they went back, and gathered them together and feasted right well in noble feast at the palace of Priam, Zeus-fostered king.

Thus held they funeral for Hector, tamer of horses.

than he could shut out of his heart Hart, tamer of lesser animals, but tamer nevertheless of much which was cunning and brave and sly. He must be *very* careful to keep shut inside himself the heresies of a defecting spirit. He was not an ascender to the sky, not a swinger in tops of trees. He mustered up a smile and Hart, mollified, grateful, slapped him on the back with the false encouragement of the true seer of doom. "You'll make it, boy, I know you will. I got faith."

The very idiocy of such a blind commitment to friendship raised Mason Raymond's spirits. His smile this time was real. For what Hart had said to him was true, he did have faith. Hart believed in him beyond all evidence of the facts. That was just like Hart, caring beyond the call of common sense.

Hart lugged over a thick rope training bag and a wire cage with a coon in it. He had Brownie and Drum on a double leash, the dogs straining excitedly at the end of their tethers. Mason Raymond would never have asked Worth to go to such trouble; it was characteristic of him that he'd done it on his own. He knew Hart would let everything down home go until the big day was over, his concentration on training Hector unbroken, nothing intruding like milking or mowing or mucking out stalls. He was trying to will his heart and knowledge into Mason Raymond. More than half dog, Mason Raymond thought, how has Mabel ever put up with it. *A very remarkable woman,* people said of her, and it was true.

Hart rigged the netted bag up in a tall pine. The bag was large enough to hold a good-sized coon; it had been thickly woven with evenly spaced small holes so that a dog could see and smell the coon inside, he would jump at the bag and try to get the animal inside, but the bag was too strong to tear, the holes too small for the coon to get hurt. Still, the whole business bothered Mason Raymond who (typical of me, he thought) identified with the coon instead of the dog. He imagined how it would be imprisoned in a small bag, hoisted up in the air and swung out over a pack of blood-lusting dogs who were leaping and clawing.

Hart, however, was enthusiastic. "A won'erful trainin' device," he said happily, pulling the coon ten, twelve feet up in the air and letting Brownie and Drum rage and tear at the bag. When the dogs had grabbed the bag and dragged it down on the ground, throwing it up in the air, giving the raccoon a good tossing, but not hurting him, Hart said, You have to let the dogs get the idea, and Mason Raymond could hear the squeaks and hisses from inside, see the terrified tumbling of the coon, and his stomach dropped and he felt sick all over.

Hector dropped to the ground and put his head on his paws.

He wanted nothing to do with the whole business.

"Bring him closer, git him up so he gits a good whiff," Hart was shouting, hanging onto his own dogs and vainly trying to yank them back.

Mason Raymond stood as if driven permanently into the earth. He couldn't bring himself to force Hector on that bag, but Hart, jumping around hysterically, more excited than his own dogs, was screaming, "Come on, come on. You don't want Lite to git the best of you, do you?" But it wasn't Lite who was on Mason Raymond's mind, it was Young John Buttes, big, strong, sure of himself; he saw his cousin's dark, contemptuous face glancing around examining the boys his own age, then the scowl changing to a smile because what he saw was pleasing—there was no one else his age who could hold a candle to him. Well, not in strength; and what did these people care about other kinds of excellence?

Mason Raymond numbly tugged at Hector's lead line, the dog looking up at him disconsolately, not budging.

"Git him goin', boy, git him onto the coon—" Exasperated, Hart grabbed Hector's rope, gave it a yank; he lay suddenly on the ground, the big dog standing over him, growling. The whole episode happened so fast that Mason Raymond was never quite sure how Hart got knocked down; all he knew was that one minute Hart had been in charge, the next minute the dog was.

Mason Raymond pulled himself together and yanked the dog back.

Hart got up gingerly and brushed himself off. "That's one of my own dogs." He looked bushwhacked. "One of my own dogs that set on me."

The hair bristled in a thick collar around Hector's neck; he showed his teeth, he meant business. He had had enough of the bag and what it represented.

Hart was overtly dejected as he transferred the coon gingerly from the net bag to its wire cage. His leashed dogs were barking and carrying on; Mason Raymond—standing uncertainly with Hector, who was once again sprawled out resting —didn't know how to make Hart feel better. In the early June freshness, windows from the house must have been thrown open; very faintly Mason Raymond could hear his mother's voice. "Please . . . please . . . please . . ."

There was a faint hope she might continue improving, possibly in time the restraints could be removed. She fought them all the time, thrashing and pulling and asking, "Why . . . why . . . why?" or begging "Please . . . please . . . please," but at least she no longer dribbled her food or looked quite so wild-eyed. A strange thing had happened to her eyes: they had become almost completely clear. When she looked at him—as occasionally she seemed to do, really trying to focus on him instead of wildly throwing her head about—there was no depth at all in her eyes, they seemed to be registering nothing; when Mason Raymond looked into them, he felt as if behind the bright, glassy, expressionless beads that served as his mother's eyes, no brain any longer ticked and drove the wheels of thought.

She had ceased being one person and become another, a stranger in whose presence he felt acutely uncomfortable, his only instinct the desire for escape; yet he forced himself to sit beside her and falsify cheerfulness, encouragement, chitchat. Sometimes it seemed to him she really might know him, sometimes not. What was most disconcerting was that when he felt she made the proper associations his presence made her sulky and irritable, as if she were blaming him. If he hadn't gotten lost . . . but of course she probably didn't even remember he'd been lost. Old and Young Docs Bronson didn't believe she had much, if any, memory. They were hoping that the brain might recover a little each day and that eventually she might be well. They were hoping, but they weren't sanguine.

"No need to keep that dog tied," Hart said morosely. "He ain't gonna run. He ain't gonna do *nuthin'.*" He lifted his disgusted face to the sky. As God had asked Moses to take a letter, and he had got out his tablets to try, so Worth, who had a Bible all his own, was demanding to know why the world went as it did and was waiting to take down the answer. "You gotta forfeit," he said. "Or you gotta git yourself another dog."

"The bet was made on this dog."

Hart grunted and creaked about gathering up his paraphernalia.

They took the cage and coon, the training bag, the two dogs up to Hart's cart. Hart was in such low spirits that he didn't even try to talk, climbing up on his wagon, the heart gone out of him, sitting a minute contemplating the humiliation ahead, then shaking his head and giving up, no remedy he could see for gittin' whupped and if there was anythin' worse than gittin' whupped by Frank Lite he didn't know of it.

He lifted the reins and clucked to the oxen—Hart would have liked horses, but couldn't afford them. Hector didn't even bother to come down and make a nuisance barking him off; he hadn't moved and it didn't look as if he had any intention of doing so. Mason Raymond had to go and drag his collar to get him up to the house.

The week before the run his uncle had a talk with him. Since his mother's illness, his uncle had been dividing his time between his own place, New House up on the hill on the other side of the inlet, and the Raymonds', trying to keep two establishments going, just as Mason Raymond's aunt had been running back and forth between her house and his. His uncle had watched Mason Raymond go off by himself every night as darkness set in an attempt to get the dog to track and tree, had refrained from asking how he was doing, but once had brought down a fresh, dead coon, Mason Raymond shaking his head, No, he didn't want it. He knew what the real problem was and there was no way to solve it. The problem was him. He didn't want to—he *couldn't*—kill, and that reluctance communicated itself to the dog; he was sure Hector felt now how he cringed from the notion of treeing some bright-eyed, human-faced coon and taking a rifle and gunning it out of the tree or (worse) going up the tree and shaking it out for the dogs to tear it apart alive. Anyway, he couldn't, because of his vow.

What was the good of going out if you didn't even carry a gun (what confidence would *that* inspire in a hunting hound, let alone trying to explain to Hart?) and Hector knew as well as Mason Raymond that Mason Raymond wasn't going to shinny up any tree and break the coon's hold so that it fell down live to be torn apart. They went out into the darkness to get out of sight of the others, to pretend. In the woods Mason Raymond plopped down glumly on a fallen log, the dog lying at his feet, silent, suspicious. Once or twice Mason Raymond tried to explain it. "I gave my word—not to kill—except in absolute need, maybe not even then. But how can I say I can't kill a coon, that it goes against my word. Who'd understand a dumb thing like that? Even Hart doesn't. All he keeps saying is, 'Jest this once, jest once, on accounta the bet.' Nobody understands. Killing is all right to them. *That's* what I don't understand."

The dog apparently didn't care. He was content to be resting, not bothering to have to fuss running after things. Even when animals started up around him, he didn't exert himself. He'd raise his head and look interestedly in the direction from which the woods noises came, but he had no blood thirst to track and kill. "We're a real grand pair," Mason Raymond said. The dog said nothing. Were they not all guests of the woods?

In the silence sounds flowed around them, insects raged, small creatures tumbled through old dead leaves, the wind sounded drunk.

His uncle in some vague way seemed to sense he had dilemmas. "You don't have your heart in this, do you?" he asked. But Mason Raymond didn't have the feeling his uncle blamed him; it was more like his uncle was just trying to understand. "You weren't scairt when you was lost in the woods—leastwise you acquitted yourself good then." A pause. Puzzled. Awfully puzzled. "Not many boys—no, nor men neither—would have got through as well as you done, but in this—your heart jest don't seem to be in it."

"It's the killing."

Cobus Buttes looked perplexed. It took Mason Raymond an instant to see that coon killing wasn't *real* killing to him. "What I mean—what I mean is that I've got this . . . this feeling about not killing, not unless it's absolutely necessary, and I can't—I don't want—to kill an innocent animal, which is what this amounts to."

"Coons ain't innocent. Got in one of them cornfields, run right through wreckin' 'nd ruinin'."

Mason Raymond didn't argue. There was no point in explaining the inexplicable. He'd tried to explain to Hart, he'd tried to explain to the dog. No one saw and the dog didn't care. He was going to do what he wanted.

"Nuthin's innocent," his uncle insisted, "and coons is maybe one of the least innocent things I know."

"They do do damage," Mason Raymond admitted. "But it's like they got their rights, too."

His uncle was looking at him with one of those deep looks that indicated he was trying to look into him. Finally he said, "You don't want to kill coons." Mason Raymond supposed that was about as close as they would ever get to it. "You don't even want to *tree* 'em?" Treeing was another matter, more like harassment, and a little harassment here and there was natural to everything. He said he had nothing against treeing but that for Hector to get the notion that treeing had any value to it, Hart had said he had to learn to like the blood, and that was where the problem arose.

"You balk at the blood? Well, I could hunt him and blood-bath him for you and all you'd have to do is tree 'em and kill that one time."

What his uncle was talking about was training against his own son. "But that wouldn't be right—for John."

"You're like a son to me, too," his uncle said.

How could such a thing be really true? He looked at his uncle. Yes, what he had said he meant. But how had he arrived at such a feeling? The point was he had it; and because he had it, Mason Raymond owed him an explanation of his own deepest feelings. He turned over all those different feelings he'd had in the past weeks—wanting to do well, wanting to win, wanting to make himself the kind of person his uncle and Hart (and he himself) could be proud of and yet not wanting to go against the word he had given in the woods. He knew he could never explain about his vow, never to anyone;

there was no one in the world who could understand such a crazy thing, no one at all certainly who had been raised around here where living off the woods was a way of life; and yet he felt his vow was right, that somehow he was closer to the woods than all these people were if he could undertake to make a promise like that. It was all so complicated, so hopeless to explain. But he had to try. "It's more than me—the real problem is—well, it's that I don't want Hector learning about liking blood. I don't want him trained because once he's learned, he'll run on his own; and if he runs on his own, I'll have to keep him tied all the time; and if I have to keep him tied, he won't be with me; and the way it is now, he's with me all the time because the only times he runs are when we go out and kind of horse around."

"Kind of horse around?"

Of course, he ought to have realized that to his uncle treeing was an important matter. How could he say to him, Once in a while Hector and I *play* at running something and he barks at a tree and I suppose there's a coon up it, but I don't really know because I don't really look, and then we both just sort of sit down and look at the tree and that's that. We've kind of treed, and then again we haven't.

His uncle sighed. Mason Raymond could tell he'd given up. He tried to be nice about his exasperation, however. "You don't either of you want to learn to kill or rather you don't want the dog to learn to kill, is that it?"

"I guess you could say that's about the size of it. Worth, he talks about bear, and that doesn't seem so bad, the bear's got a chance—leastwise if you didn't hunt him with guns, if it was just you and a dog against the bear, but this—this isn't equal at all."

"You don't hunt bear with *a* dog, you use dogs."

"Well, if—just *if*—I was going to do it, I'd only use one dog."

There was a silence, total defeat on both their parts. "That don't leave us much hope for what's ahead," his uncle said at last. "Nuthin' at all when you look at it."

"And I know you got all that money involved—"

"Own damn fault for openin' my big mouth."

"—and I'm sorry, I'll try to do the best I can, I really will—"

"That's a foolishness," his uncle said with absolute conviction, "to go against your principles for a hundred dollars."

"A hundred dollars is a lot of money."

"Maybe it is, but it ain't the end of the world, not to me, it ain't, maybe quite a chunk of it, but not the whole hog."

He didn't see what his uncle had in mind. To call off the bet, his uncle said. "You mean forfeit?"

"Somethin' like that."

"No, no, I don't want to do that, not to Lite—"

"Well, he ain't the world's most sterlin'est character, I won't argue that, and I can't say it gives me much pleasure to admit we got to lay down our silver without no contest, but—"

"Hector and I'll go," Mason Raymond said, and then, adopting a phrase of Hart's, "I don't know as how we'll win, but we'll go, we'll be trying."

"How you goin' to do that when neither one of you knows nuthin' about runnin'?"

"There's bound to be an answer someplace," Mason Raymond said hopefully, the boy whose belief in rationality had suddenly become strong because only that belief could lead him out of the darkness and into the light.

He lay awake listening to his mother babbling at the nurse, senseless, incoherent sounds which had no meaning in any universal exchange of language but which in her own mind must have measured meanings of significance because she was so heatedly raging, obviously impassioned by the nurse's efforts to silence her when she wanted to say something. The nurse's voice was the cloying, synthetically sweet one of the professional pacifier who in her heart doesn't give a damn if the patient drops down dead right now, sick people were nothing but a lot of trouble.

He got up and went to the door and watched for a moment that pitiable thrashing against the restraints. His mother's head rolled and snapped and bobbed; her arms strained and twisted; her whole body convulsed with futile efforts. There was very little they could do to make her look presentable and even that was wasted in a few minutes with the violence of her fight against them. Her hair was matted and tangled, her face distorted, bloated really, but she was getting thinner and thinner, the weight fleeing from her with incredible speed. She looked old old old. And she didn't know anyone, even him. After that first feeble acknowledgment—"May"—she seemed to have lost the connective threads of remembrance; she saw him in the doorway, he knew, because her head jerked up and she stared, glassy-eyed, through him for a brief eye encounter; but no recognition rewarded that glance. He was just a shape shaded in the doorway.

He went forward and tried to soothe her, but she paid no attention; her world was centered inside herself, the lone impulse she seemed to have was to break free; she had no time to listen to anything else, certainly not some plea to leave well enough alone and behave herself. He knelt and tried to take her hands. She wasn't even looking at him, thrashing back and forth, mouth contorted, eyes wild.

She had been a beautful woman. How did you explain it? There was no explanation, the world just whirled on its way without caring who it crushed as it turned, a woman, a coon, a dog, a boy, a whole city of people. Life and death seemed to have no meaning in themselves and yet he scrupled to kill a coon because he believed meaning existed. If there wasn't any . . . well, then he could choose to make some: the pride of being the bestower.

He would have to take the dog out and make fools of both of them, and yet this no longer troubled him; his heart had larger things to think of at this moment. He stared at her. He was her son and yet he felt no binding tie at all. He couldn't, in all honesty, have said he had any love left for her; she had become somebody else, but the truth was, he wasn't even partially sorry for her. Her hot, demanding love had made him want to escape her a long time ago and though he had tried to be a "good son," there was always something in him that resisted her—because she demanded his love and he wanted to give it.

The dog rose, as he came down the stairs, from his favorite

place on the rug (he had worn a round same-sized spot in it, blotting out a peacock) and came, pausing, stretching, yawning, a few paces toward him. He supposes we're going through one of those ridiculous nights again, Mason Raymond thought, catching hold of Hector's leash from the big elkhorn stand. Someone had killed those animals and stripped them of their horns so that people could hang up their coats. Women wore ostrich and peacock plumes in their hats, great lustrous animal skins on their backs, tucked their hands into muffs made from the smaller animals of the earth, jogged along in their carriages and broughams under the thick naps of once-living fur. People ate meat and gobbled eggs, swallowed filleted fish and savored the winged fowl of the earth and air. A carnivorous world of which he was a member in good standing.

Proud and confident, Young John Buttes lounged easily against a tree; his great black and tan coon dog with its massive shoulders and thick ugly face looked as confident and headstrong as his master. He was a vicious animal who had to be muzzled before he was let free to run because he was so untrustworthy, but he had a reputation for being one of the best treeing dogs around. "He should be," Hart said bitterly, "the blood come from my place."

Once, right at the start, Mason Raymond had tried to talk to John; his cousin had looked at him as if he were an enemy. He sees me as someone personally against him, Mason Raymond thought wonderingly. To him it's more than a bet, it's blood.

At Easter there had been no animosity from John, only what might be called pity for Mason Raymond's bumbling ways. But the bet, the bet that Lite had brought on, had changed all that.

Hart, looking from Mason Raymond to the dog, kept shaking his head; he didn't understand; for once in his life he had no anecdote to offer up—he didn't even seem to have any point at all he wanted to make—hanging back, troubled, standing next to Rivers, who was holding Mason Raymond's lantern, Hart hanging back, shaking his head back and forth, back and forth, not saying a word until almost the end when he thrust the package at Mason Raymond and said, "Here's what you asked for, damn'st thin' I ever heered tell of."

Word had spread on the size of the wager and on the two participants, and men who weren't even interested in hunting had turned up to make a wager. Lite, smiling, affable, darkly handsome, chuckling and joking, so sure of himself, popular but still not all that popular, was the heavy favorite; and Cobus Buttes, not popular at all but what you'd describe as respected, maybe even feared, but not jovial enough to be popular, saturnine, taciturn, grave, and final in a way that most men found made a space between him and them, stood to one side, as if he wanted no part of the gambling goings on, he had more important things on his mind. And then, of course, the crowd was harping on about the boy and that dun-colored dog, a crazy no-good dog and a summer boy from down Albany-way who'd got himself lost in the woods and come out (it was a miracle) and the mother gone gaga, something wrong with her blood, they said, and probably wouldn't never be right again; it promised to be quite an evening.

Rich as the Raymonds don't help you none out in the woods, Mason Raymond heard one say. Nor if you lose your health, old, limping Eben Stuart summed it up. A cursed family in many ways, he said.

Maybe that was true. His father first, then his mother, and only a short time ago himself. But he didn't accept Landing evaluation as the final judgment of the world any more; what he thought instead was, To hell with them. What do they know, anyway?

Rivers set the lantern down, turned slightly away from the light, lifted a bottle and drank. You stood next to him, his breath nearly knocked you down. Never quite drunk, but never more than half sober either.

For the first time Mason Raymond wondered about where Rivers had come from, what family he might have, what ties. Automatically he assumed whole lives for others—parents, brothers and sisters, a home somewhere, affairs of the world and heart, a place of belonging; but Rivers had always stood apart, like one cut off, as if he existed as nothing but an appendage to the Raymonds, his only function to serve them. To connect Rivers with other people, people who cared, made him a different person—one Mason Raymond felt faintly afraid of because behind what he had always taken for granted there lay complexities and mysteries he did not understand, a hidden world where Rivers loved his mother (and hence had had to hate his father) and where, without question, Rivers had to have feelings about him. Mason Raymond drew back. He didn't like to think of that half-drunk, toadlike little man having feelings for him; he didn't want any connection at all. If there was a connection, then he had a responsibility. I don't want to have to worry about *him,* Mason Raymond thought rebelliously, and that second voice inside him said, In these matters you don't have a choice.

"Turn your dogs loose," Old Doc Bronson commanded, and the dogs leapt free and bounded for the woods, Mason Raymond's moment of amazement being the instant Hector took it into his head to play the game of running, too. Of course there was no way of knowing whether he'd decide he wanted to play at real hunting or whether he'd just fool around and then lose interest and lie down someplace. What encouraged Mason Raymond was the fact that Hector had gone straight ahead, pointing like an arrow to that part of the woods where they would wander around and pretend to be something resembling hunters.

John's dog had gone right and was hollering his head off. John had as his recorders a friend of Lite's and an observer for Cobus Buttes, just as Mason Raymond was being tagged by two men whose faces were familiar though their names might be vague. Hare, he thought, was one of them. He was some recorder! He hadn't even asked Mason Raymond why he wasn't carrying a gun. Perhaps he thought that there was so little chance of Mason Raymond's winning the competition it didn't make any difference whether he carried a rifle or not.

Hart and his uncle and Lite would remain at the starting point so that there would be no question of interference or "considerations." The first dog that treed, the first boy that cooned—that is, actually brought in an animal—would be winner. He remembered the terms of the bet exactly: first one that trees and brings in a coon wins the bet. They had said *bring in* a coon, not kill one. They might have meant he was supposed to kill the coon, but they hadn't *said* so. The scattered cries of John's dog picking up scent came on the mild June air; Mason Raymond heard the dog running, excited, then losing track, silent while he was circling, then the renewed yelps when a fresh track was picked up again, the excited voicings of sighting, not finding. When a hound finally settled on trail, the sound of his voice would change; the barking would be steady and sure, the recurrent sounds of the rhythmic excitement he felt inside as he ran straight toward the quarry.

Mason Raymond lumbered awkwardly uphill through brush. Full-mooned nights were always colder than the rest of the month. During January the full-moon temperature would often fall to thirty-five and forty below zero in the deep recesses of the night and would not get above ten or fifteen below during the day. For June the weather was a little behind season—a blessing since it was hot work running and tracking —and the bugs were down, though Mason Raymond knew before the night was finished the word would have gone out, the mosquitoes would be on his trail for blood. They all, man and animal and insect, inhabited a world whose code was punish and destroy.

He tore through the brush, his ears straining for his own dog's cry. He could hear John's dog; he was still circling and looking for a steady track. Whichever dog picked up a real trail first would have the advantage. He had heard several false starts from John's dog, joyful cries of triumph when the dog thought he had struck trail; but each of these had lasted only a moment or two before a mournful confession of failure, then silence until new scent. What Mason Raymond was straining to hear was the full cry of one of the dogs truly on track.

Hector wasn't going to tell anybody what he was doing, it seemed, silent long enough for Mason Raymond to freeze and ask himself, Is he off someplace bored with the whole thing, lying down and napping?

At that moment he heard a dog give the trail cry, full, steady, sure, and long enough to be sound; and he knew, even as he recognized it as the tracking sound, that it was John's dog he heard and not his own. That voice came from John's dog and John's dog was onto something. Mason Raymond just wished it was deer. To leave trailing for deerchasing was considered one of the worst sins a good woods dog could commit—as bad as, maybe worse, than being gun shy or coon sour or what the hunters called *outlaw*, that is, a dog who took off running hard as soon as he was let loose and ran hard and fast to get far away so that he could run on his own and not for the chase. A dog like that would be gone days, come back maybe quilled, but always wise—knowing he could come and go as he wanted, there were no real controls over him. Only sensible thing you could do with an outlaw coon dog, men said, was shoot him. His running free spoiled the other dogs' discipline and you didn't want to breed and pass on bad blood like that.

No, John's dog was not likely to be running deer. Unfortunately.

Mason Raymond stopped, listening to the full cry of the run, straining to hear some word from his own dog and asking himself (now almost sure), Is that dumb dog lying around someplace resting? I tried to explain it to him.

There was no knowing where he was or what he was doing because he wasn't letting on. Whatever business he was about was his and not to be noised about. Mason Raymond cursed him, kicked, cursed him again. John's dog was hysterical with happiness, following track. In a moment or two he might tree and then it would be all over. John would have won and Mason Raymond's plan would come to nothing. Maybe Hart was right anyway; maybe it was a crazy idea. But a hundred dollars was worth some kind of plan, crazy or not. His uncle had done something extremely unusual in backing him (*against his own son,* and what he had said was, *You're like a son to me, too);* it took courage and belief in your own convictions to back someone as much of a cull as either Mason Raymond or the dog. Men respected that kind of unorthodoxy and were a little awed by it—so long as it turned out all right. But to pick something so far off and be wrong, that was the worst kind of admission of senselessness.

So it wasn't just Mason Raymond who was involved, it was his uncle, too, and of course that damned dog who was so ornery and unpredictable and, God alone knew, a law unto himself. Why didn't he say something even if it was only, Good-bye, I'm off to run deer.

John's dog was still running, a long track (thank God). Mason Raymond could picture the big black and tan with bright, excited eyes, the born hunter, maybe the best coon dog in the area, now that Hart's and Lite's dogs were off their feed, and the boy every bit a match for the dog. John wouldn't be winded, for instance, by running the way Mason Raymond was. John was seasoned. John was everything Mason Raymond was not—*he* wouldn't ever have felt any compunction about killing. So probably he *should* win. If killing and hunting and treeing and shooting and shoving were part of his nature, then certainly in all fairness he should come out ahead in this contest. Mason Raymond thought disgustedly that he could possibly challenge him to a contest reciting Homer and while John retired with the coonskin he could have the cap of laurel.

Some prize.

John's dog gave the short chops of a dog at the tree. The big black and tan would be leaping up the tree trunk giving the final signal of the chase: he had driven his coon up a tree and now it would be the turn of the hunter to come and bring him down. A man shot, and—if he was lucky—brought a dead coon out of the tree. But more often than not, the coon was only wounded; it fell to the ground with a thud and the dogs jumped it and, wounded and dying, it hissed and spit and tried to fight back while the dogs ripped and snarled and pulled it apart. One coon against a whole pack of dogs. What kind of odds were those?

Only one coon in the whole world that Mason Raymond knew of had taken on those odds and beat them, and that was Old Cassius down in Blackwood Hollow and it would hardly be worth saying that that kind of a percentage should serve as an encouragement to the coons.

I don't mind running, Mason Raymond thought, but nothing in the world could make me bring a coon down to be torn apart by a pack of dogs. And the worst, the absolutely worst part of the whole thing, was that more often than not the coon was shaken down out of the tree very much alive so that the fighting and tearing apart process seemed to take forever. A coward would have been killed straight off, but coons were not cowards; they fought—how tenaciously they loved life, how tenaciously maybe everyone did—and they reared up and clawed and spit and bit and all the time the dogs were running in from all sides and chopping away at them. And at the end —at the end (Mason Raymond closed his eyes imagining it)—when the coon went down, it was still alive and the dogs fell on top of it tearing it limb from limb and it gave these terrible, low, guttural hisses and those little screams of impotence and rage, torn apart through hisses and screams and the men shouting and pounding one another on the back and screaming themselves, only those screams were of triumph. Though the men kill coons in sport, the coons die naturally in earnest.

Maybe it was better that John's dog had treed. John would kill his coon, and that was that. Mason Raymond's notion of how he was going to handle the bet was so cockeyed that of course it wouldn't work. But wasn't it worth a try? Wasn't it worth at least a try?

Hector had treed.

Mason Raymond stood, struck dumb, disbelieving. That damned dog must have run silent, trailing, and never once let out a sound until he got something up a tree. Now he was baying clearly and evenly. It's like he almost did it on purpose, Mason Raymond thought, like he was tricking everyone, even me. But a dog couldn't do that, could he? No, of course not. It wasn't right to assign a man's motives to an animal. He heard far to the right the steady, marvelous trumpet of Hector with his foe at bay. Mason Raymond panted, exhausted, floundering up a steep grade of scrub brush, berry bushes, and a young tangle of trees. The two witnesses had fallen behind.

Mason Raymond went on, racing as best he could, shouting encouragement, scrambling and falling and feeling first exalted and then scared, for John's dog was quieting down and that meant John must be at his tree, having calmed the dog, and was now probably circling the tree looking for the coon.

A gun fired.

John had found the coon's hiding place and was pelting away at him. In a minute the whole absurd wager would be over. Mason Raymond would never have a chance to try his crazy scheme. Even Hart had said it was crazy—crazy but better than just quitting and giving in. Mason Raymond fell, picked himself up and lunged on. He'd skinned his damn knees again. The blackberry bushes were so thick that the only way he could make any headway was by thrashing through. His face and neck and wrists and arms were crisscrossed with bleeding cuts and scratches. Even his thick pants had been ripped. He plowed on. Just the other side of the thicket Hector was holding something down. Two more shots rang out. John must be shooting any old which way, hoping he'd connect with luck and topple the coon.

Coons were sly: they could wrap themselves around a limb until they looked like bark; they could curl up on a tree notch and make themselves invisible; they might scrunch down among leaves and camouflage themselves so that even the most experienced woodsman couldn't distinguish them. The only thing that gave them away was once in a while a gleam of cunning eye caught in the glance of a lantern and reflected wide and shining off the retina of the eye. If John was shooting hit-miss that way, Mason Raymond was pretty sure he wasn't quite clear where his coon was. Maybe he'd spied it and while he was aiming, it had moved; or maybe for all his peering and looking, he couldn't find it and in his anxiety and impatience he was now firing in blind hope. Whatever the reason, every shot was an encouragement to Mason Raymond, scratched and thorn-lashed, as he bungled his way clear of the berry bushes and into a small, open clearing. Under an enormous pine, Hector was howling his heart out.

Twang went another shot.

Mason Raymond sprinted to the tree, and in spite of his knees, dropped down and hugged the dog. "Good boy, good boy, where's the son-of-a-bitch coon, Heck, where's he holed up, boy?"

The dog was wagging his tail wildly and licking Mason Raymond's face. What did he care where the coon was? That was Mason Raymond's problem; he'd got him up the tree, hadn't he? Mason Raymond could jolly well get him down. Anyway, it was all a game, so what did it matter?

There was much logic to his case, but very little joy—under the circumstances.

Mason Raymond peered up seventy feet into branch denseness as *twang,* one shot rang out, a pause, *twang,* another. He sympathized with John's faith, envied it; he himself was pretty sure that if he fired from now until doomsday no animal would come tumbling down. He lifted his lantern and looked hopelessly into the green maze. A damn smart coon to pick such a tree; Mason Raymond admired his sagacity, even though it worked against him. Given the odds as they were—this big dog and he himself (not much maybe, but still the coon couldn't know that)—against a lone coon, about twenty, maybe twenty-five pounds on the average, the coon was doing well, admirably well. He deserved credit. Nobody was going to tackle a tree like that, climb sixty, seventy feet to look for a little old coon, not even the most avid hunter. Yes, he certainly deserved credit. "He ought to get off," Mason Raymond said to the dog. "He deserves to go free, a smart coon like that."

The two witnesses were cutting their way clear of the brambles, plodding purposefully toward the pine. Mason Raymond —after a cursory glance their way—took no more stock of them; so far as his own distinctions of importance were concerned, they were of no account.

He took the dog by the collar and lugged him a ways off. In the distance John could be heard hopefully pelting shot into the tree where his coon was harbored. Let him shoot all night; every shot made a delay, which worked, he considered, for him, the only time probably that not having a gun would work in his favor—if he could get Hector going again.

"Come on, Heck," he urged, "try again. Let that old fellow

up in the tree off. He deserves it. Anyway, you aren't in it for the kill. What difference does it make to you whether he gets off or I catch him?"

The dog looked at him quizzically, turned and looked at the the tree, turned back to Mason Raymond. Neither one of them paid any attention to the lumbering, panting men circling the pine and looking up expectantly.

"Go on, boy, go get another coon," Mason Raymond counseled Hector.

Hector looked at him, danced back. Mason Raymond released him. The dog took off at a dead run. "Hey, where's that dog goin'," one of the old men, the one Mason Raymond thought maybe was Hare, asked, but Mason Raymond didn't bother answering; he was too busy cutting after Hector to explain to two old men, who would never understand, about giving a raccoon the outside edge on luck.

The trees were high and cut off most of the light, though here and there a sliver of silver sliced through the leaves and left an edge of pale, shiny gray on the ground. Bugs were swarming. The faint *pop pop* of John's rifle came, muffled, uphill; he was going to cut that tree apart with gunshot before the night was through. But Mason Raymond had ceased worrying about him. Either he would blast his coon out one way or another, or he was losing valuable time. John's chances— or maybe, Mason Raymond thought, it would be more accurate to say "*his* chances"—depended upon how well the tree in which John's coon was hiding could keep that coon protected. A tall tree, a really good-sized one of seventy or eighty feet, would mean that the chances of John's hitting a hiding coon he couldn't see were miniscule. John had been firing a long time; the longer he fired, the higher the tree might be supposed to be. At any rate, the matter was out of Mason Raymond's hands. He had decided his own course of action irrespective of John's.

He could hear Hector ahead breaking trail. Behind him the two old men were cursing and saying he was crazy, ought to have his head examined, a damn fool city boy let loose in the woods, didn't know his ass from his elbow, he'd already got lost once, he'd do it again, yes, and take them with him; how was it they'd ever got mixed up in such a fool scheme anyway?

In a moment he would outstrip them and be free of their cant. Six months ago he had trembled at their judgments. Now he saw how hollow and meaningless their appraisals were. You had to respect a man's intelligence to have what he said matter. But six months ago, Mason Raymond hadn't known that. He hadn't known a lot of things, the main one of which was how complex even the simplest thing might be, that there was no *yes* or *no* about anything, you had to keep evaluating and re-evaluating over and over, make up your mind and stick with those decisions flatly and firmly and yet in a moment be ready to make concessions and reversals because compassion, not rigidity, was a better yardstick to live by than any ultimate, inflexible rules a man might make for himself.

The dog began to yelp excitedly, a new track somewhere ahead, and the gun had stopped going off so that presumably John had either won or given up and in a moment the signal —if he had won—would be given. Mason Raymond listened for a volley of three shots, a pause, another volley of three, but the forest sent no other signal than busy wings and rapid feet, screeches and quarreling cries, and Mason Raymond's dog, now firmly on track, running far ahead, uphill, on the scent of something else.

Mason Raymond rode hard on himself to keep as close to Hector as he could; he was hot and sweaty and badly bitten, his knees stung, but there was an exaltation inside him, too, in this frantic scurrying through the woods, an emotion that had to do with the slices of silvery moonlight, a monolithic forest, the howling dog ahead, and most of all with the dramatic commotion that was going on in his heart.

Somewhere behind him the two men struggled to keep up, but they were outsiders to the experience he shared with the dog, for Hector was clearly as aroused as he; he had paused a moment to howl—not a treeing howl or a scenting one, but one clear, ecstatic bay up at the moon, long and high and happy, its notes catching an echo of the tumult in Mason Raymond's own heart; he felt utterly bound to the dog in that moment, as if in all the world there would never be another living thing to whom he would be so close.

Mason Raymond stopped and lifted his head and from out of his own throat there came a long answering call, then silence, then an intermingling of man and dog voices, a long, low keening to all the elements around them, the recognition that in the end it is very hard to tell where one thing leaves off and another begins or why endings and beginnings were ever even necessary. Would it not have been better if the universe were one long, linked chain of being and their enjoined voices were like the last connective links to the whole, round, entwined world in which, in the instant they shared their cry together, man and animal and the world in which they lived were once and forever linked?

V

*H*ector *had treed again,* baying in deep, endless, melancholy loops that hung in the trees. Mason Raymond, wound round with moonlight, staggered through a sudden sidehill of chopped-up meadows and came unexpectedly out of the opening onto the crest of the hill so that below him, long, slender, and conical, lay the silver-capped lake. Men wrote poems, he knew, because of moments like this, and the urge had to do with immortality.

He went slowly across the pasture, seeing *wrath* inside his mind and then Morphis writing the word H U B R I S on the blackboard in those crooked, big capital letters he used to emphasize a point, and finally finding inside himself the same senseless kind of pride that Morphis meant, the kind that destroyed instead of created; he felt suddenly all the shame and absurdity of this wager. It was absurd for him to feel he *had* to win, absurd to force a dog against his own gentler nature to hunt, absurd that his uncle would let someone like Lite make him lose his own self-control to such an extent he was pitting his own son against his son's cousin and backing the cousin.

The wager was ridiculous, a bet based purely on pride, on

the deadly desire of one man to prove himself better than another by making a dog stand as his alter ego. It was some kind of parable Mason Raymond didn't understand, and wasn't sure he wanted to understand, but somewhere at the bottom he sensed that what was illustrated was that evil always exists no matter how hard man tries to explain it away.

Maybe it was the moonlight that was so disturbing, so beautiful that it made his heart hurt and played tricks with his eyes. The lake stared back up at him like an enormous white eye. Always at the heart of creation there seemed to be an eye. When he lifted his head, listening to the dog, he saw two shining, yellow circles ahead; his breath caught in his throat, his whole chest began to throb. Once again the woods were watching, but not as he had first thought, as menace, as danger; no, they would claim him through himself and that was all right so long as he was willing to share the claim. He would not kill. The woods must now understand that. No matter. He would not kill.

The gold of the eyes, the silver of the lake, and above all the drenching milk of moonlight; he howled for the dog to come back, his voice high and shrill, yelling for the dog to come back, and miraculously the dog answered, bounding out of the brush noisily, happily, snorting with affection, and Mason Raymond dropped to his knees and threw his arms around Hector and exclaimed, "We're all such damn fools!"

They went slowly up the hill toward the tree. Hector would run ahead a little, then stop and turn and look excitedly back, his tongue hanging out, waiting, then leaping ahead, occasionally circling Mason Raymond, nudging him to get going, let's get this whole business over with and call off the long evening. Mason Raymond was walking beside him untangling the bag. It had got somehow wrapped up inside itself—all those holes, he supposed—maybe it's easy to get tangled. The bag was big and it was going to be awkward to handle and God knew he had no idea how you stuffed a coon in a bag, especially a coon that was in a tree—you could *dump* a coon from a cage into a bag easily enough (*easily* enough?)—but how did you go up a tree and convince a coon to come, be nice, and get in the bag.

You never know until you try, he told himself.

All the crazy advice people were always giving you trying to make you do things that went against the grain—there must be thousands of things there was never even any sense in trying.

They had come to Hector's tree. Mason Raymond supposed the coon was there, though he wouldn't have put it past Hector to play a little joke on him; the dog was perfectly capable, he felt, of leading Mason Raymond on a wild-goose chase all over the woods, taking him to a tree and pretending there was a coon up there, and if he would only climb it and get it (somehow) into that net bag, he would win the bet and his uncle would be a hundred dollars richer; then he could just as easily imagine the dog flopping on his hind legs and watching with great laughter as Mason Raymond shinnied up the tree and went poking among the branches looking for a coon that was never there in the first place. "You sure there's a coon in this tree?" he asked the dog suspiciously.

To look at Hector's antics there was no question about it— not just a coon, but a big, nice, smart coon that would come right out and get in a net bag, a great coon, maybe not so famous as Old Cassius, but then Mason Raymond didn't want to go running up a tree trying to get *him* into a bag, did he?

"You're sure?"

The dog was sure.

Mason Raymond stood at the bottom of the tree and tried to get the bag untangled. It was in a bad state—first, Hart's having folded it (carelessly, Mason Raymond would have accused him) and then Mason Raymond's (just as carelessly) having jammed it in his shirt on the hunt. Finally he sat down and put it on the ground and went to work on it. He was sitting cross-legged under the trees untangling the net bag when the two witnesses came hot-footing it up the hill and caught sight of him in their lanterns. "Oh, my God, now what?" one of them asked.

He paid no attention. He was nearly ready. He got up and shook the bag out and it fell free. "It's a goddam coon bag," one of them said.

Mason Raymond said, "There wasn't anything in the bet

that said the coon had to be dead, was there?''

They looked at one another. Hare took to scratching nervously under his arm. "Now, I don't know that there was anythin' said, but it was sure enough understood it was gonna be dead.''

"Understood by whom? I didn't understand that. All I said I'd do was go and hunt coon and bring one in. I never said it was goin' to be dead.''

"He ain't gonna git no coon to go in that," the one that wasn't Hare said. "What you gittin' so worked up for? No man's gonna git a coon to go in a bag like that all on his own.''

Maybe, Mason Raymond thought, just maybe. He began to climb the tree. He had a fear of heights, got panicky when he was any distance off the ground; there was a fancy name for this—acro-something-or-other, but the thing that fancy name didn't describe was a terror so absolute that it was impossible to describe. He felt as if he were falling, could actually feel himself plummeting through the air, even as he clung, frozen, to the side of the tree. He closed his eyes. Sickness flew into every part of him and was part of this terror of falling. He couldn't catch a coon hanging onto the trunk of a tree no more than ten feet off the ground. He swallowed and opened his eyes and inched his way along the tree upward. He told his knees to let him be; they'd given him enough trouble to last all their life, didn't deserve one whit more attention and so he wasn't going to give it to them. Such a ridiculous adventure almost made him hysterical, between the absurdity and the fear; you don't shinny up a tree calling out, Here, fellow, come on, fellow, here's a nice little bag for you to get in.

The raccoon was directly above him. It looked down at him with startled eyes, as if unable to believe the crazy character frozen below staring back. Mason Raymond held on for dear life with one arm and with the other took the big piece of hard candy from his pocket. He didn't hold it out to the coon. He wedged it in a tree split maybe three feet overhead—an arm's length, but he had been growing, he had long arms now, he thought with satisfaction.

The raccoon just sat there, curled into a little ball, looking at him. It was a small coon, young, probably in its first year, with a child's curiosity and none of the craft and guile of an old coot like Cassius—thank God. Mason Raymond inched a few feet up. People said dogs could smell fear on a man; he wondered if the same were true of raccoons. And could a raccoon distinguish between fear of itself (which Mason Raymond didn't have) and fear of heights (which he most certainly did have). He wondered if there was ever such a thing as a coon scared of heights; that'd be something, all right.

He was near the candy and he took it out of the fork in the tree and moved it closer to the coon. There was now only a small distance separating him from the animal, but strangely enough it didn't run. If an animal could sense fear in a man, could it also sense safety? Did that coon know Mason Raymond wasn't going to shake it out of the tree and did that coon also know that that dumb dog below didn't give a damn one way or the other whether it got free or not?

Mason Raymond took the candy and held it out. The coon reached out and took it. Mason Raymond watched the coon turn the candy over curiously in its humanlike hands; it held it up and sniffed. It rolled its head back and forth, making a squeaky sound. Then it opened its mouth and held the candy out toward it. Mason Raymond wrapped his legs around the tree, prayed as he had never prayed before because he had one chance and one chance only, and he knew that: he threw the bag over the coon.

"You mean to tell me you brought in a *live* coon?" Lite asked incredulously. "You mean you're gonna let your uncle try to collect on a live coon?"

"Nobody said the coon had to be dead," Mason Raymond began.

"That's right, Frank," Hare interrupted. "Nobody said it had to be a dead coon."

"Oh, shut up," Lite said, furious. "You oughtta knowed better. You was out there with him. Why'd you let him bring in a live coon?"

"Nobody said it had to be dead," Hare repeated stubbornly.

"All that was said, all that was ever said," Mason Raymond

went on, "was that the first coon brought in would—"

"But you knew it was suppos'd to be a dead coon; you knew—" he turned with his arms outspread in appeal, "—we all knew that, didn't we?"

Hare was adamant. "Nobody *said* so."

"Oh my God, you got no sense at all," Lite raged. "Let him bring in a live coon and try to collect a hundred dollars off me. What you think I am, some kind of fool?"

A few men began to titter—yes, maybe they did.

"You aim to settle—to pay, or not?" Mason Raymond asked. "I don't aim to kill and no law says I have to. No law says I can't settle the bet my way neither."

Hart and his uncle were standing at one side, staring at their feet. Hart's mouth was twitching uncontrollably; he was about to burst his seams with laughter, but he was trying to hold back the torrent. He could see this was not the moment for hilarity. The other men weren't so smart; they were doubled up with laughter. "He sure put one over on you, Frank! Ain't he?" one of them asked.

"It was a setup, that's what it was, a trick," Lite raged. "Nobody wins bringin' a live coon in. Go git John Buttes outta the woods," Lite cried, "and let's see what he's got to say about this."

The best way to beat evil was to avoid it. Pulling at the leash he had just put on Hector, Mason Raymond started up the road home, paying no attention to Lite's vituperation behind him. He had come to the point where he didn't care what any of them, even Hart, thought. He'd done what he set out to do. Then he stopped. He couldn't leave the coon there. In his rage Lite might kill it. He went back and said, leaning over, picking up the bag with the coon in it. "Everybody's seen I brought it in, I'm going to take this up to the house with me."

"You leave that here. If that's your coon—dead or alive— it's gotta stay here," Lite raged.

Mason Raymond didn't answer. He turned and started off again, swinging the bag. He bent down and let Hector off the leash. He wasn't going anywhere. He'd done enough running for one night. They both had. Maybe even the coon felt the same way.

He was dead tired. He just didn't have the patience to stand arguing with a man who wouldn't understand *mercy* if you drew a picture of it in the dust.

Lite was bursting with anger. "I'm onto you. You don't fool me none with your city notions and your fancy house and your crazy ways. Whole damn family of yourn crazy—father string hisself up, mother don't know nobody, you come in here with a live coon, expect me to pay a hundred dollars for a live coon —crazy, the whole lot of you. You watch out, you jest watch out. No one puts one over on Frank Lite. You ain't no better'n me even if your family does have a big bank account and two big houses to rattle around in," raging, almost incoherent, while Mason Raymond went doggedly on his way, Lite shrieking, "My old man wouldn't have gone and done what yourn's did, your Pa killed hisself and your Ma mad as—" the syllables stumbling this way and that over each other, Lite's own pride and anger and self-esteem all in question, and he was unhinged, shouting and swearing and screaming after Mason Raymond, "Indian, that's what you are, a goddam Indian, goddam half-breed Indian with Indian ways, *trash,*" he screamed, "white trash," Mason Raymond turning, looking at him with cold contempt and saying before he could stop himself (what would be the good?), "Coward—*runner,*" hearing the roar of rage that came from Lite and understanding that he had gone too far, he had pushed the man over the point of rationality, thinking, *He hates me, really hates me,* seeing the gun lifted and Hart and his uncle running, and then the blinding flash, it was too late, the dog flopped over on his side, the blood pouring out of the hole in his head, Mason Raymond staring down at Hector, half his head blown away, his dog— *his* dog, the one thing he loved more than anything in the world destroyed by a blind, senseless act of violence and envy, thinking, *He killed him because he couldn't kill me;* and then he was running, his chest opening up in a murderous flame of grief and disbelief and helpless rage, he felt as if his heart might burst apart, toppling Lite to the ground, his hands finding Lite's throat and closing 'round; he was going to kill after all, kill with sense and meaning and feeling and—above all—joy. The hate was so terrible, so thick and dense that it

] *169* [

doubled him into darkness, going down in darkness screaming, "I'll kill him, I'll kill him, I'll kill the son of a bitch, I'll
kill him if it's the last thing I ever do."

To Mason Raymond, coming out of the darkness slowly and
unwillingly, the first things discernible were not faces, but
voices, his uncle's, Hart's, and a voice it took him a moment
to recognize—his cousin John's. "Liked to kill him," Hart said
wonderingly.

"Don't blame him none atall," John Buttes said angrily.
"Anyone calls me thin's like that's gonna pay. Anyone touches
my dog—"

"It's a law matter," Cobus Buttes said.

"Law won't do nuthin', and you know that well as I do,
Cob," Hart said. "Maybe give him a corner on a fine, but ain't
gonna do nuthin' significant, you know that."

Mason Raymond opened his eyes. "He's comin' round,"
Hart said.

"You all right, boy?" Mason Raymond's uncle asked. Mason Raymond was too weak to answer. "Had to hit you, son,
try 'nd stop you from doin' anythin' foolish."

Mason Raymond tried to sit up, but Hart held him back.
"You best take it easy," he said. "He give you a good clout."

He still couldn't say anything. "Ain't a man in the parts'll
forgit it," his uncle said.

"They'll forgit," John Buttes said bitterly.

Cobus Buttes shook his head. "I don't aim to let them
forgit."

His uncle meant well; he just didn't know human nature as
well as he thought. It wasn't their dog. Anyway, Lite belonged; he, Mason Raymond, was the outsider. *I'm going to kill
him,* he said inside his head, *I said I wouldn't kill any of the woods
things, but I never said anything about what was walking around
on two legs killing things smaller than itself—called itself a man, and
killed out of nothing more than pride and hate.*

He managed to lift his head. Dizzy and confused as he was,
he could see that Lite was gone. Cleared out. The dog, too.
*Took him away somewhere, so I wouldn't see him when I came
around, him and the coon, didn't want anything to remind me.*

Trying to be protective and politic; trying to keep me out of trouble and away from grief. *You can't do that,* he wanted to tell them.

Hart and Young John were helping him to his feet. He faltered, unsure of himself, scorched by a burning pain that ran up the whole side of his head. His uncle must have given him a really bad blow. *Not taking any chances,* he thought. *But it won't help. He thinks I'll get over it; he thinks I'll come around. I'm* NEVER *coming around.*

Most of the men who had gathered at the early part of the evening were still lumped into groups, watching. *They don't want to miss anything. Biggest thing around here since my father hung himself.* His head was on fire, but his mind went on working like a smooth, steady, well-oiled machine. *Go home, get a gun, walk into his store, stand there a minute so he sees, so he understands, blow his head off just the way he blew my dog's head off.* He pulled free of Hart and Young John and stumbled toward the road. No one could stop him; his mother was (Lite's quite accurate word) gaga and his father dead. Rivers would be swimming through his alcoholic haze. Who was there to stop him? Hart? His uncle? Maybe once, twice, but not forever. He tripped, righted himself, put up his hands to steady his head. John was right by his side, not helping him, but not hindering him either, just there watching. Mason Raymond looked at him. He saw the big square sure face hard (as hard as those granite boulders up in the hills), set, and determined. "I aim to give you a hand."

"He didn't kill your dog."

"No, but he insulted me as much as he done you. We both got the same blood so far as the Indian part's concerned."

Mason Raymond started up again, slowly, his head whirling, but his legs steadier. Perhaps half a mile, a little more, lay between the rendezvous point in the woods and his house. Go up the back steps and into the hall, take down the gun, walk sure and steady to Lite's store . . .

Behind him Hart was hollering his head off. "Listen, both you dang fools, jest lissen. He done lit out, and that's the God's honest truth. He done run off—run off the way he always does when he gotta stand and face somethin'."

] *171* [

They paid no attention, tramping slowly and surely down the road, while Hart trailed them, shouting, "He's run off, I tell you. Run off this time jest the way he run off that time and left his dog all alone with that bear. He's run off, I tell you," Mason Raymond and John paying no attention, following an idea to its conclusion. "He's done run off," Hart screamed. Mason Raymond didn't believe him. He stumbled on toward the house, John walking sure and steady at his side, and there was one thought that kept him going, *I swung in trees in a way myself, not like him, not free and easy, but I got up there, high in that tree, it's something.*

"He's run off, I tell you. Lissen . . ."

Mason Raymond and John didn't answer. They went on into the back room off the kitchen and started for the gun rack. Mason Raymond took out a gun and gave it to John. He took Old Mason Mowatt Raymond's big, heavy-handled gun. It hadn't been used in so long he couldn't remember when. His father had never been a hunter.

Hart was babbling. They passed him and went on at a faster pace for the store, leaving Hart on the porch shouting uphill, "Cob, Cob, them boys is plumb out of their minds. Cob . . . Cob . . ."

Mason Raymond's uncle didn't bother panting after them. He knew Lite had run off, so he didn't have to keep saying so; he must have figured they'd find out soon enough for themselves. Because it was true: Frank Lite was a runner, come panting into town on the run, pulled his money out of the cash drawer, got his horse, and took off, "Going South way," Eben Stuart said, "goin' like one possessed. Didn't even lock up the store. People been helpin' theirselves ever since. Ain't hardly nuthin' worth takin' left."

Mason Raymond and John still didn't believe it. They went over the back rooms of the store and down cellar and out to the barn. The looters stopped stealing long enough to watch them, and for a fact they must have been a sight worth watching, Mason Raymond loose and unsteady carrying the big, heavy gun and John sure and light, one hand hooked in the wide belt that circled his narrow waist. "Nuthin' here, he's lit out jest like Hart said," John said at last.

] *172* [

"He can't hide out forever." Mason Raymond slumped against the barn, exhausted.

"He could if he kept goin'. It's a big country—all them places out West."

"He hasn't got the guts to go West," Mason Raymond said contemptuously.

"Some people go, some people jest drift," his cousin said. "It ain't always like you make a choice about what you're gonna do."

He's always ahead of me, Mason Raymond thought, even in his thinking, three years younger and a hundred wiser. His head throbbed, spun; dull duller dullest, it said to him. He bent over and swept dizzily into space, falling. John's arms supported him, John who would never have passed out.

Later, in the moonlight, they carried the dog's carcass up and buried it in the Buttes cemetery, under Emily's larch. They even had a kind of service, standing bareheaded around the big hole which Mason Raymond and John had lined with stones. "Lord," Hart said, "bless this good dog, who was a true friend to one boy."

Morphis wrote him a note; he wanted to know if Mason Raymond was planning on coming back to the Academy in the fall. He missed him. He was very sorry about his father. *I remember,* Morphis wrote, *how you chose that line from* The Iliad, *and I thought at the time how you had found one line (one I'd missed) that captured the real essential tragedy of the poem. Hector, who is doomed, exults in his strength—for a moment. I think Homer meant here, too, that we are all doomed, but the best of us have a moment when we exult in our strength.*

There was a good deal more in the ordinary vein, observations on the loss of a parent, condolences for the loss, a final, faltering sentence—*put it in perspective,* Morphis wrote, Morphis who was the believer in the *pathei máthos,* suffering brings the only true knowledge.

In his answer Mason Raymond said he didn't know when he'd be back. He didn't know exactly what he would be doing, but there were other inadequacies in his life that he wanted to straighten out besides the academic ones. He was tempted to tell Morphis about the episode in the woods, even the vow; possibly Morphis, who, in his pedantic, bookish way, might see the links that connected these acts with larger, allegorical planes. He was a man given to parables.

With the letter from Morphis in his hand, he thought: *I have two friends, two different friends and one takes me into the woods and the other holds me up in another kind of way,* two ways of going, and no way to know which one was the right one, the one in the woods or the one with books, and maybe both were right and how could you do different and opposite things at the same time?

"I don't believe he's gone that far West," Mason Raymond said, standing stubborn and determined in front of the grunting pigs (three streaked squealers shoving against Hart's boots to get him to lean down and scratch them with the stick he held in his hand, chickens running all over the place, Mason Raymond had never seen so many screaming hens in his life, Mabel's lost control).

Hart was searching around for something, his hands rummaging through pockets. "Head's been actin' up agin," he said. "The bad weather. Never knew such a summer. Ain't been nuthin' but moisture—rain, snow, sleet, you name it and we had it. Rained all of May and most of June. Ruinin' the hayin', can't git nuthin' in this kind of dampness; ruinin' my head, I'm cross-threaded all the time, can't do no figurin' at all, that scar tissue don't let me react right when it pulls together that way."

He's avoiding the issue, Mason Raymond thought as he sat down on an overturned barrel, half its staves cracked or broken, the whole place falling in on them, he thought, but they just go on fussing with their pigs and hens. "I'm not the only one's single-minded," Hart said obliquely. He reached down and ran the thick stick over the young pigs' hairy backs; they scrunched and rotated under the stick, their high, happy shrieks squeals of pleasure.

Hart had the right to remain neutral. Still it had been his dog at the offset. "It was your dog, too," Mason Raymond reminded him.

"You want me to eliminate a man because of a dog?"

He'd expected Hart to be sympathetic. "You just aim to let him get away with it?"

"He's got a conscience same as any man."

"*Lite?*"

Hart was working the stick faster and faster; the piglets were mad with excitement. Mason Raymond got up and started for the door, which leaned in crazily, half suspended at the top by makeshift ropes and some kind of haphazard, homemade latch. He heard Hart call out. He went on walking; at the door he said, "You don't aim to help?"

"You and Young John make two. I reckon that'll even thin's out, two young'uns like you two agin a wily old codger like Lite."

"How'd you know John was going?"

"You didn't think he'd let you git all that glory alone, did you?"

Mason Raymond turned. "What glory?"

"You're aimin' on meetin' him face to face, ain't you? A regular wild-west shoot-out?"

"I'm aimin' to shoot him in the back," Mason Raymond said coldly, "just the way he shot the dog."

Hart stared. "In the back—now jest a minute, Ray. A man and a dog ain't the same. You shoot a man in the back, people's goin'—You can't shoot a man in the back."

"*Can't can't can't*—that's all I ever hear. People can't do this, they can't do that. But they're always doing it. All the things that can't be done are being done every day."

Hart had stopped scratching the pigs. They were running around in circles hysterically rooting for past pleasures.

"They ain't neither of them goin'," his uncle said.

"What you doin' down here, Cob?"

"Come to git this—" he held up one of Mabel's fancy roosters, its legs tied, its head wobbling, but managing to give out a feeble squawk of outrage. "Kam got it in her head to raise her some of these fancy-feathered chickens Mabel got off her relatives down in the mountains. So far as I'm concerned, a chicken's a chicken, but she wants them to look pretty runnin' around the place before she puts them in the pot. And as

] *175* [

long as I'm here I want to make it clear," he said, eyeing Mason Raymond, "there ain't gonna be no nonsense with guns out of you boys."

Mason Raymond wasn't going to argue, but on the other hand he wasn't going to have his uncle settle his scores. John could do what he liked.

As if his uncle read his mind, he said, "Don't think I don't know what's goin' through your head. I got a responsibility to you same as I do to John," he said. "And I aim to keep it." John, sullen, was looking at the ground, wiggling, waggling back and forth, in impotent anger. He was being shamed in front of Mason Raymond, being made to seem a *kid*. But he didn't dare talk back. Mason Raymond paid him no mind. He had his own problems.

"He shot my dog."

"He's done worse than that, probably not to your way of thinkin', but looked at in general; he's got worse crimes on his conscience."

"Conscience? He hasn't got a conscience."

"Maybe not, not as we know it, but someplace inside him, he's got at least an inkling. Can't be nobody don't."

Mason Raymond looked at the pigs. Hart still leaned absent-mindedly against a post, resting on the scratching stick, the pigs running around frantically trying to get him to put that stick in motion again. "Your Ma's not good," his uncle said to him. "She don't respond the way she should. You don't want to do nuthin' to jeopardize her in any way."

"She won't know what I do or don't do," Mason Raymond said. "It's her mind, it went with the coma."

"That specialist from Albany—what's his name?"

"Morrow?"

"He don't think she's—"

Cobus Buttes stopped so Mason Raymond finished the sentence for him. "She's never going to be anywhere near normal."

"But the thing is," his uncle went on, stubborn, "we don't know what she knows and what she don't and you go and do somethin' final, it might finish her off."

"She won't know."

"People know a lot no one gives them credit for."

"He's right," Hart agreed. "You can't put nuthin' over on most women. They got these sixth senses inside makes them see somethin' you try to hide, no matter how good you try to cover it up."

John raised his eyes and looked at Mason Raymond, waiting to see what he was going to say. *I'm the leader now*, Mason Raymond thought. Do nothing, a voice inside him said, wait and see. Lite can't let a sixteen-year-old boy (for his June birthday had elevated him indisputably, sixteen sounded far older than fifteen) scare him off forever. When he comes back—

"I won't chase after him—if that satisfies you any."

"It's better than nuthin'. When he gits back, I'll worry then."

"He's back," Young John Buttes said, leaning over his father's horse (*He took it without telling him*, Mason Raymond thought, thinking of his uncle's strict rules about his horses and seeing the horse was all lathered up). *He's been riding too hard. Riding: that's another thing I got to learn. A man should know how to ride.* John handed Mason Raymond a packet. "Ma sent it down. It's some kind of herb stuff off the Reservation. She said you could decide whether you wanted to use it or not; she didn't want the responsibility, but she thought she ought to git it for you anyway. What you reckon on doin'?"

He's leaving it up to me now. He took the oilskin packet and looked at it. His aunt had kept her word, but he wondered how she'd managed it. A week before, in the big upstairs hall, he'd stopped her, thinking how strong and tireless she looked even though she'd been running back and forth between two houses for weeks; it seemed to him she was made of nothing but grit and spirit; he couldn't ever remember her saying a complaining word, even when he'd insisted on Morrow's going back to Albany and she'd remonstrated with him that he was a specialist. "He's no good. He doesn't have the feeling a sick person needs," Mason Raymond had told her and she'd given him a deep look and gone on with her chores. So she would understand what he felt if anyone would.

Brushing a lock of thick white hair out of her eyes, she had said, "She ate better this noon, took some meat and a little mashed potatoes, and some custard."

"She's not going to get any better," Mason Raymond had said.

"You mustn't say that," she hushed him. "There's improvement. It's just slow to show because we're around her all the time. We don't see."

Mason Raymond shook his head. He was learning to be a realist. He wasn't sure he liked the transition, but he was not —nor would he ever be—the same boy who stood in the cold, pre-Christmas dawn watching Rivers ride off down the road for his father. All journeys changed men. Still the innocence of that morning lay inside his mind—the clear crystals of snow, the horses' hot breath, his mother wrapped in furs—as well as the shattered head of Hector lying in the dust. "As Lite said, I got Indian blood," watching her wince, "and if white doctors can't do anything for her, maybe Indian ones can." He saw at once she didn't understand; her face was filled with horror, with resistance. "Oh, I'm not talking about bringing a medicine man up here. I only wondered if there was any way to get some of their healing medicines."

Relief came across her face first, then perplexity.

"From up at the Reservation," he explained.

"How could we do that? You mean you think Cobus could, that he might still have—"

Ties was the word she rejected; he didn't know whether she'd ever accepted the Indian part of her husband. He waited. She was a woman who took her time. "He might," she said at last. "There's no knowing some things about anyone. He just might at that," and she laughed. "It won't do any harm to *ask.*"

He held the results of her asking in his hands. "Lite come back a couple of days ago, opened the store up yestiddy. Or what's left of it," Young John said, dismounting. He's been growing, Mason Raymond thought, seeing how tall his cousin was; his voice is changing, he's going to be big and tall and dark, and dangerous, too, he thought, *one of these days,* but he's not going to do anything now. Well, it wasn't *his* dog, he reminded himself.

They walked the horse, cooling it off, Mason Raymond looking at the small oilskin packet. His mind was running four ways at once, thinking about Lite and his mother, his mother and his aunt and his Uncle Cobus, about Young John getting on to manhood, and about his uncle and an Indian reservation more than a hundred miles away to which in some unfathomable way the Butteses were still linked. Young John was harsh with the horse, talking to it in an angry, belligerent way, the horse paying no mind, stumbling along, bored, grabbing at grass. "You gonna do it?"

Mason Raymond didn't answer. He was going to do something, but what he wasn't sure. *It* meant killing to Young John, but *it* didn't mean at this moment anything to Mason Raymond except the hate in his heart pounding up and asking the same question, *What you gonna do?*

"Pa don't know I'm down here," John admitted. "But he knows Lite got back, so I lit out as fast as I could to beat him down. Soon as this horse is rested and ready, I got to be gittin' back. He'd skin me alive, he finds out I come down here."

"I'm glad you did. When you've walked the horse out, come to the house and get something to eat."

"I gotta git back."

"You can carry something with you. You want me to get it for you?" John nodded and Mason Raymond went up the carefully pruned path toward the house. All the grounds had been trimmed and set to rights, Rivers trying to wear out his grief in work. The place had never looked so good.

He went into the house by the back door, past the maid spooning something bubbling in a big pot on the stove; he had made up his mind, or perhaps, he thought, it might have been more accurate to say his mind had been made up for him by the recognition of John's impressive height and his changing voice. "Can you give me some bread and butter and meat to take out?" he asked the maid, going into the hall without waiting for an answer. She'd get what he asked because he was head of the house now and what he said had to be obeyed or there would be unpleasant consequences. A month before she'd have questioned him and argued with him and maybe even run to his mother to find out should she, but he was authority now.

He stood in front of the gun rack. For a moment he didn't believe his eyes; all the guns were gone. They had been there this morning, he was sure of that, absolutely sure, because he had developed the habit of checking every time he went past, looking up at the gun rack and seeing his great-grandfather's gun and saying to himself, *It's* there, as if the gun were lying quietly in its place waiting for him to come take it down and put it to use after all these years of resting and waiting.

His uncle couldn't have done that, nor Hart. His mother couldn't. None of the help would dare. "Rivers," he screamed, racing for the stairs. "Rivers, I want to talk to you *right this minute.* Rivers—"

"Mr. Raymond," the nurse said, hanging over the upstairs landing from the place where his father must have launched himself, "Mr. Raymond," she said, stern, disapproving, "your mother's trying to rest."

Mason Raymond paid no attention to her. She was help, too. "Rivers," he screamed, "where are you? Answer me, *where are you?"*

"He went out about an hour ago," the nurse said, pursing her lips. "And he didn't say where he was going. He never does," she said prissily.

Mason Raymond raced back down the hall, past the kitchen maid, out the back door, down the prim path toward John, standing next to the horse watching him. "I gotta have that horse. I can't wait to saddle up another. You do that and try and catch me. I gotta catch Rivers. He's taken the guns!"

Mason Raymond had ridden now and again when he was younger, some summers, but nothing concentrated, nothing in any way sustained enough so that he could say he could ride; but he flung himself up on the horse and grabbed up the reins, wheeling the horse around, John running alongside hanging onto his left leg and hollering he couldn't take that horse, it was his father's best horse, Mason Raymond kicking out at him trying to make him let go, the horse shying sideways, Mason Raymond grabbing mane and kicking out again at John, John trying to drag him down, the horse suddenly rearing and dumping them both, galloping off and standing nervously looking back, ready to bolt again.

Mason Raymond lay winded, stunned, shaken up but not, he thought, any bones broken. John was swearing like a man, "Goddam it to hell, look what you gone and done. You ain't got no more sense than Sarton, *less* . . ."

"Oh, shut up, you little shit."

There was a moment of stunned silence, then a blow on his mouth, John flopping over against him pummeling his face, chest, belly. Mason Raymond drew up his knees and brought them against John's midsection. There was a howl. John sailed through the air, then lay still, grunting. Mason Raymond was so mad that he felt like killing John, killing Rivers, and when he got through with them he would kill Lite. But he didn't have a gun. He still had his hands, though. These he gathered together in a brain-concerted effort to murder. He rolled over and commenced to wring John around the neck. John lay writhing and gasping, too done in to defend himself. The moment—unfortunately, only a moment—was one of the most satisfactory in Mason Raymond's life. In that instantaneous happiness he even had a bursting vision of tying John up behind the horse and dragging him around in the road. He was just sorry there wasn't a parapet he could throw him over.

"Here, here, stop that, you boys. Cut that out!"

Hart was always where you didn't want him, running off into the woods when you weren't ready, losing you, telling you things you didn't want to hear, getting hit on the head by maniacs, letting houses and barns fall down around his head, leaving half his stuff God knew where, beating his brains out against a destiny over which he had no control; but he was strong, and now he pried Mason Raymond's hands loose and yanked him back while Mason Raymond raged under the restraint and John tumbled over and threw up. *He's never gonna mess with me again,* Mason Raymond exulted, *never ever. Nobody is.* He hit Hart. The old man stumbled back and went down on his knees. Then the violence washed out of Mason Raymond as quickly as it had come; he grabbed Hart and held him close, starting to sob like a small, bewildered child. He didn't know what had come over him. He was somebody he didn't even know, but how could you explain that to a good mistreated old man?

His uncle wasn't in the mood for explanations from anyone. He was furious with John about the horse, furious with Mason Raymond about the bruises around John's neck, and furious with Hart for having let the horse get loose during the fracas. "God knows where ,my best horse is," he kept repeating. "They say things happen in circles. Had a horse git 'way one other time down here, years ago. When one thing goes wrong, you let loose a whole barrelful of troubles. Didn't you see the horse wasn't tied?" he asked Hart.

"I swear to God I didn't, Cob."

His uncle sat down on the porch steps and put his head in his hands. Mason Raymond knew he was waiting for an explanation from him, but what could he say—I wanted to murder your son? Faintly he heard his voice mumbling, "I'm sorry. I shouldn't have taken after him like that."

"Wasn't your fault," John muttered. "I was hangin' onto you and hittin' you some."

What's he want to go and make me feel guilty for? "We'll start looking for the horse," he said.

"Cob, we got more problems than jest here. Down to the Landing—Lite, he's been banged up some. Rivers went after him with that old gun of Old Mason Mowatt and it went off wrong or somethin' and they're both laid up. I come up here to fetch help and come on them flailin' away at one another."

"They bad?"

"Bad enough. Rivers got the worst of it from what I hear, powder burns and shell scraps and such, but Lite, he's punctured some hisself, bad enough, but not fatal. Worse luck."

"Rivers?" Mason Raymond asked.

"I'll never understand that Rivers," Cobus Buttes said, lifting his head and looking at nothing. His eyes were white and blank. "What'dda make him go killin' without checkin' his gun?"

"He's used to thin's runnin' shipshape around here. He ain't had all my experience. The law'll be after him once he's whole agin. Don't seem right, do it?" Hart asked.

"I'm too tired to think whether anythin's right or wrong. Let's jest look for the horse. Rivers and Lite, they ain't gonna go nowhere, but that horse can go like hell once he puts his mind to it. This has been some *summer,* that's all I can say."

Rivers was hauled up to the Raymond house in a cart; he lay on a makeshift bed in back, bandages on his hands and face, holes cut for the eyes and mouth. He was going to be charged with assault with a deadly weapon as soon as he was well enough to stand trial. Lite's physical wounds were only superficial, but his pride was in a bad way. People had started seeing him as a figure of fun, and they seemed to take it as part of the joke. Rivers had taken a pot shot at him with a gun that wouldn't shoot straight. He hadn't said one word, Rivers, since he'd pulled the trigger; his silence wasn't only because of injuries, but pride, too. Always pride, Mason Raymond thought, supervising Rivers' removal from the cart and up to the house. Sometimes it seemed to him pride was the only motivation men had. Rivers' eyes looked out from the round holes in the bandages. Mason Raymond bent down and said to the white covering over his ears, "I know why you did it," Rivers moving his bandages back and forth, no, Mason Raymond didn't know. "I found it," Mason Raymond said in a low voice that only Rivers could hear. "You know, the handkerchief—my mother's . . ." Rivers didn't answer. He just closed his eyes. He kept them closed all the way up the stairs and into the back, neat, white sterile hospital-like room. Even when they laid him on the bed, Rivers didn't open his eyes. Mason Raymond pulled up the one chair and sat down. Sooner or later Rivers would open his eyes and they would talk; in the meantime, there was no place he wanted to go, not to his mother's room where she lay tossing and turning and asking *why,* not downstairs where his uncle was waiting to see how the horse was, not out to the barn where Hart and Young John were fussing with the animal, not even to his own room where he might seclude himself and ask why love destroyed so much that was decent and good, and what love didn't get, pride did.

His business was here with Rivers, Rivers who had gone to kill Lite to protect *him,* not because he cared about Mason Raymond, but because Rivers did care enough about his mother, gone as she was, to spare her the troubles a son could bring.

Later, maybe an hour or two later, Rivers opened his eyes; they were clear and bright as if all the time those lids had been closed only to give the brain behind them a period in which to rest, reason, and become reconciled to the fact Mason Raymond wasn't going away. "How'd you find it?" he croaked through the bandaging.

"I was snooping. I don't know why. You seemed—so remote from the way everyone else was, I guess I just wanted to find something that made you like everyone else. You remember that time downstairs? By the door? When you were listening?" Rivers moved his head up and down, saying yes, he remembered.

Once—long before he'd even come on the handkerchief— walking quietly downstairs Mason Raymond had surprised Rivers in the hall, his ear attentively attuned to the low hum of sounds behind the closed parlor doors, so intent on eavesdropping that Mason Raymond was almost on top of him before he realized he was being observed. "Sir," he had said, flushing scarlet, bounding back, so unhinged that he couldn't even think of an excuse to offer, standing crimson with mortification, trying to fish up some plausible reason why he should be crouched down, ear glued to a closed door. There was no explanation, of course. Even Mason Raymond, stupefied as Rivers with the painfulness of the situation, could think of nothing to say. The two of them were riveted to the peacock rug while from behind the closed door the glitter of Ardis Raymond Buttes's voice rang out, golden, "Oh, Cobus, you're just too much!" and she had begun to laugh.

He had walked past Rivers and out the front door. He had no place in particular he was going—he had just been aimlessly wandering around when he had come down the stairs, sick of reading, sick of himself, and blundered on Rivers.

He had stood on the front piazza and had heard through the half-open French doors lemony laughter from his mother. "You know I've always adored you," she was saying in a mocking voice, but behind the mockery Mason Raymond sensed truth. What could not be said in earnest might be passed off in jest. "Why, when you were away at the war, I just —just didn't know what to do with myself."

Like Rivers, Mason Raymond had found himself riveted to the spot in fascination. Later he would tell himself eavesdroppers always heard what they deserved. In the silence that had followed he imagined his mother looking up provocatively because after a pause his uncle had said, mock-gallantly but also truthful, "You know you've always been very special to me, right from the first. In this room, remember? You gave me some kind of terrible gluey mess to eat—"

"*Marrons,*" Ardis Raymond Buttes had recalled happily. "You were all upset over that horse—"

"My father's mare, all banged up because of that stallion of your grandpa's that got out—thirty years ago, at least."

"Oh, it can't be that long!"

"I couldn't have been much older than Mason Raymond, maybe not that old, time does such funny things with how you remember things, how you remember yourself; fifteen and I wanted to go into the woods, you were the most beautiful thin' I'd ever seen—"

"Oh, Cobus, I—"

Suddenly, briskly, his uncle's voice had changed, become businesslike and matter-of-fact. "You've got to do somethin' about that bottom land, Ardis. You can't let it stand fallow year after year, it'll go to scrub and weeds."

There had been no answer.

"Ardis?"

"Oh—yes, of course. What do you think I should do, Cobus, hay it?"

"No, it's been hayed thin. Why not plow it up and put in 'taters?" The discussion, impersonal, had trailed on about lime, harrowing, spring sowing. They had lost—or cut—the connection which had bound them. She depends on him, Mason Raymond had thought, she always has, and he feels something for her too, maybe she was the most beautiful thing he'd ever seen, come into a great room of heavy wood and heavy drapes, and there was a vision he'd kept, Cobus Buttes, all this time, one he wouldn't ever forget; he hadn't forgotten it thirty years later. What was there in his mother that had inspired such adoration in his uncle, in Rivers, but that hadn't caught his father's imagination? If she had cared so for Cobus Buttes, why had she married Clyde Buttes?

Now the secret was locked inside that bewildered, floundering heart whose beat was barely visible, hardly audible; he would never know; even if she lived he would never know. One more thing he would never know.

"I was in here looking, the way you were there that day by the door listening. It's kind of the same thing."

No, it wasn't, Rivers' eyes said. He was listening because he cared, Mason Raymond merely because he was curious. "Well, maybe not *the* same, but near it."

"You ain't goin' after him now, er you?" Rivers' muffled voice came from behind the bandages.

"You mean Lite?" Rivers moved his head yes. "No, not that way, leastwise. There are other ways to kill a man—maybe not so much kill him as break him down. You did worse than kill him—" Rivers' eyes glistened. "You made him the laughingstock of the Landing." Something was going on with Rivers' mouth behind the gauze; possibly he was smiling. Mason Raymond hoped so.

Mason Raymond stood up. "We'll get you off. Don't you worry about it."

"Mr. Raymond, sir, it's not me that I'm worried about. It's your Ma down the hall."

She was dying and no one, even the two doctors in the hall, father and son, knew how to stop the darkness from slipping in and taking over. Mason Raymond sat in a big horsehair chair at one side of her bed, the two Bronsons in matching uprights on the other. Three big Persian cats slept at her feet, contented. No one shooed them away. His uncle stood at the window, gazing out with his hands clasped behind his back.

His mother snored, gasped, groaned, snored again, rattled her breath, sputtered, snored again in an endless, unremitting pattern of lungs unable to right themselves and struggling to breathe the way they should. She reminded him of the dog. But she wasn't resting; she was snoring that grinding way because the air inside was wrong and her chest couldn't put it right.

She was unconscious and had been so for several hours. Another coma, Old boozy Doc Bronson said, a catchall term that meant the mind had ceased functioning and while the body maintained some kind of grip on existence the essence of its meaning was absent. The vulnerability of her organs was exposed; some alteration none of them could deal with had upset the vital balance and she was dying; yet all he could wonder was if he had ever truly loved her in the total and obsessive way she had adored him and he couldn't answer that question because he didn't know. "Oh, love me, love me, you don't know how much I love." She had always been vulnerable, first to his father, then to her love for him, and finally now at the end ugly and haggard, hair unkempt, face distorted— that was the worst part of the illness; it took a person with pride (normal, good pride) and reduced her to shriveled flesh and open-mouthed snoring, with gummy yellow eyes. It would have killed his mother, Mason Raymond thought, to know Cobus Buttes could see her like this.

The emptiness of feeling inside him was neither love nor its absence; it was more like nothing. He had lost in the woods even the ability to be sentimental. Old Doc Bronson, whiskey-breathed, leaned forward and put his head against her breast, listening for a heartbeat. Mason Raymond got up and went out into the hall; he was suffocating with a sense of helplessness. The terrible knowledge inside him was that part of him wanted her dead, the only act he could foresee that would free him; and another part of him, trembling with guilt, begged whatever powers there were to bring her back, well and safe and smothering him once more with love. As if in answer to both those pleas, Young Doc Bronson opened the door and came to his side, one hesitant hand lifted, then suspended, over Mason Raymond's arm. "She's—" He stopped, sighing;

"she's not good," he said at last. "If she doesn't come out of this soon—"

It is your fault, the reprimanding voice inside Mason Raymond said. If you hadn't gone and gotten lost in the woods . . . blackbirds, squawking, frightened, rose in a shower of funeral specks outside the window. He knew they were objective symbols of the pebbles of accusation inside his own mind.

". . . no more than a living vegetable." Mason Raymond had missed the link that had come before. He turned; the sun behind him, sheltered from him by expensive Albany glass, sent bloody colors nevertheless all over the wall in front of him, an apocalypse of some kind. He looked at the half-rotted teeth in the young man's face, watched him fumble with his watch fob. "The brain can't take long absences of activity," the mustached maw of a mouth stinking with decayed breath bayed out at him. "She's been under an awful long time to come back without damage. Irreversible damage," that black hole with its snuff-rotted teeth said pontifically.

Mason Raymond still didn't understand; his mind was busy, too, trying to sort out the symbolic overtones of blackbirds, the bloody wall. He felt clawed inside. He couldn't imagine what he was expected to say, what he was supposed to do, but he felt that some mystic pronouncement, some magic spell should come, miraculously, from him and advance her on the road to recovery. Since he was at fault in getting himself mixed up and astray, worrying her into collapse, he was responsible for pulling her out, especially since Young Doc Bronson obviously had no remedies of his own to offer. There was the Indian medicine.

"Maybe we ought to send down to Albany," Mason Raymond said, "for some help. But I don't want that Morrow back."

Insulted, young Doc Bronson hurrumphed before he stalked down the hall, bathed in bloody light, and closed himself inside the sickroom with *his* patient.

Mason Raymond went down the stairs toward the pantry where he had hidden the packet. The doors to the parlor were open and voices drifted out. He remembered his mother and Cobus Buttes in there, he and Rivers eavesdropping; now it was his aunt and uncle he paused to spy upon (whatever other term could you put to it?).

"She took advantage of your good nature, Cob, and I'm not afraid to say it even if you are," he heard his aunt say.

"She had a lot of things that went wrong for her, she—"

"Everybody has a lot of things go wrong for them."

"Well, she tried—"

"*Tried?* She always made me feel—like I wasn't born as good as she was because no one's as good as a Raymond. God made the Raymonds and then He made everyone else. She looked down on me. Oh, she didn't use those grand manners on you, I know, but on me and the children and everyone else, she queened it over all of us. You know that. Only you were always special to her, always someone apart from everyone else." There was the saddest quality in Kam Buttes's voice Mason Raymond had ever heard in anyone's voice. "And you," she went on after a moment, "you were always in love with her in a way, too, weren't you?"

"No, not the way you mean." His uncle sounded strangled. "There are all kinds of loves, Kam, you know that, you're wise. You were the only one I ever loved in any way that was important, but she was such a pretty girl, the first girl—a man never forgets his first girl, she's always got a special corner of his mind. But that's not the same as a wife."

"No, no, it's not." That sad voice made Mason Raymond feel he ought to burst in on them and say to his aunt, You're worth a hundred of her. She's pretty and sweet and man-likeable, but she's not strong, not the way you've been strong all your life, upholding so many others, even us.

Of course he couldn't do a thing like that. Instead he slipped out to the pantry and retrieved the Indian herbs, standing in the dying light of afternoon, with the blood red diluted into pink, as the blood of a dying man gushes first bright crimson and then weakens into a faint pink at the end, looking at the packet, turning it over slowly in his hands, finally opening it, the aromatic odors of the herbs flooding his senses. Nothing could hurt her now, help might come from any direction. Who in this indecipherable world knew what was good or bad for the sick and dying, for even the well? He heard his aunt's grief-stricken voice inside his heart (it was a thing of the heart, not the head) and he was crushed again by the realization that love comes in many guises, not the least of which is the disguise of salvation: never would his aunt understand the kind of love Cobus Buttes was talking about because he, Mason Raymond Buttes, didn't understand it and if there was anyone who should, it was he, he who had everything to benefit from it and nothing to lose as opposed to his aunt, who had lost so much from that divided attention of his uncle's heart and yet had survived to forgive and take what she could get, not what she might have asked had she been given the chance, but just what she could get.

The odor of the herbs rushed into the vacuum of stale air in the hall; the house seemed suddenly filled with a sharp pungent smell of strange roots and fungus barks and dark medicinal grasses and leaves that had come from secret, hidden dells. The scent was so strong that as he passed the parlor door his aunt and uncle came out, drawn by the odor to see what was happening, and as he passed them in the hall, his uncle nodded, his aunt smiled, one of those crooked you-might-as-well-try smiles, and he passed upstairs and into the sickroom where the two Bronsons whispered advice back and forth to one another, advice that probably served no other purpose than to puff them up, and he leaned down, as his aunt had told him to do earlier, and put the herbs in the empty saucer by the bed and took another handful and scattered them over the sheets, letting them settle in little, miniscule, dark patches, almost forestlike, on the bed covering, and the strong, strange smell, an Indian smell, filled the room and startled even the Bronsons, tongueless for the moment, looking across at him with frowns of disapproval. They didn't have to ask what he had done; they had lived in these parts all their lives and knew.

Toward dawn Rivers, still bandaged but partially recovered, limped into the room and stood next to her bed. He stood there a long time, big globular tears falling off his cheeks, his hand clutching the stolen handkerchief to his chest. He had come to give it back, though giving it back meant giving up his most precious possession. Finally he tucked the handkerchief under one limp hand. When she was buried, Mason Raymond insisted the handkerchief be left in that hand. He valued other people's emotions even if he seemed to feel none of his own.

The minister had finished, looking smug and self-congratulatory on such a splendid departure oration, smug and happy, saying, "In the Book of Life she must now be registered as having entered the Eternal Home." Mason Raymond rose and prayed (as admonished by that beelike voice), knelt and prayed (as advised), walked and touched the coffin and knelt again and bent his head and prayed once more (this time on his own, but none of it with any credence), stood (with his aunt and uncle) beside the coffin as it was borne from the parlor out to the long, ornate black carriage, the black horses with their black-feathered panaches (ordered specially from Glens Falls) standing, bored, under the bright, golden, late June sun. His only moment of surprise came then; Rivers was sitting on the brougham beside the driver provided by the Seward Brothers establishment, as were the folding chairs, palm fans, memorial cards with a picture of Christ ascending to the Golden Throne (and a small advertisement card, *The Seward Brothers would be pleased to discuss any burial problems you might have. Please indicate your desires on these memorandum cards or stop by the office at your earliest convenience. All information kept in strictest confidence*), the burial diggers, and—for an extra fee —green matting from the house to the hearse for the body to be carried over, "royally," Mason Raymond had commented, remembering Agamemnon's home-coming, but of course no one, least of all the Sewards, got the allusion; a pale, half-bandaged Rivers, eyes riveted ahead, hands folded formally in his lap, who didn't even flinch when the body went into the back with a thump and the whole carriage wobbled; then stiffly standing up, a lopsided figure whose solemnity looked silly in such dark garb and all bandaged that way, swinging himself stonily down to help Mason Raymond's aunt up to the casket where, following local custom, she put the family wreath (gladioli, the flower of death) over the casket and watched, anchored by Rivers' trembling hands, as one of the Sewards

] *191* [

slammed the glass door on the carriage shut and then leaned forward and put his weight against the door and shoved. It had stuck.

All his life Mason Raymond had been trying to love his parents the way he felt he should and not succeeding and feeling weighed down with guilt because he couldn't muster the emotions he should; or maybe that wasn't true either, maybe what was true was that he had wanted them to love him in a way they couldn't, just as his mother had loved him in a way that had been oppressive; possibly you had to be free to feel, not goaded or forced. Yes, he cared for her, but he still wasn't sure that could be called love, real love. Maybe he wouldn't have ever known there was such a thing as love if he hadn't read the word in books.

He ought, he supposed, to have performed some meaning-ful rite for her, placed her in one of those holy coffins that had holes bored in the bottom so that when the casket was sus-pended over a pit all the body fluids dripped out, leaving the bones free, the bones then removed, scraped, dried, polished and strung back together bone by bone with golden threads and hung for veneration in some sacred spot. Yet the grave-yard on the hill was a shrine of sorts, to the blind belief that the dead did influence the living. There were places in the world (or so Morphis had said and Mason Raymond had no reason to doubt him) where men appeased ancestral bones by human sacrifice, catching a victim off guard, with a knife quickly piercing cheeks and tongue before any curse could come, the throat slit so that the blood might run into a bronze or copper coffer, the blood poured over the bones to give strength from the living to the dead. In time, so many sacrifices were made that the bones turned black. A pagan people, Morphis (a good Methodist) had said, ignoring the fact he and almost everyone else Mason Raymond knew participated in what Mason Raymond considered barbaric sacrifice. It was the blood and bones of the God's slain Son they consumed, wasn't it, in order to purify themselves? He had raised his hand and then put it down, thinking better of what he had been about to say to a classroom of good young Christians, but not before Morphis had seen the look on his face, cleared his throat and passed hastily on to the week's lecture about the Propagation of the Faith Among the Heretic and Infidel. The class was asked to cough up a portion of their allowances (or, if they felt singularly moved and pious, the whole shebang) to bring The Word to Pagan Shores. Then they rose and rendered "God Be Merciful Unto Us" and "Great Is The Lord, Our Maker."

Great is the Lord, our Maker, praise ye His holy name with joy and gladness, joyfully give praises,

Praise Him ye nations, fall down before Him, let all mankind adore Him and praise His name. *Alleluia.*

Informal discussion of the missionary work of Africa and China, Morphis announced, would follow Assembly. As an incentive cookies and punch would be served at the *end* of the question-and-answer period.

Mason Raymond hung his head and remained in his seat while the others filed out. They were so obedient, so trusting; he both envied and pitied them, their innocent belief filling him with confusion and disgust. They were always lining up to light candles and make their way through the night in Christian certainty that their candles were lighting up the dark of ignorance, and yet he felt they were the untutored ones, never *once* wondering if the heathen Chinese and pagan Africans wanted their solicitude. Yet he had never had the courage to confront their numb allegiance to what was told them. They accepted. They always accepted. It seemed to him only *his* heart rebelled in soft, murderous anger against the lighting of his candle and the trudging off into night to some terribly tacky shrine where the uplifting speeches were both endless and boring.

Closing his books over-noisily, Morphis hung back; he should be galloping off to monitor the whisperers, doodlers, paper-throwers through Civics and Ethics. Glumly Mason Raymond rose and lifted his own texts—those books of wisdom in whose final word on everything he was beginning more and more to doubt.

"Well," Morphis said.

"It's all a lie. They're no more heathens than we are, killing each other over slaves most people wouldn't have in their own homes."

"The peculiar institution," Morphis said ironically as if he were making an adult jest Mason Raymond should appreciate and applaud.

"Everything's 'peculiar' one way or another," Mason Raymond said with great feeling.

"You aren't going to win any converts with condescension. Your father sees a Great Future before you, and the youngsters you patronize now won't forget or forgive you fifteen years from now. That could maim your future."

"There's such a thing as the truth."

"*The* Truth? And what is that?"

"How would we like it if a lot of Africans or Chinese suddenly started pouring over here telling us we were savages and murderous and cruel—which of course we are."

Morphis sighed with the despair of defeat. "If you must think like that, don't say it. Otherwise you'll end up like I am —reprimanded for being late again. Stop in my room tonight and we'll talk if you feel like it."

"What's the use? What I think won't change anything."

"You never know, you just never know. That's what keeps us teaching, the hope for change."

"Look what they did to Galileo—to say nothing of Christ. Nobody talks about that when The Word is mentioned. Or feeding Christians to the lions—although I suppose of course the argument would be the feeders were pagans and in need of *the* true Light."

Morphis leveled his books under his arms and said, "You'd better stop by tonight." He plodded toward the door, an unhappy, overweight, underpaid anomaly. Mason Raymond admired him but he didn't want to be like him: Knowledge had not freed him. That's what, Mason Raymond supposed, Morphis himself had been trying to say, that the open mind was in a position of great exposure and hence great peril. Practice disguise. Go in stealth. Hit the enemy from hidden places. Guerrilla warfare was an American invention. The colonists hadn't presented themselves as open targets for the British; they skulked behind trees, took pot shots, darted from one cover to another. If you were British, you called that cowardly; if Colonial, smart. There were, Morphis was saying, tactics of the mind as shrewd and successful as those of the Continental Army. He must learn not to lay himself open, an easy target.

Yet something more was involved besides Morphis' appreciation of his budding intellect; the sad discovery he had made that night in Morphis' master room was that there were demands every man had to fulfill, no matter how much he tried to suppress them—in a word, nobody lives in the intellect alone for very long without paying for it. Morphis was paying. He sat in a thickly napped worn chair, his fat legs crossed, his fat hands folded, trying to explain to Mason Raymond how grievous his life was in the midst of such an antediluvian society (antediluvian? before the Flood, Morphis said, antiquated, old-fashioned). With that word, that carefully chosen word, he had established his authority. Mason Raymond listened, though he had supposed the point of the evening was to be *his* talking, the pouring out of *his* apostasies and iconoclasm. No such thing. Morphis was in one of those expansive teacher-pupil moods where the font flows forth. Mason Raymond hunched up listening, listening, listening, Morphis so carried away with the eloquence of self-elucidation that he overlooked completely the fact that the purpose of the evening had been misplaced.

Morphis was explaining himself to Mason Raymond. This required a detailed review of his childhood (hostile parents; athletic, nonunderstanding brothers and sisters; an ignorant, dictatorial school life); Morphis had been miserable, unappreciated, persecuted, and (of course) heroically right.

They passed, an eternity later, into his young manhood, a spectacularly misspent number of years in various institutions of higher learning where Morphis' brilliance had raised the envy and animosity of his instructors. A pause for a lecture on *hubris,* which Mason Raymond was beginning to recognize as Morphis' favorite subject. Morphis was the shining example of the bright boy born to poor parents. He had no money for the good schools and, though he was bright, he was no genius. Scholarships passed him by. This he also blamed on the unorthodoxy of his ideas—and the fact that he was fat. He had to drop out of the academic race and rest on the sidelines of the Academy. The academic pack was leaving him behind and, as he complained bitterly to Mason Raymond, he hadn't even the consolation of a wife or family nor the hope of recovering his breath and trying to regain the race and catch up. He felt *finished* (his own word).

The melodrama of this pronouncement left the master marooned high and dry in an emotional oasis of melancholy. Morphis ceased speaking, his eyes watery with the emotion of the moment; he sat in inner isolation gazing ahead into the nothingness of his future, a man for the moment dead to all calls of hope from the heart.

The whole spectacle seemed mawkish and self-indulgent to Mason Raymond, who was still smarting from the fact that he had come bursting with his own complaints against the world, only to find he had no audience before which to perform; but there was also no disputing that in certain ways Morphis' emotions were genuine, he was miserably unhappy, a fat lump of unfulfilled humanity bypassed in a provincial little school from which—even Mason Raymond saw this—he would never progress. At twenty-seven or -eight he had plunked down with a thud into his niche in life; from there—and it was so small, so insignificant, that was the tragedy—he would never move again.

Mason Raymond rose, an emotional exhaustion of his own emptying him even of any perfunctory response. He had lived Morphis' life over again with him, suffering all the petty indignities, the small, cruel injustices, the brutal blows of one minor defeat after another, until they had both come to rest, failures, here in this tacky room with its ruined furniture and bleak, faded drapes and carpets. For the first time he recognized that it might be better to die young and glorious than to live a long and meaningless life. Achilles' choice came to mind; Achilles had chosen the short, fulfilled life.

But most hadn't the choice. Their lives just happened. Morphis, for instance, would never have chosen this existence; he had slipped into it even as he struggled against it, a man being propelled toward his fate instead of shaping it himself. How many men were in control of their lives?

Look at his mother: very little—*very* little—of her life was of her own making or choosing, only really one event he could think of, her marriage. He was back to the central question—why Clyde over Cobus Buttes?

His uncle, who had managed somehow to shoo all those terrible Seward people off so that just the family remained on the hill at the family graveyard around Emily's larch, a family affair—Rivers and Hart and Mabel were adopted family—stood quiet and solemn and distracted, and he, almost as if he were there and yet not there, was someplace else inside his head. How much of his life was of his own making? Or Hart—with his thirty-six skins of coon cut into a cap, what would he have said: *I chose that boy to come out and hit me on the head.*

A cluster of those who cared circled around the open hole with the box below, covered with gladioli, shovels stacked neatly at the head of the grave, and all of them at last rid of the formalities from required, mercifully divested especially of the Seward Brothers, Amos and Elmo, who had been scandalized over the burial plans. Their main concern was over who would—well—"do the dirt."

"Do the dirt?"

"Yes, you know—" embarrassed—"cover up the—the coffin."

His uncle had looked at the two brothers as if they were lepers who had lost their bells. "I guess I can shovel a little dirt," he said at last.

Mason Raymond had asked that there be no usual graveside prayer, certainly not that terrible ritual dust-thou-art-to-dust-returnst that made everyone break down. Now his uncle looked at him, stepped forward, and began to read from the Bible.

There was no question of the twenty-third psalm, the obvious choice. Cobus Buttes was reading from the Song of Solomon, not really appropriate, but Mason Raymond had left the choice up to him and if he thought the Song of Solomon was right for reading, then it must be right,

. . . the king hath brought me into his chambers: we will be glad and rejoice in thee, we will remember thy love more than wine: the upright love thee,

and when he had finished, standing with the open book in his hand, Mason Raymond trying desperately to think of some kind of sacrificial rite he might make in obeisance at the grave and all he could think of was himself, his own selfish need to break free from all the massive outside forces here that were crushing him to nothingness, to insignificance, thinking *I must break free and go out into the world and find something more to myself than what is here. There is a distinction between being a stranger who comes to a new place and doesn't fit in and a stranger in a place one has lived all his life,* the eternal selfish child, he thought, who in the midst of his mother's death can scheme only for his own life, standing watching the pages of the book flutter in a gentle wind while his uncle stepped forward, closed the book, and knelt on the freshly turned earth and said in a clear, sure voice,

Lord, take this Thy servant and use her well,

scooping up a handful of the fresh dirt beside him and sprinkling it over the coffin,

Whom we relinquish, earth; take forth, sky and sun and heavens above,

and then bending his head in prayer a moment, rising, rising, slowly, so slowly Mason Raymond wondered if he would ever get to his feet; then finally standing, looking down, slowly turning, sighing, saying, "All right, Hart, Rivers, we're ready;" and the three of them took up the shovels lying neatly at the head of the grave and began to cover the coffin with the sure, steady strokes of men used to dealing with plows and planting.

Two

The Carolina Mountains
Fall, 1869

"There is great pleasure in some sinning."
—Source unknown . . .

I

Rivers, scarred, not just physically scarred but cut to pieces way down inside where it mattered, had brought them to the station, handing down Hart's battered valise, the knapsack and gunnysack, creaking down himself, standing there with his face a sight, saying, "I want to thank you, Mr. Hart, for all you done. I ain't had the chance."

"Only wish it were more," Hart said, snuffing with disgust. "I'd like to see the end of that rodent Lite once and for all, but it ain't likely. We ain't none of us seen nor heard the last of him; his kind you don't git rid of so easy."

"Still," Rivers persisted, "if it hadn't been for you and Mr. Cobus—"

"Only wish they'd put him behind bars—*permanent*—instead of lettin' him off so easy. I mean, they ain't a man in the vicinity blames you goin' after him, not even that law man hisself," recalling, no doubt, as Mason Raymond was, the confrontation in court when Lite and Rivers (still half-bandaged) had been hauled up before the hard-of-hearing judge hollering "just-i-fi-able pre— var— i— ca— tion, what do you meant jest-i-fi-able pre—var—i—ca—tion?"

Cobus Buttes began to talk about the wager, the dead dog.

It was demeaning to Mason Raymond (and, he presumed, to Rivers) to have to drag his uncle and Hart to court to fight their battles, but who cared what *he* had to say? Hart and his uncle were respected. People might laugh and call Hart "Tall-tale Hart," they might make jokes about his absent-mindedness and his ramshackle life, but they liked him and honored the wisdom that was in him, which was more than was in most people; his word carried weight. Whatever deficiencies he had, falsehood was not one of them.

And Cobus Buttes was like a law unto himself. All the Butteses up on the hill were. People did not mess with them. Even the judge wouldn't; he leaned forward, hand cupped to his ear, listening carefully, pretending to weigh the evidence, but in reality (Mason Raymond saw quite clearly) really asking himself, How riled up is Buttes about this? Riled up enough to kill him (looking at Lite) hisself, maybe even me? He's been to war, killed a lot of men, come home a hero, got his name on a plaque in the post office, you kill that many men, one more or less don't make much difference. "What's that you say?" screaming both because he didn't hear right and because he hadn't been listening. "Speak up before the bench."

The bench! Pompous as well as dense in the ears. But Cobus Buttes didn't raise his voice, talking low and slow and dangerous, a man not to be messed with. He had reached his point of no return.

Lite, dancing about on his toes in frustration and anger, kept trying to interrupt. "He pointed a gun at me, point-blank, and *fired;* only reason I'm standin' here tellin' my story today, the gun blew up in his hand."

The judge tried to quiet him (he didn't want to rile Lite any more than he wanted to get Cobus Buttes's dander up; it was one of those cases where you were damned if you did and damned if you didn't; Mason Raymond didn't envy him), telling Lite he'd get his turn, the bench would hear him in due time, sighing and leaning forward, straining to hear as Cobus said, "He shot that dog for no good reason at all, there's a dozen men testify to that."

"Shootin' a dog ain't the same as shootin' a man."

That was when Hart had said, loud enough for everyone to hear, "Depends on the man. I've knowed a lotta dogs were worth a darn sight more than the men that owned them."

"Not in the eyes of the bench," rapping for order and trying to get Lite to stop jumping around; he was in perpetual motion under the steam of his rage, and he hadn't smiled once the entire time, a man who could feel power slipping through his fingers and no way to close his hands and stem the escape.

Rivers wasn't even called upon to give his side of the story. For a fact, Rivers hardly seemed to matter, though it was Rivers who had done the shooting and got the blast and burns and stood before them on trial, baffled, bandaged, becalmed, the only one in whom rage had abated, as if action had released the well-spring of his anger and now in the leeway of passion, he stood objective and outside the storm raging around him. He was not the point; the point was the principle involved, and the principle lay somewhere in man's unwritten rights and what had to be done to protect them. Did a boy have a right to turn his back on a man and walk down the road without expecting his dog to be shot from behind? And if a man took it in his head (a man like Lite) to shoot, what rights did the boy or those close to him have to stop a man from behaving like that? The law's punishment (which everyone seemed to acknowledge, except of course Lite) was inadequate, but as "the bench" said, leaning forward shouting at them (assuming apparently that if he were hard of hearing everyone else was faulty in the ears as well), "It's a good thin' for this feller—" pointing at quiet, scarred Rivers—"that gun did go off on him. You can't jest look the other way with murder. He kin go conditionally, subject to stayin' here and reportin' in and stayin' away from this feller—" pointing at Lite—"and you keep away from killin' other people's animals, you hear? Case dismissed."

Looking back on the past few weeks, Mason Raymond felt his life had been cornered by what Hart called "crafty men" —lawyers and doctors who to Hart's way of thinking automatically ought to raise suspicion. Hart was grateful to the medical fellows for cleaning the slivers out of his skull and gluing it back together, but he still had powerful doubts about his payments for that mending. "Them fellers, them law and medicine men, you don't see them borrowin' at the bank," he said. His wisdom had come firsthand, he said, what with all his dealings with doctors and lawyers and banks, and he wanted to share it with Mason Raymond. The whole thing came down to—he said—the fact that of all the three virtues—loyalty, compassion, and courage—the first came cheapest. He commenced to laugh, his laughter coming in great whoops that wound around Mason Raymond and entangled him in Hart's affection. Then Hart began to holler. He had sighted Cobus Buttes and his boys on the wagon coming around the corner downstreet.

John looked just like a grown-up man, sitting ramrod straight with his arms stiff by his sides, full of self-importance because he was taking part in a real-life will-reading, even if it wasn't his. He was a glory-gainer, always would be. Mason Raymond envisioned him flaring forth in life, bright and quick as a special commemorative comment; his light would leave a mark, no doubt about it, and maybe that was about all anyone could hope for, a brief, gasping flash that was remembered.

He went up to the wagon and held up his hand (as he had been taught a gentleman did) to his aunt, ignoring the quick, disgusted glance John gave his fancy Albany clothes. Real men didn't wear coats like that, even to a will-reading, John's face said. "Mason Raymond," his aunt said, slipping her steady hand in his and getting down (you couldn't say gracefully, she was beyond grace; letting herself be helped down was almost as if she were granting a dispensation; gracious as the Papal Father she dropped to the ground, touched him briefly on the cheeks with her lips—he had been blessed), then turning to Rivers and beginning, the concerned woman, to berate him for not tending to his face. "You haven't been putting that salve on," she said accusingly, switching roles: she was Florence Nightingale now, taking on the Crimea.

No other woman in the world, he was sure, was like her.

That was perhaps in his mind when he had begun going through his mother's things (they were such opposites), a job that his aunt had volunteered to do but one which somehow he felt obliged to perform, possibly, he thought at this moment, a debt hanging over him from his snooping and finding her handkerchief among Rivers' things. He wanted her private things to remain as private as possible.

He dreaded going into that silent room (why? why? *why?*); yet he had accepted the obligation (please . . . please . . . *please*).

He thought now of the bound black and tan book; she had bought it in some foreign country; the red letters in the middle said DIARIO. He opened the thick cover to the date of the first year, 1860, the year before the war had started. Mason Raymond juggled figures in his mind. He must have been six then, for he was seven the year the war started.

I'm sorry, he says, but I've had too much to drink, I can't. He says it in connection with his love making, or lack of it, but really it's an epithet for his whole life.

And, really, what's the use of going into it, it's the same old repetitive story. He got drunk Friday night at the party the Elvings gave, falling down in the hall. Saturday morning Irving Elving came over to have a talk with him, and he came down looking sheepish and said he had a terrible head, he was sorry if he'd done anything to—well, he said, you know, put a damper on things.

Irving tried to make excuses for him. They sat down and began to talk about how things would shape up in the next election. I felt Irving was trying to give him a warning. Saturday night when the Ewells and all those other people came over, they didn't know what to make of him. Invited for dinner, they sat all through the meal shaking their heads—oh, not openly, too polite for that, but inside, in their private hearts where they can really condemn. I went upstairs early, I just couldn't bear it. I stood thinking about how it was back at school, how handsome and clever he was, and how my whole world had seemed bound up with the dream of marrying him; and then I thought of a few moments before when I'd finally snapped at him in exasperation and he had turned and gone out to the garden, and I thought, what a relief.

May Savage and Caroline Irving sat and tried to be polite; we kept hearing him crashing about outside, and our conversation would stop and we would smile embarrassedly at one another and a minute later we'd try to think of something else to say.

Suddenly I heard Caroline Irving gasp. She had her hand at her heart and she was all white. I looked up and there was Tip at the window making faces. I looked at him for a full minute and then we all went on talking and just ignored him, pretending he wasn't there, the way you treat a naughty child.

August 28: We had a bad argument about that woman he's keeping over on Sanford Street. He kept denying it until I said did he think I was a fool, people *talked.* He got mad and Mason Raymond started to cry. He was so upset. Between the women and the drinking I don't know what to do.

September 8: Yesterday the nerves in my whole face ached. He came home early in the afternoon—"I've simply *got* to talk to you." He has run up all these debts. It's the woman of course but it's more than that. He doesn't want to talk specifics. What he wanted was for me to pay the money he owes and leave him alone. Finally he said he'd stop drinking for good if only I'd help him out this once. Those were his words—"Help him out this once." I wanted to ask about that woman, but I was afraid to. But I have Mason Raymond, I have Mason Raymond. I mustn't forget that and give up. He said two such funny things today. One was "Mother, don't forget to remind me the roses are in the oven." He was drying the old ones, the yellow ones the Irvings sent, for sachets. And then, later, "Remind me on Monday about the solar system, will you?" He had to take some things to school for some classwork.

November 4: Casually (as he's getting dressed), "Oh, I didn't keep to my promise. I was downtown with Irving and I had a couple of drinks. Nothing to worry about." I felt stunned. I couldn't say anything, I just sat down and looked at him and he went on tying his tie. I felt as if I didn't have the strength to deal with him anymore.

December 20: Back together of course. Part of love is, I guess, pain, at least for some people, and I must be one of them.

Mason Raymond thumbed through the book. He saw that there were a lot of dates crowded one on top of another in through here, as if his mother had had to go to her book to write to relieve her feelings. On *December 22,* in a handwriting unlike hers, his mother had scrawled:

One o'clock, shaking, after the most terrible scene. He came in here tonight looking awful and started to put his arms around me and something just snapped in me, I struck out at him, right in front of Mason Raymond, I couldn't help it—this beautiful day when Mason Raymond and I have been bringing ornaments down from the attic just ruined by his behavior, a symbol of so much of our life this past year, all because of this drinking, that woman, his gambling, and I tried to make it all right by taking Mason Raymond in my arms, as if he hadn't been hurt by all this, as if love was something strong that had made us all secure instead of wrecks, but I wanted to abuse Tip and debase him the way he's hurt and humiliated me, to show him up for what he really is, and for one moment I could understand how a woman could take a knife and thrust it into her husband's heart and not regret it one bit—and poor Mason Raymond was in the doorway crying, I couldn't concentrate on anything except my anger and hatred, I wished him dead, removed forever out of my life, so that I would never have to look at him again, I would never have to go through another day like this, he would be obliterated forever, someone I would never have to be unhappy over again, because so long as he was alive he could get me back with his empty promises and hopeless pleas, and something in me would take him back, I hated that thing in myself as much as I hated him, it was what had undone me again and again, and as much as I struggled against belief, I would start over, trying, believing, only to be caught again by his weaknesses, I would be in this state—worse, for it would get worse and worse—and one day I would do something violent and irrevocable because I was unable to stop myself, I was consumed in hate—and helplessness.

It was looking at his eyes—those eyes full of all the alcohol he had had that afternoon—swollen, red, veined, fuzzy, and frightened—those eyes that did it.

Mason Raymond put the book down and paced toward the window, staring down the beautifully trimmed green lawn that at this moment Rivers was fussing with, thinning bushes out by the gate, and he thought, She started out with everything, and this is what it came to. He knew of course that his father drank—all the men Mason Raymond knew down in Albany drank, it was expected of them—but he hadn't understood and seen how much his father had relied on alcohol. How could he have been so blind? You don't see what you don't want to see.

He went back and picked up the book and opened it to the

next entry, which was marked *December 24,* the night before Christmas. The holidays seemed to have been a special time of the year for undoing his mother and father; they could not perhaps sustain what should be with what was and they broke under the image they couldn't sustain.

Two thirty in the morning and I heard someone in the hall and I stumble (this is just a minute ago) through the freezing darkness; it is Tip, standing there looking at me and then taking hold of me, I love you, do you know how much I love you, how are you, how's Mason Raymond, oh I miss you both so, you're my whole life, you know that, don't you, my whole life, my teeth chattering, and so weak are we—or am I—that I took him back. Maybe it had something to do with Christmas. We should all be together at Christmas.

March 6: [Why, Mason Raymond wondered, the long silence in her book?] Heavy rains, high temperatures, like spring—all the snow is gone, although the lake is still frozen at the Landing, Cobus writes. Seeing Tip every night now, he is trying to come to grips with his problems, isn't drinking, has promised to break off with Sanford Street, hasn't (that I know) run up any big bills lately, and I am puzzled by my reaction. Maybe there's been too much emotion for us. One minute I feel close to him again, another I'm cold, standing off, judging.

A line entry which had nothing to do much with what had gone before read, *Beautiful, beautiful May mornings.* There was no date, and the entries for that year ceased there. Under that last entry *Beautiful, beautiful May mornings* his mother had written in big figures 1 8 6 1. The first entry was in March,

March 7: Friday I felt very shaky, at noon went to bed; was no better Saturday, and all anyone talks about any more is the war. I don't want to think about the war, I have enough problems of my own. He is gone again (Sanford Street?) and I lay in bed with my throat throbbing, feeling hot and feverish and choked up and Mason Raymond kept asking from five o'clock on, "Where's Daddy?" and by six of course I knew he wasn't going to come home for dinner. If he isn't home by five thirty, he has been drinking.

I waited until after midnight. I sat first with Mason Raymond and read to him; then I went downstairs and turned down the lamps, sitting in the darkness waiting. At eleven I went around and latched all the doors. I sat in the darkness waiting and waiting until at last I heard the carriage pull up. He tried the front door and found it locked. A soft knocking. I sat, silent, in the dark. Louder knocks. Then a tour around the house calling my name, pleading at first and then angry, shouting outside there in the darkness, "If you want to live alone, goddam it you can, but not here. Go up to the Landing where you belong." Finally more knocking, then a pause, then I heard the carriage being brought out again.

I felt very calm, empty but calm, very calm. I think it was because I kept asking myself that if our places were reversed, would I have acted the way he has done all these years? And I knew with absolute certainty that I would not.

March 9: I have been reading and reading, sometimes two, three books a day. And through some a sense of life pumps, as if warning me, You are letting yours go, there is the house in the country away from everyone, but you'll have Cobus, go there, go there, it is quiet and peaceful there, don't be frightened.

There was a long silence in the journal again, no entries, then months later:

September 28: Cobus has gone to war. I always thought I could count on Cobus and in some ways I can, but he won't love me the way I want, Tip won't love me the way I want, only Mason Raymond loves me the way I want and he's only a child. The war, Cobus at war, and the things he said to me before he left . . .

October 3: I touch up my hair now—have I remembered to record that? Little dibs and dabs here and there in the front where it's going gray. *Gray* hair—and I am thirty-one. All human beings need love, and I've wanted it so much . . .

There were no more entries for this year. When she was happy, she apparently felt no need to write—or so Mason Raymond guessed. There was an entry for the passage of yet another year:

1 8 6 2

and only one entry for this,

March 14: I sit here with no plan at all for a future (how many times, I ask myself, has this happened and isn't that a reflection of my own choices, my own weaknesses, my own pride?)—no way to believe again that Clyde [it was the first time in the journal she had used his father's formal name] will ever put his life in some kind of order. There are bills being sent here for him, bills bills bills. Why should I pay *his* bills? But that's what's expected and of course I will, I always do. The effort, the effort of these next few hours, how can I get through them—or the next weeks, the next months?

The book had been idle for almost four years before she took up her pen again. Mason Raymond wondered what in her inner life had taken the place of that second voice of hers that had spoken to her in these pages, trying to comfort and understand and accept. Possibly she had come to action. Somewhere in here they had moved permanently to the country. She had tried to cut herself off from the presence of all that pain.

He thumbed through the next years, all of them somehow familiar now: her hopes and disillusionments with the shaping of her life and always at the back of both those hopes and disillusionments, his father. She had never truly understood his father would not change, or if she had understood that with her mind her heart had stood stubborn against the recognition. Over and over in the pages he saw how much she had come to rely on Cobus; Cobus was her substitute for the twin brother she couldn't control or have.

Mason Raymond went to the last year,

1 8 6 9

September 21: Woke very early, around six, with the sun flooding in. Suddenly felt good. Alive. Exuberant. Weather is still quite warm, although it's autumn light falling in the window. Determined to get up and get some joy from this day. Will go up to the woods, will go over to the New House, perhaps even think about buying another cat, I thought, and then remembered I'm back in Albany and all my feeling of joy fled. Back here with him.

October 1: Have been back nearly a month now and the first days went well, but the past week he has been touchy and irritable. He has money worries. He has no money in the bank, can't borrow any more, and when he came to me this time, I said, "I'll see." Let him suffer for a change. I'm the one who's always been the one who has had to before. "I *must* have some money," he said this evening. "Please, Ardis. *Please.*" "I'll see," I said and went in and closed the door. He can wait, yes, he can wait.

October 31: "Ardis," he stopped me in the hall, "I've got to talk to you." We went into my room. It was dark there, no one had lighted the lamp. He sat down and folded his hands and looked at the floor. He really looks very bad. He said, "Ardis, I've got to have some money, just a thousand dollars or so, to keep these people from—" He looked at me. "I'll think about it," I said. "I've had a lot of expenses up at the house this year." How wise my grandfather was to insist on everything settled and in writing before we married. If I hadn't had all these special considerations, I wouldn't have anything to fall back on. But he put it all in fool-proof legal ways. He knew, I thought for the first time today, he must have known. But he never said a word against the marriage, never once. He knew, I thought, he knew there was no talking to me—then.

November 15: He wants to come up to the house. Maybe he thinks it's Christmas and he can talk me out of the money. I'll give it to him, I suppose. I always do. But not before the end of the holidays. I've learned that much. He won't drink up there so much if he's waiting for the money. No, I won't give him the money until after the first of the year.

December 10: Mason Raymond and I leave for the Landing tomorrow. Am sitting at my desk in the front room with a warm winter sun pouring through the window and down the hill, glittering, a white-topped view of the city. It has been snowing. The world outside is all white and inside warm, Clyde lying on the couch with a cold, Mason Raymond in his room working with his solar experiments. I am doing all the odds and ends for Christmas before Mason Raymond and I leave. Things have been *very* stormy for the past week, but after an incredible scene, they have calmed. He is not drinking—for the time being at least, and all is tranquil and for an instant happy. Part of this no doubt derives from the fact that for the first time in our lives he HAS to do what I want or he knows I won't give him the money. It is easy to be hard with people you don't care anything about any more. The Janus face of love,

she had written as the last entry in her diary.

He stared down at the lake, at Rivers limping up toward the house with the big cutting-shears in his hand. Mason Raymond thought about his mother sitting at the desk on the other side of the room going through her bills, looking at her diary, turning over in her mind the subtle torture of the husband who had tortured her. Two weeks after the last entry in her book she had opened the door to the front hall and found that husband swinging. Had she blamed herself? He would never know. She had not written out those hidden thoughts in her book. He would never know how she felt about his father's death, just as he would never know so many things that it seemed to him at this moment he needed to know. But that was one of the difficulties about life: it didn't tell you the secrets you needed in order to make sense of its tangles. He only understood one feeling inside him very clearly: he wanted to get away from this house and the pain that seemed to him to stain its very walls.

Hart had been so nervous about missing the train that he'd got them to the Ft. Edward (Ft. Ed'derd, it was called locally) station a full forty-five minutes ahead of time. He was either a day ahead and a dollar behind or a day behind and a dollar mislaid. When Rivers had driven up to the Hart place, Mabel had come out to berate *them* because Hart was driving *her* crazy. "He's been up since four o'clock this mornin'," she accused them, "sittin' on his va-lise waitin', gittin' up and openin' it up and goin' through and takin' stuff out and puttin' it back in, who can git any rest with a commotion like that goin' on? He's all wore out before he even gits started."

Hart came charging out of the house bawling they'd better git underway they was going to be late, plunging past Mabel who cried, "Pay me some mind, old man," and throwing his gear into the wagon, climbing up, turning and shouting, "Look after them pigs and don't let nuthin' happen to them, they's growed enough now for one of them to make it through," yanking his coonskin cap down around his ears and shaking his head, "Carolina," he said, a man going to the Promised Land of Plotts, a man who after years of making do with used, worn-out, discarded, or damaged had at last arrived at the point where he was buying *new.*

"You ain't et a thin'," Mabel said, handing up a sack.

Hart opened it. *"Eggs?"* he asked incredulously.

"They's hard-boiled, you old fool, you ought to have sense enough to figure that."

"I don't want 'em," Hart said, handing them back. "I ain't hungry and a sack of eggs ain't gonna do nuthin' but git in the way. We got enough troubles without havin' to worry about hangin' onto a whole lot of old eggs."

"They ain't old! I gathered them eggs fresh this mornin' with my own hands—"

"You're holdin' us up, woman. You want us to be late? You want us to miss the train?"

"Oh, git on with you, you're worse than a young buck, runnin' all the way to Carolina lookin' for some old dog and talkin' him into your foolishness, too." She was smiling, happy for Hart, one of those people who can only express sentiment in anger. She waved until they were out of sight, standing in the road calling to Hart to keep an eye on his things, he was bad enough on his own, but with all those Schenectady and New York rascals she didn't see he stood a chance. "Won't come home with a stitch on his back," was the last thing they heard her say.

Now they stood in the bright October sun forty-five minutes ahead of time with nothing to do. "I always said I would," Hart said suddenly, "And by God I am. Mabel, she's a great one for gettin' a look into the future, gits Crane's wife to tell the cards, and I ain't disclaimin' their powers, ain't sayin' some of them thin's as were predicted didn't come true, but I ain't sayin' neither that given enough time some of them was bound to work theirselves out, but I always said I'd go one time and try one of them fortune tellers myself and, by God, settin' out on a journey like this it certainly don't do no harm to hear somethin' about what maybe the future's got in store. You mind eyein' the bags?" he asked Rivers. "We jest gonna run downstreet and see mabbee we kin look ourselves up one of them women does palms, or cards, or one of them tricks."

What could Rivers say? He certainly, Mason Raymond thought, had no interest in having his future told; for a fact, maybe he didn't have a future at all; for Rivers, everything he cared about had happened in the past.

Hart was ebulliently wending his way down the dusty Ft. Edward street as if someone had just said to him,

> *Born to nobility,*
> *You are spellbound*
> *Frog-Prince.*

He had his hat on (of course) and he sauntered with the air of royalty incognito, moving his coon-skin-capped head from side to side in acknowledgment of the recognition due him even if the locals hadn't yet penetrated his disguise. When he stopped to make inquiries about where he might have his future predicted, he raised, however, unroyal suspicions. One small boy fled instantly, and one man turned out to be deaf and dumb—or struck that way by Hart—but at last they found a sullen old farmer who reckoned they were looking for the likes of Mrs. Merriweather, "You go up yonder a piece, and when you come to the yeller house, you're there. Cain't miss it. There's raspberry bushes all along one side and lots of laundry hangin' out back. When she ain't readin' the future, she's hangin' over the washtub."

Hart set out with purpose, beating up a trail of dust. He was like a man possessed—and, a moment later it came to Mason Raymond this was the exact truth: he was possessed. He was going to the Promised Land to get himself his Plott dog.

"Mighty nice-lookin' lady," he said now as they stopped by the raspberry bushes and saw a woman pegging out wash. Her outstretched arms had hiked up her skirts. She turned and sized them up right off as customers, left the laundry and came down the walk, waving them in. She was strong and powerful (filled with power was perhaps, Mason Raymond thought, a better way of describing the feelings she inspired in him); and on his own he would never have gone up the path, but Hart went without hesitation, never even paused at the kitchen door. Mason Raymond followed him, almost banging against the square table that filled most of the open floor. It had a pile of neatly folded white linen handkerchiefs stacked on it, and two chairs on either side, where Mrs. Merriweather was motioning them to sit. "Which one goin' to git read first?" she demanded, fixing Mason Raymond with one of those woman looks that made him hot and heavy in the body and crimson in the face. "Not me, him," he mumbled, pointing at Hart.

"Take one of them handkerchiefs," she directed Hart. "It don't have to come from the top, better if it don't, jest take any one you want from off the pile, roll it in a ball and put it in your hand and squeeze it hard as you can. You ain't squeezin' hard enough. That's better. All right, you can drop it on the table."

She went to the stove and took out a cupful of ashes, sat down, and dusted the handkerchief with the ashes. Where Hart had squeezed the cloth, lines appeared where the ashes settled, lines that ran back and forth and in some places crisscrossed. Mrs. Merriweather took her time studying. Finally she said, "You goin' on a journey," and Hart, whose boyish blue eyes brightened, turned and puckered his mouth in approval to Mason Raymond. She guesses that the same as everyone else with any sense would guess it. We're strangers, we obviously were walking up from the station, of course we're going on a trip. What's so marvelous about telling us what anyone in his right mind would already surmise? "You hit that right on the head like a hammer hits a tack," Hart said. "What else you see there?"

Mrs. Merriweather pointed here, there, outlining shapes. "You see the lines of that head? That's a man's plucky, hardy, robust, full of expeditions, adventurous, going on a big trip. And you see that one? That's a man profligate and vicious, abusive and violent, resentful, choleric, rude, fierce, and wild. And he's to stay put. And them two heads is pressed together which mean them two men, they natural enemies.

"And those two souls, they in this struggle with one another, they can't abide each other. In one case the ties were taken up and broken when they were found to hamper and that's where selfishness come into control, selfishness seldom been equalled, and that going to work itself out in a web of destiny. In the one case the keynote been truth and liberty and in the other fear and bondage.

"You see how that line run down there? That shows the impulse and self-will and the perverseness, and that other line, that says the shot is never worth the powder expended. The intentions are excellent, but the means are lacking. The ideals are of the very highest, but ideals they remain, ideals that are always sacrificed because they cannot be lived.

"Some people are pioneers and some destroy so that others may build. Look here. No better picture could be chosen to depict the warfare between God and Satan than this map describes. In more sense than one are body, soul, and spirit in this case fleeing from the Devil, which means, in plain language, that the spirit is in combat with evil, with the lower self." The widow looked up at Hart. "The only mistake is in taking up too big a load, for this is what has been done in this case. While one soul is viewing all life and its possibilities with joy and hope the other is making bitter reflections on the past and bad plans for the future. The whole secret of the difference between these two maps lies in this one difference. This line is all spirit, ideality, desire, energy, but this one is buried amidst the weakness of a poor, angry spirit. The workman Satan has usurped the place of his master the Sun, but is yet unable to carry out his plans.

"But this life is a matter of changing places." She bent over, looking more intently. "You will go on a long journey and you will endure much that you do not understand and all the time, forgotten by you, will be one who continues to build an evil edifice and to turn stones and burn bricks to make a bad building. And this man, in the end he will undo all that you have done and he will take from you something very precious, very very precious, so precious that I cannot tell what it is. And here is a tree and here—" she looked at Hart— "here is a cross."

"A cross, what's that mean?"

"Well, it might mean a crossroads or it might mean—some kind of sacrifice. What I do see is the sign for life and the mark for the heart's wishes and these go together. And I see the sign for trial and tribulation and a man who undoes what others have been working to erect. Shake the handkerchief—do it carefully, I don't want ashes all over my floor. There, that's good. Now let them settle. All right, let's see." She stared down at the handkerchief. "There will be many episodes put upon you on this journey, many testings. Many men will do to you strange things and you will go and see many strange places, see many strange things, things that puzzle you, men and women that are not like any you have known, and beasts, too, there are animals here, many animals, but I cannot tell of what kind, and the men and beasts come together and meet and their lives intertwine." She got up. "You leave what you want. I don't charge," she said. "But you can leave something if you want." She went out quickly. Hart was still staring at the crumpled, ash-stained handkerchief on the table as if great mysteries were hidden there.

"How much you going to give her? Hart—*Hart*—"

"What? Oh. You think a quarter's all right? You think that's enough?" he asked anxiously.

"That sounds pretty fair to me."

"You're sure it's all right? I wouldn't want to insult her."

"You don't have to leave anything if you don't want. You heard her say that yourself."

"Oh, she said it all right, but she don't mean it."

"Well, leave her a quarter and let's get back. It's getting near train time." Hart was acting almost as if he had forgotten the trip.

He got up, distracted, his mind obviously preoccupied with problems he was trying to solve. "What do you suppose she meant by crossroads?" he asked. "You got all that good schooling. If someone was to say to you, I see a crossroads in your future, what would you take that to mean?"

"She didn't say crossroads; she just said cross."

"That's right, she did, didn't she? I ain't religious, not in no final way—you know, hymn singing and gittin' down on the knees and all and when it comes right down to it I use a lot of words ain't in the Bible and do a lot of thinkin' ain't what you call orthodox and a cross, that's sure enough a religious sign. How come you didn't squeeze no handkerchief of your own?" he demanded. "This here trip is a combined venture and what she didn't see in mine she mightta seen in yours."

"You think I cheated you out of knowing part of your future, Hart?"

"You ain't got the proper respect, and that's a fact."

Rivers was sitting disconsolately on Hart's faded old rucksack; he rose respectfully and awaited instructions, toadlike, with the marks of the powder burns etched into his face and those bad scar burns on his hands. His eyes had the faded, detached look of one who has given over believing in good. But he believes the devil is real enough, Mason Raymond thought.

The train was coming in and they gathered the baggage together and stood, soot- and wind-blown, as the engine rumbled past. The railroads had been allowed to deteriorate during the war and though the government had given them a lot of help (more, some people thought, than they deserved, all those special privileges out West) there were still many branch lines (like this one) that needed attention. Down South he had been told things were in a hopeless state, but an inconsequential thing like a broken-down railroad wasn't going to deter Worth. Seeing Mason Raymond's mother dead there in the front parlor no more than a few months after his father and both of them a danged sight younger than he ever even remembered had put the energy of ambition into Hart. He saw (his own words) it was now or never. "I'm gonna git me my dog," he had told Mason Raymond, "come hell or high water. Ain't no time left to pro-crastinate. You come with me, it's the chance of a lifetime, boy. They don't let you into them mountains 'less you got connections. Mabel's people, they give me the names to look up and I'm goin' and you come with me and git yourself an education you won't never git out of no books."

Mason Raymond handed the last piece of luggage up to Hart; he turned and held out his hand to Rivers. "You're in charge now," he said. "You'll do fine, I know you will. Just hang on until I get back."

"Don't you worry none, Mr. Mason, sir. I'll do jest like she would have done. I don't think there's anythin' she'd want that I couldn't think through. I wouldn't never do one single thin' she wouldn't have wanted, you know that." Mason Raymond knew that—because of the handkerchief. Handkerchiefs, it seemed, played a large part in his life.

"Who'd believe thin's could git theirselves up so different?" Hart asked, staring incredulously out the window. "It's a whole 'nother world out there."

The changing scenes didn't seem particularly unusual to Mason Raymond, just the habitual long, rectangular, red-brick mills, the smoke stacks, the streams bubbling with waste pouring out of the ends of huge, open pipes, farmers stopping their plowing now and then to look up. Only the children took time to wave. He had seen the same scene a hundred times traveling back and forth from Albany. But Hart had never been on a train. He was filled with wonder—and respect. He wore brand-new overalls, stiff and obviously uncomfortable; his everyday ones were worn smooth and easy from all the washings Mabel had given them, but they were not fittin' for his great journey. He had gone and bought new. *New* was going to be the keynote of the journey for him. He had his thirty-six coonskin hat clutched belligerently between his legs; the passengers had laughed when he got on the train and he'd stopped dead, staring 'til the laughter broke in their throats; but as he went down the aisle, snickers had followed him and in his seat he kept the hat anchored on his head a long time before he finally deigned to take it off and clutch it tightly between his legs.

He had started in the aisle seat, but his curiosity was so continual and he squirmed and wiggled so constantly in his efforts to get a better view that Mason Raymond had insisted on changing places with him. His hands clutched his hat; his eyes behind his big glasses on the bailing twine never stopped ransacking the scene for philosophical implications. The world unraveling outside this window was a revelation; he just couldn't get over it. "All them people bunched up on one another like that," he said as they clattered through some remote country town, small by city standards but large to someone used to the scattering of stores and houses that made up the Landing. "Livin' right on top of each other like that, piti'ble critters." It was a wonderment for him equal to the lighthouse at Alexandria or the Colossus of Rhodes.

"My life's been the farm, the land," he said. *"Most people's is."* He looked out the window, pale, hesitant, shy. *"Your uncle's right. The War's changed all that.* Took men off the land and put 'em in cities, and when the War went, they stayed put, workin' in the factories, the mills, workin' with machines instead of land. *The whole country changed, because of the War, jest like Cob said,"* he said, staring out the window. *"We was one kind of people before and another after."*

"Mills," he said. "Machines."

Later, when they flashed past a crowded, dirty little town with its red brick rectangular mill belching smoke, he got angry. *"It ain't right,"* Worth Hart said, "a man does the work ought to git the money, not some man markets it and makes more money from the marketin' than the man who done the work. Don't put theirselves out none, don't soil their hands, but they's the ones that git rich, comin' and goin' like bees in a hive but none of them makin' the honey."

Quieted, he looked out on the smoky surface of a lake, tumbled and violet under the violent fall sun. Mason Raymond wondered if he were mourning all those marginal farmers who hadn't been able to stay put; there were better ways to chase the dollar than tangling with rocky land where brambles and berries grew, where foxes ran on the few remaining tumbling stone walls and adder's tongue overgrew the orchards.

The train rattled past dark patches of woods, great expanses of empty, lonely space, the train whistle howling at deserted crossroads, limitless, open, lonely stretches waiting, waiting, waiting for what, no one knew; tractless and vast, somewhere West the magic names called to Mason Raymond, rivers and mountains and buttes, canyons and gulches, the names lay thickly in his mind, names drawn out of a life that was foreign but which drew him on in a dream that was enclosed between two great bodies of water where strange, hard, tough men talked of washes and waterholes, badlands and gaps, notches and mesas, peaks and creeks, of a nation out there beyond the mountains that he didn't have any idea of because if the truth were known he only lived in one of that nation's small pants-pockets.

If that land over the mountains was strange and unknown to him, this flat run toward Schenectady was just as peculiar to Hart. Mason Raymond had made the trip so many times that he took it for granted; now he was seeing it, really seeing it, because of Hart. Hart's vision was of smoke and noise and strange towns and machines (this machine in particular gobbling up the countryside). The whistle called now and many came; lonely women in farmhouse doors shading their eyes and watching the great metal monster pant by; men, distracted from their tilling, looking up, shaking their heads as they stumbled over the broken sod; a horse bolting now and then; and cows, big humps of brown and white or tan and black, throwing their heads and looking at the big, long, black smoking animal puffing by.

It occurred to Mason Raymond that maybe he'd never seen the landscape with the same kind of wonder with which Worth gazed out, the childlike joy in the unknown; perhaps he'd never been a child, but had been born a little old man, he thought disparagingly, and even when he was small, somehow he'd understood that his mother and father didn't want a child, they wanted someone strong and competent and "no bother," and somehow, he saw, someone on whom *they* could lean. What was so terrible to him at this moment was that he could not, in looking back, remember one single instance in his whole life when he'd really been allowed to be small and silly and completely cared for.

Mason Raymond stared out at a nestling of honey-colored cones, hayricks humped up beside a lonely house, wondering if his deciding to come on this trip with Hart wasn't just more than wanting to get away from that house where so many terrible things had happened; wasn't it more like trying to be a child again, going back to re-create some of the spontaneity that a child feels because in so many ways this crazy old man in the coonskin cap had retained the innocence of the child?

"I'm hungry. I wish I'd et before we left. Too excited to put food down. Mabel standin' there jawin' at me, don't forget this, don't forget that, who can put food down at a time like that? She would, though. Never seen sech an eatin' woman. She kin pile it in any time. One time I was arguin' with her to beat the band and she jest set there and et a sandwich. Beat anythin' I ever seen, sittin' there arguin' and eatin' at the same time."

"We'll get something to eat when we get into Schenectady," Mason Raymond said.

"Sch—nec—ta—dee," Hart said wonderingly. "I never thought I'd no more see Sch—nec—ta—dee than I'd live to see the day these feet would be walkin' down the streets of New York City. It's a marvel come to a man like me. Sets you wonderin'—or it would if my stomach would jest leave me be. Thinks my throat's been cut. We got to look sharp though, don't want them city people takin' advantage of us 'cause we're not accustomed to their ways. Still, I forgit. You had plenty of experience along them lines, you're fit to git us through, I reckon, without too much exposure to tricksters and thieves."

Hart leaned back and closed his eyes, resting them, he said, they were all tuckered out with the sights. In a moment he was snoring, deep and confident, his mouth open, the breath roaring up from his chest. Awake or asleep, he clutched his coonskin cap in his hands. People passing in the aisle stared down at him, then passed on, shaking their heads; it takes all kinds to make a world, but there were limits.

The steel rails of the tracks pulled them along more swiftly than current, drew them over s   a section of the land that sometimes Mason Raymond had the illusion as they sat enclosed inside the iron horse that all of America was speeding past their eyes, and they were being given a view into the heart of the country, from the disappearing small farms, doors flopping open to sun and wind, to the teeming towns with their continuous flow of food for the mills; Hart was right, they had left behind at the Landing a world that was almost blocked out of existence. From the train window Mason Raymond could see that the kind of life represented by the Landing—one of farmers and shopkeepers, tradesmen, artisans—was dying.

The future lay in the large towns, in the buzzing, smoking mills. The future lay brooding, napping, quarreling, worrying, occasionally laughing, in the crowded slums of the city; it was caught in the palms of those rich men who eased themselves into brocaded chairs in big, wealthy mansions up on nob hills and dreamed finances and furnaces and squeezing corners of markets unheard of a hundred years before.

Mason Raymond remembered the excitement in May about the tracks from East and West linking up at Promontory Point, thought of all the skirmishes between the determined railroad men and the angry Indians, seeing in his mind the mounted cavalry of the army guarding the railroadmen mile by mile as they lay out track. They had Chinamen out there in the West working on those railroads. Mason Raymond had never seen a Chinaman, nor a calvaryman, nor the kind of Indians they had out West which were different from those in upstate New York, different from his grandmother; the West was full of different people of all kinds, pony riders and plainsmen drifting from place to place with the buffalo, and those Indians traveling on horseback with two long poles dragging behind fastened into a point, making a triangular carrier in which the tents and stores were transported. Those Plains Indians lived in tents instead of long houses. They had Western names too —Dull Knife, Man Afraid of His Horses, Santana, Red Cloud, Crazy Horse. *Crazy Horse.*

"Sche-nec-ta-dy, Sche-nec-ta-dy," a voice shouted from the rear of the car and the train plunged into brick and mortar, smoke and confusion, women beating rugs out of their windows right over the train tracks, men wielding picks along the railings, and down in the streets pedestrians sagging under parcels and tools and great loads of produce. A small, dirty brown snake of a river unwound between houses and streets; boats, barges, great hulls of ships, slipped over the sluggish surface toward the sea.

Almost everyone in the car was standing, fussing with parcels and bags. Hart slept on, rhythmically blowing noise out his nose, rattling the breath at the back of his throat. Touching him, Mason Raymond felt the body heat, the strange woods sense of him which would never be washed off; the smell of the hot, moist manure of barns and the wet, hairy hunting scent of dogs. A line began to form in the aisles. "Worth," Mason Raymond said, shaking him, "Worth, we're here."

Hart's head jerked up; his eyes opened onto the terror of the unknown. "Oh, Gawd," he gasped. His head swiveled around looking for something familiar. He was close to panic, bobbing up getting ready to run—anywhere, so long as it meant escape. "I been caught with my pants down," he said to the fates and rose, a desperate man ready to risk all, then sank, defeated, down into his seat. "I plumb forgot where I was at," he said weakly.

Mason Raymond stood up and began getting their things together. "Let them madmen trample one another," Hart said. "We ain't got no reason to git ourselves wrung out in the crush. We ain't in any big hurry."

"I thought you said you were hungry."

Hart stared up at him. "That's right, I was, wasn't I?"

They were the last ones to leave their car, standing in the steam and roar of the engine, Hart gazing up at the man in the cabin a moment before he lifted his head and yelled, "Nice trip—many thanks." He turned to Mason Raymond. "He done a credible job runnin' this thin'." They shouldered their satchels and ruck-sacks and limped down the ramp toward the station. Whenever Mason Raymond sat for a long time, his knees bothered him, and Hart just naturally seemed off-gait. They bobbed up and down going out with the flow of people washing into the depot.

Mason Raymond had planned maybe to go over to Albany and the Academy to see who might be around; he had missed school more than he realized, especially Morphis, waddling between the lectern and the blackboard talking about Oedipus and Antigone, Agamemnon and Odysseus. The colorless eyes behind the fat folds would shine when Morphis spoke of *hanartia* and *hubris,* a man who lived in the past amidst high wedged shoes, painted linen masks, long flowing robes, and plays whose meanings had seemed as far removed from Mason Raymond as the maenads who, Morphis said, ran barefoot after the fleeing goat, seized it and tore it apart alive, devouring the bleeding flesh in honor of Dionysius, god of the grape, god of fertility of the fields, he in whose honor tragedy had sprung. Tragedy means goat song, Morphis said, his eyes cloudy with reverence.

"We learn by suffering," *"Know thyself"*—saying (Mason Raymond could picture him, calm, enormous, godlike, Dionysiac, even almost to the cluster of grapes he ought to be clutching in his pouched hands), "you see it, for you it's there." Leaning over Mason Raymond with his eyes gleaming, "That's a start. You mustn't let your sense of balance go simply because you see there are other things in life besides the exercises of the mind."

Morphis would be back in his small, book-shambled, dark room, that blot of darkness lighted by rickety lamps whose pools of yellow light fell on the chipped statues of Socrates and Aeschylus; his world was imprisoned between the pages of books and illuminated by scattered fragments of another time and place where, even if he had been born into the right century, he would never have fit in. The Greeks believed in a fine body as well as a well-honed mind.

Mason Raymond's own body was changing; the complex interworkings of his system had finally shifted gears, he was moving toward manhood in sudden lurches and fits and starts, and the worst part was how embarrassed he felt: he would have liked an overnight emergence of hair, beard, voice, and (what he thought of as) "the rest."

Mason Raymond had assumed he could leave Hart for an afternoon and go over to the school; now he saw how impossible the whole notion was. Leave Hart where? And with whom? Hart was as dependent upon him here in the city as he had been dependent upon Hart in the woods.

Now Hart stopped and dropped his knapsack and stretched, snapped his suspenders. "There's always some man bitin' a dog, some mystery needs unravelin'. Lord, look at those people *pushin'*. Let's eat."

People were crowded around a counter, were bunched around tables, and were forking food into their mouths. Mason Raymond thought (almost reverently) of Morphis and the buttery biscuits; it came to him how unlikely it was he would ever go back to formal study; he was a different person now, no more the shy scholar than Morphis would ever be one of those pioneers out past the Missouri, lashing a mule to get going and get him to the Divide and the beginning of a new life.

Hart sat down at a corner table, grumpy and ill at ease, looking at the menu. He kept moving his glasses up close to his eyes, then pushing them way down on his nose; he didn't seem to be able to get a proper focus on the lettering. Finally he laid the card down and said, "You do the orderin'. I can't make up my mind." But he was hungry enough. When the food came, he set to cutting the pot roast into small pieces and running his fork over the meat until he had practically pulverized it. "My store teeth," he said apologetically, and for the first time Mason Raymond realized there *was* a difference in the way his face hung together, more filled-out like; he'd never thought of Hart as toothless before—not toothless, he had some of his bottom teeth, but all the uppers were gone. A sense of propriety (you put in your teeth to go to the city) guided everyone apparently. He passed over to Hart the mashed potatoes, the gravy, the peas with the life boiled out of them. After coffee and doughy pie, Hart was expansive, almost happy, chattering about getting to Asheville (as far as they could go by train) and then working their way into the mountains. Mason Raymond was going to take to that country, it was like the back side of Paradise, Mabel said, and one thing you could say about Mabel, she didn't know the look of a lie. He began to reminisce. He come into the church social, she was sitting with her people, he took one look at her and was hooked, she just sat there and reeled him in. "I don't know what she ever seen in me," he said, picking up the piece of paper the waiter had put down in front of him. "She could have had her pick of the litter and she took the runt." He let out a roar. "It's my hat," he yelled. "They think I'm some kind of country rube because of my hat. I may be backwoods, I may wear overalls, I may wear a country cap, but I—am—not—goin'—to—be—took," Worth Hart bellowed. "Git me someone in authority. I will not—repeat—will not be put upon."

"Just a minute," Mason Raymond began. "Hart, just wait a minute—" His voice staggered, flopped, scrambled to right itself, clawed its way up the scale, and broke. Hart paid no attention; he was too busy rising to his feet and blowing like a bull. All over, people suspended their meals and gazed happily at the theatrics. Hart was purple with passion, shouting for the po-lice, waving the check over his head like a banner around which the disinherited of the earth would rally and seek revenge for their wrongs.

Mason Raymond sprang up, seizing Hart by the arm, trying to stop him from pummeling a man who had had the temerity to tell him the check looked perfectly proper to him. "All right? All right? You say it's all right to be charged for BREAD? Let go of me," he shouted, furious, trying to shake the waiter loose. "All right? You call it all right to charge a man for BREAD?"

"But, sir, if you looked at the menu—"

A policeman shoved his way through the crowd, using his nightstick to wedge the curious apart. Hart shrieked into his face, help, he was being robbed; the manager shouted he was being cheated; Mason Raymond tried, hopelessly, to suggest some kind of compromise.

"Pay extree for bread and butter, for a full-up of coffee— why don't they charge for the water if they don't throw nuthin' else in. Why don't they charge us for the water we drunk? Why don't they put down the air we breathed while we was settin' in here eatin'? Why not add those itsy bitsy pieces of rags they give us for napkins, the seats we sat on, the—"

"We're going to miss our train, Worth, if we stand here arguing. It's what we ate—it's fair—"

"I lived over sixty years on this here planet, a boy I tried to help come up behind me for no reason on this good earth and hit me over the head with a hoe, like to kill me; I worked hard every day of my life and I can't never see my way clear to get shut of the bank. What's *fair* about anything—but there's sech a thing as what's right, and it ain't *right* to charge a man for bread when he eats meat and 'tatoes; it ain't right to charge him for a second cup of coffee—I may be poor, I may be backwoods, but I ain't downright dull."

"*You took what you wanted!*" Mason Raymond hollered.

"Now pay for it." His voice, to its credit and his eternal gratitude, stayed on pitch. "Here," he said, grabbing the check, "I'll pay. But for God's sake, *stop—making—a—scene!*"

Hart sat grumped up, sullenly viewing the darkness wrapping itself around the train. He was not speaking to Mason Raymond. Mason Raymond had betrayed principles, Hart's hunched shoulders said. Mason Raymond had sold out, Hart's hunched shoulders said. Mason Raymond didn't believe in taking a stand when a stand had to be taken, Hart's hunched shoulders said. He had not only been taken, but he had also been betrayed.

Once Mason Raymond tried to explain, to justify. Hart turned his back on him and scrunched down, acting as if he were going to sleep. They rode all the way to the outskirts of New York without exchanging a word, Hart brooding on his principles and Mason Raymond giving him the chance to feel righteous and rejected.

But on the outskirts of the city, Hart began to fidget. He stared out the window at the endless monotony of buildings, the cluttered streets, the angry, belched spit of smoke from factory after factory, finally slumping down in his seat, clearing his throat, his whole attitude one of demoralization. In his despair his resolve began to break; he deigned to talk to The Betrayer. He was wounded, he had been deceived, but he was going to be magnanimous about it. His was a performance of great intensity; Mason Raymond admired it and stored certain gestures and expressions for future use.

He was still mad, Hart pointed out, but he was willing to give Mason Raymond a second chance; he was willing to forgive and forget, but Mason Raymond must see he had been wrong to pay that bill . . . if Hart had left it at that, Mason Raymond would have let the matter go, but Worth insisted on going over again the whole scene and, as he detailed each of the humiliations and Mason Raymond relived each of his own degradations, Mason Raymond began to smart all over again from the dramatics of Schenectady. He looked at Hart, an expression of anger and disgust and his own outrage at last filtering through. Hart's voice died. He turned his back and didn't say another word, even after the train jerked spastically into the station and crunched to a halt and they rose and handed (silently) one another bundles.

They struggled down the long aisle of the train and came out on a narrow, cold corridor, a kind of passageway into the main station which was crowded with carts for moving freight and people's luggage, people and porters and men hawking candy and buns and cold drinks. Hart had his coonskin hat on over a truculent just-you-dare-smile expression. People gave him a wide berth. He looked wild.

Mason Raymond could see Hart was trying to work things out in his mind, going over plans slowly, methodically, the way a man in the woods did, getting ready to break trail in the city. Hart plodded along toward the station with the same dull determination he used when he was uncertain in the woods, but the enormity of the space, all the people, the hiss and roar and noise of the trains were too much for him. He dragged up center station, unloading his baggage, snapping his suspenders, shifting his fur hat, kicking a bag around, standing, watching, sizing up, figuring, figuring. Finally he spoke, "She never saw nuthin' like this in that there handkerchief of hers, I'd lay odds on that." He turned slowly, examining the space around him. "Where's our gunny sack?" he demanded, beginning to get excited. "We've gone and left the gunny sack some place. Did we have it afore that fracas up there in Sch—nec—ta—dee?"

Mason Raymond tried to revisualize the Schnectady episode step by step, the policeman shouldering Hart along, Hart resolutely resisting, the excited people shouting and gesticulating, his own acute sense of distress which had first tongue-tied him, then set up a counter-reaction in which he couldn't seem to stop talking; Worth's violent insistence that he wouldn't let Mason Raymond pay, he didn't care if they both of them went to jail, then his astonished look of bereavement when Mason Raymond insisted on settling up; the frantic struggle to catch the New York train, Worth's not speaking to him: where in all this was the lost gunny sack with its precious dog papers, one copy for Worth and the other for Salonski—the man who had to have copies of all the dog papers in case of loss, so there would always be a permanent record of the Hart breeding? Where were Worth's monuments, the most important things that would outlast him, his instruments of immortality? The only thin' worth doin', he had once said proudly (looking at his streaked pigs) is somethin' that will outlast you.

In the gunny sack were also all those letters of negotiation that had gone back and forth between Carolina and the Landing, the carefully copied pedigrees of dogs Hart was interested in looking at, the sole reason for this odyssey which, though only begun, seemed to Mason Raymond likely never to end, in sum all the reason for Worth's whole life—characteristically toted around in a gunny sack and characteristically left God knew where.

Yet he must be careful not to put Hart in a panic. But you do not stem, Mason Raymond was learning, primary instincts. Hart, already agitated, now appeared pushed to the edge of hysteria; in his imaginings some brakeman in the Schenectady railroad yard was already burning his precious papers. The flames danced up in his eyes; the shouts coming from his mouth might have been "Fire! Fire!" He began to wave his arms wildly, to bellow; onlookers were gathering; it was going to be Schenectady all over again.

Mason Raymond recognized the impossibility of dousing a raging fire with a bucket of water. Though a crowd washed about them, curious, Hart's dramatic energy was not dampened. If anything, outside interest spurred him on. He raved, fur hat clutched in his hand, face red with sweat and heat and despair, dancing about in a fit of desperation, a storm of pain, bitterness, disappointment, shouting, *We left them somewhere in Schenectady, oh my God, we left them somewhere in Schenectady, oh my God, what are we goin' to do? We left 'em somewhere in Schenectady.*

He *looked* broken, boneless, battled beyond his resources; he stopped jumping around and stared into space, mumbling, a man utterly undone. "Oh my God, all my *papers* . . ."

Mason Raymond just couldn't stand any more. The pot roast and mashed potatoes, peas and pie of Schenectady rose in his throat. He listened to the intense pounding of his own heart and he tried to get hold of himself and take charge of both of them. He gripped hold of Hart and hung on. His despair must have been evident. "You're all white," Hart said in a panic. "You sick? You gonna pass out? Oh my Gawd, don't pass out—not here, not in this big, crowded place we don't know nobody. Don't do that. Here, hang onto me."

"You wait here," Mason Raymond got out.

"Where you goin'? What's got into you, leavin' me here in the midst of all these thieves and cheats 'nd murderers—wait just a minute, don't go off, wait for me—"

Mason Raymond sprinted across the station and through a door, the one he thought they had come through after they'd gotten off the train. A dark, cavernous well of baggage, boxes, crates, carts, threatened to swallow him up. Someone shouted angrily, "Here, you—" He turned and bolted back into the big station. People pushed and shoved. He scanned innumerable identical doors with numbers and signs looking for the one he and Hart had come through. How was it possible to be so confused in such a short time? Hart's hysteria had unnerved him. Also he hadn't been paying attention. All these hurrying mobs of people looked too intent and preoccupied to pay attention to him; he saw no one in a uniform that promised authoritative information. There were just too many problems, none of which he had foreseen. The only thing in the world he really wanted was to be free of everything, back home, safe. He didn't care if he ever saw Hart again. He didn't even *want* a dog.

"You lost, boy?"

The man looked shabby. Mason Raymond debated telling him anything, but what could be the harm of just asking where the Schenectady train came in? He had not counted on the tall, skinny man insisting on showing him. Uncomfortable and uneasy, he followed. The platform was deserted, huge, abandoned carts blocked their way. "It's all right, thank you very much," Mason Raymond kept repeating, "I can find it myself now. Don't go to any more trouble. You've been kind enough, really. I don't know how to thank you, but I'm sure I can manage by myself now. You see—" then unexpectedly the tall, cadaverous man bumped against him, nearly upsetting him, and they fell against one another, fumbling for balance, and when Mason Raymond righted himself and turned to apologize the skinny man was smiling with a wide, gashed-looking grin, breathing heavily through widely spaced teeth, his hands fumbling in front of him with his fly, crying out, "Wait, just wait, look—"

Mason Raymond knocked against a cart, pain filling the hollow of his back. For a moment he was sick again; then he wheeled about and stumbled, tripping, momentarily looking back into the black pit of the station, thinking, *I just can't take any more* . . .

He could smell the awful acridness of the oozing under his armpits, the emancipated glands that were part of becoming a man; they had begun to function lately; the smell of nervousness and nausea and excitement and, of course, fear came from them; he felt a tremble run the length of his body and he recognized the feverish heat of fear all over him, soaking his clothes. His eyes fell on a pile of valises, cartons, sacks. "Here—" A hand took hold of his shoulder. "What you think you doing with that bag?"

"I'm getting our gunny sack."

"We been onto you kids for some time now, comin' back after the train's emptied and pretendin'—"

"It's *ours*. I can prove it." He put a fist to his breast as if to suggest the fulsomeness of his heart.

"You'll git your chance, don't you worry none about that. You jest come along with me—"

"I came with it right here in—the man I was with is back in the station. You can ask him if—"

"Oh, you're a bunch of beauts, you boys are, with your excuses and ruses."

Mason Raymond's chest felt as if it were filling with smoke. He knew instinctively there was no arguing with a man like this: he was Authority Doing Its Duty. "Listen," he said, insistent, "there's a man back in the station who came in with me, an adult, he can tell you—"

"Don't give me none of that. Don't think I don't know you kids is smart enough to bring along an alibi. You're not puttin' anythin' over on Edward M. Garrison, you aren't."

"I'm not trying to put anything over on you, I'm just trying to make you see that this is my gunny sack—well, not mine, but the man I'm with, it's his, and—" Finally he said, "I don't know what I'm going to do, I just don't. I swear before God I don't. I just give up. I'm not going on one more moment." He fell down—there was no other way to describe it—on a clutter of boxes and threw his head in his hands. At this point he didn't care what happened.

The man still gripped one of his arms fiercely; Mason Raymond let it hang loose, unprotesting. Let them call the firing squad; it might be easier in the long run.

"How do you explain the fact that sack's with freight."

"I don't know how it got there. I don't even care," Mason Raymond said. "We left it on the train. Somebody must have put it there. But it's easy enough to see if I'm telling the truth—just open it up and see if what I say is inside is there."

"That's private property. I can't go around opening up someone else's private property."

"But I tell you, it's ours, my friend's and mine. It's all right to open it."

Edward M. Garrison scratched himself with his free hand and stared down at the gunny sack, scratching again in the manner of one who depreciates the property value of what he sees. A well-made suitcase he would never have tampered with, but a gunny sack—still, there was the matter of protocol, of rules. He wasn't supposed to open passenger goods. Mason Raymond twisted his hand free and held it out in imitation of the kind of appeal made by one unjustly accused. He felt foolish, but a new worry had started to nag at him. What if Hart started to panic and bolted God-knew-where.

He began to babble. It was the worst stratagem he could have adopted because the man could not keep up with his dislocated sentences. He thought of the skinny little man with his pants flapping open on what in the dim light looked like two shriveled little apples. Why wasn't Edward M. Garrison chasing real criminals like that?

There is no logic to law or life, a voice inside him said.

He looked at the railroad official and thought, He's as confused as the rest of us. We're all of us mixed up. The whole

Goddam world is mixed up. One lousy, mixed-up mess.

"Oh my Gawd, *here* you are. Oh, I tell you, I thought I'd never lay eyes on you again. Oh, boy, what have we got ourselves into? You've found it!" Hart leaned forward and seized the sack. "Oh, thank Gawd for this favor. I don't mind tellin' you I thought we'd been burglar'd sure."

"Not burglar'd," Mason Raymond said. "But damn near bugger'd."

They came out into faded twilight, a gray which seeped away in the soft light—lamps were being ignited all around them. They began to walk. Hart had the gunny sack and his ramshackle suitcase, Mason Raymond a satchel and duffel bag. The noise all around was a steady throbbing, like a giant heart vibrating against the stone ribs of the city. They were swallowed by an overhead El, weaving through the creaks and squeaks of carriages, weaving in and out among people pushing, shoving, elbowing them aside. They walked first in midtown with its great shops, its row of millionaires' mansions with thrusting turrets and bristling spires, Gothic gargoyles and fancy footmen, handsome men and powdered women in expensive, oiled carriages. Finally they turned back, retracing their steps past the fine houses, the finely dressed crowds, the lavish shops, the great town houses, past furriers and florists, the confectioners at which were stationed doormen in beautiful uniforms and big polished boots, past running servant girls with the sashes of their enormous aprons flying.

"You look around you," Hart said, pulling up, panting, "and it makes you take stock, don't it? I wouldn't want to say" —he surveyed and evaluated iron and stone—"out of *me* has been created *this.*" He was thinking, Mason Raymond felt, of his own house and land, all that junk (which would one day come in handy if he only waited long enough); he was picturing, too, Mason Raymond supposed, his wife standing with the pullet eggs in her hand, pondering now the eternal ambiguity—though it is good to go far, it is best to be home safe.

"We're only going to stay overnight," Mason Raymond said encouragingly. "We'll be off first thing in the morning and you'll be in the hills looking for your dog before you know it." Hart was worn out. He was tired himself, but there was also something exhilarating about the lights and noise and excitement; on his own he would have thought this an adventure, but he could see Worth was only interested in getting off his feet. Adventure for him lay far away from man-made things. Here he looked abandoned and forlorn, his coonskin cap tucked away in his duffel bag, finally (it seemed to Mason Raymond at least) ashamed of this backwoods symbol of his upbringing. Such size had diminished himself in his own eyes; he admitted now his own insignificance and only asked (the expression of misery on his face seemed to say) to be allowed to eat and sleep and get on his way. It wasn't in his mind to *bother* anyone.

People were bristling past them, shoving them aside, bumping into them. Hart retreated toward a building and took shelter on its stoop, finally sitting down, surrounded by his battered satchel and duffel bag. He looked ready to weep, a strong man who was going to cave in and break down. Better keep him going, Mason Raymond thought, or he'll give up. "Let's walk down there," Mason Raymond suggested with synthetic heartiness. "That looks like a spot where we can get some grub."

"What makes you say that? Don't look no different than any of the other places we been jackassing ourselves to all these hours without success. Look," he cried suddenly, springing up and grabbing his bags, bounding off down the street. He had found a policeman, a great, massive Irishman in blue uniform whom he waylaid against a barber pole and into whose hairy ear he was pouring out his problems.

The blunt, Irish face lowered itself for an inspection of the wild, tumbled hair, the bright, young, blue eyes, the store teeth slipping and slurring Worth's words. Hart sounded half drunk but—worse—he looked poor, and for the law the poor were always suspect. In the land of plenty poverty was an admission of failure, possibly moral weakness. Hart was crying he had to git hisself settled, he was jest plain tuckered out, he was all stove in. Without answering, the policeman dodged

away, swinging his stick. Hart was left standing next to an
unsteady old man with large billboards strapped on either side
of him.

SWAYNE'S TAR & SARSAPARILLA PILLS
A PATENT CURE
FOR AILMENTS OF THE
CONSTIPATED BOWELS, TORPID LIVER,
INWARD PILES, HEADACHES, COSTIVENESS, FEVERS,
YELLOWNESS OF SKIN AND EYES,
INDIGESTION; DYSPEPSIA, AND ALL
DERANGEMENTS OF THE INTERNAL VISCERA.
UNLIKE MANY PILLS
SWAYNE'S TAR & SARSAPARILLA PILLS
DO NOT IRRITATE THE STOMACH OR BOWELS,
BUT KEEP THE SYSTEM IN A HEALTHY CONDITION
BY AROUSING THE TORPID LIVER TO HEAVY ACTION IN
EXPELLING BY THE BOWELS & KIDNEYS
THE MATTER THAT POISONS THE
FOUNDATION OF LIFE.
BUY TODAY, FEEL ALIVE TOMORROW

"Lookin' fer some place to stay, er you now, poor lads?
Thar's a decent place not fur from here, if you don't mind
family ways."

Hart was piteously grateful, wringing the advertiser's hand
and going on, volubly, about their trials and tribulations. The
sign-board carrier was sympathetic, moving his head up and
down empathetically, uttering little oaths of exclamation at the
horrors Hart enumerated. He was a County Cork man himself, the sign holder said, and could understand how the gentleman felt. The world was a terrible wicked place for the
innocent. You follow me, he said, for the best beef this side
of the Liffey.

They fell into line, the sign boards banging first their owner,
then swaying out to slap Mason Raymond or Worth. Mason
Raymond was too tired and appalled to do much except stumble along; he saw himself chained to fate, the subject of one

impossible adventure after another in search of expiation for some crime he had committed maybe a century before, in another life, or perhaps just for having been born, but how this had brought him to the pavements of New York City in a shrill sea wind trudging behind some crazy fool in banging billboards (raising his voice to assure them in a breathy voice rusted with strong spirits that he was taking them to a first-rate capital place, but cheap, cheap; he was happy, only too happy, to give them directions for a little—well—remuneration), Mason Raymond did not know.

A small mist, almost a rain, had begun to fall. They walked against that and the wind, through streets growing shabbier and shabbier, the few hollow-eyed faces that passed and the strange words Mason Raymond heard hardly inspiring confidence. He took it as an omen, too, that here nobody seemed in the least put off by Hart's hat now confidently restored to its owner's head.

He felt as if they had crossed the border into a foreign land. Abruptly, the billboards became stationary, the man inside tugging at Hart's sleeve and pointing downstreet toward a sign that said ROOMS — MEALS. Hart kept trying first to ignore the insistent tugging, then to shake the man off. But the hands were firm, with the insistence of a very thirsty man. Mason Raymond was not going to have another argument about money; he took out a coin larger than he had intended but resigned to its being the only end to an impossible situation, and quickly handed it over to the grasping fingers. A moment later he and Hart were standing alone looking down the deserted street toward those faint, dispirited letters: ROOMS — MEALS.

"Well," Hart said uncertainly, backing up and looking disconsolately into a store window in which hung great fists of cheese and long fingers of sausage. Hungry and exhausted as he was, Mason Raymond had sense enough to see he and Hart were in trouble.

"This is no place for us," he said.

At that moment he heard footsteps and he knew—he absolutely knew—trouble was upon them; but before he could cry out a warning two large men were closing in on them so that escape was impossible. Mason Raymond stood for a second in the confusion of Hart's oaths and his own uplifted fists, under the threat of shouts and blows, watching the little man at the end of the street raising his billboards up and down in excitement and screaming, "Git 'em, lads, give it to 'em;" then Mason Raymond was running alongside Hart, his heart making a terrible slamming inside his chest. He could feel pains shooting all up and down his side, his knees throbbed and his head felt light, but he kept running, fleeing frantically between tall, elongated buildings that dipped down and tried to snatch him up, hearing Hart pounding behind him gasping and shouting—"Run like hell, son, they mean business." He ran, faster and faster. Then he stumbled and fell and as he looked up the little man who had so kindly led them into this trap bent over him and began to beat him with one of his billboards. He felt himself going down, down, down, hands scurrying back and forth, feverishly searching out where he might have money hidden. One of those clever, swift hands found the "hidden" little pocket; Mason Raymond heard a triumphant shout, then felt a blow, another and another . . . until he no longer remembered anything except a void of darkness inside his head and outside the noise and anger and grunting of men dragging him, inert, along the street.

Blood flowed from his nose, his tongue, a great gash in his head. The ground was sticky with rain and grimy deposits of oil, slippery with his blood; he had to get up and look for Hart, but it was impossible to raise his head. He felt as if a spike had been driven into his skull and if he moved ever so imperceptibly the nail would pierce some vital part of his brain and he would never move again. Yet he managed to call Worth's name.

No answer.

He listened for breathing.

No sound.

Inch by inch Mason Raymond raised himself painfully on one hand trying to control the exploding lights flashing on and off inside his head. Eyes surrounded him. For a moment he thought, Dogs, but the eyes were not voracious or filled with the look of the abused, not the eyes of abandoned animals, but small, frightened ones receding in a soft, liquid melting as the lights inside his head swallowed him up, and he moaned and leaned forward spitting out blood and pot roast, peas and parts of pie.

He fell back and looked up at the city sky, or what he could see of it, a small, gray-black flag covered with mist raised above the crisscross of tenements above him. "I'm hurt," he said in a strangled voice. "Go—get help."

Without looking he knew his money was gone; his satchel, no doubt, as well. He tried, once, twice, a third time, to get to his feet. High, childish voices began chattering excitedly. Though he could not identify the foreign words, the tone was unmistakable: even children recognized helplessness when they saw it.

Concentrating, he propped himself against a wall. Fifteen or twenty feet away Hart lay stretched out.

"Need help," Mason Raymond said thickly. Then his legs gave way under him; he folded up, going down, as one hand, too small to do any good, tried to hold him up. He went down, closed his eyes, and let the lights inside his mind ignite him. Burning, burning, he went down into the conflagration.

His eyes were open but he couldn't focus; he had to rely on his ears. His ears told him Hart was somewhere near because the voice was unmistakable. "Lay off me," Hart was shouting. "Don't poke at me like that. I got thin's out of place down there."

A constant jabbering was going on, most of it unintelligible, but every now and then someone would bend over him and commence questioning him in English. This came to nothing. He had very little helpful information to pass along even if he'd been able to talk coherently—getting any sound out at all was almost impossible, but as soon as he did say something a great hubbub broke out and he could sense excitement and gratification. Apparently no one had thought to call a doctor.

He lost consciousness again, then came to as he was being lifted up; he struggled to tell whoever was carrying him that Hart must not be left, they must go together; carried bumpily down one flight of stairs, then another, jiggled and bounced and bumped against, one of the men carrying him uttering angry, guttural words Mason Raymond took to be the sounds of swearing; he was still struggling to tell them Hart must come with him; then he was shoved into a carriage which took him not as he expected to a hospital but to jail; he was apparently either dangerous or dying, for he was isolated in a small room where, having given up completely (he could not see there was anything else he would have to do to hit bottom) he passed back into the fire and the darkness, burning, burning, down in the darkness, long reaches of pain catching him even there in the blackness and smiting open his skull in long bursts of red flames, the spike was being driven right through the center of his brain; white-hot flashes glanced rhythmically from the blows, flowing through that hollowness that was neither sleep nor waking, only the awful pain inside his head, and he thought, I can't live through his. My brain can't take it.

He lay rigid and tried to reason with the pain. *You've got to go away,* he told it. *I can't take any more.* But the pain paid no attention; it had plans of its own. Intermittently, and briefly, Mason Raymond wondered what had happened to Hart; then he even stopped speculating on that. His sense of responsibility was disintegrating under the powerful, piston-like blows of all-engulfing pain; the only interest he had was in trying to outwit the omnipotence of the pain, in trying to die before it could punish him further.

Occasionally a brief glimpse from his other life flew up out of his memory, and he had a momentary vision of Lite's handsome, laughing face in the lantern light, of a dog whining, the light glancing off the eyeteeth of its open jaws; he saw bare feet, then mud, and then the white, hot light of the spike drove through his forehead burning deeper and deeper until everything else was shut off except the scream that took hold of him and ended in the clasp of a hand across his mouth, a voice saying, "Hold 'im down. I know how it feels—I been over that road myself, and though it's a considerable time back, I still recollect how white and hot it kin be deep down there inside your head." Hart's voice, Hart was there, Hart knew—the pain even seemed to draw back a little in recognition of that stubborn old man sitting there, hanging onto Mason Raymond's hand and repeating over and over, "Hold on, boy, jest hold on. You git through the next twelve hours, the doc says you got it made. We got our dogs to git. Jest hang on. This is a different kind of schooling you're gittin', the kind I guess they call The School of Hard Knocks," and, unbelievably, Hart began a cackling Mason Raymond recognized as a form of laughter. Laughing!—he would have liked to murder Hart, but he was too weak and sick even to curse him, put one of those eternal spells on Hart and all his own, like the one wrought down upon the house of Atreus, punish Hart and his for all eternity—The School of Hard Knocks! *Oh my God—*

Later he felt Hart's hands calming him, explaining, "It's you, son, down there doin' the prayin'. It's you was sayin' 'The Lord Is My Shepherd,' don't keep tellin' me to stop it, you don't want to hear it, because it's you doin' the recitin'. Ain't no minister here," and Mason Raymond lay back thinking, *Like I was reading over myself, just the way he did.*

Hart bent down and took him in his arms and held him as gently as if he were one of his wounded animals, hurt and in need of confidence, a dog who had lost his leg in a trap and hobbled home or a young lamb born blind and bleating to know where to go and what to do in a world it couldn't see, Hart cradling him and crooning, "Gonna go South and git ourselves the best damn dog they ever was, you and me, folks come from miles about to see that there dog. 'Now ain't that a wonder?' they'll say. Jest hang on, boy, jest hang on a little longer. If I done it, you kin. Weren't no timider coward in the whole of the North than Worth Hart until they laid him as low as he could git and he found out it weren't so bad as he'd imagin'd. Go down in darkness, boy, but come back . . . come back . . . Go down in darkness, but walk your way back home."

II

*I*f *they could only* stay on the train, they would be all right. But the trouble was they couldn't stay on the train. They were constantly getting on one train, jolting along for an hour or two, stopping or slowing almost to a stop, then picking up speed, stopping or slowing again, and then having to change. The trip from Washington on was a nightmare of stops, starts, changes, poorly repaired tracks, often ancient cars, sudden spurts of decent railing, then more of the war-damaged sections that did your bones in and rattled the teeth right through the top of your skull. And his skull wasn't in very good condition to begin with. The whole of the top of his head itched where it had been sewn up and he was forever trying to scratch to get some relief, burying his hands in the bandage and rubbing like someone who had gone out of his mind. People stared and backed away. Mason Raymond had assumed the war had made people nonchalant about wounds, but apparently enough normality had returned to make a man in a head bandage a curiosity. Besides, between his bandage and Hart's coonskin cap, they must have made quite a pair.

Burnt ties, twisted rails, burnt-out bridges and water tanks, trestles and depots, dilapidated cars and decrepit engines made the trip slow and exasperating. They made ferryboat crossings at unbridged streams and occasionally had to leave the train for wagons, old military ambulances, or coaches; everything was skyrocket high and Hart groaned and swore and almost wept over the prices. But they kept going. He had his dog to get. His dog, his damned dog.

"Oh, there's somethin' special ahead," Hart promised, patting Mason Raymond for reassurance. Mason Raymond made no response, pressing his bandaged forehead against the gritty glass and seeing the raw mudflats spring past; the stink was terrible, but the birds—big, swooping giants whose names (of course) he didn't know—drifted up and down over the swaying marsh grass and promised a kind of peace he no longer, since New York, believed possible.

What he was trying to do was to thrust out of his mind all those crowded images of the hospital stay, the frantic messages back and forth to Cobus Buttes for money, the appearance of Rivers, looking (if possible) worse than either of them, his face and hands scarred still—a dark red—his body getting bigger while the flesh on his arms and legs seemed to have shrunk away so that Rivers more than ever resembled a toad, a scarred toad now, leaning over the hospital bed (as Mason Raymond had once leaned over Rivers' bed and stared into Rivers' bandaged face, life ran in parallels), breathing heavy, liquory disapproval of the ways of the world, and then, still sighing, sitting on the single chair beside Mason Raymond's bed, Hart having sprung up from it as soon as Rivers came through the door carrying the money package from Mason Raymond's uncle, sitting solemnly on the edge of the sole chair in the room, shaking his head, "Can't trust nobody in this world no more outsiden family and them friends that's closer than family. How long you gonna be laid up?" Rivers asked.

He was a fast mender, Mason Raymond assured him. He didn't want Rivers fretting. He'd be bad enough as it was.

"He couldda sent the money, your uncle couldda," Rivers went on, "but he reckoned as how I should come down and take a look at you myself and see how bad a fix you was in and stop over with you 'til you was mended. You sure got a knack for gittin' yourself banged up," he marveled. "At the rate you're goin' you'll be all wore out by the time you hit on twenty."

"He's learnt it from me," Hart said. "He's done took over where I left off. Them fellers give me a bum time in my side," he said, pointing, "but thank God they left off my head."

"Your Missus sent you these." Rivers handed Hart a sack.

"They ain't eggs, is they?" Hart asked suspiciously.

Rivers shook his head. "I believe she said they was cuttin's from her dogwood tree."

"Beatin'est woman I ever knowed. They got dogwood down there."

"Not this color pink, she said."

After that first burst of conversation, Rivers had subsided into moody silence, sitting voiceless (but breathing heavily, so heavily he might have been suspected of having lung trouble or of having—as Hart thought—let the drink get the best of him), regarding Mason Raymond with impatient affection.

Now, setting out the last leg of the trip, he thought to himself, All right, all right, the trains were bad, but it was at least safe on the trains. The Asheville train was running uphill and Mason Raymond closed his eyes and dreamed of a long, endless track running all the way across the land and on that track a train, a good, safe train running out into the heart of the great plains, out to the Platte and the Colorado, Laramie, Little Medicine, and the Sweetwater.

The train jolted into the Blue Ridge hills they had been waiting for ever since they'd crossed the Mason-Dixon line and Hart had settled back against the train-green seat and said with satisfaction, "We're down South."

Yes, it turned out, they were, but not as Hart had envisioned it. He sat in disbelief riding through rubble and burned-out lands and seeing the ravages of war for the first time and beginning to comprehend, looking at Mason Raymond saying, "I never know'd it was goin' to be like this."

The train rattled and groaned on. The track was in bad condition, but it was nothing compared to the scenes outside —houses emptied and left standing open or burned out or overrun with people camped around. Sometimes beside the tracks white men stood—just stood, sullen, emotionless, watching the train jolt past. After a time Hart scrunched down in his seat and closed his eyes, blocking out that ruined world outside.

Mason Raymond's head ached. He stared numbly at the devastation, at the weed-choked fields that ran on mile after mile. Nothing was fenced in. All the fence posts had gone for firewood for one side or the other. Churches were battered and dilapidated; desolate factories stood silent and smokeless on the ridge of desolate towns. There seemed to be no livestock at all; not one cow, not one horse did Mason Raymond see the first hour after they crossed the border. In one field he saw a man hitched to a plow instead of a horse, with his woman behind the handles.

And yet, now at this moment, when the great blue rise of mountains began to emerge before them, the hazy and mysterious Smokies, they both began to take heart. They got off the train happy and expectant; they were in the mountains at last. Yet if Schenectady had hated them, New York had hated them, it turned out Asheville hated them most. White people stared through them, blacks cringed and babbled incoherently, soldiers eyed them suspiciously; it was a town given over to hostility. Once Hart was tripped. "Deliberately," he said, not fighting back now, but humbled—No way of knowing what would happen to them (he said later).

The year before there had been an outbreak of violence in Asheville, a riot started by Negroes and worsened by whites, in which one black had been killed, and the town had still not put itself back together. When Mason Raymond and Hart tried to get information on how to get south to Waynesville, a man they had never seen before began to scream at them that they were carpet-baggers, damnyankee Union Leaguers who wanted to squeeze the lifeblood out of the South. *This is the hog trough of the world,* he shrieked into their faces, *and it's you people made it that way.* Then he disappeared, Hart and Mason Raymond standing stunned, the very pavements under their feet breathing up at them that they were enemies, men to be watched and to be hated and, if possible, to be hurt. A second later a large cordon of blacks pushed through, knocking Hart sideways and shoving Mason Raymond against a stand of newspapers where the white vendor screamed and flayed at him, beating him back against the blacks who elbowed him back into the newspapers, people crowding and shoving and cursing him; then he was suddenly marooned, only the vendor studiously ignoring him, placing pale white hands on his periodicals and busily straightening them. *Only the train is safe,* Mason Raymond thought. *Every time we get with people in a town, it doesn't matter where or how big it is, size doesn't really matter, what makes the difference is the people crowded up on one another, every time we get to a town it's all wrong, everything goes wrong.*

Hart hung onto him for dear life. "We gotta git out of here," he said. "We gotta git out of here fast. Even if we gotta walk. This ain't no place for folks who ain't armed."

Armed by what? Mason Raymond wanted to ask—not that the *what* mattered; they weren't armed with anything anyway except possibly the terrible catastrophe of innocence.

He wanted to be back on the rocking, bumpy, bone-harrowing, safe train that coughed and sputtered and lurched its way, hesitant but sure, along those tracks that ran wherever you wanted to go (almost), out into the vast expanse of land that was becoming this country, some place clean and new and fresh where everyone could start over and make a new world. Too much bad had happened here.

His head was itching like crazy and he scratched frantically, feeling the ridge of stitches along the back of his skull; the wound must be closing well because he had fewer headaches, but there would be a scar—a line of bumpy tissue across the top of his head. He didn't mind; he'd be more like Hart, Hart bumping along frantically ahead of him trying to outdistance all the dangers that were panting at his heels.

"I'm not walking to Waynesville," Hart shouted over his shoulder, "and neither are you." He grabbed a man passing and spun him around. "Listen," he said, "where can we rent a rig to git to Waynesville?"

There were blacks—singly, in twos, bunched together in forlorn groups—all along the road. Sometimes a white man would hail the rig, it would crunch to a halt, the man, worse-dressed than some of the blacks, would ask how much it was to such-and-such a place, the driver would tell him, the ragged white man would shake his head, the cart driver would shrug his shoulders, and they would jolt on. Hart said he couldn't believe it. He'd never seen people so money-and-pride poor. He'd never seen a rig like this neither, he said. Jest boards on wheels and us sittin' on the floor like trash. Mason Raymond didn't bother to answer. With all the bounces and jolts, his head was killing him; he couldn't understand why Hart's wasn't acting up. They had been in this wagon God knew how long and at the rate they were going he'd have done better to have died back in New York and be done with it.

Wagon was a pretty grand name for the contraption—just as calling the animals that pulled that pile of wood and wheels horses was an elevation in stature undeserved. The two old, bony beasts that stumbled and wheezed and panted and lurched were so beaten down that every four or five miles the driver had to get out and rest them; otherwise, he said, they wouldn't make it. Like everything else down here, he said, spitting, they broke down. "Ain't nuthin' serviceable or decent or useful left, jest derelicts and no-accounts and poor dumb animals like these." He pointed at the horses and then banged on his leg. It was made of wood and created a heavy, dull sound that rhymed with despair.

When the one-legged veteran came to a rest stop, he hauled the cart up and thrust his game leg over the side of the wagon. It stood for a moment straight out, like a pointer. The rest of him took a moment to come after. The driver always stopped where there were people to watch. You give a leg to your country, you want at least to get a little appreciation back.

He was watched, but gloomily, morosely; no one talked. At the Landing men came together to "pass the time of day," but here it was as if there was no time of day to pass. Their driver was right: the world had broken down.

When they got to Waynesville the place was shut down, as if there wasn't any use in lighting up the night any more, nothing out there but things people didn't want to know, the whole South was being swallowed up in a darkness no light could ever make friendly and free again. And more blacks—

not doing anything—just standing around in the darkness looking dumbfounded. Getting free, as they just seemed to have realized, had only made things worse instead of better.

"Don't none of these people belong nowhere?" Hart asked and the answer appeared to be, no, they didn't, they'd been freed, but no one knew for what or to go where. Most of them, it turned out, couldn't read or write, didn't have a trade or money, didn't even know who they were. When they'd been freed, they'd thought, a lot of them, maybe that meant they'd been freed from work; what they couldn't seem to grasp was that being free maybe imposed worse obligations on them than being held in bondage. Their dumb puzzlement was the pain of beginning to see how hard being free was going to be with their own whites down on them and the Northern ones come to help them either expecting too much or not caring really at all, just wanting to line their own Yankee pockets. Didn't make any difference what kind of white you were, you still didn't understand. "The whole Goddam thin's jest out of hand," Hart mumbled. "People jest ain't got no inklin', not back where we come from, and if you was to tell them, they wouldn't believe you. The problem's jest too big," he kept saying, "I jest can't take it all in." He took out his store teeth and put them in his pocket; such an act, Mason Raymond saw, was in the nature of restoring him to himself.

They hoisted their gear down and moved toward a small light upstreet. "Nuthin' lays good inside me," Hart complained. "I jest feel uneasy all the time." He stopped to knock the dust from his boots. It flew out red as blood. Red dust, red ground. "Beats anythin' I ever seen," Hart said. "How they ever grow anythin' in it?"

Autumn here didn't blaze either; it glowed. The muted colors lay translucent in the soft evening light; a great bird dropped out of the sky with half-closed wings and disappeared behind an arc of trees; Mason Raymond smelled wintergreen and clove, and somewhere someone was playing a small organ or perhaps an old dulcimer. The golden notes floated on the evening air over the blood-red earth. He had Hart's loneliness on him now, that sadness which has no name, but which, even as the door upstreet opened, and he saw people coming out

and he and Hart went up the path and into the "parlor,"—
horsehair furniture, Bible prints, and the place for the casket
left open under the far window—his heart constricted, he felt
all the loneliness there ever was enclosed inside; even this
stumpy-faced Southerner twanging his suspenders and chewing on a dipstick of snuff, saying he was mighty pleased to
make their acquaintance and there was vittles left, plenty if
they didn't mind "biled" bacon and greens, grits, okra, and
berry pie, laughing and letting loose his suspenders again with
a *twack,* showing he knew "biled" hocks and greens was just
about the best fodder there was; all this made Mason Raymond feel more lonesome than he had felt while he was lost
in the woods because this was in many ways a more lost and
alien world that those woods. There were all kinds of woods
to get lost in, he guessed.

"You folks down here visitin' or plannin' to stay," the
Southern hotel-keeper asked, suspicious of their accents, trying to find out if they were just strangers (Yankee strangers,
which was bad enough) or some of that carpetbag trash (still
a man couldn't be too careful, it didn't do to go against the
government), Hart flourishing his coonskin cap and saying
proudly, "We come for a dog."

The man regarded Worth with the respect he accredited the
demented. He treated Hart gently as befitted one with a grave
injury, but he showed them to a back room, nevertheless,
where he could keep them out of sight.

Hart sat down on the bed. "How's your head?" he asked.
"Mine's full of protest. It'll need some attention by and by, but
I'm used to bein' a headache victim, I don't panic no more.
You new at this sort of business and expect more from your
head than I do."

Mason Raymond gave him no answer. In the corner was a
stand with a basin and pitcher. No water in the pitcher—there
was a big crack where it had all leaked out into the basin. He
plunged his hands into the water around the pitcher and
splashed his face. A dull, red ache suffused his head, almost as
if that red had been transferred from the earth outside into his
basin here. He didn't want to eat, he didn't want to talk, he

didn't want to do anything but lie down and go to sleep. They had been in that wagon almost nine hours. And he couldn't stand the itching one more minute. "I'm going to take these bandages off," he said, pulling at the binding around his head.

"That medical man said you was supposed to leave them be until next week."

"I can't stand the itching, it's driving me crazy, and look at this," he said, holding out one end of the bandage which he had untwined, "it's filthy."

"Little honest dirt never hurt no one."

Hart rose and went to the window. He peered out. He bent over. His body seemed suddenly cut in two. He began shouting. Mason Raymond just wished he'd mind his own business and quit trying to be "neighborly" with these people; they didn't want to be neighborly or pass the time of day with damnyankees, but Hart, Hart couldn't seem to get that through his head. He was full of good intentions, too full of them for Mason Raymond's taste.

There was a chair in the room over near the bed, but it looked lopsided and rickety; Mason Raymond was afraid to sit down on it; he flopped on the bed (no spread to worry about, just a rough, gray old blanket) and closed his eyes. Let Hart bellow out the window if he wanted; Mason Raymond was too tired to care; but at least his head felt better—cooler, for one thing, easier to scratch, for another. He shouldn't get annoyed with Hart; Hart was all he had—besides, of course, Rivers. Rivers would stick with him like a burr for the rest of his life. And there was his Uncle Cobus, his uncle's family. Still he felt incredibly alone. Sometimes it seemed to him he didn't think or feel like anyone else in the world. Maybe he ought to write to Morphis. No, the Morphis part of his life was over. "What is it, Hart? What's going on down there?"

"Bunch of fellers—" Hart's voice sounded odd. Mason Raymond opened his eyes and sat up. Oh God, something was wrong again. "It's none of our business, let it be. They don't want a lot of Northerners butting in, you ought to know that by now."

"Maybe not, but somebody'd better butt in. They got a

nigger down there they holdin' onto and harassin'. Leave off harassin' that nigger that way! Leave off botherin'— Stop that!''

Mason Raymond sprang out of bed and rushed to the window. Four men were poking a bent-over black man with what looked like sticks. The man was jiggling around in the dust trying to get away from them; one after another of the men poked and prodded him, laughing and shouting. The Negro was trying to explain something, but none of the men badgering him were paying any attention, and the pleas were incoherent and muffled to Mason Raymond because the harassed man had his arms over his head. "Leave off," Hart shouted down at the men, "leave off!"

One of the men raised his stick and Mason Raymond saw it was a whip; the end came down across the black's back. Hart gave an outcry of indignation and sprang back from the window, banging his head; his language was the most inventive —even from Hart—that Mason Raymond had heard in a long time.

Then Hart raced across the room and yanked at the door, disappeared into the hall. There was no choice; Mason Raymond pounded after him. He and Hart stumbled down the stairs and out into a back storage room; the screen door was open and as he and Hart tangled with one another trying to get it unlatched, Hart kept screaming, "You leave off, you hear, leave off pesterin' that old man!"

He got through the door first and threw himself on one of the white men, Mason Raymond helplessly grabbing another. The odds were hopeless: four against two, and these four were big, bull-like men, the kind used to starting fights and winning them. The struggle was formless, banging and pummeling this way and that, typically, Mason Raymond thought, without plan, Hart's enthusiasm leading them into the heart of something (like the woods) he hadn't given a moment's thought to. One of the men hit Mason Raymond with a rocklike fist across the jaw. He started to drop, but threw himself against his opponent, the two of them swaying back and forth, hanging onto one another in an embrace like that of lovers, only the man was hitting Mason Raymond in the stomach every now and again as they danced about in the dust.

The Negro scuttled down the alley and out of sight; one of the white men cracked his whip and let fly, and Hart gave a yelp of pain and threw himself over the man he had been fighting and on top of the man who had struck him. They went down in the red dust. That left Mason Raymond with three large-bellied, bull-necked men; it took them very little time to bring him to his knees. He expected them to use their whips on him, waited fatalistically; one thing the trip had taught him already was that nobody put a premium on innocence: it was only something to take advantage of. Hart and he crouched side by side on the North Carolina earth looking up at the four savage Southerners. At that moment the war became a personal affair to Mason Raymond. "I'll git the law on you," Hart said through anger so thick it blunted his speech. "You lay a whip on me once or you touch this here boy one time and you won't never see the end of the trouble you're goin' to git from me. Up where I come from we hear tell about men like you, but I wouldn't never have believed it if I haddana seen it with my own eyes."

Hart got up. He was covered with red dust and there was blood on his mouth. "Leastwise," he said, "that nigger got free."

One of the men began to laugh. "A runnin' nigger," he said, "ain't gonna git very far in these parts."

"Yankees," another said, "Damnyankees. Union Leaguer niggra-lovers come here lookin' fer trouble, you gonna git it, we kin provide you with plenty of it."

"Four men pickin' on one," Hart said contemptuously.

"You wanna keep that kind of talk up, you gonna git yourself in more trouble than that nigra," said another of the men.

Hart began to laugh. "In a pig's eye," he said. "In a striped pig's eye."

"Worth—"

"You come down here, Yankee, to tell us how to run our business, that it?"

"You think four agin one is fair, you *need* someone to tell you how to run your affairs."

"We got ways of dealin' with interferers—we got—"

"I don't doubt that one bit. Like as not round up another four or five like yourselfs and come back 'nd gang up on us, I don't disbelieve it one bit."

Why didn't Hart stop agitating them for God's sake? Someone fired a shot. All of them, all six of them, Northerners and Southerners, started. Mason Raymond heard the second shot as he ran, the four men running beside him, Hart somewhere in back.

Oh God, Mason Raymond thought, I wish we were out of this. At the end of the alley, he stopped, winded, his chest heaving. The New York trouble had left him weaker than he'd realized. Hart's sixty-one, Mason Raymond thought, and I'm just out of the hospital, we shouldn't be mixed up in all this. But just try and keep him out.

The four Southerners sped off to the left; they had the advantage of knowing where they were going. Mason Raymond watched them jog down the street, big, larded men whom the war had scarcely trimmed down at all, products of the poor man's diet of potatoes, rice, grits, and gravy, and all that heavy homemade bread made of coarse flour. "Which way them shots come from?" Hart asked.

Mason Raymond didn't know. He only knew one thing for sure; the safe, the wise thing to do was to stay out of this. Inside his head Morphis pointed out that there were sins of omission as well as sins of commission. Mason Raymond was in no position to dispute this (and anyway who could?), but he would have said there are also extenuating circumstances when—to quote the old adage—discretion is the better part of valor.

A distinction most often made by the guilty, Morphis said inside his head.

Against the darkening sky a flame leapt up. "They're burnin'?" Hart asked incredulously.

"Listen, Hart, this is none of our business—"

"None of our business?" Hart turned on him. "I'd never thought I'd stand 'nd hear you say a thin' like that, not you, boy, not you who been closer than a son to me 'nd better in some ways than my own flesh and blood—what do you mean, this ain't none of our business?"

What, indeed, did he mean?

"You kin stay here or you kin go back, it don't change my goin' none," Hart said and started off down the street toward the flames and smoke burgeoning up against the sky.

We should never have got off the train, Mason Raymond thought. You always have to get to the end of the journey, you know that, the inside voice said.

He trotted beside Hart, not knowing what to say, trotting, silent and ashamed, into the small square where the man drooped against the ropes wound all the way around his body and who was already bubbling and crackling in the consuming flames.

They tramped out of the boardinghouse the next morning, up the road toward the golden-yellow tulip trees, the beech and birch and basswood of the mountains, into the rich red sumacs and sourwoods, the crimson sassafras, scarlet maples, wine-red oaks, the purple sweetgums, Hart trying to strike up some talk by enumerating every species, pointing out to Mason Raymond the characteristics of each, giving a little lesson in nature lore, Mason Raymond thought, looking at him sullenly, tramping along, not able to speak, the only thing in his mind the blackened Negro body of Plato Guy and the big, crudely lettered sign nailed to a post driven into the ground.

ALL BARN BURNERS AND WOMEN INSULTERS,
WE THE WHITE BROTHERHOOD
HANG BY THE NECK
OR BURN IN THE FIRE
UNTIL THEY ARE
DEAD, DEAD, DEAD

W.B.

This nigger was Plato Guy, a Union Leaguer

Mason Raymond and Hart crossed a stream and rested under some great willows (even Mason Raymond knew a willow), Hart consulting a map Mabel's people had sent up to him, and they turned to follow the path wandering beside the stony bed of the creek, past wheat and corn, the cornfields everywhere, not just in the valley hollows but also pinned precariously against the steepest slopes of the mountainsides. Beans were planted in the corn, a convenience for the beans: they could climb the stalks. Hart, trying still to be conciliatory, was saying didactically that corn was the heart of a mountaineer's life—gave him food, moonshine, fodder for his cattle.

How could he talk about corn when they'd just come from seeing a man burned alive? Didn't he understand? Of course he understood. It was he, Mason Raymond Buttes, who hadn't really understood anything about the war—to be truthful, hadn't even much thought about it except in terms of his uncle being away and then finally coming home safe, as if that return demonstrated that war wasn't really all that serious, his uncle had come back all right, hadn't he? Oh, it was true maybe other men hadn't made it back, but Mason Raymond hadn't known those other men so they didn't count. But there had been a war without mercy out there, a war which returned home men who could shoot and burn another man, men whom the killing had made so strong in their convictions that they were a source of fear to Mason Raymond because they were so sure of themselves and so intolerant of others that they could back up their faith with whips and guns, could post the kind of signs that he and Hart had seen and tried to ignore all along the outskirts of Waynesville and Asheville:

THE TIME IS COME!
DEPART, YE CURSED!
WE CANNOT LIVE TOGETHER!
TAKE WARNING AND GET OUT!
K.K.K.

DEAD MEN
MAKE
NO TROUBLE
K K K

WORK IN DARKNESS
BURY IN WATERS
MAKE NO SOUND
STRIKE HIGH AND SURE
VENGEANCE! VENGEANCE! VENGEANCE!
TRIED, CONDEMNED, EXECUTED.
FEAR IS DEAD !!!!!

K K K

They were going up from flat land and into the blue mountains, the Great Smokies Hart had been so keen to see, scrambling over huge boulders, tripping over shale and roots,
struggling up, up the steep slope, over knife-edged ridges,
feeling their way along precipices and ravines, panting for
breath, enjoying the deep blue spindles standing upright
among the fallen leaves, the closed gentians, the bonnets of
goldenrod, the purple and white wild asters, the feathery
helmets of queen of the meadow, and inside Mason Raymond's head the image: a burned black man and those four
white ones holding whips. He didn't know which was worse
to remember.

Hart *was* demented. He was sprinting along, stumbling,
happy, singing ever since they'd broken over the rise.

> *"Oh, the bear went over the moun-tain,*
> *The bear went over the moun-tain,*
> *The bear went over the moun—tain,*
> *To see what he could see . . .*
>
> *To see what he could see,"*

bellowed Hart,

> *"To see what he could see . . ."*

waving his coonskin cap and running, waving and running and
hollering his heart out. "It's like I always dreamt! Jest look at
them blue hills."

Mason Raymond saw the rippled mountains, the high hilltop orchards, smelled pine and balsam and beech and more

pine, always pine; the sun beat down on him like honey, he could *feel* the gold; he heard the birds and scratched where the gnats were trying to carry him off; his heart was beating right through his breast with pain and the acceptance of knowledge, which meant sun, and the sense he would never be the same again, he had been broken open and could not be put back together and though he was repaired he was not whole, a boy who knew finally and at last that there was evil here in the world and it would never go away and it could concentrate itself in men like Lite and those four Southerners with the whips, and in that dwarflike man with the billboards in New York; yet the air was so clear here he felt as if it were an offering. Then, as if part of a plan in honor of which he had made this terrible journey, the gift at the end of the quest appeared (he was free at last of deceit and fraud, knavery and trickery, being cheated and hounded and harassed): he saw a small cabin down in the glen, tumble-down and paintless, but looking just as he had imagined it would look, pure—that was the only word to describe it, pure—because it wasn't painted; it wasn't near anything at all, it lay just by itself, away from everything, huddled softly in the green folds of the meadow, a little feather of smoke rising and fading against the bright blue sky, and there was Hart running forward, waving his fool coonskin hat over his head and shouting, tripping and shouting, burst-open with relief that he'd finally got them through to the Promised Land, yet Mason Raymond stood in the hot, autumn Southern sun and said to himself, Don't trust any of these people, they're not like us, I don't care how good or right they may seem or even if they're Mabel's relatives, don't trust one of them, they aren't like us.

Hart had run almost to the cabin door, shouting and bellowing and letting this old woman who was supposed to know everything there was to know (according to Mabel's relatives) know also that he had arrived, though why she would care Mason Raymond could not figure out; maybe she hadn't even been told he was coming, these people said one thing and did another, and even if Mabel's relatives *said* they'd told her Hart was coming, Mason Raymond didn't put much stock in their *doing* it.

Mason Raymond had never in his life seen anyone as old as the stooped little woman coming out the door and standing on the end of the ramshackle porch in front of the tin cans of herbs and flowers, wiping her hands on a gunny sack apron, hair flying this way and that, shouting at a bevy of ducks squabbling near the porch, shouting at the dogs worrying the ducks, shouting at a hog trying to break loose from its chinked pen, shouting at last up the road to them, her words lost in barks, groans, grunts, quacks, Hart waving that crazy hat and shouting back.

"I knowed company was acomin'," the old woman said. "Sneeze 'fore breakfast, someone's comin' 'fore night. Got me right busy with the light. I been through a bad spell, sometimes so lonesome it's like I been off here all by myself all my life. God bless you for comin'."

"Worth Hart, and this here'n one of the Raymonds from Buttes Landing, Mason Raymond." *I'm still one of the Raymonds to him, Mason Raymond thought.* "We come lookin' for dogs. Bear dogs. Mabel's people—the Wald'rups, they was supposed to pass the word along we was on our way."

"You come to a good place. Best huntin' dogs in the world in these hills, bar none. You name your best breed b'ar dog in the whole world and I reckon there ain't any can touch what's been born and bred in these here mountains. Come in, come in, I got to see to the vittles."

Hart began an explanation about Mabel's ties with the Wald'rups and how they—at least some of them—still held to these parts, holding out the dogwood cuttings he'd carried all the way from New York, held onto through that whole terrible train ride, watered and tended on that rickety railroad southward over the mountains and carried in his knapsack right out here into the heart of the mountains, and Auntie Dirk said she'd heard of them, the word didn't come direct, but it had been passed along; her not knowing them direct didn't make no difference, folks come to her door didn't need credentials, but thank ye anyway for the cuttin's, I do love to tinker with growing thin's. One of her neighbors had sent her over a hog's head that mornin', maybe God hisself had sent it because they was comin' and she needed provisions, it was

] 259 [

like a miracle, their comin', she had been so blue and down
with lonesomeness lately. And here they were, God sent;
she'd been tryin' all mornin' to yank out these here hog eyes
and they wouldn't come loose no way.

Hart said he was a hand with hogs, been butcherin' and
sausagin' and jointin' since he was skim off the top of the
cream, no more than seven or eight and helpin' out with the
big men. They would make a fine pair, he said, her with her
cookin' and him with his pullin'. They bent over the hog's
head and started poking and prying.

"We need to git the eye out whole," she said. "You damage
it, break it up, then th' black stuff runs 'nd runs. Let me reach
my hand down in 'nd see if I can't pull it out. Eustis, his hands
was so stout they could pull hogs' eyes out no trouble atall.
Well, you can't call a man back twenty-five years. No use
tryin'. The grave hangs onto its prize. I think I liv'd the firmest
I could 'nd done the best I kno'd; then no one can't want to
go back 'nd git his life over 'gin. You ain't got it comin'. Good
men dyin' every day."

"I got it." Hart held up the eye. "Them dogs out there—"
Auntie Dirk took the eye to the door and threw it out; it hit
a tree and hung, bobbing, from a branch, like some kind of
larva in the cocoon, the black eye swinging in the milky case-
ment of the cocoon. The black man burned in the white-hot
heat of the fire; Mason Raymond watched and watched, unable to turn his head away.

"Oh, it's a high, clear day," she said. "It'll make a good
huntin' night. Can't many have the courage to come down past
the road no more. War drove everythin' off, men 'nd animals.
And varmints in these hills, from both sides, hidin' 'nd then
ridin' down on the unsuspectin' 'nd thievin' what don't belong
to them off the innocent. You want to keep a sharp eye. You
ever heard of the Lowries? They's thiefs 'nd vagabon's 'nd if
they git their just deserts they'll be put in the penitentiary, but
the way thin's is goin' here now, you watch 'nd see, they'll be
voted into office, next thin' you know one of 'em 'll be Gov'-
nor.

"Last Christmas I made fudge. Sav'd for the chocolate, I did,
'nd then cook'd up a batch of the thickest fudge you ever laid

eyes on. I thought somebody'd show up. I cooked beans 'nd bread 'nd a tart, too, but nobody come. Afraid of the roads, afraid of the thievin' 'nd the shootin' 'nd them that's the same breed as the Lowries, don't people go from one to 'nuther no more the way they used to. Grieves me. I miss the music, she said, oh, how I miss the music. I ain't heard "Thyme" now in, oh the Lord don't know how long. I was sittin' with the folks down to the Rosses', they was all a family then, seven big handsome boys they had, two gone in fightin' 'nd gaugin' 'nd two gone in the war 'nd one run off to the city, 'nd the two that was left was a little light in the head, but once, oh, it was a manly family, them boys set all the girls' hearts to flowerin'; they'd stand against a wall, all lin'd up, lookin', you know, lookin' the girls over, 'nd all the girls would be lookin' back, they was so well-made. Everyone 'cept me said I'd marry Tom Ross. He was big 'nd strappin' 'nd come up all the time with spoonin' on his mind, but it wasn't in me. I lik'd his looks 'nd I lik'd his walk, 'nd I wanted to like somethin' else in him well enough to say yes, but it weren't there.

"Dances we had all the time, 'nd music, people walk over the hills 'nd git together 'nd play 'nd dance 'nd oh we did sing, 'nd there I was at the Rosses' 'nd I kep' sayin' to myself, Why you got such an independent turn of mind, why you holdin' out for somethin' more than that fine boy over agin the wall; but it weren't no use arguin' with myself, I knew it weren't. I didn't have the feelin'.

"And in walks this lad, oh, he was a hard, handsome thin', with a wild brown thicket of hair 'nd blue, blue eyes, 'nd he looks at me 'nd he says, loud enough to let me hear, said to someone, I don't recollect who, it's been so long ago, I don't know that thyme, do I?

"I didn't know what he meant t'exact, but I understood. And the feelin', I knew it right out, like a cold 'nd then a hot shock run over me. Flu feelin'. I was tremblin' lookin' into his blue eyes, 'nd I never know'd what he meant, carryin' on like that—I thought he said, *time*. I thought he meant *time* when his turn come to sing 'nd he stood up 'nd took the floor 'nd he stood there singin', 'nd I thought he was sayin', like you know, the hours 'nd minutes, time, 'nd all along it was the herb he was talkin' about, 'nd even after I knew it was the seasonin' he kept singin' at me, all that summer, every time there was a do, he'd git up 'nd sing this song, 'Thyme,' 'nd I never knew what it meant. It weren't until after I'd lost my own he explain'd it to me 'nd then it was too late 'nd it didn't matter no more, I want'd him to have my bonnie, bonnie thyme. What eyes he had," she said, lifting her head, and for a moment her eyes seemed to mist over as she told about the past, seventy, maybe more years before; she was watching the man with the music making it for her, for her alone, and Mason Raymond was both attracted and repelled by the strength of her emotion. He envied her that memory, but its ability to move her, too, seemed to him exaggerated, sentimental. People didn't love all their lives and still care about an ancient room and a song he'd never even heard of and come close to sobbing because once someone had given them "a feeling." But he recognized, too, that part of his annoyance came from envy: he had never experienced that binding sense of being she was talking about, he wasn't even sure he knew what she meant about "that feeling." Who'd want to feel like he had the flu? He wanted to say to her, *Love destroys,* but she was an old woman and it would be cruel to kill her convictions. He knew that. Thyme, carrying on about thyme. What *was* thyme?

"Oh, I do love sweets, I'm plain silly about sweets," she was saying. "But it was funny nobody come because it was jest like this mornin', the sneezin', I was dead sartain someone was comin'. We made a good life here, Eustis 'nd me, but it's lonesome now, all to lone. When it comes snow 'nd storms 'nd thing's like that, it's not good, but I wouldn't go nowhere else in the world. A man died 'nd went to heav'n onct. He went walkin' here 'nd there, lookin' it all over, 'nd when he come on a man all fetter'd down with a ball 'nd chain he stopped, 'nd he look'd at that man 'nd he didn't understand. How come a man had ta be ball'd 'nd chain'd in heaven, he ask'd, 'nd the man he looks at him pityin' 'nd says, A man comes from the Carolina mountains *got* to be ball'd 'nd chain'd or he'd run right back first chance he got. Heaven can't compare with them Carolina mountains.

"I was born here, gonna lay down my last here. You wait 'nd see. Death don't fear me. And I don't fear him no more. Only one thin' I's afraid of in this world. B'ar. I'm afraid of b'ar in the worse way 'nd I carry me an axe every time I goes out alone in any direction. A little hand axe. And folks, they say, What you gonna do wi' that? 'nd I say, Kill me a b'ar. I've liv'd here eighty years 'nd I've seen as many b'ar as there were years, 'nd Eustis like to die off one, trapped him down in th' blueberries 'uz ripe, 'nd he feedin' on them, that b'ar, don't you know? Was right over there, up on top a' th' mountain 'nd got Eustis out in the mornin', it did, it was such a fine, clear day, 'nd he went along with his pail lookin' to git some honey 'nd he come on these blueberries 'nd the b'ar he was jest sittin' 'ere, it 'uz real early—just crack a' daylight when he got 'ere —'nd you know that b'ar come at 'im out of the blueberries, oh, he 'uz a dandy! 'nd he raz'd him across th' he'd 'nd that place never did close back, one sid'a his head run from that day to the day he died. Eustis, he had a awful hard time, with all 'at sickness 'nd ever'thin' on him."

Hart took hold of her hand—grabbed it, was more like it. She was seized with silence, as he had intended, and he bent over and put his head almost to her hand, began talking about his own wound, about how peculiar it was, Mason Raymond had a scar lining his scalp, too. They were linked, the three of them, he said, making Mason Raymond bend down so that she could finger his scar as well.

She and Hart were shaking their heads and murmuring in reverent tones about how, yes, there were signs, you couldn't never deny that. He would have liked to ask them if the morning he was shot and burned Plato Guy had had some kind of sign.

Hart was working the saw on the pig's head, worried about breaking it on bone. He wasn't trying to direct the discussion now, he was just letting it take its own course. Sooner or later he was hoping that it would come around to where he could grab it and swing it in the direction he wanted it to go.

"Don't hit that other eyeball, you can he'p it. Eustis took them out clean as a whistle," Auntie Dirk assured him. "Don't hit th' eyeball you can he'p it. That old black stuff run all over.

I hope you never has t' live by you'n'self. In one way hit's a
joy 'nd in another hit's a poison. Nobody t' lend you a hand.
Oh, hit's come out!"

She took the head and put it to soak where, she assured
them, it would come out white as winter and she'd put it
through the grinder and cook it, juice and all, with sage and
black and red pepper and some thyme, she said, smiling, I put
a little thyme in anythin' 'at'll hold it, 'nd they would sit down
'nd eat it hot. Hart didn't care about the cooking; he was after
her about the dogs. He'd never given up hope of taking
control over the conversation, though long ago Mason Raymond had plunked down on a stool and surrendered himself
to despair. How's come she still kept such a parcel of dogs
since she didn't hunt? Hart asked. She turned them loose
every now 'nd agin, she said, jest to let them run 'nd so she
could hear them call; it reminded her of the old days. She
asked Hart if he wanted to take them out, and he was tickled
pink, he made an absolute fool of himself dancing around and
claiming he'd give his honor 'nd his heart to run a pack of dogs
like that.

That night, full of hog meat that had been bubbling three
or four hours on the wood stove, and corn pone cooked up
in the Dutch oven, the three of them started out. There were
six dogs with them, savage with impatience; they kept turning
back, their jaws snapping, deep growls in their throats, springing toward Mason Raymond and Hart, trying to topple them
and run free. Hart was raving. "Real bear dog at last," he kept
telling Mason Raymond, who wasn't much impressed with
how extra-fire wonderful they were, "You ain't seen nuthin',
boy, til you seen Plotts run." The dogs didn't look any bigger
or better or heavier than the regular coon dogs back at the
Landing, maybe they were even finer-boned, skinnier,
smaller, closer down to the ground than Landing dogs. They
had powerful shoulders, yes, but there was nothing really
special about them Mason Raymond could see except maybe
their heads, which were *not* like the heads of Landing coon
dogs; *finer* was the way Mason Raymond would have described the bone structure, whatever that meant. And what
good would a fine head do them killing bear?

After a time, though, he became impressed in spite of himself. My God, they had power for all the "fineness" of their bones; they were pulling, tangling with one another, tangling with Mason Raymond and Hart, tearing Mason Raymond's arms right out of their sockets. If he'd been by himself, he'd have given in to them, turned them loose and good riddance, but Worth set a lot of store by this hunt. "You're gonna see somethin' tonight, all right," he kept boasting, while Mason Raymond hung back, both diffident and angry at the same time. How could he blurt out again to the exuberant Hart, sprinting along, singing,

> Oh, the bear went over the mountain,
> The bear went over the mountain,
> The bear went over the moun—tain,
> To see what he could see . . .

that he didn't see any sense at all in this killing. They weren't going to eat the meat; they weren't going to cure the skins; they weren't going for any other reason than the pleasure of the kill, and Mason Raymond didn't find any pleasure in that, didn't intend, for a fact, to do any killing—Hart knew that after all that had happened; but, no, he was too pig-headed and stubborn to believe it, too excited and too driven by a single-mindedness that encompassed nothing but hunting and killing to give any consideration to a sixteen-year-old boy's problems with moral distinctions. He said Mason Raymond was going through a stage, he'd get over that the way he'd get over his skin and cheek eruptions.

Mason Raymond fell, jumping up at once to make a grab for a leash that had gotten away from him and shouting at Hart to watch out, he'd let go of one of the dogs and the damned thing was running for all he was worth straight up for the woods and they'd never catch him. He felt like explaining that one free soul was a danger to everyone else.

It was no use. They weren't going to catch that dog if they ran with the wind and mist. Mason Raymond sat down on a stump. He recognized rebellion when he saw it and he had never witnessed a clearer case, even if it was in himself. He let the other two dogs go, slipping their collars so that they'd be really hard to catch. If Hart wanted to kill, there were at least going to be enough obstacles in his way to make the odds a little evener for the coons than he'd counted on.

The commotion up ahead was now extravagant. Dogs were tracking every which way, howling, barking, baying, while Hart shrieked and hollered with them, even bayed occasionally himself. A second later Mason Raymond heard the dog voices weld into one long, full cry of hound on hunt.

Resigned, he rose. Time, it is a precious thing, and time was running out for some of the animals of the night, creeping cautiously along, foraging, or running excitedly on their own trails, unaware of the dogs running them in full cry through the dark night.

What'd you come for in the first place? he asked himself.

He didn't know all the reasons—there were so many: to get away from home, to forget what had happened this past winter and spring and some of the summer, too—maybe to please Hart who was so set on going and turned out to be afraid to go alone. "A long journey like that," he said in lieu of an open plea, "and me an old man and no experience in travelin' ways, it goes against the grain throwin' myself into a void like that without aid. You reckon you might want to tag along—for the experience of the thin'?" he asked anxiously.

He'd have found some other fool to share the expenses and experiences if I'd said no. The point is, you are here, the voice said, and Mason Raymond answered it without hesitation, But no killing on my part went into the bargain, and that is that. He's got to accept that. I'll tag along but I won't carry a gun. The sins of omission and commission, the second voice inside him said.

Oh, shut up, he answered it. Hart's not going to do any hunting tonight anyway.

Don't make any real decisions, let them be made for you— that's a fine way to run your life, isn't it?

Why don't you leave me alone? All the time pick pick picking.

You take a lot of reminding. Whose fault is *that?*

He lay with his head on his arm watching the shadows flicker on the crude walls of the one-room mountain cabin. He remembered Auntie Dirk saying as she rocked in front of the fire, I was born 'nd rear'd on Smoke Knoll, I come here with Eustis when I was thirte'n 'nd I been here ever since. Ain't no part of this country for twenty mile 'round I don't know. I've hoe'd corn here 'nd huckleberri'd 'nd syrup'd here. And I've made baskets, lots of 'em. And footmats 'nd beds outa corn shucks. And rais'd high as seventy-five bushel a' goobers 'nd 'taters over 'n't field over there. I've hogg'd 'nd cut wood 'nd rais'd my brood here. My child'n, some gone off 'nd some lay here on the land 'nd some lay God hisself alone knows, old soldiers never die, it's the young 'uns do, but I'm here still, on this here land Eustis 'nd me put our hopes in 'nd I don't never aim to leave it 'til I'm carried off 'nd laid over there next to Eustis 'nd that ain't *leavin'*—Yes, he felt safe here, just as he had felt safe on the train, and he thought how really temporary safety was, he and Hart in that iron car plunging over the land but not a part of it, safe only because they were cut off from people, but distance was not depth; you couldn't create anything in a railroad car. And that, he thought, seeing the fire leap and die, leap and die, was what he wanted his life to be about—creating, as Auntie Dirk had created—as she had learned every hollow and hill, kept the dogs for the pleasure of listening to their baying, kept the flowers and herbs for the pleasure of their smell and sight and feel, grew her tub of thyme in the strength of remembrance, kept her cabin because it was part of her, Lonely sometimes, but hits a joy, too, she had said, and he understood this; for he had watched her rise, old, bent, rheumatic, straightening the bones in her back with both her hands, getting her legs going slowly, rickety with age, moving over the bare wood floor slowly, then standing to rest in the sillway in a patch of sun, standing barefooted on her porch gazing down-glen where the sun spangled the Appalachian trail and the mist rose sulkily over a wide stream in the distant valley; just as Hart stood there and knew, too, though he had never set eyes on these mountains or valleys before, yet it was like they were a part of him because he, Worth Hart, had dreamed them somewhere inside, because

] 267 [

somewhere out there was the dog he had come for, there were hunts yet to be run, coons and bears to be treed, and a house —shabby, falling apart, surrounded by debris, but his own— to which he would bring back his mountain dog, joining Carolina to Buttes Landing, constricting the world and making it smaller, taking back in a way, too, Auntie Dirk, because what was held in the mind was as real and certain as that sun rising lazily over green valleys and misty glens and mountain smoke. Nothing ever stayed except in the mind.

He had stumbled somehow onto an answer and had known it for a brief instant and tried to grasp it, and it had slipped away from him even as he clung to it: *He that maketh me to lie down in green pastures . . . he that leadeth me beside the still waters . . .*

In the morning when he awoke she was trying to get into her walking shoes. These were old, cracked, half-broken brogues, men's shoes with slightly rounded, squarish toes and thick leather heels, run over, Eustis' once, she said, but like new when he went, she said, so she had stuffed them and they were as good as new for her, better, broken-in that way, she'd hold them up with the best and not be ashamed. They were going to put up some of the souse and bread and carry some eggshells filled with maple sugar boiled black and put in the shells to harden so that it was easy to carry, and they would walk aways over the hills to see Grady Lamb, he had a dog or two worth seeing.

Hart, dancing up and down on the hard-packed earth in front of the ramshackle front porch, kept trying to get her going; she was a slow mover, old, creaky, yes, that was true; but there was also something hesitant about her manner—she wanted Worth to see the dogs, that much was certain, but it seemed to Mason Raymond she didn't necessarily want to take them over to Lamb's herself. She kept finding one unimportant chore after another she just *had* to do before they left.

Worth was like to lose his mind if they didn't get going soon, and finally—as if even Auntie Dirk could see she was trying his patience past endurance—she hobbled out on the porch, took down her sun-bleached bonnet, and reckoned as how she was set to git goin' if it wouldn't molest them none to fetch along the noon vittles with the rest of their garb.

They ate at sun high under the shade of an enormous beech —cold souse and the buttermilk bread and some small, warty, tart apples Mason Raymond had never tasted before; she spread everything out on a linen towel and bent over the food to make a "beginning," as she called it, simple, but to the point, "O Lord thou knowest how I need this," and then proceeded to verify the assertion—and after she had wiped her mouth and laid back against the thick beech trunk, she let out what was the matter. She and Grady were friendly—but cold friendly, she said—on account of Faith, her sister.

There had been three girls—Faith, the oldest; Hope, who had died at birth; and Auntie Dirk, who after some discussion had been allowed to be Charity even though everyone said she didn't look like no Cher'ty. His woman was Faith, she said, looking at her hands, gnarled as the wizened apple Mason Raymond held. We best git goin' or we won't gain it afore sundown. Worth and Mason Raymond were left to puzzle the matter out for themselves. It seemed a sort of parable, a mountain allegory—Faith, Hope and Charity and not the least of these had died at birth.

For her age she was spry as some of the young crop, she said, using her stick, a thick staff Eustis had cut for her when she had her hip fall that year before he died. There was little talk, just that steady, paced walking Mason Raymond was later to identify with mountain people, men and women used to going two–three miles of a morning to look for lost livestock or to tend an orchard, who thought nothing of going four, five miles to berry or nut at some favorite spot, who traveled over the ridge eight, ten miles on Sundays to church service or on Saturdays to some sing-fest with good strumming and frailing and singing, whose nearest neighbor on one side might be fifteen, twenty miles east or west, or nobody at all north and south within a day's walking.

There was a time for talking and a time—apparently longer —for silence. She walked, bent and silent, almost as if she weren't even conscious of the two men at her side; she wasn't in the mood for chitchat. All she said at one point was they'd had some deserters from both sides in these hills during the war 'nd a couple of years after, but there were no nigras to speak of, nigras didn't take to the mountains, they stayed more down to the towns. The war, she said, the war was a bad time. I give two of my own to it.

She didn't seem to hold their Yankeeness against them; then it occurred to him she wasn't Southern in any way he thought of as Southern, didn't talk slow and Southern; and her manners weren't plantation ways, they were mountain-farm manners. There was a world of difference. Being part Buttes he understood that.

They came over the knoll into a thick patch of raspberry bushes, with the broken, blood-colored earth of a road separating the hilltop into two thickets, and they stood in that narrow path, too slender to be called a road, and looked down on the log cabin, the smoke rising from the thick chimney that took up almost all of the side of the house nearest them. Dogs were running out on tethers from everywhere, barking and jumping into the air as far as their leashes would let them. "You shoot twice in the air to let 'm know it's friends," she told Hart while he gave her a quizzical look, but did as she said. "We'll wait here. You don't want to go hurryin' in on Grady Lamb."

They stood on the knoll, looking down on the inferno of dogs below. The smoke rose lazily; the dogs bayed until Mason Raymond felt their throats would burst, and the sun slowly, slowly, inch by inch, moved down toward a meadow and another hill far on the other side of them.

"He likes to take his time," Auntie Dirk said. "He ain't one to be pushed."

"Maybe he ain't home," Hart suggested. "We been standin' here a good quarter of an hour and there ain't been a sign of life. Be hard not to know you had visitors 'round the way them dogs are carryin' on 'nd me shootin' 'nd all."

"He's down there with that little glass he puts up to his eye 'nd looks out 'nd people way off look big as life. He stands 'nd looks 'nd it takes him a while to make up his mind if'n he feels up to company or if'n he don't."

"And if'n he don't."

"He'll run us off. The door's openin' now. You watch. He does it real slow. He don't make up his mind complete 'til he's got it all the way open. His mind hangs in the balance. Don't make no sudden mov'ment, you'll make him nervous. He suspicions people got too much ambition in 'em 'nd mean him harm."

"Cher'ty, is that you up on my hill?"

" 'Course he knowed it was me. He seen me through that little glass. You stand still." She took a few steps in front of them, leaning on her staff, taking her time, in no hurry to answer the obvious.

"It's me, Grady, me 'n' a couple of men want t' see your'n dogs."

Grady was standing on the porch, a shotgun in his hand, just standing there looking uphill, not saying anything, not moving, not even shifting his shotgun, while Auntie Dirk, resting patient against her staff, looked down on him, waiting.

"If that ain't the dangest thin'—"

"Cher'ty, is that you up there on my hill?"

There was a note of impatience in Auntie Dirk's voice. "You *know'd* it's me, Grady. You kin see me plain as day in that little spy glass you got, you know it's me. Ain't no one else so bent 'nd broke 'ud walk over to see you no more."

"Who's them two strangers with you?"

"Two fellers want to hunt, heer'd you got the best dogs in the mountains, ask'd me 'n' I told them it was true 'n' brun' 'em over to see for theirselfs."

"Wily old witch, ain't she?" Hart said in admiration.

"What kind of fellers?"

"You know you ain't suppos'd ask that in these parts, Grady, you don't never—"

"Thin's all chang'd, Cher'ty, you know 'Cession done chang'd everythin'. Old laws don't work no more."

"Not with me, nuthin' ain't chang'd. A man come to my door, he gits food 'nd lodgin' 'nd no questions ask'd. I 'spect the same I go walkin' out in the world. I don't 'spect t' stand 'n a hill 'nd shout my lungs out afore I'm ask'd even down to the yard."

They waited. The sun slipped down another inch; long

velvety shadows began to run over the meadow, Grady standing on his porch looking up at them silent and still.

Finally Auntie Dirk turned and started back to Mason Raymond and Worth. "Ain't no good. He's 'n one of them moods cain't make up his mind one way or t'other. Stand in the sun all day won't cast no shadow, he won't make up that suspicionin' mind a hisn. And one of th' nic'st men in th' parts 'fore he 'ad his trouble with Fa'th. Sour'd 'im like old milk, it did. Ain't ne'er been sweet 'nd sound since, e'en ifn he got hisself anoth'r wom'n."

"Cher'ty—Cher'ty, whar you goin'?"

Stopped and turned. "Home, where I kin rest m' feet."

"You kin rest yourn feet down to here."

"Well, why didn't ya say so?"

"You didn't give me no time."

"It's all right," Auntie Dirk said. "Only don't go 'n move too fast. Walk slow 'n easy so he kin see yourn men of small ambition. He don't put no trust to outsiders, 'nd I guess he got reason, considerin' it was that Ten'see boy come out of the woods 'nd made him all the trouble."

They walked in single file, Auntie Dirk leading, Hart behind her, and Mason Raymond bringing up the rear. Grady didn't come out to meet them. He stood on the porch with the shotgun in his hand watching them come; when they got near the porch, Mason Raymond could tell a lot about the Lambs. There were no tins of herbs, no pots of geraniums, not even a wooden rocker for sitting and looking at the sun. The porch was bare except for some wood by the door and a dented tin coffee kettle on its side, rusted so badly that Mason Raymond could see where a hole was eaten through.

" 'ftern'n, Gr'dy."

" 'ftern'n, Cher'ty."

"This here'n is Mister Hart 'n' his nep'ew, Mas'n Ray, come down from up North."

"How d'you do," Worth said pleasantly, and Lamb said nothing. Mason Raymond didn't know what to say, so he said, "Sir," and stood behind Worth and waited.

"You come huntin', that it?"

"We'd pleasure ourselfs to do it with you," Worth said. "We heer'd you got the finest dogs—"

"You heer'd right."

Worth's voice sounded discouraged, but he was giving it a good try. "I come a long, long way lookin' for a dog to take back—"

"None of my dogs is fer sale. Not to you, not to nobody, esp'c'ly not to some damn'd Yankee."

"Well, I didn't reckon you'd want to part with sech val-u-able animals, seein' how your dogs earn'd sech names for theirselves. I don't blame you wantin' to hang onto quality stock like you got. It's advice I come to git from you—not dogs—if'n you're willin' to part with some of that. You bein' sech a well-knowed dog man I reckon'd the thin' was I come to you you'd set me straight on some matters I been turnin' over in my mind."

He knows a thing or two himself about how to deal with these buggers, Mason Raymond thought.

"Well—" Lamb said, "I don't know as words kin cost you much." You believe that, you'll believe anything, Mason Raymond thought. Grady Lamb turned to Auntie Dirk. "You reckonin' on evenin' over?"

"I cain't git back on this light, Grady, but if'n we're puttin' you out—" He didn't answer. "Mr. Hart and the boy had a pow'rful hope to go out with you woodsin' tonight."

He thought. He turned it over in his mind. "It's a poss'b'l'ty," he said. "I'll turn it over and think on it, but it's a distin't poss'b'l'ty."

They were not asked in. Apparently Auntie Dirk found nothing curious about this. She settled herself on the porch steps while Grady took Hart and Mason Raymond out to show them sleeping space in the barn, undoing her brogues and calling after Grady, "You look better'n last fall, Grady."

"I been down to the bottom 'nd start'd t' rise agin," he told her. In the barn he was a bit more friendly. "The husband—Eustis Dirk—he was all right, but them Bounty girls were all a pack of trouble to the men who took up with 'em. She give her old man a fierce time while he was up'n runnin' 'nd I reckon she told you what her sister done to hasten my end."

"No, she never said a word," Hart said, "and that's a fact."

"Asham'd, I 'spects, though shame don't run much in that fam'ly, and *that's* a fact. I been took by women all my life," Grady Lamb said sadly. "Had three—'nd all of them were a relief when they went. One was full of woe 'nd one misery 'nd one was a Catholic." Mason Raymond wondered which was woe, which misery, and which was the Catholic.

"You kin bed down here, we got some comforters up to the house to put over'n the hay. My woman ain't well, ain't been right since the boy went off in the fall—gone to the city like all them t'other fools. Ain't no place fur man nor beast, folks don't treat you right there—"

"And *that's* a fact," Worth said fervently. "They robb'd 'nd beat us so bad this boy like to die and I had to pray 'n promise him back. Offer'd to help us 'n then led us into this alley and laid our skulls open 'n then run off with all our money. Only reason they didn't git some of mine, I had it sewed in my underdrawers and if they'd a had time to take them, they wouldda done it, too. Man ain't safe nowhere in them city places."

"My boy, I wish'd he'dda heer'd you say that. What we told'm done no good. He'd got his mind set to go 'nd he went, don't matter he was the only male 'un Emma 'nd me ever had. All them young 'uns runnin' off to try and git rich off machines in the city, it won't bring then nuthin' but perdition and grief, and *that's* a fact for you."

He stood against the back of a stall and looked them over. "We'll vittle you and it'll set all right with your bones if'n you don't mind plain fare. The woman, she ain't up to a lot of eff'rt, the starch done gone off her. It's a good night fer huntin', rain yistiddy give the dogs some good tracks fer scentin'. We'll run after the light's good and gone, up in the hollow—coons aplenty up thar."

"Any bear?"

"Always chance it in these here parts. You keen on b'ar, is you?"

"I got bear in my blood," Hart said. "You git some dogs

runnin' bear, I'll run with them and they'll give out 'fore I do, I'm that keen on bear."

"Good b'ar dog 'round here."

"That's why we come. Mabel, my missus, she got family in these parts—"

"That a fact? What's thar names?"

"Mabel's mother's side of the fam'ly was Wald'rups."

"Nervy bunch, every 'un of them got his nose to somebody else's bus'ness."

"That's them, a turrible rackety lot, but God almighty, you shouldda seen this dog they brung up to me after my head was busted open. Feller workin' fer us, wasn't too right in the head, he took a notion to flay me with a hoe across the head and went and done it, near kilt me, I got the ridge yet, here, feel—" Hart bent his head and Grady touched the scar ridge wonderingly. "Brains come right out of the bone. Weren't one soul in this world thought I'd make it 'cept Mabel. She had the faith." At the word faith, Grady stepped up and put his hand on Hart's back. "Ain't many good women left," he said. "Ain't many men lucky 'nough to meet up with one."

"Said if I got up and about, she'd git me the one thin' I'd always had my heart set on, one of them North Car'lina bear dogs, and she done it, and you know what I gone and done, o'nery dumb old fool that I am? I hunted that thair bitch afore I got a litter off'n her and she got kilt on her first run. Wouldn't git away from that bear, no matter how hard I tried and called her off. I'dda gone in for her myself and fetched her out, only three men, they held me back. Next to losin' Mabel, losin' that dog's the worse loss I'm ever gonna experience in this here world. In the next, that's another matter— but here and now I felt I lost my soul when I seen that dog go down. Now I got me another chance to git me one of them dogs. It's like a miracle; men don't often git no second chance 'round. This boy 'nd me come all the way down here from up past New York Cit-y, way up past Sche-nec-ta-dy, to git us a couple of good bear dogs."

Grady shook his head. "Come through war-struck country, lookin' for dogs, and you a couple of Northern'rs could have git your heads shot off and no one say a word. Yankee heads go cheap 'round here, 'nd th't's a fact. You that crazy on dogs, you're gonna see real dogs run, you'ar. Yes, sirree, you got somethin' in store for you. You nev'r seen dogs like mine in all your life, I'd lay my hand on the Good Book on that and swear 'til the day I die, and I'm not a swearin' man."

A big globe moon hung low in the sky. Auntie Dirk had gone out to the barn to make up the beds and turn in herself. Mrs. Lamb had never appeared. Mason Raymond had wondered for a time if she existed at all, Lamb himself being so peculiar, but Auntie Dirk had assured him she was indeed a fact, only she didn't take to her, "M' sist'r left a bad impres'ion on this house for the whole Bounty fam'ly," she said. "She don't crave much to look on me, Emma don't, and you Yankees with m' don't add none to the attraction."

Somewhere in the dense night an animal cried, a bird rose in a whir of flight, the three men spoke softly though the dogs were running noisily, their high, excited voices lunging out of the night, a quarter, possibly a half mile ahead. "They're on to somethin', you kin bet your brogues on that," Lamb kept saying. "We'll git ourselves three, four coon afore the night's gone."

He was right. The dogs treed first in a big pine; the yellow eyes of the coon were quite clear high in the needles, where the animal clung fearfully to the branch, which swayed from side to side as the coon tightened its grip. Lamb told Hart to give it a try. It was a pleasure, Hart said, to use a decent gun. His was always coming apart. Had a sentimental feelin' for it though; his Pa had give him that double-barreled shotgun as a wedding present, and he set a lot of store by it, bent and beat-up as it was. Pretty accurate, too, all thin's considered, but nuthin' like *this*. This here is a first-rate gun, he said, shooting and missing. Never have been able to hit the side of a barn.

Lamb took the gun and began to whistle through his teeth. He took his time sighting the coon. He was going to show off, get that coon in one clean shot. Mason Raymond caught his breath in his throat. It's not me doing the killing, he kept telling himself, I'm not responsible, it's not me. How responsible, the voice asked, is the onlooker, and Mason Raymond was still feeding the voice syllogisms when the coon came crashing down through the branches and landed amidst the dogs, apparently dead, for it made no sound as they tore it apart. It was at that moment that Mason Raymond knew he was not going to bring back a dog. Some people, he told himself, are born to stay East, and some are born to go West; some to kill, and some not; some to own pure hunting dogs and some to forgo that favor. I'll forgo the favor.

He wasn't even going to try to explain to Hart. When the time came, he would just say he'd changed his mind, he couldn't take a dog back, he might be going back to school, he might be going out West. Hart would argue that Rivers could look after it, and Mason Raymond knew that no doubt in the end, Hart, with his fine logic, would get the truth out of him, which was unfair, because the way he felt was nobody's business but his own; he didn't want to tell Hart out in the open that a man who threw coons to dogs was, to his way of thinking, not the kind of man he wanted to be.

The dogs had gone into a swamp and though the three men eventually floundered their way through, the tree where the dogs were barking was flush against another, the branches of both intertwined to such thickness that the coon was impossible to sight. Grady and Hart both shot into the foliage hoping to get it moving or even catch a lucky shot, but though in the end Worth even climbed the tree, the coon had to be given up. Half an hour, the two hunters agreed, was time enough to monkey around; there were plenty more coons in the woods, maybe even, Hart said hopefully, a bear they'd come on. Mason Raymond tramped behind the two hunters trying to disassociate himself from them. Should there be a Great Recorder he didn't want it on his record he was one of those pulling a trigger, and mistakes (especially in the dark) were easy to make.

A fine distinction, his conscience said sardonically. If you object so strongly, why are you along at all?

I don't know, I don't know, Mason Raymond thought. Because of Hart, because I owe Hart something I can't put in words, a debt there's no way of repaying except to come South with him and help him find his Plott hound. It's not a choice between right and wrong.

All the meaningful decisions never are.

The three of them stumbled and slipped until they came upon a pine, tall and bare, dying or dead already, stripped clean so that they could spot the coon easily. He was three-quarters of the way up, a big granddaddy of a coon, hanging on to the trunk with his arms wrapped around the tree. He looked down into their lantern light with wise, bright eyes, as if he had outrun a lot of dogs in his day but realized he'd picked the wrong tree for escape. He even gave a shrill little kind of moan when he saw them, a kind of warning or pleading from between his teeth. He was big and he looked half-human, hanging up there peering down into their lantern light —*knowing*. Mason Raymond started to say something and then stopped. People would say, Don't pay no mind to that old man come lookin' for a b'ar dog, he won't kill if that city boy asks him not to. Ain't no hunter won't *kill*.

Lamb was overjoyed. "You ev'r seen anythin' the like of him?" he demanded, dancing around the tree gazing up at the big coon looking down at him. "Ev'r seen anythin' so siz'ble in your life? You ain't got no coon like that up there wh're you come from, I'd be willin' to stake my life on it, and that's a fact. You shoot," he said to Hart, giving Hart the honor of the kill. "That's one shot you can't miss."

Hart didn't miss, but he didn't hit clean either. The big coon came tumbling through the bare branches and hit the ground with a thud. It got up and tried to fight off the dogs, clawing, dodging, making a strange, hissing sound. The dogs yelped as its claws raked a nose or caught an ear, but the coon was no match for the circle of excited hounds. Mason Raymond watched the dogs pick it up, tear at it, let it go, go for it again, toss it in the air, drop it, circle, and attack. He was sick, groping about in the dark for a tree branch. The first he found was too thin, the second rotten, and the dogs were still tearing at the coon, still running in, tearing, moving back as the coon tried to fend them off. Hart and Grady were watching, leaning in against the lantern light, talking, Hart peering intently at the dogs to see how tenacious they were and Lamb leaning back and lighting up a corncob pipe.

Mason Raymond ran over and grabbed Hart's old gun. He brought it down on the coon, but as he hit the gun came apart and while he'd hit the coon, he hadn't killed it. It jumped back, bloody, its fur matted and torn, and looked at him with dimmed eyes. My God, wasn't it ever going to die. Why didn't one of the men shoot it? It wasn't right to let a thing like that live. It wasn't right.

Mason Raymond picked up the butt of the barrel and brought it down with all his strength across the coon's head. The brains popped out just the way Hart's brains must have popped out when the hired hand hit him with the hoe. "Holy Christ!" Hart said and Grady came over and said it was a good big fellow. Mason Raymond was panting, his breath rattling out of his chest in long, jerky sobs. In the woods he had eaten the eggs, and now he had killed. He thought he was going to be sick. All his insides were heaving up. Grady picked up the dead animal and slung it over his shoulder and tied its tail to some twine that he took out of his pocket; as he walked, the dead coon swung back and forth, back and forth under the distant, peaked light from the moon and stars.

Mason Raymond could hardly move for the trembling in his legs. He felt the way he had in the woods when he was all lost and light-headed; he felt the way he had when Lite had shot Hector. The terrible sensation that was running through him was one so murderous that he could have turned and yanked the dead coon off Lamb and beaten the man until he lay numbed and helpless in the swamp. He'd have left him, too, left him lying there to die and he'd have gone right past Hart without a word and left him, too. He never wanted to see either of these two old men again.

He trudged along behind them trying to work his weak legs. He was holding two dogs. The animals strained and pulled trying to break free until Mason Raymond's shoulders ached, his arms felt unhinged. The dogs, suddenly excited by some woods scent, were jumping and barking and straining so that they pulled Mason Raymond over; he lay in the fetid mud having an instantaneous vision of Morphis, book-laden, stopped in the hall just before that Christmas vacation when he and his mother had come up to the Landing to get ready for his father. Mason Raymond had been asking him for some suggestions for vacation reading, and Morphis had said, smiling, "Why not Trollope and Sterne?" The books were still in his room, unread (they ought to be posted back to the school). He could think of Morphis quite calmly; he could even think of his mother quite calmly (she had been dead really when she went into the first coma, the woman left after that was not his mother); he might even picture his father swinging over the stairs quite calmly; but there were two things he could not stand to think about calmly: the burned black man and the torn coon Grady had swung over his shoulder.

The three of them broke through brush and brambles up a rise where, over a long, sloping field of corn, they looked down on a round coin of a lake shining in the moonlight. The wind shuddered softly through the field, the stars winked high in the black dome of sky, and below, flat as if it had no dimension at all, the lake lay silver-capped, still, immutable, and untouched.

He had killed. He had brained that coon with a blow that was both willed and wanted. The desire to end pain was the only thing on his mind at the moment he brought Hart's gun butt down on the coon's skull. But desire had nothing to do with deed. Again and again a man arrived at killing. Out of need, out of anger, out of desperation. He had eaten the birds' eggs. He had burned with the lust to kill Lite. No amount of pleading or logic in the world could have stopped those first hot moments of wanting to seize something and let Lite's life run out under its force. And he had killed the coon. Out of mercy. But motive didn't matter. The coon was as dead as if he had killed it in the kind of anger he had felt for Lite, in the kind of need that had driven him to strip the birds of their young. Death was final no matter how it came. Why should motive matter?

He threw himself down, lying stretched out in the long grass, staring up at the spiky points of stars. Even the dogs were quiet, lying, with tongues lolling, beside him. In the hush Mason Raymond could hear his heart working. The voice inside that usually told him, sardonically, what he was trying to avoid knowing, was stilled; his heart pumped and beat and something so large inside was swallowing him up that he would not have been surprised if it had destroyed him the way he had destroyed the coon—out of pity perhaps, but whatever the emotion, it would be a final one.

He lay with open eyes, breathing in and out that terrible, killing pain, waiting for what was going to happen to him, the silver circle of water below, the high, arched sky overhead with its planets and suns whirling at such rates even his heart couldn't keep up.

And all the time Lamb, who had settled down beside him, kept talking and talking. "I had jest about the nices' little place you ever did see 'nd we was gettin' along fine," Lamb said, "famous for a fact for what we was doin' with what little we 'ad, we 'ad ourselfs fifty of th' prett'est white-legg'd hens you ever did see, plentiful'st lay'rs, couldn't nearly col'ect the eggs as fast as they thro'd 'em out. And then this Ten'ersee feller he come over the mountains, he said he want'd work, he was tir'd 'nd hungry, all that thair walkin', 'nd out o' mon'y 'n' tir'd 'n' would we put 'm up for a spell? We was gittin' to th' po'nt we 'ad more 'n we could hold ageth'r ourselfs, we could use anoth'r good pair 'f hands. Been better astay'd small than ambition ourselfs so hard we couldn't no more keep up with wh't we 'd.

"This Ten'ersee feller he stays a week, 'nd then anoth'r week, 'nd then th' third 'un a friend tipp'd me off he 'nd the missus was meetin' up back. About ten o'clock th' night I went to woken up 'n' Faith she was gone from th' bed. I git up 'n' pull my suspend'rs up but don't put on no shoes. I went real quiet through the house 'n' she warn't thair, so I commence acallin' her 'n' acallin' her. No answ'r, you know, so I waits quietlike with that thair gun on the porch maybe 'n' hour, maybe more, 'nd then I sees them comin' ov'r the grass. They was aholdin' hands, she 'nd th't thair Ten'ersee feller, stoppin' 'n' touchin' ev'ry once in a while. Thair minds wasn't on nuthin' but theirselfs. They n'ary give me a thought, they was so bent on touchin' one anoth'r. They nev'r seen me atall, me sittin' thair on the porch waitin' with th' gun.

"They got almost t' th' porch 'nd then Fa'th she sees me 'n' she says, 'No, Grady, no, don't,' 'nd runs 'n front of 'm so I cain't shoot him, 'nd he sees me 'n' takes off 'n' I shot at 'm, but he jumps th' fence 'nd was gone. I nev'r did know wheth'r I hit 'm or not.

"I said to her, 'If you think more of 'im than you do me, you go with 'm.' I says, 'Me 'nd you is done, woman, you kin b'lieve that, for hits a fact.' She cried 'n' said it warn't her fault. It wair mine. I was so busy I nev'r paid her no mind. She was lonesome 'nd low with all the work 'n' me nev'r payin' her no mind. She said she was repent'd 'nd I said, all right, I'd give her anoth'r chance. But you know when I took her up to bed she commenc'd cryin' 'n' finally she says she cain't help it, she cain't love me, she'll leave me 't the light, 'n' that's what she done, took some of her thin's in a satchel 'n' went out, 'n' they tell me later she 'n' him met up 'n' went off togeth'r 'n' ain't no one heer'd from 'em since."

In the darkness Lamb struck a match and worked over his corncob pipe. "Dogs, they give back twic't what you give, but people—people don't give nuthin' but sorrow 'nd wrongin'. This woman's a good woman I got now, but Fa'th, she had my feelin's, don't you know, and she jest took all the good givin' part out'n me. You ready to call it a night? Seems to me 'em dogs done all you could expect fer one night. I always did admire a good treein' dog, one didn't git sidetrack'd when he start to run.

"But it's b'ar you interest'd in, ain't it? Then I reckon you got to git over to Perk'ns Holl'w and see old Hobe Perk'ns, ornery as he is. Ain't no other reason to take 'm on 'cept his dogs. He's a powerful miser'ble man, Perk'ns is, like he'd done lock'd up with his money 'nd his god 'nd he don't care nuthin' else comes along. 'Cept his dogs. His dogs is 's religion 'n' that's th' truth, though he'd like to have you think counter-wise. He got the true religion to lean on 'cause that kind of salvation's free. His dogs and his Lord, he's like a two-head'd man. They's kith 'n' kin to him. Ain't got neith'r woman nor blood of his own to share. I always thunk them dogs of h'sn was so keen in the woods 'cause he kept 'em on sech short rations. They was lookin' for *meat.* I'd give you a dog myself, but I don't have one I kin spare. I don't want to leave me short-handed, and Perk'ns, he breeds to trade 'nd sell. I ain't never been able to part company with nuthin' I raised on the place. Hit's a weakness in me, tryin' to hold onto my own thin's. Some thin's you cain't hold onto.

"You git'n early start 'n' don't lag, you be thair by noon. You reck'n on puttin' up here on your way back, you hear? Git a night or two of huntin' in 'n' I'd take it a favor to see what kind of dog you come up with. I always did take to a fair man 'n' that's a fact, be he Yankee or home bred. I'd say you was a mighty fair man," Grady Lamb said to Hart. Mason Raymond he just ignored. He knew Mason Raymond didn't know the difference between can and can't.

Hart wanted to give Auntie Dirk something and he couldn't make out what; he asked Mason Raymond to turn the matter over in his mind; he was educated, he'd been to school, maybe he could come up with something appropriate; but a woman like that, walk up and down all them hills that way to give them some guidin', at her age, she deserved some sort of recognition. Money of course weren't no good. Woman like that'd be unsettled you handed her currency for thanks. But an expression of feeling, that was different. Only Hart couldn't come up with what would be appropriate. His experience with women was limited, especially in the givin' department. He never had no trouble with Mabel, he just kept replacing her wedding ring. She was always slipping it off and it was going astray somewhere. Once or twice a year, at the big holidays, Hart sent away from the catalogue and ordered her a new one. She'd had fifteen or twenty different wedding rings; he never ordered the same one twice. Women liked a change. That way, too, there was an element of surprise in what she knew she was going to get. She knew it would be a gold band, but what kind, that she didn't suspect. The best one had had real hearts and scrolls engraved so deep on it you could make them out real plain, but that hadn't saved it none. She'd only had it two months or so when she lost it manurin'. They'd turned over at least a couple of hundred pounds of old manure and moldy hay and never seen a glint of it. "You ever hunt for a weddin' ring in a manure pile?" Hart asked.

A little later he sat down, chewing on a piece of straw. "Women all like jew'ry," he said.

"Where we going to buy any jewelry around *here?*"

"The way I see it, we could pick off two crows with one firin'—give her some hard currency she could always fall back on and yet give her somethin' kind of pretty she could wear 'round her neck 'nd be proud of. You still got some silver, ain't you?" Hart knew he did, he didn't even wait for the answer. "What I got in mind is this, we take one of them silver pieces of yourn 'nd pierce it 'nd put it on a chain—"

"Where are we going to get a chain?"

"That's where my contribution come in. You give the silver, I give the chain. I wore a chain with a medal on it all my life. Got it when I was confirmed."

"Confirmed?"

"Me and the church had a partin' of ways. Mabel, she weren't one of their elect 'nd didn't choose to join up so they give me the choice, them or her. Weren't a hard choice to make all thin's considered 'nd to tell you the truth I'm pretty sure Whoever's Up There sees it the same way. I know I would. Any rate I kept on wearin' this. Habit. Was the feelin' behind it, not the formalities interested me. But a person shouldn't hug thin's to him. Funny that woman never seen this in those handkerchiefs she lay'd out. She sure saw a lot of the rest though, all that business about travelin' and troubles and changes and all. The cross. You recollect the cross? We had plenty 'a crosses to bear this trip. I tried to recollect her exact words the other day and they done slipped away, but I know she said we was goin' to have a big type of trip, and that much she hit fair and square. You willin' to put up one of them silver pieces?"

"How you goin' to punch a hole in it?"

"We'll drive somethin' through. Grady'll have a device we can make do. Only I wouldn't say too much if I was you about it bein' for one of the Bounty girls. He ain't what I see as a forgivin'-and-forgettin' man."

When they walked up the hill with her, they gave her the medallion as she put out her hand to shake good-bye. She stood with the coin and chain curled in her arthritic old hand, staring down disbelieving. "For me?" she said twice, then turned, shaking her head incredulously. "Old woman like me," she said and hobbled away. Then she stopped and said in a clear, sweet young voice, "I thank you most kin'ly, Mister Hart. And the boy—you don't know what this means to an old lonely woman like me." They could hear her singing, her voice old and crumbled, but happy, as she walked along, fading up into the gold and green of the hill,

> *Once I had a sprig of thyme,*
> *I thought it never would decay*
> *Until a saucy sailor chanced upon my way*
> *And stole from me my bonnie bonnie thyme . . .*

III

Lamb didn't even offer to go part way with them. He and Perk'ns weren't walkin' friends, he said, meaning they wouldn't walk any way to greet one another. But he drew a map in the dust, using a stick to make the three hills they would have to go over, the ridges and the branch in the road by the big spruce where they were to keep to the right, and finally he sketched in the creek they would have to cross, the short cut after the bridge, and Perkins' place up the knoll where, according to Lamb, the best bear and the best bear dogs in the mountains ran. They'd know the place sure, Lamb said, because of all them dogs Perk'ns had and the big cross with the burned-wood sign JESUS SAVES AND DAMNS.

"A cross!" Worth said happily, jabbing Mason Raymond. "That woman was right. There is a cross in our lives."

"Hobe Perk'ns' Jesus done more damnin' than savin'," Lamb said. Then he shook his head, no, they'd never find it on their own and he gave out a call.

"Been holdin' back on us," Hart said as the girl came down the porch steps, swinging a pouch. "Said he had a son, didn't say nuthin' bout no daughter." Lamb apparently thought he had held back a real treat, keeping the girl out of sight in the house with her ma for these two days. Showed how mountain-shut-off Lamb was (he stood on the porch cackling with glee how he'd put one over on them); the girl coming down the path with her chicken-wing arms and turkey-long legs, two bumpy little breasts poking up into her homemade butternut, so hopeless it made Mason Raymond want to laugh, and she didn't even have the sense to know it, nor her father either, cackling away, she swinging her nut-brown hair and smiling up into the sun as if all the world were waiting out there to open up to her. Thirteen or fourteen at the most, Mason Raymond thought disgustedly, a kid. "I'm suppos'd to helpen you over to the Perk'ns place," she said, looking Mason Raymond up and down, measuring him as if he were going to go on sale. Defiant, too, he thought, a regular scrapper. He felt like laughing in her face, she put such a store on herself. Instead he held out his hand, polite, and offered to take her pack. "I can manage the poke," she said with a bob of the head, a quick flash of flying hair. "I don't need no help from nobody."

"Lamb is the livin' end," Hart said and turned ready to start off.

"Don't let on to that Perk'ns you come to pay good money fer nuthin'," Lamb warned, "or you'll be there 'til Kingdom come. He'll git his Jesus to gouge more and more outta y'u. Ain't nuthin' like a religious man fer miserin' money. You come back right off, Della Mae. Don't you hang around none, you come right straight back, you hear?"

She didn't answer, walking, swinging her hair, not even looking back. Lamb said, disgusted. "Cain't do nuthin' with her. Women got no business actin' smart like that. You come *right* back," he shouted after her. "You hear? None of your sass now, none of your sass, you hear?"

The girl was walking fast, she was a good walker—long, straight strides, jumping over rocks and brush almost automatically, and happy, lord she seemed happy to be out in the woods and on her own.

She went first, then Hart. Mason Raymond walked behind Hart. He wanted matters perfectly straight right from the start. He wanted to make absolutely clear he had no interest of any kind in her. But she wasn't paying any attention, only woods-conscious of what was going on around her, stopping once to snap off some sweet birch for them, showing them how to chew on it, the fresh tart taste of wintergreen freshening their mouths, then stopping later to open the "poke" and distribute corn pones dipped in sorghum molasses, Mason Raymond trying not to be too finicky, but he had heard the molasses was extracted and boiled, juice, bees, and all, and then put up.

They ate, at least Hart and the girl did, as they marched along, the girl pausing now and then to point out to Hart evidence of bear—a clawed tree; bare patches in the high, dry grass where a bear had raked out a place to lie down and rest; a little farther on, spore; then a rotten log which had been torn apart in a search for insects and grubs. At the raspberry bushes Hart was particularly attentive. Bear loved berries. But she shook her head. "Too near the house." Mason Raymond looked around, as Hart was doing. There were no houses. Yet over the next rise he saw a board roof and one hewn log wall of a shack, and a little farther on a woman by a spring with a three-legged iron pot, the pot boiling over a fire, the woman down on her hands and knees beating clothes against some rocks. "It's easier to take the wash to the water than the water to the wash," the girl said, hallooing, waving, but walking on, showing as politely as she knew how that she wanted to be friendly but she didn't want to stop.

They got lost late in the morning, must have taken a wrong fork, the girl said. Mason Raymond looked at her sharply. Maybe she meant to take a wrong fork, but she looked back at him forthrightly, shaking her head, puzzled about how she could be so *dumb*. They should start to climb after that short cut at the bridge before they would come out to Perkins Hollow, she said, but this road went straight through flat, scrubby country, the kind good for very little except hunting, certainly not worth planting and of very little use for grazing.

They could see hills to their left, but ahead stretched low, flat, stubby fields.

Hart grunted and stopped. Then he sat down and without

saying anything broke off some tobacco and passed it to Mason Raymond. Mason Raymond took it even though he didn't want it. Chewing would put the girl in her thirteen- (or fourteen-) year-old place. The girl stood, watching. He imagined her impressed though she seemed to be paying very little attention, fiddling with her skirt and twisting a strand of hair in her mouth. Just showed how young she was: girls, babyish girls, were always sucking on a strand of hair.

Hart chewed, silent, looking at the landscape; Mason Raymond knew Hart was trying to make up his mind and he didn't want to push him. The trip had taken away some of his confidence and Hart was going to need a lot of decisions made well to restore it. Now he was chewing on his lip; he kneaded a portion of his tobacco between his fingers, shredding it and then forming it into small balls that he rolled over and over until they formed a tight sphere of black. Yes, he was worried.

"We gone wrong somewhere," he said at last, looking at Mason Raymond and the girl to see their reaction.

Then, before Mason Raymond or the girl had a chance to answer, he shouted, "Git down." The girl dropped immediately, but Mason Raymond could only stand, staring. A roar sounded over Mason Raymond's head. "Scramble," Hart shouted at him, clambering toward rocks and bushes a way off.

Instinct moved Mason Raymond. He found himself without memory of the journey, crouched behind a rock. Another shot ricocheted off a wizened beech directly opposite him. Hart was hollering, shouting his head off. Mason Raymond could count the pauses between shots for reloading; there would be two quick firings, then a pause; in the pause Hart kept hollering they were harmless, leave off the firing and let them explain.

"Like as not it's one of them gangs," the girl said, crouching. "Left over from the war—you know, deserters don't care which side they git from so long as they git."

The afternoon subsided into bird calls, a hot sun, the big, silent beeches. "Don't move," Hart warned even though Mason Raymond had no intention of moving. "I seen the glint of the barrel when whoever it was rais'd it to fire. Good thin' it weren't rainin' and there wasn't no sun to show him up or we'd be goners sure. Moonshiner, mabbee, and we come on his still."

"It's a gang," the girl said. "Probably the Lowries. We're all goin' to be kilt. Don't matter to them who they kill or why," but she seemed totally unfrightened by the idea, as if dying were of no personal consequence to her. Mason Raymond found it impossible to share her indifference; he had a high stake in staying alive. He still had a large part of himself he wanted to explore. On her back, looking up at the blue sky, she seemed to be waiting for the archangel to come to fetch her back to where she had wandered from, as if life were an accident and she had somehow made the wrong crossing and chosen the far side and would have to relinquish her ticket to go on.

She had large, brown eyes, good teeth. She lay so close he could smell the wintergreen. Once she turned her eyes—not her head, just her eyes—and she looked at him; then she went back to concentrating on the sky. In that long look he saw he was wrong about the eyes: they weren't brown at all, but more like yellow—tawny.

Mason Raymond, Hart, the girl all lay, hot, sweating, waiting. "Don't git up," Hart kept repeating nervously. Finally Mason Raymond said irritably, "I'm not going to get up, don't worry."

"I worry, I can't help it, I'm responsible for you." He was testy, which was a good sign. You got Worth Hart's dander up, he was a man dangerous to monkey around with. "If we was home, I'd lay nine to five it was Lite. Trouble with this world, there's Lites everywhere. We's *friends,*" Worth hollered into the hotness, into the stillness.

"They won't believe you," the girl said.

"Friends, man, *friends,*" Hart shouted. "Takes 'em forever to figure out the *whys* and *wherefores* of a situation in these parts. I'm liable to die of thirst while that there feller makes up his mind we don't aim to do him no harm. You got any suggestions?"

"Let's sing," Mason Raymond said.

"Sing?"

"Well, it worked in the swamp. Kind of allayed *our* fears,

maybe it'll calm him some. Singing men don't mean anyone harm. Might even take us for a couple of traveling preachers, you never know."

After a moment Hart said, "What you want to sing? You got somethin' appropriate in mind?"

"What's that one about the valley, the one with the girl leaving the valley?" After a hesitation, Hart sang hoarsely,

"From this valley they say you are goin',"

and Mason Raymond picked up the next line, a little unsure of the words, but putting a lot of enthusiasm into the rendition,

"I shall miss your fair face and bright smile,
But remember the bright Mohawk Valley,
And the girl who loved you true . . ."

they sang together. They got stuck on the next stanza, so they sang the first four lines again, louder, more heartily. The girl didn't sing at all. She lay waiting for the worst. When they finished, they lay still. Then Hart picked up "Onward Christian Soldiers,"

"marching as to war,
with the cross of Je-sus going on be-fore,"

he and Mason Raymond sang; there was power and conviction in their singing, then silence again. "Why don't we try one of those mil-i-tarry songs, the flag-salutin' kind," Hart suggested, "and then we kin all stand up and salute. He can't shoot and salute at the same time."

"Come out 'n' show yourselfs."

"Think we dare it," Hart shouted back, "when you got that there gun?"

"You ain't never gonna git out of this valley alive ifen you don't."

Mason Raymond stood up.

Hart tried to pull him down, but Mason Raymond fought

him off. "Mister," he said, "I ain't got a gun and neither does the man with me. I'm gonna walk—"

"You fool," Hart hissed, "git down!"

"—walk right out in the open so you can see for yourself." He shoved Hart's hands away. Hart grabbed him around the legs. Mason Raymond was floundering, but he kept trying, kicking and telling Hart to *let go.* The whole scene was absurd, absurd and terrifying. He kept waiting for the bullet's impact.

"He's only a boy," Hart was shouting frantically. "Don't shoot, he's only a boy!" He had given up his struggle with Mason Raymond and he had got on his feet himself. "Look at us—jest a boy and an old man, neither one of 'em with a gun. And this here harmless girl." He reached down and yanked her up.

"Walk—closer."

The sun seemed terribly hot; perspiration was pouring forth all over Mason Raymond. Hart was babbling about how his wife had relatives here in this mountain country, the Wald'-rups, he ever heard of the Wald'rups, words tumbling head-over-heels in a race for survival, saying how Auntie Dirk had put them up and how they'd been hunting with Grady Lamb and were on their way to Hobe Perkins'—

"Hobe Perkins? Stop whar y'u ar. Whatcha want to see Hobe Perkins for?" the hidden voice demanded.

"Lamb he told me Perkins got some of the best bear dogs in the county—"

"He got the best b'ar dawg in ANY county."

"I jest hope you're right and we git the chance to—"

"Y'u don't need to hope none. Y'u jest take my word fer 't, and who should know better'n me, Perk'ns?"

"Mr. Hobe?" the girl trilled, but Perkins paid no attention. Mason Raymond had begun to see that with a few exceptions women weren't what you'd call honored in these parts. Wash, work, wean, that was about the sum of it.

"You Perkins? What the hell'nd tarnation you want'nd go shoot at us fer? We come to see your dogs, pay you a sociable call, come a real long ways—all the way from upstate New York, and that's the god's honest truth—and all we had in mind was admirin' them hounds we hear you got, and what do you go and do? You go 'nd shoot at us. You call *that* hospitable?"

"I ain't interest'd in bein' hosp't'ble. I ain't interest'd in people traipsin' ov'r my place. Never knows what strang'rs got in mind, skin you, most of 'em, first chanct they git." Perkins apparently hadn't even seen the girl, just as if she didn't exist. Hart let out his rage. "Don't you see we got Grady Lamb's girl with us? How come you don't notice that?" Hart cried. He went unanswered except for the light, thanking touch of the girl's hand for a moment on his arm.

"Thin's 'as differ'nt afore the war. Man could come and go unmolest'd, trust his neighbors, not have to be on the lookout all 'er time for renegades 'nd looters, barn-burnin' niggers. Nowadays man cain't afford to take nuthin' fer grant'd. Thairs been a war atwixt God and His Commandments 'nd the Devil 'nd his holpers done won and we done lost."

He's one of those Bible-beaters, Mason Raymond thought, taking up his gun in the name of the Lord.

"I kin appreciate the *whys* and *wherefores* of a man bein' nervous nowadays, but to shoot at a man afore you even know where he's from and what he wants appears to me—"

"I didn't aim to hit you."

"Humph," Hart said skeptically and sat down on a rock. "Oh, bother and tarnation, I musta left my tobaccy back there in one of them places we stopt to rest. Mabel's right. They give you bones and muscles to hold you all in one piece. Otherwise people like me'd be discardin' theirselves all over the landscape, wouldn't git halfway through a life whole. You wouldn't have a quid on you, would you?"

"Never touch the filthy stuff. Devil's work, makin' a man addict'd to the evil weed. Revelin' 'nd car'ousin' 'nd chewin' on Satan's plants, poison yer body, black'n yer soul. If God ameant man to smoke, he'd a made it clear there to Adam in the Holy Place. If he'd ameant him to tipple he'd a made a special stream there in Eden for that thair specific purpose and that thair one only."

"Maybe He give him grapes 'n' grain to help 'im exercise his 'magination," Hart suggested.

"Sin 'nd error stamp'd 'im from the start, there in the sacred grove," Perkins said. "Ev'r aft'r it's been sweat of the brow, the temptation of women and drink and poisons of the soul, Satan's lures . . ."

"I'm thirsty, and that's a fact," Hart said. "There a stream, pure or otherwise, 'round here?"

"Down a piece, mebbe half a mile."

"You shoot a man for goin' for water?"

"I told you. I didn't plan to shoot you, jest put some respect en you."

"I'm filled with reverence," Hart said, rising. "Re-ver-ence and de-hy-dra-tion."

Perkins led them into a thicket of tulip, hemlock, chestnuts, enormous golden, crimson, and mauve trees, a great grove of golden beech the color of the girl's eyes. She had drifted back (or Mason Raymond had drifted forward) so that they were walking side by side, following Hart and Perkins through the spruce and pine, the enormous tulips, some beech almost two hundred feet high, eight, nine inches in diameter, a smooth, silent forest of trees that provided, Mason Raymond could see, an ideal spot for hiding. No wonder so many from both sides had taken to these mountains to get in what licks they could. Up home, even at the Academy, he had never paid much attention to what was happening down South, never taken a side on the issue of Restoration or Reconstruction, the problem seeming far away and unrelated to him, as it seemed to almost everyone he knew, at least at the Landing; there were some Radicals in Albany who sided of course with Stevens and Sumner and the rest—most of their names were vague to him —who wanted to make the South pay for its sins. Lite, of course, was one of those who was naturally unwilling to forgive and forget, always talking about getting even, making "them" live to regret the day "they" ever started anything.

"Johnson babyin' 'em," Lite would growl. "He's a Rebel hisself at heart, everybody know that. Carolina-born, Tennessee-brung up. A Southerner at heart, he ain't gonna go agin his own."

He had not thought of Lite really since he and Hart had set

out from the Landing. Did those who deserved them in time receive their just deserts?

It would be comforting to believe so. There were many lies it would be comforting to believe. The world went around with lies. Love, lie lightly in my heart, he thought, I have seen how much harm you can bring.

He looked at the girl kneeling near the water in her mousy homespun butternut. She was wearing that hapless dress because of the time and circumstances of her life; it was a symbol of the aftermath of a war which had devastated her land so badly that it lacked even the old-time barks and leaf dyes to color the linsey cloth and even if these had escaped the gun and grapeshot, there was no time to collect them because there were more basic problems that must be attended to; no indigo to predye the wool before it was spun (hence, he thought suddenly, the old expression "dyed in the wool"), no time— nor energy—to take the pains to cut a pretty dress, to decorate it; only the basics, the most basic of the basics, was there time for, and not always even that; thus this willowy girl bent over the brook scooping up water in her hands looked shapeless and graceless because, outside any control of her own, a war had stomped across her mountains shaking the foundations of those mountain lives, of the people who grew their corn and goobers in the crisscross patches that quilted these blue hills, a war so violent that men, like Perkins, carried a gun, shot first, and asked questions later.

Still she was not, he saw, without pride, nor was she even, perhaps, aware of all the limitations put upon her, standing up suddenly and shaking out her long, tangled, nut-brown hair, looking up matter-of-factly and saying, "Gonna be an awful storm."

With everything else there had been to contend with, including nearly getting shot, Mason Raymond had not noticed; he looked up into a sky boiling with black, elephantine clouds, zebra stripes of light on the green glade by the stream. She was accurate almost to the minute; a violent bolt of lightning sliced through one of the elephants; it broke in two and poured out a roar of rage; rain slid down, red, like blood, first as fine little nails that pierced the earth lightly, then as heavy bolts that broke it in bits and pieces; torrents ran red. Leaves dropped heavily, chunks of earth flew up, branches sagged, split, dropped; lightning poured through the black clouds, electrical charges sundered trees, split canyons, fired the blackness from one second to the next. No more than a minute separated the girl's remark and the whole earth being rent to pieces. Next to him a gigantic band of light dropped, thunder roared, the earth opened up, and the girl next to him fell as if shot while phosphorous lights shot through the rocks in the stream. He could hear nothing. Torrents of natural rage—rain, thunder, lightning, steam, wind, spray—flew up all about him. The bolt that had dropped the girl had deafened and paralyzed him. He stood riveted to the earth, a witness unable to move, unable to cry out. Hart and Perkins were struggling toward the girl but kept being torn back by the force of the gale.

Wind was ripping the whole mountainside apart, lightning igniting fires in three or four canyons ahead. Smoke poured up, black, thick, unstoppable.

Mason Raymond's head was ringing as if someone were striking one clear note inside his skull. He felt no sensation at all; he was all sound, clanging like a bell. The dead girl lay stretched out stiff as stone under a rhododendron dripping rivulets of rain, her hair wet and matted, shrunk all up into spirally ringlets. She looked weightless, and light as death. He felt nothing. Emotion had stopped when his nervous system had jammed—sound only, that's all he was, the ceaseless alarm of a ringing bell.

"We have anger'd Him," Perkins shouted into the wind. He grabbed hold of Mason Raymond and began to shake him. Sound deafened Mason Raymond's brain; he felt himself engulfed in the ceaseless tolling inside his head. He fell forward, Perkins catching him. "Have you anger'd your God?" Perkins cried.

Hasn't everyone? Mason Raymond thought, and then, coming back to himself, the shock subsiding, *Leave him alone, he's just one of those religious cranks you find wherever you go.*

The girl was dead; that was the terrible fact to center on— a few moments before crouched down, lapping up water, shaking out her hair, lifting up her tawny eyes to look at the dark sky. *Never mind God being angry with me,* Mason Raymond wanted to say, *why shouldn't I be angry with Him?*

Hart clasped him close, trying to warm him, or perhaps driven by instinct—what we hold close we give life to—kept clutching him. "I wish to God I'd never set out on this fool trip, that's what I wish—it's pride done me in, that's what it is—wantin' to have somethin' better 'n anyone else."

"Kneel down 'nd pray, Brother. Kneel down 'nd thank God you done seen the light. Kneel down 'nd confess you done disobey'd Him. 'With God all thin's are possible.' Matthew, nineteen, twenty-six." Perkins was bent over the girl, half-blessing her, half-blaspheming. Mason Raymond couldn't sort out what his real attitude was; maybe he didn't know himself.

"If that woman had only give me the true picture of it when she read them handkerchiefs, I'd have never set foot outten the state, I swear to God, I wouldn't. That woman, she *held back.*"

"Pray, Brother, pray, it lies in God's hands."

Hart was of that breed of believers that feel prayer helps, but it's also a good idea to raise up the medical man as well. Right now he was trying his own hand at doctoring, holding Mason Raymond close, literally trying to breathe life back into him, Hart's mouth pressed up close to Mason Raymond's, Hart pumping air into Mason Raymond as if Hart saw his lungs as a giant set of bellows with which to enforce life.

Mason Raymond could breathe all right, he just wasn't moving or speaking. He blinked his eyelids back and forth to let Hart know he was coming out of it. What would they tell the girl's father? You couldn't just walk up to a man and say, I'm sorry, sir, but while we were walking over to Perkins your daughter died of lightning striking amiss.

Kneeling in the rain, Hobe Perkins prayed. "Jesus heals and mends," he said. "O Jesus Christ, only Begotten Son of Christ, have mercy on these miserable sinners. Have mercy. Hear me, Father and Son, and come. This is your faithful servant Harold P. Perkins callin'. Ask and ye shall receive, it is said, and I'm here kneelin' and askin' and waitin' to receive. 'In Thee, O

Lord, do I put my trust; let me never be ashamed: deliver me in thy righteousness.' Psalms, thirty-one, one."

"That kind of familiarity is like to breed contempt," Hart said. "Bring that girl in outta the rain." He was dragging Mason Raymond toward a shelter, a hollowed-out place in the hills that appeared to be a shallow cave, but as they got closer showed a deepening, as if that maw were cut deep into the heart of these smoky hills, a large, black mouth that went down, down, down, into the underworld. The entrance looked like a huge, guarding face, the tumbled masses of stone suggested a mammoth head with bulging eyes, high cheekbones, a long, Cherokee aquiline nose, and that carnivorous mouth waiting to swallow up the unsuspecting, to deliver them (if one took Perkins' admonitions seriously) down into everlasting torment and damnation, sinners in the hands of an angry god.

Hart was hauling and Perkins was hauling and praying. When Hart stretched him out on the floor of the cave, he closed his eyes and just gave way to death. Maybe Perkins was right, maybe he was going to give up the ghost and go under; he didn't even care, death was no longer an enemy. The racket of the rain, the howling of the wind, the reverberations of thunder inside the cave walls, the flashes and strokes of fire— were these not the proper passage into some nether world where he would be free of his troublesome body and its need to become hairy and sexual and filled with still stranger and stronger demands? He hadn't even got used to the old problems, how could he deal with the new ones burgeoning within him? Not just abandon the body—though God knew that would be a relief—but relinquish forever the terrible dilemmas that pestered him day and night, reminding him time and again he was not someone who could either count on himself or be at ease inside his own kind of casing.

He wondered if Lite had ever paid his uncle the hundred dollars he owed him. *There* was a parable for you.

"Oh, son, you do love me, don't you, baby, you'll never know how much I care for you." She leaned across the polished table and grasped his hands in hers so harshly he was filled with pain. She did not hear

his cry, too immersed in her own emotions, eyes swimming in tears, mouth trembling in its contrite act of confession. "You're all I've got. Pappa's gone—if only he had lived," she cried of her grandfather, "it would have made all the difference, he'd have seen you got what was right, you were named after him, he loved you, and I was his favorite, I was," she insisted, though Mason Raymond had not said she wasn't. "'Ardis,' he'd say, 'the others may be prettier or sweeter or more disciplined, but there's not one of them stronger. Be strong, it's the most important thing.'

"But he was wrong. I'm not strong, I never was. He wanted me to be strong, so that's how he saw me; but it wasn't really so, he was only trying to wish it so."

Gratitude filled Mason Raymond as she released his hands; he slid slowly away from her so that she couldn't get hold of him again. He could take listening to her, but he wasn't going to bear being grabbed and squeezed like that.

But she had forgotten him, drifting away from him, living a moment years before, a young girl deferring to her grandfather because she adored him and because he was all she really had. Her own father had "declined" and had been taken South somewhere (perhaps near here) for a nerve cure that never took. He did not come back, a relief, she had once confessed to Mason Raymond, because he was "peculiar" and a harassment to them all, someone who had been a burden and death had unburdened them all of him—as simple as that. Blood bonds did not necessitate love. She had respected Old Mason Mowatt Raymond and hence loved him. That had nothing to do with blood; it had to do with being protected and coddled and cared for.

But her love for him was of different substance. She certainly did not respect him (nobody did), and yet there was no denying she was in an excess of passion, leaning across the beautifully polished table, imploring, "Promise me you'll always be with me—"

An easy promise to keep since she had left him first. Apparently he was now returning. Death, then, was a returning. There was his father (holding in his hands a coiled sash). "You'll see, boy," his father said. "You'll see it all one day." His father was dressed to go out. The first thing Mason Raymond did was look at his feet. He had his shoes and socks on, and he was smiling—affably—his mouth one long, open slit of teeth, smiling and happy, just the way he'd seemed that night when he'd put his napkin down on the table and allowed

*as how he would be spending the holidays with them at the Landing;
and for that reason Mason Raymond didn't trust him. He had
learned that handsome, smiling men often meant him harm. Like Lite,
Mason Raymond thought, as alike as two peas in a pod. He looked
at his father and his father looked back at him, and then after a
moment his eyes left Mason Raymond's, he stared at the ground.*

*And there in the background (fuzzy, difficult to distinguish) stood
his great-grandfather, old Mason Mowatt Raymond, and—raising
up his head, perking up his ears, unable to believe his good fortune,
the dog. Hector sprang up and bounded toward him. Mason Raymond
dropped to his knees and engulfed the dog.*

*Hector smelled of woodchuck, of the wet floor of the forest, of a hazed
sun, and possibly of swamp. Mason Raymond clung to the dog; that's
where his love had gone, to a dog. "Why'd you have to get killed,
Hector?" and the dog lapped at him with his wet tongue, trying to
tell him; but whatever message he had to give about the inner workings
of the universe was lost as Mason Raymond struggled to hold onto,
to understand, and the dog, and Hector wiggled and squirmed—that
damn dog wanted to play at a time like this. Here I am going down,
dying, Mason Raymond thought, and all he's got on his mind is a
game of catch. "Listen—" But the dog was gone, they had all disappeared, he was all alone in the muggy swamp, standing all alone
looking out over the desolate swamp.*

*Maybe there was some kind of sorting out that had to take place
—you were ferried up or down (which direction you went told you
what was in store)—and you were assigned a circle, something like
that—you didn't, Mason Raymond supposed, just come and go at
will. At any rate, he wouldn't be going alone. There was the girl.
She'd been hit, too.*

Where was the girl?

She was lying next to him, her eyes open, her body rigid.
Hart had wrapped her in his own coat, and he was trying to
talk her back to the belief she was still alive and going to stay
that way. He kept encouraging her to relax, lie still, not fight
for life but just let it come; and she kept staring back at him
with wide, terrified eyes, struggling to do something with her
inert bones, but they had been through too much, they refused
to respond.

"You wasn't struck direct," Hart kept telling her. "You 'n' him was jest within range, that's what done the damage, but it weren't no direct hit."

Mason Raymond moved first his fingers, then his toes. They responded, not much, but enough to show him he wasn't really paralyzed; mauled a lot by that electrical charge, but not done in permanently. He started to close his eyes and rest, then remembered that vivid vision where he'd gone down into the depths; dreaming couldn't hurt you, could it? He forced his eyes open. His mother and father were dead, but he was alive, looking at Hart bending over the girl saying, "You jest rest yourself easylike, we ain't goin' noplace, not in this rain." Mason Raymond couldn't raise his head, but he was alive; he could hear—it was blowing up a terrible storm out there.

"You reckon you could stir up a fire?" Hart asked Perkins, who—though grumbling—reckoned he could. Mason Raymond could see the top of Perkins moving about, gathering up rocks to make a backing for the fire so that it would throw heat. "Have to go out in all that damp to git any wood," Perkins said. Everything in the cave seemed unreal, Perkins a shadow of himself and the world outside shadowy and far away. "Out in all that anger," Perkins said.

"Mind you don't git struck," Hart told him.

"I ain't aimin' to git hit. I got my righteousness set straight a long time ago, I ain't one of those hard sinners takes sinnin' so serious he cain't see the light. Lord don't punish them what walk in His ways. 'I am not ashamed of the gospel of Christ: for it is the power of God unto salvation . . .' Romans, one, sixteen." Pause. "But then I wasn't aimin' on nuthin' like this this mornin' neither. Cher'ty Bounty—all them Bounty girls —bring a man peck of bad luck. Ungodly. O Lord, when thou mark iniquities, Lord, who can stand?" He paused in the mouth of the cave. "Comin' down daggers 'nd spikes, the Lord rainin' down His righteousness."

"I'm goin' to try 'nd git her to breathe right," Hart said, and Mason Raymond had a vague notion of him bending over, talking about it was that or let her die, but he was jest as glad Mabel wasn't around to see him pressin' his mouth agin a young girl's, and then he heard Hart breathing in and out that exaggerated way, heaving his breath in and out of the girl, *huh* huh, *huh* huh, *huh* huh . . .

He heard a low moan and a cry—Hart's jubilation—and then a sobbing and a strange retching sound; Hart saying, "Oh God, she throwed up," and Mason Raymond thought, I'm so tired, I can't keep my eyes open, but I can't close them either because if I do—yet the next thing he knew shadows were dancing up and down on the wall of the cave, flames from the fire leaping up, then dying down, and Perkins had taken his hands and was clasping them in his bony fingers, leaning over him demanding, "Pray, boy, pray for deliverance. God gives and God takes away." The firelight flickering on the wall of the cave, Hart and Perkins, all unreal, but the girl lying beside him (both of them wrapped in Hart's coat for warmth) was real, and he jerked his hands free from Perkins, Perkins leaning so close to him Mason Raymond could smell his breath, the same fruity odor his mother's mouth used to give off, thinking, He's sick, too, maybe got the same thing she had, while Perkins prayed fervently, his raspy voice calling on the Lord to come and fell every mortal man with light, Mason Raymond inching next to the girl and taking her hand in one of his, it was cold and malleable, but underneath that limpness he sensed life; and she murmured as he touched her and she shifted slightly toward him, seeking out warmth, sighing in her dreams, Mason Raymond listening to the God-driven man over him praying and lamenting, thinking,

You don't know nuthin' about life and death, Old Man.

In the night he woke and the girl was on one side of him, Hart on the other, their bodies close; Hart knew enough to crowd flesh to flesh to give them all heat; for a moment Mason Raymond thought Perkins must be on the other side of the girl, and his heart tumbled and gave a sharp, hard pain; then he thought, No, Perkins wouldn't let himself be tempted and tormented in such a way, he was probably lying on the damp cave floor, cold and alone, bound up in his own inflexible righteousness.

There was also a clearing in his head. He was very conscious of the fact that he was next to the girl and very, very conscious of liking the warmth she gave off, but Hart gave warmth as well; there was something more to it—in their linked hands, for instance, and the soft sounds that came from her mouth. He turned his head slowly and looked at her, hair dried long and heavy, lying over one cheek, the tawny eyes closed away from him, the long, slender cheeks pale but creamy, the mouth partially open, having difficulty with breathing.

She made small, snuffing, animal sounds. Her body moved first in, then out, occasionally a deep protest against something he would never know catching her breast and heaving it up, pained, in conflict with that inner world. Once her hand fluttered in his, and he gripped harder, trying to reassure her. He knew what it was like going down into that underworld.

He could lie like that all night, reassuring her in her sleep, the fire dancing on the dark cave walls, the groans of Hart abusing his arthritic bones on the hard earth floor, Perkins gurgling and snorting in some dark, personal, God-induced corner of his own, the girl and he really apart from everyone and everything, their hands linked in both conscious and unconscious worlds, reaching out over the chasm of knowing and withholding to touch.

She opened her eyes, all yellow in the reflection of the fire. Questions rose, unasked, on her lips, which were trembling with sound. Her hand opened in his, then closed. She watched, unblinking, while he looked back at her. Nothing moved but their hands, opening and closing against one another. Mason Raymond's heart beat so violently his whole chest heaved with the effort; he was light-headed with the exertion just to keep breathing, he thought he couldn't bear one more moment the bitter, wondrous throbbing inside his lungs. He wanted to say her name, but he couldn't remember it. He saw that she was trying to say something to him, too, her lips moving, but nothing formed there that seemed close to sound, just those small gasps and truncated sighs, and her hand moving in his, her hand moving back and forth, back and forth in his.

"Lord God, Creator, Preserver, and Ruler of the Universe and all the Nations of the Earth, lead us forth to safety and the resolution to follow Thy ways. *How long will You stand aside?*" Perkins demanded. The three of them looked up from where they were crouched by the fire, not sure which one of them Perkins meant was standing aside.

Hart had been out in the gray morning rain looking for food. He had come back with a squirrel, which he had gutted, skinned, and spit. He was rotating the scrawny body slowly over the fire, worrying about the stick maybe not being green enough and burning through and dropping their meat in the fire. The girl was propped up against a rock, Hart's woods coat around her. She was turning his coonskin cap over and over in her hands. She had not spoken at all, but her eyes went first to Hart, then to Mason Raymond, then back to Hart, as if trying to ascertain from their eyes if she was safe.

"Animal meat," Perkins said, gesturing toward them, "comes from God alone and man has no right to snatch it from Him."

"This girl needs food 'nd so do we," Hart said gruffly.

"You shot 'nd kill'd one of God's creatures."

"You hunt, you shoot, you kill, what you jawin' about?"

"You didn't give no blessin' first."

"Mabbee I shot 'nd bless'd at the same time. How you know what goes on in my head?"

"The Lord knows. 'Ye are my friends, if ye do whatsoever I command you.' John, fifteen, fourteen."

"Well, you aimin' to eat or ain't you? This is one skinny squirrel, but it's better'n nuthin'."

Perkins didn't answer. When the time comes to eat, he'll eat, Mason Raymond thought. The girl's continuous yellow-eyed watching unnerved him. She was wary of him. Did she know the change in feeling for her that had come over him? Her eyes said, You're goin' to do me some harm, and his said, No, I'm not. Yes, yes, you are. She searched his eyes trying to find out why he was changed and how he might hurt her. He tried to look open and honest and trustworthy. Her hands never stopped turning over that crazy coonskin cap.

Maybe some key to him was here in this cave, in the firelight, the sizzling fat running off the squirrel into the fire, in that crazy cap turning in the girl-whose-name-he'd-forgotten's hands, in her yellow eyes and long, dark lashes, in the tremendous flood of feeling suffocating him.

Hart turned the squirrel rhythmically, talking more to it than to the three of them. "Git myself a dog and Mabel a couple of fancy pullets and *go home*—if I ever see home agin."

"I got dawgs, good dawgs, up to my way," Perkins insisted. "Best in these he'ar mountains, but I ain't partin' with them to no man don't hold fast to the Bible."

"Show him your skull, boy," Hart said.

Mason Raymond looked away from the girl.

"Show him that ridge on your skull," Hart insisted. "Here, you, Perkins, you git up and run yer hand over his head, don't make him bend down none, he's shaky enough as it is; you jest git up and feel that ridge he's got there."

Perkins' bony hands traveled over the scar tissue twice— once, hastily; the second time, exploring. "Now, come here 'nd feel this," Hart said.

"They's both alike," Perkins said wonderingly. "As alike as two babies spit out of the same womb."

"That's a sign," Hart said, "a spiritual sign. You don't want to go agin no spiritual signs."

"How you know that ain't devil's work, how you know that?"

"Because," Hart said triumphantly, "it ain't no base place, it's the head, and the devil can't touch the head or heart. He has to put *his* signs on feet and back or some hidden place like that. This here sign is God-given, meanin' me and him is linked, and you know what we're link'd by? We're link'd by sufferin', that's what we're link'd by. And what is sufferin'? Sufferin's part of the Passion, that's what it is, so these is God-given signs. How long *you* gonna stand aside?"

"Cleanse my heart and lips, O Lord," Perkins prayed. "You'll git you a dog," he promised Hart. "Make us to grow in love, He said."

"I'm much obliged to you," Hart said, lifting the squirrel out of the fire and bringing it up close to his eyes to examine it. "Blood still runnin' in the joints. Ten, fifteen more minutes.

I'm so hungry I could eat a horse 'nd chase the driver. Seems to me all I been on this trip is hungry. Reckon Mabel's up home settin' one of her bilers on the fire right this minute 'nd cursin' and flayin' me for runnin' off and leavin' her with all the chores. That woman sure has put up with a lot off me all these years."

Mason Raymond sat nearer the girl, not close enough to scare her, but close enough so that he felt within range of the invisible limits of her world, on the rim of that unseen circle everyone draws as a protective territory against the unknown.

She shuffled uneasily, watching Mason Raymond with widening eyes. Needed eggs and cream and biscuits running with butter, no meat on her at all. Their worlds were so different, what could he say to her?

"Grub's on," Hart shouted. "Here, you, Perkins, let them have first druthers—here, boy, give this to the girl. Mind you don't burn yourself, it's strong from the fire."

Mason Raymond tossed the leg joint back and forth between his two hands, blowing on his fingers. When it had cooled, he held it out to her. "She's too weak to hold it," Mason Raymond said helplessly.

Hart and Perkins, mouths greasy and hands stained, stopped chewing for a moment, staring. "I'll feed her," Mason Raymond said quickly, "and then eat."

He tore a small piece of hot flesh from the bone, blew on it, and held it up to her mouth. Her head wobbled forward. He moved closer, within the magic, private, territorial circle, and waited while her head flopped back against the rock. Very carefully he inserted the meat between her lips. Her teeth were apart; he could feel her tongue wrapping around his fingers licking at the meat. She was sucking on the meat, she was sucking on his fingers. "Chew," he said.

Her head went faintly back and forth. "You can't chew?"

A faint movement of the head, this time forward. She couldn't chew. Mason Raymond took his thumb and forefinger and grasped the meat inside her mouth, gently taking it out. He began to shred it. Her eyes never left his; he was shredding blindly, looking into the yellow flames reflected in her eyes, and she was watching him, wary, for any movement that might alert her to harm. "No one's going to hurt you," he said, then held up one of the thin slivers of meat and put it against her closed lips. Her lips parted, her tongue darted out; he put the meat in her mouth, her lips brushed his fingers, taking it in.

He took another shred of meat and held it to her lips. How beautiful you are, he told her with his eyes.

IV

Two days later they stumbled out of the cave into ground fog and a drizzle, earth running blood-red everywhere. Newly formed narrow rivulets were bleeding out of the ground; there was no knowing how much water had fallen, but an awful lot, and it was falling still, running red everywhere they looked. Perkins, standing in the mouth of the cave, was red to the ankle already. Beads of what looked like blood stood out on his pants; even his face had red drops all over it. Mason Raymond was weak, but sure he could make it a mile or two, which Perkins said was all it was to his place; but he was worried about the girl, who could scarcely stumble forward. He wanted to prop her up but he was embarrassed, standing watching her lurch about while Hart, all elbows and thumbs, tried to give her a hand. They're going to go down, Mason Raymond thought. He took hold of her arm —and he was worse than Hart in his clumsiness; she fell against him and grabbed hold, clinging to him, her head buried in his chest. Either he'd grown or she'd shrunk in the last two days, she was so small and weak, all fluttery like a frightened bird. He didn't know what to do with his arms; he was afraid to hold her. He held them outspread, and she sank against him, slipping down. There was nothing else to do but hold her up. He ordered his arms to come around her, and she lay within that embrace crushed and helpless. Yet he could feel the beating of her heart. "She ain't gonna make it," Hart said. "Take her back inside."

They lowered her against the same rock that had propped her up for the last two days. She melted over and around it, fluttering her hands. "She's plumb tucker'd out," Perkins said. "Cain't drag her nowhere weak as she is, it ain't human."

"Well, we can't jest leave her here neither, helpless as she is. Oh Gawd," Hart cried, "I'm never goin' anywhere agin if I kin jest git back up home." He knelt in front of the girl, surveying her. "She needs help and she can't make it 'nd we can't leave her here alone, and that's about the sum of it. I'll be thunder'd if I know what to do."

"You could leave us both here," Mason Raymond said. "I could tend the fire and look after her. It'll only be a couple of hours and you could get help or bring a horse to get her back."

"Schoolin'll do it ever' time," Hart said, slapping his thigh.

"We cain't leave them two out here alone," Perkins said. "They's man 'nd wom'n, conceiv'd 'nd made in sin."

"Oh, for Gawd's sake," Hart interrupted, exasperated. "It's broad daylight, we're not goin' to leave them overnight."

"Devil makes as many sins at noon as midnight."

"You got an evil mind," Hart said, "and that's the size of it. I *know* this boy. He ain't gonna do nuthin' wrong."

"Cain't trust NO man, all of 'em conceiv'd in sin, come forth in evil, spend their earthly days committin' it. He ain't no different from the rest."

"Well, I wouldn't molest no young, sick girl if I was left to look after her and neither, I hope, would you, and he ain't gonna neither."

"I will take no re-spon-si-bil-ity."

"It's her Pa I gotta answer to and I ain't got no qualms at all about takin' the re-spon-si-bil-ity. Man ain't *born* bad, he grows that way. You don't trust nobody, the way you see human nature, all bitters and gall."

The two men stood looking at the girl. "You ain't afraid, is you, girl?"

She looked at Hart. Mason Raymond's whole life hung in the balance. Her head moved: no, she wasn't afraid. But her eyes looked afraid.

"We'll git you some more wood afore we go 'nd stir up a brisk fire, no need you wearin' yourself out and gittin' wetted through in this rain, Ray. We gotta wet ourselves, but we'll be movin' and keepin' warmed; but you're gonna be still sittin' here waitin'. Gonna be cold all right, that temperature's been fallin'. I'll leave the coat—" He sounded uncertain though; the weather had turned awfully cold.

"You keep it, Hart. We'll be warm enough. We're protected here. We get a good, strong fire going, we'll be all right, don't you worry any."

"It won't be for long," Hart said, but he still sounded uncertain.

"We'll be all right, don't you worry. Really. It's good and sheltered in here and there's lots of wood already, you get a little more, we'll make out fine. Like you say, you aren't going to be gone that long."

Hart put on his coonskin hat. The girl had relinquished it with great reluctance, but after all it was his hat. He smiled, toothless, down on her. "It's my good luck cap," he said. She closed her eyes. "Jest exhausted," Hart said. "Poor thin'. Well, we'll git the wood 'nd git goin'. Sooner we go, sooner we'll be back."

Mason Raymond looked at the girl. She was paler than she had been since she'd suddenly dropped to the ground and lain as if dead. "She's jest wrung out," Hart said pityingly as he brought the first load of wood and stood a moment, dripping red rain, watching Mason Raymond feed the fire. "You sure learn'd a lot these last months. Wouldn't even know you was the same boy—you ain't for a fact, neither the same nor no boy. Grow'd almost man-size, you have."

"Well, we've seen a lot." He had thought he could never look into a fire without that one remembrance of Plato Guy being burned alive, but now he knew that there would be two memories that would fire-flood his consciousness, one good, one bad: the black man burned and blistered and the girl gazing up at him with yellow eyes.

"A good part of what we been through I couldda done without. We're 'bout ready to git away. You sure you're gonna be all right? That girl looks plumb took. She oughtta have a coat."

"I'll make a good fire. Don't worry, Hart."

"I can't help it, I'm responsible, I worry. I was born to worry 'nd that's the long and short of it." At the mouth of the cave, just as he was ready to leave, he said, "One of these days, I'm gonna have the pleasure of knowin' you're the one's responsible. Won't that be a turn of events though? As alike as two from the pod, he said, and there's some truth in it at that." Then he was gone, dissolved into rain and fog, gone as cleanly as if he'd never been there at all, neither he nor Perkins, just Mason Raymond and the girl and the fire there in the cave, with the rain beating down outside and the earth running red and here inside the red flames of the fire, the yellow flames in the girl's eyes.

He had built up a good, strong fire and he was warm, but he was crouched next to the heat, feeding sticks and branches into the flames. She was a little distance away and it worried him that she might not be getting enough heat, that she'd take a chill and—he moved back and he got cold right away. "You're too far from the fire."

She looked at him.

He couldn't move that big rock she was lying against, and she couldn't lie on the bare floor. He had his coat and she had a sweater, but both of these were lightweight and hardly large enough to make a good, comfortable bed. "I'm going out and get some more wood."

She didn't answer.

He stood in the mouth of the cave gazing out into the rain, looking at dripping trees, base-line scrub, a heavy canebrake, the refuge of animals driven from places where men had moved in and stripped the wildness of its protective covering, panthers, wildcats, bear, wolves. Great beeches dripped the red, coppered rain. He'd be soaked through in a matter of minutes, but there was no alternative. He plunged out, rain pelting him; it was raining harder than he'd thought, coming down in buckets, a real deluge. He darted back to the entrance of the cave and shucked his jacket. No use getting it soaked. The cold got him right away, and he ran, trying to work up body heat, rain and cold hitting him like blows. He felt weak, sick. I will not faint, he told himself.

There was a big pine with fine, heavy, low branches just ahead. In the cave, making his plan, he hadn't considered how he was going to cut through thick branches. He'd just thought he'd twist and pull; he hadn't realized how big these branches were, how thick their wood. I can't yank these off with my hands, he thought, and ran on, searching. He ran in a straight line, never deviating to right or left. It wouldn't do to get lost. He *couldn't* get lost. He couldn't leave the girl there in the cave, so weak she wouldn't even be able all by herself to keep the fire going. And she'd get scared. He'd better not run too far even in a straight line. He might think he was going in a straight line, but he might have gotten off it without realizing it. He knew a thing or two about how easy it was to get lost. He stopped, turning back to look for the cave.

The forest had swallowed him up. All he could see were big, dripping trees, the tangle of the canebrake. *I can't get lost,* he told himself. Up ahead he had spied a pine he thought would be about the right, manageable size. He stood, shivering, debating. Finally he said, To hell with it, and turned and ran again.

The pine was medium size. One tree in a thousand: one with the will to survive, the runt of a litter of gigantic pines all around that had managed somehow to soak up enough water and light to pull through while weaker ones all around dried up, shriveled, and died. Just like it survived for me, Mason Raymond thought.

He ripped the two lowest branches off easily, two good-sized limbs that had thick needles; they would make fine covering. But the higher branches didn't come away as easily. He pulled and yanked and twisted, but he couldn't work them all the way free. He got them half-twisted through so that they hung down, but couldn't break them off. He stood, panting, dizzy, then bent over and spit up squirrel. His stomach knotted and he felt a spasm in his bowels. He let down his pants fast and the explosion came. When it was over, he lay down on the wet red ground and just let his body heave. Fireworks were exploding behind his eyes. He had fallen forward on the pine branches and they scratched, but he was too weak and woozy to move. He was drenched, and cold, and sick sick sick.

The girl was back in the cave, alone; the fire needed wood; he felt numb with the wet and cold. If he didn't move soon, maybe he never would be able to get up. He sat up, feeling as if he were whirling around and around. He tried to stop himself and couldn't. The world was falling away all around him. Bile came up from his stomach and he spit it out. His pants were still down. He tried to bend over and pull them up and the vertigo was so intense he fell forward on his knees, vomiting. *You've got to get up.* He leaned back against the pine and blanked out for a minute. Sitting up that way, he'd thought maybe he could work his pants up easier than if he had to bend over and he struggled with them, hitching them a little ways, resting, then working them up a little farther. Hart was right: if he ever got back to the Landing, he was never going to venture out again, the world was crazy. But that wasn't true either; it was as if he was born to go out toward the magic names, the canyons and creeks and arroyos and plains that existed so strongly in his mind that he had made a map of the western country inside his head.

He got to his feet, fumbling with his buckle. He had the shakes and his stomach was threatening another upheaval, but he put both hands on one of the half-severed pine branches and pushed, swinging back and forth; he heard a crackling sound, but the limb didn't come away. He swung again, there was a snap and the branch hung loosely by one long, sinewy cord. He twisted and turned, stopped and spit up, twisted once more, and rested. He wanted to scream and shout and curse and cry in the awful, engulfing frustration he felt, but all he had the strength to do was lean weakly against the tree and pound it with his fists. Then even that effort was too much. He just closed his eyes and rested, shivering, nauseated, defeated, dying of thirst. He would have given an entire month of years of his life for his mother's fancy canteen. But that came from another world, a long way away.

After a time he roused himself and worked at the limb again. "You son of a bitch," Mason Raymond said through clenched teeth and took both hands and yanked with all the wobbly strength he had left; the limb hung on mockingly. "Goddam son-of-a-bitch-no-good-limb," he said and took a few steps back and ran, enraged, and grabbed the branch and swung out. The limb snapped free and he crashed down, banging his elbow. He couldn't have cared less; the son of a bitch was free.

When he staggered back into the cave, dragging the three tree branches, he must have been a sight. The girl started up, sitting bolt upright and staring at him with her mouth open. She even said something, but he couldn't make out what it was. He flopped down in front of the few dying ashes of the fire. The cave was an underworld of icy blasts and he was worn out and now he had to try and build the fire back up enough so that he could get dried out, get back enough strength to fix up a place for the girl. Her face looked troubled; not against him but for him; she could see how bad off he was. "Your name—what did you say your name was?" Faintly he heard her whisper. "Della—Della Mae." *Della Mae?* What kind of name was that? Just hopeless. Everything was hopeless. How did he keep getting himself in predicaments like this? His cousin John would never have been in a fix like this. His cousin John would have taken control right away and *managed* things. He shoved himself up and began fussing with the fire. Hours seemed to pass. Why wasn't Hart back? It'd be just like Hart to get himself lost or in a fight with that religious maniac or something; the whole world was out to get him.

A little lick and spit of flame began to rise and fall; it didn't give off any real heat to speak of, and real heat, a good, roaring fire, was what they needed. He fed the finicky flame slowly, painstakingly, encouraging it to take hold. He was so chilled that his teeth made an awful knocking noise in the big cave. The girl started to move, very slowly, toward him. He was too done in to argue with her; anyway she needed the fire as much as —maybe more than—he did. By the time she crept close to him, he was shaking so violently he couldn't manage his hands; most of the sticks weren't going in the fire and it had died down, was threatening to go out. She began teasing it up again, leaning against him (or was he leaning against her?) and pushing wood on. "The pine's for covering," he said weakly. "For us." He was terrified that after all his work she might throw it on the fire. He let his teeth go a little while and then clamped down on them and said, right through his teeth, "We put my coat down and your sweater, and dry those branches and put them over us, we'll be warm."

He was soaked and if she got close to him, she'd be drenched, too.

Time passed—a lot of it, he supposed, since he had no concept of minutes or hours any more, just warmth and cold; he had been freezing and now he was a little warmer so time —a lot of it—must have passed. He felt better, his head clearer, his stomach less queasy, so that meant he'd been using time to recuperate. Hart should be back. Why wasn't Hart back? The girl was lying beside him, that's why he was warmer. She was curled up, nestled into him, her eyes closed, her breath regular, in and out, even, and he was afraid to move and wake her, afraid not to move and in his stiffness alert her even in her sleep that he was awake and solid as stone, frightened out of his wits to be this close to something so different —my God, why didn't Hart come?

He didn't want to get mixed up with some mountain girl with one of those foolish double names all these Southerners seemed to give their girls. Supposing she woke up and felt the fire all over him and recognized the whole melting inside him. And yet the feel of her was wonderful, the light touch of her wonderful, wonderful; he was filled with the ache of his wonder.

She had gone suddenly very still, as stone still as he was. He held himself tight and jammed his eyes closed, feigning unconsciousness. He tried not to breathe, but the air built up inside him and threatened to blow him up. He gasped and opened his eyes. Her eyes were wide open, eyes yellow like

] *315* [

that bobcat who'd spied him picking berries and whose un-flinching stare had looked at him and seen right into the heart of him (but that bobcat had been wrong, the woods hadn't got him, the cave was getting him, where had that been in that lunatic woman's handkerchiefs?). Her eyes were warning, I'm going to get you. Then an instant later he saw nothing but fear. Maybe he'd only imagined that confidence because she was so frightened that her whole face began to pucker up. He was scared half out of his wits; how come *she* looked scared? Her eyes were terror-wide, her hands fluttering.

They fluttered toward him and he went from being hot all over down into the depths of ice. Her hands had brushed against his; he didn't understand; those hands were almost seeking. He took hold of them with his mouth trembling near hers; and then her eyes closed, and he closed his. "You care for me?" she asked against his mouth.

The first time he didn't think he heard her right. After all, who was he to know anything about caring; but then she asked again, her voice very clear and precise, both their eyes opened, hers beginning to fill with tears, and he wanted to curse and push her away; but he couldn't, he saw her eyes all filled with tears, he couldn't bear the pain and doubt in them. He put up one hand and cupped it around her head, drawing her head down on his chest. "Yes," he said, "I care." Maybe this hot, flushed anxiety was caring. Whatever it was re-sponded to (came from?) her because as she moved even closer, he felt such a flame run up over him that he was afraid he would be burnt out by that inner fire. He would know then what the black man had felt.

She looked at him, her eyes swimming in happiness. She'd hold him like this for the rest of his life and even as he thought, Oh God, he was moving his mouth up to hers and she was touching him and murmuring, and, oh God, he was going to be a man, he couldn't help himself.

They were sleeping (thank God, clothed) when Hart stamped into the cave. "Goddam man fell down on me and hurt his goddam leg—here, what's goin' on here?" Mason

Raymond sat up, brushing sleep out of his eyes. The fire was nearly dead. "It's all right, Hart, we're just trying to keep warm." It's all your fault, he wanted to say. You should have got here earlier. "Where you been?"

"Goddam man," Hart squatted, automatically starting to build up the fire, "fell down and hurt his goddam leg, had to lug him more 'n a mile 'nd then see to his missus who was cryin' and carryin' on like the world was comin' to an end. This has been the goldarnest trip any man ever went out on. What I want to tell you is that when I see that woman, I'm goin' to tell her to pack up her hankies and put them away for good; she ain't seen nuthin' like what we been through. How could he go and bust up his leg?" he demanded. "Here, girl, drink some of this." He handed her a clay jar. She lifted it and drank.

"You've lost your glasses."

Hart looked down at the broken bailing twine dangling around his neck. "If that ain't the absolute, livin' end. One of these days there ain't gonna be nuthin' more left to lose. You drink some of that, too, boy. Make you perk right up."

The girl gave Mason Raymond the jar without looking at him. He was afraid he might touch her. How could they be so shy of each other when only a short time before—well, he didn't understand much else, why should he be expected to understand that? Only one thing he would have been willing to bet on, this wasn't going to be one of those cases of live and let live.

He took a big swig and felt the flush rise in his temples, the fire flare up inside. He moved a little closer to the fire, holding onto the jug. Deferentially, the girl hung back. Before she'dda fought me for her part of the fire, she was such a scrapper, and now it's like she's giving it up willingly, it's her gift to me, to show she cares. Women are always giving, and that giving is always a bad sign for a man. He handed the jar back to her.

"Tripp'd over a goddam root and hurt his goddam leg and I told him to git his goddam god to fix it and he told me to take my goddam tongue 'nd pluck it out because it offend'd Him. His old woman's worse than he is. The two of 'em are plannin' to pray in the Second Comin' and be the only ones on the Reception Committee. What a man has to go through in this world to humble hisself."

The girl gave Mason Raymond the jug back and he finished it. Hart had the fire going briskly and he was taking another poke of corn juice out of his jacket. He drank first. Mason Raymond didn't blame him. "That leg ain't broke, jest dented up some. You don't look so spruce yourself," he said to Mason Raymond. "She looks better'n you do."

"I got numbed getting in these pine coverings. It turned bitter cold."

"I got a horse tied up outside," Hart said. "It ain't more than a mile or two, but it was one long haul cartin' that Jesus man." He grinned. "Someone gits all fir'd up with the word of God, puffs hisself up with sech a load of pride in his own salvation he jest weighs others down. It's one of those queer philosophical turns," Hart confessed, "that are so hard for a man to understand, like how most of the good seem so dry 'nd dull and most of the damn'd so sprightly an' in-ter-estin'. You ready to raise up, girl, and go on?"

"I guess so," she said meekly. Mason Raymond wished she'd stop that submissiveness. Hart was going to suspect something was wrong if she kept on acting so unnatural. She had started the trip so independent, sassing her pa and all, and now she was mild and meek as a docile wife. How could I ever explain, Mason Raymond wondered. I didn't intend any wrong, I never meant to touch her, something just happened, something over which I didn't have any control. I didn't want to touch her, but I couldn't stop myself. Why didn't you get back when you should have? None of this would have happened if you'd come when you should have.

Hart said they could take turns riding the horse. "We're goin' down to Perkins' and beat him out of a dog," he said to Mason Raymond, "and then we're skedaddlin' for home jest as quick as we can. I had enough of this travelin'. Don't let me forget some of them pullet eggs for Mabel, though. Pack 'em in meal and put 'em in a box and tote 'em back and they'll hatch right out, no trouble atall. She'd take to some of these fancy roosters run around here."

Going through all these trials and tribulations, he'd *earned* hisself a dog, Hart said, but God knew whether he was going to get one or not. "What you waitin' fer?" he asked the girl.

She ducked her head and darted behind, trailing them. "What's come over her?" he asked Mason Raymond. "Women is always doin' somethin' mystifyin'." He was shaking his head as they went out into the rain, which fell in a steady, moody way, as if the sky were sullen and mad about something and wanted to show its rebellion. "Gonna wash the world away, or at least that's what that Perkins's predictin'. Probably down there buildin' hisself an ark. Won't git no animals to go aboard with him though, too rackety. You ride first," he said to the girl.

She wouldn't do it. She didn't argue, just moved back and shook her head, stubborn, no, she wasn't going to get up on the horse, and bit her lip and stood, pouting, in the rain, driving Hart to despair. "If these ain't the beatin'est people," he raged. But he couldn't budge her resistance.

Mason Raymond told him to calm down; he'd talk to the girl and see what could be done. Hart took the horse off a piece and stood in the rain sulking. Mason Raymond went up to the girl to try to persuade her to ride, but before he could say a word, she burst out crying and said, "You don't care none for me atall!"

"Please," Mason Raymond pleaded, "don't carry on so, he'll hear you."

"I don't care if he does. I don't care about anythin'. Why should I after what's happened?"

"Nothing bad has happened," he began.

"Nuthin' bad? Is that your idea of nuthin' bad? Yes, yes, it is," she said passionately. "That's exactly your idea of 'nuthin' bad,' you're like all of them damn Yankees, no good through 'nd through, ain't only damn Yankees, all men, they only think about raisin' a girl's skirts and—" She began to sob in a horrible, hearing way; Hart was staring at her apprehensively and Mason Raymond was half out of his mind trying to calm her. "I didn't mean it the way you're taking it. Maybe I didn't put it right—"

"Oh yes, yes, you did. You put it jest right for the way you feel. It wasn't nuthin' to you."

"It was, too. It was a lot. You know that."

"No, no, I don't."

They were standing in the rain gazing at one another and her eyes were melting and his anger was, too; they stood looking at one another, and Mason Raymond could feel the tension and excitement starting inside him and beginning to gather momentum when Hart shouted, "You two goin' to stand there jawin' in the rain all day?"

"Please ride on the horse."

"You want me to? You really want me to?"

She walked along beside him, obedient, going up to the horse and climbing on. Hart grunted and then looked at Mason Raymond. Whatever made me think I could put anything over on him, Mason Raymond wondered. He's a hundred times smarter about human nature than I'll ever be.

Mason Raymond was weak, but the liquor had given him some strength and more courage and when, after a half mile on Hart said it was his turn to ride, Mason Raymond said no, he felt fine, leave the girl on. They went wetly on. Twenty minutes later the girl said they were going the wrong way, they should take the other fork. She got down, her hair dripping, and stood in the rain, pointing, explaining. Hart said all right, they'd go her way. She wanted Mason Raymond to ride and he didn't want to, and she and Mason Raymond stood there in the rain discussing the matter while Hart went crazy. Finally, in deference to Hart's sanity, she got back up on the horse; when they came in sight of the house, they saw the cross and heard the fiddling. The horse pulled up short and stood between Mason Raymond and Hart, his ears pricked forward, listening.

"They're dancin' in there," Hart said in disbelief.

The pounding of feet, steady and happy, beat time with the fiddle. Occasionally voices could be heard. "Singin' 'nd dancin'," Hart said as if such a thing were beyond his ability to conceive. "I drag a man a mile through the rain with a bung'd up leg 'nd he takes to singin' 'nd dancin'?"

The horse began to jog on, almost in time to the music.

"Wild'st thin' I ever hear tell of, a man dancin' with one bum leg."

"You don't know he's dancing," Mason Raymond said.

"It's a service," the girl said. "They do a lot of singin' 'nd dancin' 'long with the prayin' when Preacher Perkins gits goin'."

"Whole country's goin' foolish," Hart said. "All start'd with that crazy icebox Seward put out all that good money for. Seven million dollars for ice 'nd snow. Whole country's infected, it's in the air. Look at them two—what's their names —even tried to corner the gold. Done all them widders 'nd orph'ns in."

"Fisk and Gould," Mason Raymond said.

"I do love singin' 'nd dancin'," the girl said wistfully. "Ain't been much 'round here what with the war 'nd all. We was took bad early in the fightin' 'nd it don't seem to me thin's has gone anyways but down ever since."

"Singin' and dancin'—I don't think I can take much more," Hart said. "I been through so much already." He stopped, hauling the horse up, looking at the house. "Still he promised me a dog and a God-abidin' man like that ain't likely to go back on his word. Ain't Christian—and I can quote Scripture good as him to prove the point."

Drenched, bone-weary, hearing the twanging of tambourines and the shouts of the God-driven, they went on. A mighty saving was going on. The echos of *Amens* crowded the corners of the cabin. Hart shouted, but no one inside could hear while the rafters were being raised in holiness.

He went up to the window and peered in, motioning Mason Raymond to come have a look. People were down on their knees flailing their arms about; children were running up and down singing and shouting and praising. Perkins was bellowing over flutes and penny whistles and tambourines to let Jesus in, He was knocking at the door, Perkins said, and a woman, standing on a chair imploring the sinners to be born again, saw their heads and began hollering, "He's done come! Glory Halleluh! He's done come!" A tall, lanky man stood stark still, eyes glazed, still as a statue while in a circle around him men and women beat time with their hands, chanting, "Let the

Lord *speak,* let the Lord *speak,* let the Lord speak *in strange tongues."*

Mason Raymond banged on the door.

There was a moment of silence, then a mighty shout. "He done come!" Perkins screamed. Mason Raymond could hear chairs overturning, women and children shrieking, men braying that the Judgment Day was on them, form the lines, form the lines.

It's going to be a mighty let-down, Mason Raymond thought, when they see it's only me and Hart and a half-dead girl. No room at the inn, he thought.

Behind Perkins people pushed and shoved; the noise was like a volcano going off. Mason Raymond just stood there. He couldn't think of anything to say. There wasn't much that needed to be said anyway; neither he nor the girl nor Hart was surely the Lord, and that they could see for themselves, and sometimes saying you were sorry was just adding insult to injury.

"He saves them that asks," Perkins cried, clasping Mason Raymond to him, crying against Mason Raymond's cheek, " 'He that hear'th my word, and believ'th on him that sent me, hath everlastin' life, . . .' John, five, twenty-four."

Perkins hobbled out to the barn with them even though there were forty or fifty others who could have shown them a spot in which to bed down. It turned out Perkins wasn't so much interested in their comfort as in their miraculous signs. He made Hart and Mason Raymond bend over so that the faithful could crowd about and run their hands over the scar tissue. Mason Raymond was too tired to do more than endure, but Hart seemed to enjoy all the attention: he kept helping people's hands find the right path down his skull. A couple of semi-sensible women had stopped hallelujah-ing and had dragged off the horse and taken the girl under cover. Mason Raymond was glad to have her taken away from him and then again he wasn't; his feelings about her were all mixed up, but he was absolutely clear about how he felt about Hart: it was all Hart's fault, every single bit of it. He was the one who wanted the dog, he was the one who had been gone so long, he was the one who had got them to come on this crazy trip in the first place. But he couldn't go up to Hart and say, That girl is going to make trouble for me, and it's all your fault.

He kept straightening up and looking around for the girl, and people kept shoving him and imploring him to let them have a feel of his head. He sat down, closing his eyes, letting those strange hands massage his scalp. He wondered if he could get some of the Saved to say a little prayer for the burned black man.

"You feeling better?"

She was lying on a mat covered by an old, ragged quilt, the stuffing coming out of three or four long, jagged tears; and her eyes weren't yellow, they had darkened into a deep, velvety brown.

He knelt down beside her, not knowing what to say or do. "You want me to stay?"

Hart was going through how the hired hand went into the woodshed and saw the hoe and just took it into his head to hit Hart and one woman said, "Lord Almighty," and Hart stopped, waiting for the drama of the spectacle to take hold. In the pause Mason Raymond said, "I'm going to move our gear over by the girl," and didn't wait for Hart to agree or protest; he really wasn't interested, Mason Raymond saw, he had gone on with the boy walking out of the shed and up to the porch steps where he was painting and the boy took the hoe and hit him over the head.

Mason Raymond got two lumpy corncob sacks and lugged them over to the end of the barn where the girl lay. The women on either side of her kept sneaking glances her way, but they weren't unfriendly, just stand-offish. He put a sack of shucks on either side of her and started smoothing them down and she watched as he covered these with hay. He made a big fuss about putting plenty of straw over both places. There weren't enough quilts to go around; at least no one had offered him one. Most of the people apparently had a kind of sleeping sack they brought with them, as if they met and sang and prayed often enough to make it worthwhile to carry their own bedding. She was sick enough, he understood, to be special. Someone had given up his bedding for her.

He got her some water in a dipper and she drank a little, and then she went to sleep. He stood looking at her a long time wondering what he was going to do with her. He couldn't take her back and he couldn't leave her, either.

In one corner a man was tuning a banjo; he was bent over the instrument, tenderly plucking first one string, then another, tightening tuning pegs at the end of the neck, strumming a chord, working with the tuning. He was a big, strong man, twenty, twenty-five, with thick black hair and when he raised his face he had blue, blue eyes (a handsome, well-made man); he looked just the way Mason Raymond would have liked to look, handsome and strong and sure of himself; and when he turned to look at a girl sitting on a bale of hay near him, his look was steady and sure, he wasn't embarrassed to stare into a woman's eyes. He began to run his hand over the instrument. Music, slow and moody and full of desire, flowed from his fingers. He was telling that girl on the bale of hay that he wanted her, and he wouldn't have to go through any of the confusion of words, he could let the music—the music and his eyes—do the wooing. The girl knew it, he knew it, it was all planned. The man would play and sing for her, and then they would get up and wander out into the dewy night and the man would embrace her and hold her next to him, and the woman would move her head back and forth against his cheek because she was happy to be in his arms. Maybe that was the only true time men and women were happy with one another, when they were in one another's arms; all the rest of the time it was strain and not knowing what to say or saying the wrong thing, or just messing everything up one way or another because most of the time one person was in one mood and another was in an entirely different one, and there was no way to communicate; but that man playing his banjo knew all this from past experience and he wasn't going to let the shortcomings of talking hold him back; he took up his instrument and it was like some kind of spell because as he started to sing, low and sensual, a song full of implication, it was as if Mason Raymond had been transported back in time to another room and another man and woman.

Thyme, it is a precious thing,
Thyme brings all things to your mind,

the man sang and the woman looked back at him, and as Mason Raymond moved toward them, listening, looking, the man sang,

And it's thyme bring all things to an end.

The woman was smiling, she knew what the man was really saying to her and she had taken the message in and looked at it—not very hard, she had already made up her mind—and her smile said, Yes, yes, it's all right, and he went on singing,

Once I had a sprig of thyme,
I thought it never would decay . . .

And he was smiling, plucking his banjo, running his hands automatically over the strings with such subtlety and surety that Mason Raymond marveled, and looking at the woman, he already knew what was ahead, he was smiling in anticipation, maybe—probably—savoring the anticipation because, as someone (was it Hart?) had said, The chase is always better than the kill—smiling and singing,

This sailor he gave to me a rose,
A rose that never would decay,
He gave it to me to keep me well reminded
Of the night he stole my bonnie thyme away.

Thyme, it is a precious thing,
Thyme calls all things to your mind,
Thyme and all its labors along with all its joys
And it's thyme brings all things to an end . . .

People had begun to hum, to stand up and watch the scene in front of them, as if they wanted to witness the ritual of love, that moment of recognition that suddenly flashes between two people when they know what it means to be in a new world,

] *325* [

one which contains only yearnings and hopes and imaginings and fantasies of one another. He will go out and hold her, Mason Raymond thought, and they will be close and care. "You care for me?" "Yes, I care."

How could that be? He didn't know. Maybe the strength of their feeling—strong feelings, even the wrong ones, had meaning. The strength was what mattered. People did what they swore they wouldn't do, Mason Raymond knew. And something in him swelled and went bleak; he was tender again for the girl, the tenderness coming from the music, from seeing the look that woman gave the dark-haired, blue-eyed man, and he wanted them to love forever even though he knew that this moment was doomed, was passing even as it happened and would never come back, these two would never again re-experience that instant when the man looked at her and sang,

> *Thyme, it is a precious thing,*
> *Thyme brings all things to your mind . . .*

If their eyes promised everything and their hands had lives of their own with which to reach out and touch, and if they were no longer themselves, but a part of each other, it was also equally true that while Mason Raymond envied them, he was giving thanks to be free of such commitment, for his mind told him what his heart refused to believe, words that had come from his mother when she was in the Landing one day and saw a young boy and girl swinging hands together down the street, oblivious to all else save each other, and she had stopped and watched a moment, shaking her head in pity, and then she had said very slowly and clearly, "I hate to see it begin because I know how it ends."

He had cared, yes, but, not the way the eyes of that man, putting his banjo aside and rising, coming toward the girl, said he cared; he had only cared with a part of himself that belonged to hunger and thirst and the very strong desire to be free; to live as one wanted to live, alone, not tied to another human being because he didn't want to be engulfed by an emotion that swept away all reason, that would have turned

him back to the girl lying on the pallet and bade him bend
down and hold her to him and say, I want to take you back
with me. What was in him was the sudden, strong urge to go
forth and see and be free and wander to where the magic
names were, out there far over the mountains where the new
land began, one of long hard plains and a thick blue sky and
canyons of gold and hard-grained men riding the prairies.
Maybe that was what he was supposed to learn in his initiation
into life this year of his growing, that his place wasn't here at
all but somewhere over the mountains out West where he
could retrieve some substance of self that the East would never
yield up. Finding himself was not—at least now—in a girl, and
that was the meaning of what that other young man, leading
his girl toward the starlight and darkness, believed his essence
to be at this moment: finding himself in love for a woman.

I hate to see it begin, Mason Raymond thought, because I
know how it ends. Maybe that's the center of feeling for
someone: to forget how it ends, to believe that kind of end
exists only for others and that you and yours are freed from
the law, that you two only will go free and be the ones who
will end as they began, still caring for one another, still being
somehow blind with the force of fantasy. It'll never, never
happen to me, he thought. There's something inside that will
always say to me, I hate to see it begin because I know how
it ends.

And yet he knew how it was that Auntie Dirk decades ago
could have looked up and fallen in love instantly with a young
man who walked through a door and how it was that this man
and woman, shut off now from everyone else, could believe
themselves blessed; he was just sure it would never happen to
him.

He lay down and pushed straw over him. The hay scratched
and tickled him; he felt prickly all over. He thought of his big
feather bed at home with its fine linen sheets, its big, plump
pillow. The girl didn't belong in that bed, but why should she
be lying on straw on a barn floor? Come to get a dog and bring
back a mountain girl. He could just picture Lite smiling that
square smile of his and his cousin John lounging back and

looking her over; that kind of inspection she could not pass. All right, he thought, angry, words *are* important—maybe the most important thing there is. It's words keep her (looking at the girl) and me apart. Maybe some people (that dark-haired, blue-eyed man bound outside in the dark to his woman) can do without them; maybe a long time ago, when things first got going here, you didn't need to be able to put things in words, all you had to do was clear and plow and work and subdue the land; but those times are over and the time for not needing to know how to say things is passed, too; now words can be everything, everything.

Not everything, the voice inside contradicted him, some, but not everything. Just remember that: to make it halfway between two worlds, halfway between the books and the land. Can I do it? he asked the voice, it seems such a lot, to be able to balance both, but the voice wouldn't answer him. Maybe it didn't know.

He scratched and turned, wiggling, trying to get comfortable. Damn hay.

He was still and miserable and he couldn't get to sleep for all the light. The lanterns were all flickering high (keep away from sin, he thought, sin is for the dark; God is love, he wanted to cry out to them, and then he said to himself, What do *you* know about that?) and he got up and wandered back and forth, trying to put himself at ease. He felt so uncomfortable being Mason Raymond Buttes, a boy who'd taken a girl and now only wanted to get rid of her, and she was sick and all, it wasn't right. He knew it wasn't right, but he couldn't make his feelings change simply by knowing what he ought to do; all he wanted to do was what he felt like doing, and that wasn't being responsible for a girl with two mountain names. She looked spent (Hart's word). Thinking of Hart he knew that Hart would never have tried to get free; he would have owned up to "what was right" (whatever that was. You know, you know, the voice told him. And the voice was right, he did know) and he tried to make himself feel better by pointing out that Hart was a different kind of person, *he* wasn't Hart, he was someone else. Words, he said to the inner conscience, trying to pacify it, offering it up *words* as a rationale for not behaving the way he should. What he meant was that he had the right because of his schooling to go scot free where others would have felt the necessity to pay a price, is that what he meant? Oh, come on, he told himself in disgust.

He ought to do something for her. He wandered around looking for a rag. He had an idea he would find one hanging (the way towels and wash cloths hung on the rack in his room next to the pitcher of water and matching basin); finally he had sense enough to borrow a scrap of cloth from a woman tending a fussy baby. He took it to a trough of water and wrung it out, looking over to the spot where the man had picked up the guitar and started to play and the girl had sat on the hay watching him. Their places were vacant. He thought of them under the stars. He hoped they were still out, away from everyone, happy—he wanted them to be happy, he wanted that terribly.

The girl was quiet as he sponged her face. Something in her had broken, the girl part of her maybe just as the boy part of him was gone. Her eyes were sad, filled with loss. She was too adult to cry, but that's what she wanted to do, he could see. Well, so did he.

How had he gotten them into such a mess? By growing up, that's how. Why in the world had he ever wanted to grow up? He hadn't known what growing up entailed—stupid, stupid—and now he couldn't go back, it was too late. And he'd made it so that she couldn't go back either.

"I'm sorry," he said.

He wished she'd quit that goddam nodding. Yes yes yes, her nodding head said, and meant nothing. Nothing meant anything any more if they couldn't go back to before that one long, lost embrace, and they couldn't go back.

She took her hands out from under the quilt and held them out to him. He washed them off.

Hart came over, eyeing the performance. He had tact enough not to open his mouth. Then he started nodding. "Oh, for God's sake," Mason Raymond said irritably.

Hart lay down and turned away. Straw was sticking out of his hair. His whole body shook. Laughing. He's laughing, goddam him.

"I wanna go home," the girl said. "I git home, I'm never gonna leave agin."

He moved the quilt up around her neck and got up and took the borrowed cloth back. The man and girl were standing at the door, just standing there looking at one another, not talking, they didn't need to talk, just standing there staring into one another's eyes, and Mason Raymond wanted to rage at them, You'll see, just wait, you'll see.

He passed an old couple sitting on a bale of hay; the man was reading from a Bible, and the woman was nodding (everyone was nodding, it was the year to nod, apparently). They looked up and stared at the stranger (damn Yankee intruder) and Mason Raymond tried to smile. They looked away. Down the aisle the woman who had lent him the rag took the cloth and he tried to thank her. He might have been black the way she glanced at him and then turned down the corners of her mouth, shrugging. Could these people see into him? Could they see all the bad things that were going on and had gone on and they didn't want anything to do with him? Maybe it was the war. He would like to think that. It would be better to have people hate you because you were a no-good Northern Yankee son of a bitch than because you were just a plain no-good son of a bitch.

He went to the door of the barn and slunk out into the dark night, glancing up at Perkins' house where a light burned in the window and above that the cross stood high in the moon. He'd have to make some commitment; he knew that and rebelled against the knowledge, but he faced the judgment of that inner voice that couldn't be buffaloed. It *knew*.

All right, he told it, all right, I'll do what's right.

He went back and sat down beside the girl. She was sleeping; he'd have to wait until morning.

She was sitting up when he awoke; steam rose from the thick mug held up to her face; her lashes trembled as she lowered her eyes and blew into the cup. Inside his head his mother gave him explicit instructions about *never* blowing on anything to cool it. "It's not *polite*," she said in her northern accent.

"Your friend, he went up to see Preacher Perkins about them dogs he's so keen on."

Now as well as never. He banged away at the straw that clung to his clothes.

"You guilt-feelin', ain't you, about what happen'd? And you reckon'd on—" she faltered. "You do, don't you?"

"Do what?"

"Reckon on tryin' to make it right? I cain't go North with no Yankee. My people'd never forgive me doin' a thin' like that. They could git over some thin's but never that. You ain't one of us. You—" She didn't seem to know who he was. Who did?

He wondered if her eyes could go back to their original color if—if, as she was now saying—"nuthin' took." Finally he got himself in hand and said, "What if it—"

Tears came suddenly into her dark eyes and she blinked them back angrily. "Nuthin' jest cain't happen. I cain't have somethin' like that happen, I jest cain't."

"You can't know now and it wouldn't be fair to leave before you know."

"I don't want nuthin' to happen because if it did—"

She looked sullen and detached, a person determined not to let bad things happen to her. The angle of her shoulders said, I will not let bad things happen to me. You could not argue with that kind of irrational faith. He just wished he had her belief. "We got ways of doin'," she said. "Ways of our own."

In his misery he turned away. She's had to learn to be hard in order to survive, he told himself, and only half believed it. He didn't want to believe a thirteen, fourteen-year-old girl could be so manipulated by the world around her that she could put on a face like the one she now had. "We ain't *dumb* jest 'cause we mountain born," she said.

"Nobody said you were dumb."

"You don't have to say it, you thinkin' it. You don't fool me none. You got that look says, 'I'm better'n you,' and you believe it. Well, you ain't no better'n me, I don't care what you think."

Well, at least she was getting back to normal, scrapping again.

"Because," she said, her eyes flashing, "you ain't so smart, let me tell you, you ain't got so much to brag about, there ain't a man in these mountains couldn't best you beddin'. Little peanut thin' on you ain't even worth mentionin'."

He backed away from her, shamed and humiliated, raging inside himself. He would like to have hit her, right across the mouth, right across the mouth that had spit out those words —he was right after all, it was words could do you in—hit right across that outraged mouth screaming at him, "Little bitty tool like that ain't nuthin' to feel high 'nd mighty over, ain't no bigger than my little finger, and so green it don't even know what it's made for—"

He hoped he never saw her again in his whole life, but he knew he wouldn't be able to blot out her words, ever. Is there any goddam thing I do right? he asked himself, stamping down to the barn, furious, red-mad with rage. It's this goddam place, he thought, these goddam people, burning Negroes, sending a pack of people out to run praying and screaming around like this: Hart was right, it was the living end.

He stood, stamping in the doorway, like a horse penned up in a stall. Hart was marching perky and proud across the rain-red earth. Goddam bloody earth. Burn niggers. Turn little girls into bad-mouthed old women. Raise up a bunch of religious nuts. Peanut-sized.

"He's parting with a prince, boy, a prince of a dog."

"I don't care if I ever see another goddam dog as long as I live," Mason Raymond said.

Hart's mouth dropped open. What else in the world was there except great dogs, princely dogs, dogs that went down like Argos in myth and legend, dogs that outlived men in the annals of mountains and valleys where men and animals became a part of one another? What did Mason Raymond mean, he never wanted to see another dog as long as he lived? He was sick—mountain fever, sure as anything, fevered right out of his mind so bad he didn't know what he was saying.

Hart grabbed hold of him. "We gotta git you back home quick," he said. "You ain't yourself. But I ain't goin' no place 'til I git you a dog. That's what we come for, son, a dog for you and a dog for me—and a couple of fine young pullet eggs for Mabel."

"I tell you, I don't want a dog, I don't want anything except for everyone to shut up and just leave me alone."

Light dawned, and with light, knowledge. Hart began to cluck, running his tongue against his teeth and making a disparaging sound. He understood, his nodding head indicated, he understood only too well.

"And stop that goddam nodding," Mason Raymond raged. "Stop that goddam nodding and clucking and just leave me alone."

"You been baptized," Hart said sadly. "I was hopin' it could be postponed, but sooner or later we all got to git initiated. I was jest kind of hopin' that with you it could be postponed a while."

"Nothing's ever postponed," Mason Raymond said, "so long as it's bad."

V

They had to ride back in the post and produce car because the dog couldn't ride in a regular car. South and North had strict rules about their railroads. That was a comfort. It reinforced Mason Raymond's newly won view that you can't say people are all basically good or all basically bad, that one place threw out good and another bad. There's a mix-up all the time goin' on, Hart would say. All right, North or South, you had to ride in back—certain regulations, it seemed, covered everyone, regardless of geography.

There was no question of Mason Raymond and Hart riding up in front and the dog, in a crate, put in back. Hart wasn't going to pen his good dog up in a crate, and he wasn't going to be separated from the dog either. The dog's name, according to Perkins, was Singalong Stonewall, and Hart was aghast at the idea of a dog with a name like that. What would happen if you, he asked, was to git yourself out in the woods and have to call him. Who was goin' to run around shouting Here Singalong Stonewall, here Singalong? Disgust made him self-righteous. I don't care what *you* call the dog, Perkins had said, I'm jest tellin' you the name we give him. How's come you give him such an o'nery name? Hart wanted to know, and—swelling with assurance—Perkins had answered: We like to elevate all we come in contact with. It is the way of The Word.

Tramping away from Perkins' place, Hart was still worked up about what to do with the dog's name. Finally he stopped in the midst of the woods and said, "What was the name of that man who stood at the bridge?" He was staring ahead at a little wooden crossover that spanned a brook. It took Mason Raymond a moment to realize Hart meant Horatio. He was going to call this dog Horatio, Hart said, because he was sure to be a stander-at-bridges.

After the first leg of the trip, Hart had shortened the name to Ray-shi, and by the time they got to New York Hart and the dog had almost blended into one single unit; they marched confidently through the station, the dog's head up, the ruff of fur round his neck flared out in anticipation of danger, a low growl in his throat to warn off interlopers. Hart seemed to fear nothing, striding confidently beside his great dog through the parting crowds, up to porters to ask for information, even ordering food in a restaurant where, he confided to Mason Raymond, let them give him any sass and he'd sick the dog on them.

Mason Raymond had bought Hart a gun, a real beauty of a gun in New York. "My sweet Winchester," Hart called it and handled it like it was a woman, gentle and reverent with it and a little in awe of the beauty and craftsmanship. "God Hisself couldn'ta made no better," Hart said blasphemously, cradling his gun against his bosom.

All along the trip—which to Mason Raymond seemed even longer and more exhausting than the one down, though mercifully they were spared some of the incidents that had punctuated that journey—Hart enjoyed himself extravagantly. Mason Raymond doubted he even felt the bumps and jolts; he was too busy nattering with the postal sorter, sharing bread and thick slices of sausage with the dog, laughing fit to kill over old, mealy jokes. He wove elaborate stories around their epic journey, recounting how he and "this boy" (Mason Raymond was furious, his pride was struck a bitter blow, being called a boy and after all he'd been through at that, "this boy" indeed) had gone through a mighty store of trouble to fetch this here dog, stand up Ray-shi and let the man see what a real Plott hound looks like. The big brindle stretched and turned fierce eyes up to the praise. He understood every word Hart said and even, Mason Raymond concluded, inspired a few of his own. They were an impossible study in pride, that man and dog, and they preened and puffed before each other in a way that made his heart sick. He would be so consumed with disgust that he would march off to the rear of the rackety car and sit humped up in indignation, thinking to himself, I swear to God, I don't know how I can stand them both one more minute. And that dog has got fleas.

Of course Hart vehemently denied such a thing. His dog would never have such a mundane disturbance as fleas. So the dog sat and thumped and humped himself up and occasionally yelped and Hart ignored his misery because he was too proud to admit that even the mighty have lice.

The walk out of the mountains to Waynesville had been bad enough (who wanted to remember he was possessed of a green, unready tool with which to make his way in the world?), Hart yammering the whole cussed way about how great *his* dog was until, in a fit of rage, Mason Raymond exploded, "He's not *your* dog. Perkins raised that dog and you wouldn't even have him now if it wasn't for the fact we both got knocked over the head and got the same kind of scars."

Hurt, Hart banged along nursing his bruised pride. If Mason Raymond wanted to act that way, let him, his silence said. A *man* overlooked such childish behavior. Hart even took out his store teeth and reset them to delineate the difference between them.

From Waynesville to Asheville, Hart sat in the back of the cart with his dog, studiously avoiding Mason Raymond. Let him sulk, Mason Raymond thought, he did it coming down, why not going back? Anyway, what do I care? But the truth was he cared a great deal. He knew Hart didn't understand why he hadn't got himself a dog. "I kin talk that Perkins feller out of two," Hart had argued, "and then we'll have real prime stock up there to home. You git yourself a female bitch dog and I'll have this first-rate pup and we'll raise ourselves the best danged dogs anybody ever seen. What do you mean you 'can't take the responsibility'? What responsibility is there to having a dog?'' Hart just couldn't grasp the idea that Mason Raymond wasn't going back to the Landing and stay put. ''You might go away? You been away. You kin see fer yourself there ain't nuthin' but trouble in travelin'. Don't do nuthin' good fer a man; all the benefits is negative. You git yourself a good female bitch dog and you and me be the envy of the whole county.''

Not to want to be the envy of the county was beyond Hart's comprehension. ''What do you want to be then?'' he demanded and (naturally) Mason Raymond didn't know; he sat benched in on himself, the cart jolting by the burned barns and ruined bridges, the tumbled-in farms and the abandoned plantations, and put the question to himself; he put it again and again up for grabs between Asheville and the Landing, turning it over this way and that to see what he might find on the underside. His problem was that he couldn't take one answer alone as a solution to his dilemma. He wanted to go and he wanted to stay. And in going he wanted to go half a dozen places and in staying he wanted to try out half a dozen lives. But he had to settle somewhere, light on one answer; he couldn't flit from life to life, trying first one and then another until at last he wandered luckily onto one that suited him to a T.

Hart was one kind of person and he was another, but it was even more complex than that. Hart hadn't really had much chance for choice; he had been born into a time that demanded certain things of him and he had given those back. But times had changed and with those changes people were altered, too—something else was asked of them than had been asked of Worth Hart or Guthrie Buttes, or even Old Odder Buttes.

There was no longer any need for Odder Butteses at the Landing—and if one appeared, he would be out of his time; he would be a misfit now. Men had to be weighers as well as doers.

Hart's ideas were the ideas of another time, another country —but the times and the country had changed and something new was expected of Mason Raymond. He stared out at all the long brick factories they passed in the cities and even the smaller villages; the war had speeded up the machining. Soon they would be in Albany, Schenectady, Ft. Edward (Ft. Ed'der), home; Hart doesn't see all the alterations (for that perhaps he is lucky), but I do, Mason Raymond thought. There's the me that's wanting to go back to the Landing and live there, fit in—no, I could never fit in, I know that already —and there's the me that wants to stay in Albany, go back to Morphis and the schoolrooms, the books; but that me is gone, too, left behind somewhere months ago; the trouble is that I don't know what I want to do with all those selves inside me that are pushing to be let out and given a chance to explore the world and find themselves.

I'm not John Buttes, I'm not Hart; I'm not my uncle or even my father; there are many kinds of trees on which to swing (if I just knew their names, he thought sardonically).

"How about Mrs. Merriweather—you want to pay her a little visit and report on how well the trip went?" Hart looked at him, frowning. After a moment he said, "After what we been through compared to what she told us we was goin' to git, it kind of strains your faith in future-readers, don't it?" Hart lugged his gear into a pile by a post where the dog was tied up and sat down on it, cradling the box with the meal-packed eggs carefully in his lap. They were waiting for Rivers, and Mason Raymond was beginning to worry maybe something serious had held him up, but Hart's faith in life (now that he had his dog) was complete; a moment before he'd told Mason Raymond to stop fidgeting and enjoy the nice weather, it was prob'ly the last nice, really good day they'd see in quite a spell. It was Hart's terrible, complacent pride in himself and in his possession of the dog that was so offensive to Mason Raymond and had prompted him to begin badgering Hart— first with that business about Mrs. Merriweather and her hand-kerchiefs and now with an observation that there was no doubt about it, the dog had fleas. Ray-shi was thumping and scratching in a fit of irritation and it seemed to Mason Raymond there was no way (as Hart had been doing all trip) to deny the dog was infested. Hart even now wouldn't admit something so commonplace on his great dog. Pride again.

Mason Raymond turned and gazed down-road wishing Rivers would get the hell here; it seemed to him he had been away forever, though in truth maybe two months, a little more in all—but he and Hart had been so close all that time that they were beginning to wear out their affection for one another in minor irritations. And he didn't want that to happen. He was ashamed of having baited Hart the way he had.

Home. He turned the word over in his mind. Maybe. Maybe the Landing was home, but it didn't feel like home. Certainly the place down in Albany (which was giving so much trouble getting sold) wasn't home. I've got enough money to do almost anything I want and my trouble is that I don't know what I want to do. Too many choices, he thought.

He remembered suddenly the cold-rimmed morning Rivers had rushed the feeding of the horses and how his mother had laughed instead of being angry; he thought of Rivers as he hopped up behind the horses and inside his mind he saw the great, plumy puffs of breath rising mistily as the horses snorted and threw their heads. Not quite a year ago. He thumbed through his memories looking for one of the boy who stood in the new snow all bundled up in that greatcoat, and Mason Raymond could not put his hands on a proper image, the right feeling, that would give him back that self he had been that day. He was totally (or so he imagined) another person.

This life is a matter of changing places. He remembered that now, too, probably because just a moment before he had been teasing Hart about the handkerchief-reading and the memory of that reading had brought back to him Mrs. Merriweather and her kitchen. For months he had forgotten about that handsome *(well-made)* fortune teller, and now in a moment she was filling his mind, he could actually picture her bent over the table studying the ashes scattered on the white linen; he could hear her say, *Some people destroy so that others may build.* And because his mind saw handkerchiefs, his mind also saw Rivers: Rivers was forever linked inside his head with his mother's handkerchief.

Rivers would never have to leave the Landing, even when

he was old and work worn-out. Mason Raymond made that promise to himself. I must write some kind of legal thing, he thought, in case anything happens. "Do you suppose he's ever coming?" Mason Raymond asked irritably and Hart said companionably, "Set down and rest your bones. It's a fine day to wait. Ain't many days you're let jest set in the sun. Take advantage of it, boy. Be happy when you kin."

Rivers was drunk.

He stumbled down off the buggy and grabbed Mason Raymond. "Mr. Mason, sir," he burbled, squeezing Mason Raymond and spraying him with alcoholic fumes. "Oh, sir, I'm so glad you come back." He clung, a threat to both their stability, and he looked like a terminal case, bloated, scarred, stupified with drink. Mason Raymond unwound him and Rivers lurched left, staggering, half falling, righting himself, and giving what explanation he could: "Slight in-dis-po-sition." He sank down on the luggage and covered his face with his scarred hand; strangled sobs filtered through his fingers.

Hart was nonplussed, all his bravado wiped out in the face of such a fit. Mason Raymond seized Rivers and hoisted him to his feet. They swayed together like young lovers. Rivers stank of old wine, new booze, and the sour-sweet odor of apples. He must have been down cellar and into the hard cider. He wept unabashed, clearly beyond any appeal to pull himself together and "straighten out." Mason Raymond hauled him over to the buggy and propped him against its side. He was furious, baffled, and—incredibly—all set to laugh. The list of indignities a man could commit was endless and all of these ended in clutter, confusion, and chaos. The only way in this world to stay clear of trouble was to isolate yourself off from other people. "Let's get him back up," Mason Raymond said to Hart.

"It's gonna be mighty crowded in there, Ray, all this stuff we got and the dog 'nd all. How's come he didn't bring the cart?"

How's come indeed? How's come anything? "Put the dog on your lap," Mason Raymond said and then he started to laugh, he couldn't stop himself; he was looped by laughter,

doubled over with it. He had a mental picture of boozy old
Rivers passed out against Hart, Hart sitting stiff and righteous
with that big hound on his lap—hardly the triumphal entry
Hart must have been envisioning all the way back from
Carolina. Weak from laughter, Mason Raymond leaned
against the side of the buggy letting all his animosity and
irritation leak out. When he was cleansed, he would try to
make some kind of apology to Hart, but in the meantime, in
the meantime—

Hart waited him out, solemn with injured dignity. Finally
the two of them took hold of Rivers and tugged and hauled
him back up into the buggy. The only thing Hart said during
the whole maneuver was, "Wonder he ever made it," for
when Rivers reached the seat he reached it with the desperation of a done man, falling back in a gargle of groans, his head
folding forward on his bloated breast, a snaggle of snores
rising out of his beetlelike body. "He sure is a sight," Hart
marveled. Even the dog had been awed by the performance,
standing tied near the bags observing the whole, righteous
business as if it were proof once more of man's inability to
control his own destiny. Animals managed better. You didn't
see dogs drunk.

Ray-shi refused to get into the buggy next to Rivers, rearing
back and baring his teeth to show he was *not* to be messed
with. Hart started a tug of war, the dog on one end, the man
on the other, the fleas in between. Mason Raymond gathered
up the gear, letting them settle their own issue. Finally he got
up in the buggy and waited; he could see this was going to be
a long session.

He sat in the warm autumn sun and waited for Hart to give
up or for the dog to back down. Mason Raymond wasn't any
expert on animals but any fool, he thought, could see there are
times when an animal wants to be enticed into doing what's
good for him. You might, Mason Raymond wanted to say, try
sweets instead of sweat. *You* talk about pride, he wanted to
say.

Hart was sweating and he looked done in; Mason Raymond
took pity on him and got down out of the buggy. "Listen,
Hart, don't try to force him. Why don't you try getting up in

the buggy and letting him come up on his own accord?" Hart was in a towering rage, stomping about telling Mason Raymond he didn't know a goddam thing about dogs, especially hunting dogs, they had to be led, *led, goddam it,* you couldn't jest let them go do what they wanted. Then he threw himself down on the side of the buggy and just stared at the dog. The dog stared back.

Mason Raymond climbed back in the buggy and waited. Sooner or later one of them was going to give. It would be Hart of course, but he couldn't be hurried. That damn pride again.

"Don't jiggle her eggs," Hart said irritably. "You're jigglin' these here eggs somethin' awful. Can't you drive this thin' more even?" He was still smarting, Mason Raymond knew, from his defeat with the dog, but in deference to the end of a long journey Mason Raymond slowed the rig down, even though the horses weren't doing anything but a walk now. Hart just wanted to flaunt authority a little in front of the dog.

At the turn Mabel ran out to meet them. She stood in the road shaking her head in some kind of eternal female exasperation, and she said, "I knew it, I jest knew it, I see you got jest what you set out for." Albert was waiting for his father, too, hands on hips, bobbing up and down trying to get a good look at the new hound. He kept saying over and over, "That's some dog, that sure is." Miranda, standing in the midst of trash and litter, cats and a tumble of young dogs, waved her apron and cried, "Welcome back, Pa, welcome home."

Hart jumped down, hauling the dog with him, bending over to give a peck on the cheek. Mabel was radiant with happiness. "Them pigs all pulled through. You kin rest your mind easy there." She looked up at Mason Raymond, ignoring the snoring Rivers. Ladies did not take account of drunkards. "This here old man give you a peck of trouble, boy?"

Boy, Mason Raymond thought.

"Enough," Hart said, "enough to keep him on the jump."

"You comin' in?"

"Not now, thank you just the same. I want to get him

home." Mason Raymond nodded down at the snoring man.

"He's been hard took of late," Mabel Hart said, pitying. "He ain't been the same since your Ma was took. You look different," she said after a moment. "You growed up."

"I ain't lettin' no bygones be bygones, and neither is this boy," Hart said, standing in the Indian summer sun and holding his ground. "I said I wasn't never goin' to set foot in Lite's store agin and I ain't, I don't care what the occasion."

Old-timers like Eben Stuart and Old Doc Bronson, four or five of the other hunters whose faces Mason Raymond recognized, were ragging Hart about his dog. They kept saying there couldn't be no dog as good as Hart said this one was, it didn't make any difference to them Hart had fetched it all the way back from some hills way down there South. A dog was a dog, and while some dogs were more dog than others, still there were limitations. This such a splendid dog, one of them said sarcastically, why don't you run it with Lite's and see which one is king of the roost. "I ain't runnin' nuthin' with Lite," Hart repeated. No one said anything at all to Mason Raymond, they didn't even acknowledge him; once Mason Raymond would have cared desperately; now he simply lounged against the side of Lite's store and thought, It doesn't matter to me any more what they think. My uncle, and John, they're Butteses, but I'm a Raymond and I reckon I want to be more Raymond than Buttes. He wanted to be what he was, not the reflection of someone else, even if someone else was stronger and wiser. He had a way to go yet; his was a young, green tree. But he knew one thing for sure: he was one of the Raymonds.

Hart didn't contradict Crane, sluggish in a chair, tilted against the porch railing, drawling, "Woods is free, you can't keep Lite out of there, Worth, bear dog or no. Your dog may be the wonder you claim, but I gotta see it to believe it. No offense meant."

Two of the other squatters grunted, flailing at late, lazy flies. Lite had kept out of their way ever since they'd come back and Hart's dog had become the talk of the town. Even forgot my father, Mason Raymond thought. Even Rivers was interested, once he got sobered up again. He'd come down with Mason Raymond to look at the wonder and he'd stood there looking at the chained dog and then he'd said, "Well, he looks all right," but his voice had been full of misgiving. On the way back he'd finally got the courage to ask Mason Raymond if the dog was really all Hart was claiming or if Hart had just got carried away with himself. "He's pretty good," Mason Raymond said. "I saw him run once in those hills he came from and he was pretty good chasing coon. I've never seen him on bear, it's only what we hear tell."

"I wouldn't lay no wager on it. He ain't all that impressive looking." Rivers looked down at his hands, the backs of which were ridged with powder burns, great scars—some white, some still pink—crisscrossing. "You reckon on my fittin' up a little fence 'round your Ma's grave? It looks so bleak up there the way it is. I thought I put a little fencin' 'round, plant some ivy and flowers, it'd give it—you know—a better air."

Mason Raymond started to speak to him about all the time he spent fussing with that grave, then thought better of it. He had been meaning to tell Rivers he thought he ought to go away for a while—take a vacation was what Mason Raymond meant, but who could use the word "vacation" with someone like Rivers who spent all his spare time fussing with a grave. Time, it is a precious thing, he wanted to say to Rivers, and Rivers would probably say back to him, Time, it brings all things to an end. His mother was right: *I hate to see it start because I know how it ends.* Little bitty peanut of a thing . . .

Eben Stuart, who was getting senile, had been babbling about how Lite was willing to forgive and forget. "You want to get out on that hunt, don't you?" one of the old men laughed. "You reckon your old lady's gonna let you go, Eben?" "She ain't old, that's her trouble," another laughed. "Young gal like that needs a lot of attention, you don't give it to her, there's others that will."

"You tell Lite not to let me catch him out alone in the woods where accidents happen, that's all I got to say,"Hart said. "Let him keep to his corner of the lake and I'll keep to mine."

"He wants to run and watch, you can't stop him," Old Doc Bronson pointed out.

Hart spit. "Man like that don't have the sense to know when he ain't wanted. Come jest to spite you. A dark, square man," he said with great intensity.

Crane moved his chair upright and said, "Lite, he been braggin' he got a forty pound coon his Walker treed last week."

"He's always braggin' about somethin'," Hart said.

"Albino, too."

"He killed a white coon?"

"Gonna tan the hide 'nd hang it onto one of the walls of the store, one of them novelties attract folks in to buy," Eben Stuart said.

"Ain't no excuse," Hart said. "I been huntin' these woods forty-some years and ain't never come on no white coon yet and if I did I'd leave it be for others to see instead of shoot."

"Claims he shot it out afore he knew what color it was."

"He's always claimin' somethin'!"

"Well, he says, Hart, ain't nobody in these parts got a dog can touch his Walker dog; he was kinda lettin' it be knowed he wouldn't mind runnin' that Walker dog of his'n agin your bear dog from down there in Carolina, but if'n you ain't gonna have the fancy to—"

Hart spit. "His dog couldn't touch mine."

"That's what you say," Stuart said. "That's not what he say."

"Let him put up or shut up," Hart said. "I don't do no idle talkin' and I don't do no idle braggin'!"

"It's a powerful dog," Crane said. "Biggest damn dog I ever seen. Run all night and don't seem to tire none. That Walker dog of Lite's, he's not like no regular coon dog."

"Lite says he kin run anythin' he's ask'd," Stuart agreed.

"Lite says, Lite says—"

"You reckon on bettin' him?"

"I ain't reckon on doin' *nuthin'* with 'im. I got better thin's to do than to run agin a man shoots other people's dogs—"

There was a silence. None of the men looked at Mason Raymond. "—shoots other people's dogs and runs hisself when his own dog corners bear, leaves a good dog to git maul'd 'nd runs, hightails it out 'cause he's a coward; he runs, that's what he does."

Luke Hollister, up from Albany visiting the Bronsons, started up. "He run? When'd he run?"

"His dog had this bear cornered—not treed, but cornered —and Lite, he run 'nd left that dog. Wouldn't have been nuthin' to git a shot off, but he hightailed it out and run, scairt. And shot this boy's dog when it beat his own dog fair and square. Don't surprise me none he killed a white coon. Nuthin' surprises me about Frank Lite, nuthin'." He looked around the porch. "I'm takin' my dog out tonight and any of you want to run with me is welcome. We're runnin' coon tonight, a sort of preliminary to the weekend runnins. Come the weekend I'm bear trackin'. Anybody want to see a real dog on bear is welcome—but don't brin' that critter Lite along. I had enough run-ins with 'im, I don't want anuther this late in life."

"You reckon they'll come?" Hart asked Mason Raymond as they walked on toward the post office. Ever since they'd come back from Carolina, Hart had a thing about mail. He was corresponding with Lamb and Perkins and had even sent a letter to Auntie Dirk, said it pleasured him no end to get a letter postmarked Asheville. The girl had been no sorrier to see him go than he was glad to be gone. She hadn't even come halfway down the path to say good-bye. Tramping back down that red-rust mountain road, all Hart had said was "Whatever happen'd to turn that little girl so sour on you—no, don't tell me, it's best mabbee I don't know, then I can't feel olig'd. Scrappy little bit of calico, weren't she?"

Hart would never know.

They halted near the new blacksmith's, the Crane place, Mrs. Crane on the porch looking anxious. "Worth, you seen Les 'round? He's got two customers waitin' 'nd I ain't laid eyes on him since breakfast."

"He'd be up at Lite's, gittin' the last sun of the year with the others. You want, we'll walk back and give him a call."

"No, don't you bother yourself none, you got other things on your mind."

"Don't put us out none, jest on the way to the post office, any mail I got kin wait, ain't likely I got no trust fund comin'."

Les Crane's wife began to laugh. "No, I don't reckon none of us do, worse luck, but don't bother. When you gonna let me look at your palm?"

"One readin's enough. I ain't in no hurry now to know when the tree's goin' to fall."

"Years yet."

"Mabbee, mabbee not. My skull says not. Been actin' up somethin' awful lately 'nd the weather been good, can't blame it on rain. You got your ways and I got mine. I got this here head tell me when times ain't so good. Ain't right for a man to see too much anyways."

She was a beautiful woman, full-figured, with a big bust that made her sway from side to side from the hips up, and strong, steady legs. It seemed impossible to Mason Raymond to imagine her *caring* for Crane. But what did he know about love? He never used the word love any more. He had banished that word from his speech and thoughts. A bad word. Its destructive powers he feared, something to keep away from; if you stayed out of its way maybe it couldn't hurt you. It had hurt everyone, everyone. Look at his mother. Look at Rivers. Look at what had happened with the girl. He must be very careful not to get too attached to Hart's dog. And even as he chided himself, he knew that he had become attached; he and Hart spent hour after hour grooming the dog, talking to it; the dog was companion to both of them in a way people couldn't be. He and Hart and the dog: they were a special, separate part of the world where no one else, not even Mabel, intruded. They walked on, he and Hart, special in their separateness from everyone else. Yet he would never use the word love, he had made a promise to himself that he would never again use that word. Banish it. Stay away from it. Protect himself from its powers.

He and Hart pulled up short; his uncle was coming down the opposite side of the street in what Cobus Buttes always referred to as "the supply wagon." He must be in town putting in winter goods. When he came to the intersection and started to make a turn, Cobus Buttes caught sight of them and hollered.

John, he's got big, Mason Raymond thought, he's going to

be a big man. He was always big. He doesn't have to prove anything; he's his own proof. Yet he felt a tie to John; they had once set out to kill a man together.

"Ain't tradin' with Frank no more," his uncle said to Hart, getting down off the wagon. "Tryin' that new place, the Harrolds'. Not so much variety but the atmosphere's easier. Where you headed, Hart?" The two men began to talk dogs. Cobus Buttes's two younger boys jumped down and commenced running and jumping, scrapping with one another and whining. "Sart done this to me," "Lyman done that, Pa," their father ignoring the tattling while Hart described the runs he had in mind.

John Buttes, still atop the big old cart, looked down on Mason Raymond, neither friendly nor feuding. He doesn't hold it against me I beat him on the dogs, Mason Raymond thought, but that didn't make him any chummier either. We're so different, and I'm nothing to him really, just somebody he has a blood connection with and has to pass the time of day with once in a while.

He was going to shoot Lite with me, Mason Raymond marveled. But I don't know him at all. He's not the same boy who used to swing out over our heads and taunt us because we were on the ground. He's someone else. He examined John curiously: had he ever had a girl? Yes, of course he had, and that girl wouldn't have made fun of him.

"No more out of either one of you," Cobus Buttes warned the younger boys. "I don't want no more of that tattlin' out of you. Saturday, Worth, that when you have it in mind to run bear—you want to go trackin' bear come the weekend, John?"

"With that new dog of yourn, Worth?"

"Goin' to break him in coonin' tonight. Like to have you with me then. Makes me feel more confident somehow know I got a couple of friends I kin count on."

"We'll be there," Mason Raymond's uncle said, leaping back up on the cart. "Too bad you can't git Lite mixed up in a bet, Worth," he said, chuckling. "Do him good to git a good lickin' again."

"I wasn't aimin' to have *nuthin'* to do with him. He's the poison in paradise."

"Wouldn't let him off for nuthin' on earth, I were you."

"But you know, Cob, that's like acknowledgin' evil."

"You know any other sensible way to deal with it?"

"I ain't never learn'd *no* way to deal with it, let alone understand it. Best thin' all around is let it alone, keep out of its way, maybe it'll keep out of yourn."

"The way I see it, the bad thin's of this world is always searchin' us out, ain't no way to escape them."

Back at the house, Hart and Mason Raymond started fussing with Hart's animals. First they tinkered with the streaked pigs, moving them; Hart said he thought they'd do better in the upper barn now the weather was turning nippy; they rounded the three squealers up and beat them up toward the barn. It was a nuisance because one or another of the pigs kept breaking loose and running off, raising up a flurry of hens; there would be screeching and Mabel coming out of the house hollering and once one of the pigs got lost for a time and they had to go around lifting up junk trying to locate it. They found it asleep next to two sheep who were standing looking at it in wonderment. Prob'ly never seen a striped pig before, Hart said. Then they went down to the place Hart had the dog chained. Horatio was standing, stretching, as they came around the corner, and when he caught sight of them he began to wiggle and wag his tail. Mason Raymond forgot his adult pretensions and dropped down, hugging the dog. He had come to fill Hector's place, no matter how much Mason Raymond had thought no dog would ever again mean so much to him as the old, tan dog with the black-tipped tail. He spent many afternoons brushing and fussing with the dog, talking to him, telling him things he wouldn't even have told Hart.

He was suddenly aware, walking up the path, looking at the gray-boarded clapboard house settling into the four o'clock sun, that he was lonely, lonely for company his own age; his friends were an old man and a dog, and sometimes (though not so much lately) Rivers who still polished and mended (now mostly drunk) in the back-stairway room, Mason Raymond sitting across from him watching. They rarely talked. Sometimes Rivers hummed a little under his breath, not even aware of it, Mason Raymond supposed; he had a terrible voice, Rivers, gravelly and off-key, but there was something nice nevertheless about the humming and the way Rivers' hands wandered knowingly over the leather searching out nicks and strains.

Mason Raymond caught himself humming too now and again that song he'd brought back from the mountains—

> *Oh, thyme it is a precious thing . . .*
> *Thyme brings all things to an end . . .*

He thought about the girl. She was not a happy subject to let his mind dwell on, but there was no getting away from her; she had a life of her own there inside his head. He went up to the Hart house feeling blue, his mind full of theories about where his hands and mouth had gone wrong in the love-making. He wondered how you were supposed to recognize when you got off track in such a mystery. That was one area he believed you couldn't get lessons in. Maybe you just lived and learned. He'd have to *hope* so.

His uncle and John were late, and Hart fidgeted, waiting. He was so eager to be off that he was willing to strike trail before dark even though any self-respecting coon wouldn't be out for an hour or so. Probably had to do with Lite, standing out on the border of Hart's property, just standing there, not saying anything, not venturing onto the place, just standing there watching and waiting.

He's come to watch, Hart said angrily, hopin' somethin' bad will go wrong. Like he's standin' there puttin' the evil eye on me. A dark, dark man, he said, spitting. You run up to the house and git some tobaccy, will you, boy? Don't pay no mind to that old coot, he ain't goin' to jinx us, boy, and that's a promise.

Still, Lite made everyone nervous, just standing there, not intruding, not pushing in, not even bringing a dog, just hanging around, observing, a shadowy figure on the outskirts of the action, poised, waiting, in that odd, high-toed stance peculiar to Lite, as if he were waiting to spring. Don't mean nobody no good, Hart predicted.

"Where you gonna run?" Crane asked Hart.

Hart said maybe he'd try up pasture, in back, where he was sure there were plenty of coon. "How's come you don't go up to the Hollow, take on Old Cassius, your dog so special?" Eben Stuart asked, making a kind of chittering noise in his throat, laughing. Lite had put him up to that, of course, and now it was Hart who was caught, who couldn't wiggle out of a contest he'd never even had in mind because if he let that challenge go by he'd be admitting his dog couldn't even take on a big coon let alone a real bear. Old Cassius, one of the other men said, letting a low whistle out between his teeth, Old Cassius.

"Yeah, how about that, Hart? How about your sick-ing that dog on that old coon and gittin' rid of it for us onct and fer all?" Eben Stuart was such an old fool he'd do anything Lite told him.

He's going to be too proud to say no, Mason Raymond thought, watching the expression on Worth's face.

"No one in his right mind'd take a good dawg up to that Hollow," Crane said. "That ain't a coon up there. That's the devil hisself."

Someone had to explain to Luke Hollister who kept asking, "What's so special about the Hollow?" while Mason Raymond sat down, thinking, of course, that damn fool's got no more sense than any of them when his pride's involved. He'll run that dog in Blackwood Hollow against that old coon and get him killed just like the last time, and he'll be right back where he started, and I'm not going to say one word. He'll live, but he'll never learn.

"Hart, you ain't," Crane protested.

But Worth Hart wasn't arguing; he was waiting; and when, a quarter of an hour later, Cobus Buttes and Young John rode up and tied their horses, Mason Raymond was hoping that his uncle would talk Hart out of it. Hart might listen to him where he wouldn't listen to other men. Mason Raymond didn't want the dog to die. He had strong feelings about Horatio; he cared —all right, damn it, he did care. He didn't want anything to happen to the dog, but he wouldn't say so. Hart wouldn't pay any attention to him anyway, and people might think he was a crybaby about that animal, especially after what had happened to his own dog. So he was hoping his uncle would talk some sense into Hart. "You take Ollie, Ray, and I'll run Ray-shi." Mason Raymond took the female. She was whining and scattering her energy running and sniffing with no plan or reason to her, just female heat and drive—Della Mae in the mountains.

What are you so condescending about? I didn't notice *you* holding back and acting sensible like that big brindle over there. If anything, you were rutting worse than she was. Mason Raymond hauled up on Ollie's leash and said, exasperated, "Stop it!" Part of his annoyance with her was really not with her at all but with his uncle who should be talking Hart out of this craziness but was only standing there, shaking his head, saying, It ain't a good idea, Worth, but not objecting strenuously enough to make any alteration in plans. If he wanted to argue, really argue, Mason Raymond thought, he might change Hart's mind. Why doesn't he say something? Why's he just standing there mealy-mouthing that little remonstrance? Can't he come on stronger?

Ollie was paying no attention to his attempts to calm her down, jerking and pulling and leaping and straining. The men were filing after Hart, Mason Raymond's uncle walking beside him, not arguing, but giving him a look which maybe said more than words. But Hart didn't have to answer a look. John Buttes came over. "He's crazy," he said and then took the leash from Mason Raymond and ran with the dog in a great spurt of energy. "She'll quiet some now," he said, handing the dog back. "She jest wanted a little run to work off some of her steam."

The Hollow was maybe a mile and a half, two miles uphill. Since it was all climbing, the distance seemed farther than it might actually be. The men began to string out; beads of lantern light formed half a necklace against the mountainside. Indian Hills. There was very little left of the Indian here. But out West, there a few bands of warriors still resisted. The magic names—

He and John moved up toward the head of the band. His uncle had finally started arguing with Hart, telling him he should have better sense than to be tricked into a set-up like this. Hart paid no attention. "You got a gun?" Mason Raymond asked John. John looked up. "I don't shoot any more," Mason Raymond said. John was giving Mason Raymond the same kind of look Cobus Buttes had given Hart when he heard Hart was going up to the Hollow with his brand new bear dog and look for Old Cassius.

There's a lot you don't know about me, Mason Raymond wanted to say.

And there's a lot you don't know about him, his second voice said.

At the bottom of the Hollow, Hart hauled up to give the two dogs a chance to get side by side. Mason Raymond had to pass Lite to reach him. When he got abreast of the store-keeper, Mason Raymond slowed down and again said to Young John, "You got your gun?" John nodded. "Then you walk behind him and keep an eye on him and see there's not another mishap like the one we had with Hector."

Hart's pride had got them up to the Hollow and now they would all see what the dog could do. It seemed unfair to Mason Raymond to have to rely on an animal to retrieve your honor, but then men were always using animals to boost themselves. A good horse, a fine dog, even some silly thing like one of those Persian cats of his mother's—all these were *for* something, not just owned for themselves. Why did people use animals to enlarge themselves? He didn't understand, but he identified with Hart, bent over scratching the ears of the big brindle, whispering a little into his ear, telling him, Mason Raymond supposed, things he ought to know—like what matter of raccoon that was out there, not the usual everyday run-of-the-mill raccoon, you understand, Horatio, but a big monster of a coon that's a dog killer and you want to watch out, you want to be on your guard, because this coon is smart, smart and crafty, it'll take you in a minute if you don't keep your eyes open, and you best keep 'em open if you want to git one up on that granddaddy of a crafty coon, 'cause he's killed dog after dog, and though you ain't no regular dog, that you ain't, you still want to watch out.

The dog's head was cocked to one side. He was listening, all right, and Mason Raymond would have been willing to bet he understood. Cobus Buttes was still trying to argue some sense into Hart, his words heated by now, Hart fondling the dog and listening, the thing already decided, what was the use of all these words? Now it was too late.

The Hollow was heavily wooded with second and third growth, covered now with a low blanket of ground mist. Mason Raymond, slowly being enveloped in fog, had little feeling about what was coming, though most men said the will-o'-the-wisp gave you signs. People were always looking for signs—like Hart and that crazy business with the handkerchiefs—because they were afraid of the future. Mason Raymond didn't know whether he was afraid or not at this moment, but one thing he did know: he would have liked to postpone it. He was cold, he shivered a couple of times; but there was no premonition, good or bad, running over him saying *Do* or *Don't.* Spells and readings and divinations and all the rest, what good were they, anyway? He had poured the Indian herbs over his mother, hadn't he, and what good had they done? "John's carrying a gun," he said to his uncle, "and I asked him to walk behind Lite. You got your good new gun, Hart?"

Hart didn't answer, which meant *No,* he didn't have it, he'd mislaid it someplace. Even that waywardness didn't give Mason Raymond any sensation of foreboding because Hart's old gun might, looked at in certain ways, be a good sign, not a bad one. You carried your lucky old gun on the important runs.

Hart reached over and unleashed the dog. Horatio ran fast, fast and silent; that was one of the odd things about him, he wasn't much of a barker. Tied up at Hart's, he was silent in the yard when the rest of the dogs were raising a terrible racket. He only sounded once he'd picked up a true track, then opening with a couple of chops, silent again, then the steady, full cry of a dog near treeing, and finally the chops at the tree.

The men stood huddled at the foot of the Hollow, the mist closing in, waiting to hear from the dog. Ten minutes passed, fifteen, with no signal from the running dog. Two men put their lanterns down and tucked their hands under their arms for warmth, dancing back and forth to keep the chill away. "He's on to somethin' sure," Hart promised them.

"What do you mean 'on to somethin',' he ain't made a sound."

"You'll see. Them with confidence don't need to make a lot of noise."

"Come on, Hart, let's move out 'nd see what's goin' on. It's cold lyin' up like this."

Hart didn't move.

Five more minutes more passed, six, seven, the men stamping about and suggesting this and that, Hart straining for sound. "He's trackin', he's trackin'," he said suddenly. Mason Raymond had heard nothing, but he knew the old man had senses he'd never developed. "Cob!" he cried. "You take the lantern, and Ray, you hang onto that thar dog 'nd see she don't slip away." He ran into the mist; Mason Raymond could hear him crashing ahead long after he was out of sight. Just like a cow in corn, Hart had said to him a long time ago. Now he heard the dog, heard clearly what Hart had heard silently a few moments before.

He held onto his frantic dog as tight as he could; she, too, knew something he didn't and was straining to break free. Lite passed him, slippery and silent, dancing forward in his high-toed gait, Young John behind, tracking him, the gun half-pointing. He would only need a second to aim and fire.

The men fanned out, flailing about in the fog. Mason Raymond held onto Ollie and swam through the fog. One minute he would sink in thick, white mist, the next he would bob up in a small pocket that was so clear he could see stars winking overhead. A shadowy, vaporous figure of a hunter would rise before him, then drop down into the milky mist. He flailed toward the sound of Horatio's call; somewhere out in that vast, inpenetrable sea of fog, the dog and coon were going to meet.

He heard shouts, voices yelling back and forth to one another, men crashing on either side of him, ahead of him, behind him. He pulled himself up and tried to work himself free of the leash, he could hear Horatio treeing; then he was running, running so fast that Ollie could scarcely keep up.

Horatio's bawl was straight ahead. Mason Raymond heard the hollering get more intense, more frantic, almost hysterical; the men were tumbling in from all around and were under the tree—it must be Old Cassius, no other coon could excite them so. He ran on, listening to cheering, then more hollering, yanking the dog and striking out at the fog as if he could break through it, bellowing to Hart to wait up, he was coming, emerging into a short clearing with the men walling off his view. But he could hear the sound of the coon, the hissing and snarling, an enraged *whirring;* then the men rolled back and Mason Raymond flew forward, shoving his way through, swimming through bodies and fog and tree branches into the circle of lantern light and the big, brindle dog shaking something back and forth, back and forth, while Mason Raymond hollered and no one answered, and then he saw the coon, the biggest damn coon he had ever seen; it was thrashing and scratching, clawing and chewing, blood from both the coon and dog shooting out in the darkness, spattering men and foliage; and the dog first throwing the coon back and forth, then running with it thrashing in his jaws. Horatio dashed it against a tree.

It went limp for an instant, then raised itself up for one last cry and the dog threw itself on the coon and all Mason Raymond saw was thrashing, and then the dog leapt back and the coon lay still, the dog's head cut and scratched, its jaw laid open and bleeding, one long, jagged gash along its near shoulder dripping a colorless fluid along with blood, but victorious, the proud, torn, bloody, but confident killer. Hart knelt over the dead coon looking at it; no one spoke, gazing at Old Cassius, who must have have weighed forty, maybe fifty pounds, and all that weight the residue of the wisdom and craft of the woods, of the ability to stay alive, to survive where others had fallen, a mythic animal who had kept hunters and their dogs out of the Hollow for years, and who now lay, a lump of limp meat, too old and tough to eat, too mangled even to turn into a trophy.

How, Mason Raymond wondered, how could they be proud?

Pride, said Hart, real pride came only from bear. Old Cassius had been a big coon, yes, but, after all, only a coon. Coon wasn't bear, no matter how big. Now they were going for bear.

There were crowds there in the Saturday dawn, men from half a hundred miles away come up on foot and cart and horseback to gather in the clear, cold, Saturday dawn to see Worth Hart's Carolina Plott go into bear country—the place you could always be certain of coming on fresh tracks—run bear and tree and hold it for as long as need be until a man came and shot it down and dragged it out of the woods for other men to see.

"*Git down,*" Hart told one of the Landing dogs, cuffing him. The dog slunk back, not whimpering, not really hurt, just rebuked—properly, to Mason Raymond's way of thinking. He'd been jumping up and making a nuisance of himself. Horatio never did that. He was trained.

The air was cool in the early flush of dawn, a relief after the long, sulfurous Indian-autumn night. Funny how long a false spell they'd had. Mason Raymond thought of how Hart had tried to pacify him at the station by telling him to rest his bones and enjoy himself, this kind of weather never lasted. But it had, day after day of heavy honey sun sweet to the skin and eyes, even the mouth—you could almost taste it.

They were all waiting for Cobus Buttes. He was late, but then he had a long way to come. The dogs slunk around the debris, most of them black and tans or blueticks. They were coon dogs and wary of bear. "You watch my Ray-shi," Hart said proudly, "and see what a real bear dog can do." The best chance of jumping a bear, Hart said, was to split the hunt. Someone started to give him an argument, but the other men were gathered around Hart; the hunt would be split, one party going up one side and the other circling around to keep any animals between the two packs of dogs. If there was a bear in there, he wouldn't escape the trap.

Even in the desultory talk, the occasional joke and laughter, the lazy murmuring of dawn noises, there existed the tenseness, the men knowing that in a few minutes they would be trailing the excited dogs on the chase, running, breaking cover, trying to keep up with the howling hounds, pushing themselves harder and harder, tired and hot and thirsty, but unable to stop because the dogs were running and you couldn't blow dogs off when they were running, you didn't know how far they were going to run or how long, you had to keep up or run the risk of losing a dog or discouraging the whole pack, and good dogs were important for the success of the hunt, the dogs maybe more important than the men. Mason Raymond stood by the porch stanchion looking out into the dawn and thinking, Why aren't there any books that talk about what a day like this is? Why wasn't someone writing about people like Worth Hart and Charity Bounty, Hobe Perkins and Grady Lamb? They were far more real than The Lady of the Lake and those rustics William Shakespeare always had running around in his plays for comic relief. "The greatest of the Tudor propagandists," Mason Raymond's history teacher had called the great playwright and had nearly given Morphis a heart seizure.

Imagine, Mason Raymond thought, even trying to explain to a class—any class—at a school a sunrise like this and men and dogs like this. They wouldn't understand just as once he hadn't. The teachers at the Academy maybe didn't even know what being American meant. They thought it was acting like a well-bred Englishman. That was really what they were trying to teach their pupils: to be American Englishmen.

But Americans didn't talk like Englishmen. They didn't think like them or act like them. They weren't in any way like them at all. They were themselves—or lots of selves. Because the Americans Mason Raymond knew here at the Landing weren't like the Americans who lived in the mountains down South and he didn't think they were probably much like the Americans out West, they weren't like city or even town people. There were lots of Americas, maybe so many that it was impossible to grasp the whole and say "This is it" because it wasn't it, only a part of the whole; but there must be some way to bring all of it together, the farms and towns, his uncle's place, the Landing; and the big cities with their fancy houses and their terrible, poor towns, like Albany, or Schenectady, like New York; there must be a way to capture the North and

South, the West, the mountain people and the ex-slaves, the farmers and the mill workers, all of them, and say, See, *this* is it.

This is better than books can ever be, Mason Raymond thought, I don't care what anyone says. The trouble with Morphis and the rest of them is that they never stopped doing the reading and started doing the living. Living for them is secondhand. They've never really tested themselves against anything they can't control. There's no danger if you do all the manipulating.

"You take that thair dog," Hart said, "and set yer mind to what yer doin'. Yer mind been wanderin'."

Mason Raymond flushed. He would always be the dreamer, he supposed. He took hold of the rope leash and talked to Ollie, trying to quiet her. Hart wanted to mate her with Horatio. He thought he could work up a combination coon-and-bear dog. I got me some striped pigs, didn't I? he asked. But when Mason Raymond pointed out that Plotts would hunt coon as well as bear, he said, That ain't what I'm after. What I want is them coon dogs to be as keen on bear as they is on coon. I want to upgrade them, so to speak.

Mason Raymond saw downroad to where his uncle and Young John were swinging along rapidly, their guns thrust over their shoulders. They came up, laughing, sharing some secret joke between them; envy struck Mason Raymond a blow that left him hollow. His father had never once in his whole life been casual and close to him the way Cobus Buttes was with his son.

Yet John was decent enough to him, edging up familiarly, even clamping him 'round the back. He doesn't think I'm completely hopeless anymore, Mason Raymond thought, and if he doesn't, maybe that means others don't either. John's opinion, it sometimes seemed to him, was the most important one in the world because it was given critically; with his uncle and with Hart, affection often overrode objectivity; and of course the truth was he would have liked to be John—and yet Mason Raymond found it impossible at that moment to think of one single thing to say to him. Being near was enough. He acknowledged the fact that more than likely all his life he would be, in one way or another, standing in John's shadow because John was to his mind what he would like to be. He's just strong, Mason Raymond tried to argue with himself, but, no, it was much more than that. He's got a way with him I'll never have.

"Which way you figure the bear goin' to run?" Cobus Buttes asked Hart.

"Your guess and mine ain't goin' to influence their thinkin' one way or t'other," Hart said, "but I kindda like it high myself—somethin' about bein' way up high and lookin' out pleasures me."

"I vote high, then. How about you, boy?" He was talking to Mason Raymond. He had included Mason Raymond among the men, the ones who helped make decisions, even if he still called him *boy.* Everyone called him *boy;* maybe it was more habit than definition. "I like it better in the hills. You can see more from the rises," he said.

"Ain't never fergit that swamp nor that windfall, has you?" Hart laughed. "I was always proud of you, the way you kept yourself together when you got lost in the woods that way and I reckon I never said so out-and-out. Funny how it is a man uses so much language up durin' his lifetime and says so little that counts. The real thin's we want to say we can't git out, too embarrassin' maybe. I remember when I knew I was all filled up with feelin' for Mabel, couldn't never look at another woman, I couldn't figure out no way to tell her. Been shut up like that most of my life, been holdin' back fer fear with all the good thin's I wanted to say, but I was proud of you, Ray, you knowed that, don't you?"

Mason Raymond didn't know what to say. He couldn't say back, I loved you so much, Hart, too, and I never knew how to tell you, I never said half the things I should have. I don't know how.

There were lots of dogs, two to each man. Only Hart held his single dog. Horatio, he said, was worth twice two dogs. Hart took off his lucky coonskin cap and bowed his head. "Almighty Gawd," he said, "make us fair in the trackin', humane in the kill, and modest in what we expect. Amen." He clumped his coonskin hat back on his head, coughed, spit, and was ready to move out. He would pray about bear because they had earned his respect, but coon he just took for granted. Mason Raymond read a message about men into this, but he didn't have time to turn the notion over in his mind because Hart was waving his hand, they were ready to get away.

Packs of dogs flew out and the Landing hunters grabbed onto their leashes, trying to restrain them—Old Doc Bronson (but without his son, the one who had worked with Mason Raymond's mother); half-blind, half-lame Old Eben Stuart; Crane, the blacksmith; that man Hare who had been with Mason Raymond on the big betting hunt; and even Lite, smiling and walking high on his toes, balanced between life and death, as if he hadn't quite made up his mind which way to go.

The men fanned out, the dogs sniffing the ground for a strike. It had been raining for two days and the sky was still full of broken clouds in the pink suffusion of dawn; the dampness helped the ground hold the scent, and there was not too much wind. Wind dried the track and took the scent away. But there was a low ground mist and the dogs looked like monsters emerging waist-deep out of the milky, white mist. Hart was running ahead, talking to his dog, encouraging him, though Horatio needed no encouragement, he was excited enough scattering leaves and brush as he searched out a scent, backtracking, running first one way, then another, yanking and pulling and pausing, trembling, head lifted, listening with his keen sense of hearing, listening for sounds the men couldn't pick up, tongue hanging out as he panted, lowered his head, and began to run again.

"He's got somethin'!" Hart cried excitedly. "Look at 'm, he's onto somethin'!"

Horatio had caught the scent, he had jumped bear. Hart turned him loose and he was going full bore, his voice strong in the track song. He ran so fast that he was soon almost out of hearing. Panting, running, their own dogs still chained, the hunters followed Horatio's lead, first through a field and then onto a wide, plummeting stream of rocks, foam, slashing white water; a rock ledge at one end and at the other birch, maple, poplar, pine, reed-lined spring holes, and the wild weeds that seemed so close to flowers.

The dogs were hysterical wanting to be turned loose, and as the hunters released them they bounded forward wildly, their voices urgent, the men galloping after, stumbling, tripping, sprinting, gasping the cry, "Bear goin'!" breathy but jubilant, "Gotta bear goin'!" "Bear on track," "We've got a bear goin'!"

It wasn't one bear, but *three.* They ran a half an hour circling before they split into three straight paths, all different. The bear-green bluetick dogs and the black-and-tans kept switching trails, doubling back and forth, the hounds' warbling, treble voices coming first triumphant and sure, then broken and troubled, but Horatio and Ollie kept moving out in a steady, straight direction, belling with confidence and authority, Hart and Mason Raymond floundering after, and in their wake, cursing and falling, Lite shouting, "Let 'em run, for God's sake, let 'em run. You're a maniac," Lite said, "a mad, old maniac."

Hart ran on. "You can bet on that," he said. "Jest stay outta my way."

Horatio ran on. The men began to fall off, one by one; but Hart, like his dog, kept on; Mason Raymond, the bitch dog dropping behind him, dragged on; and behind Mason Raymond, cursing, tripping, but somehow managing to keep up, Lite every once in a while shouting at Hart to let that fool dog run hisself out if he wanted to, but there was no sense in killing the rest of them. "Bugger off yourself if you want," Hart shouted back. "Won't be no loss."

Hart crossed a creek, Mason Raymond and Lite trailing, following the riverline maybe a quarter of a mile until the briars became mean and thick, and then they all pulled up, listening to Horatio's high, long bawl somewhere out ahead. Hart began to carry on. "I done left that new gun you give me," he said to Mason Raymond, stamping about. "It's done gone sure as my name's Worth Hart, that good, expensive, new gun you give me—and I don't know where I set it down." He sounded grieved beyond death. He started tracing back,

Lite pulling up short, watching. "You left it back, Hart," Mason Raymond said. "You never brought it to begin with." Hart was scrambling about in the bushes searching through the thickest bracken Mason Raymond had seen. It seemed impossible that either a bear or a dog had gone through here, but he and Hart and even Lite had somehow managed to tear their way through.

"Nuthin' to do but use my old gun," Hart said, "maybe pick up trail the other side of the mountain. We could take horses in some," he said, brightening. "Maybe it won't be so bad as it looks."

What he meant was that they had lost the dog; he just didn't want to say so.

They plodded back, Lite tagging along, not saying anything, just stalking them, Hart, irate, blaming his own stupidity, the river run, the dumb gun, toe-busting logs, the woods, every dingblasted thing he could think of connected with hunting, but mostly himself, tramping back, wet, cold, leading the way, and so down the last thing Mason Raymond was going to suggest this time was singing.

Hart didn't blame him for not carrying a gun, at least. He'd accepted the non-killing feeling in Mason Raymond and while he might have thought it queer, he didn't try to pressure Mason Raymond into carrying a gun the way he did. I suppose I was excusing my own not wanting to carry one, Mason Raymond thought, by buying him that Winchester—but he didn't think the gift was all expiation. He had really wanted Hart to have a decent gun. You get a great dog like Horatio, you ought to have a good gun. Now Hart had gone and brought his old gun by habit.

Mason Raymond couldn't understand why Lite didn't call it quits like the rest. Somehow it was as if everything were predetermined: the beech tree with the bear marks, the apple trees with their pulled-down limbs, the bear spoor covered with whole berries and nuts, the place where the bear had passed through the tall grass, and the matted-down area where he'd lain down. There was the same hot breath and the heavy odor of the dogs, rank and fetid from the woodchuck smell where the dogs had rolled in dead chuck to camouflage their own smell; the same heat and mugginess, flies and midges; his feet were rock-bruised, and yet he ran on, stopping only back at the house so Hart could shout to Mabel, who stood with her hands on her hips, shaking her head, shaking her head, they were all dog- and bear-crazy, she had long ago given up on them; and then they were back slipping on the wet floor of the forest, which never seemed to change here with the season, so deep into the heart of the forest that light could barely sift through, and there remained in the damp darkness a permanent carpet of brown, slippery needles under the big pines, Ollie panting and stopping to drink dirty surface water, the ground sweating, the men limping, but then picking up speed as once again they heard Horatio's high, clear call as he ran the bear, and the three of them—Hart, Lite, and Mason Raymond—running after, all just some dream, with Hart pushing on, shoving, not caring whether Lite (or Mason Raymond) kept up, bent only on bear, his dog running and treeing and him coming in at the end, killing.

The dog was out of earshot again. Lite had pulled up, panting, in back of them, and when Mason Raymond looked back he saw him lying on the flat ground licking water off the leaves and logs, he was so given out for thirst. His own rasped breath was coming in hot, painful gulps. Hart'll run until he drops, Mason Raymond thought. Sixty-some years old and running stronger than any of us. He won't stop 'til the bear's treed and dead.

He took a last look back at Lite and forced himself on. He couldn't run but he could stumble. He wanted Hart to know they'd won. Lite couldn't keep up. Hart *had* to know that.

Hart was leaning over a log talking quietly to Ollie. She was lying on her side, her eyes half-bulged out of her head in heat and fatigue and the astonishment of collapse. "It's all right, girl," Hart kept saying. "It's all right. You done your best. I'm gonna tie her," he said to Mason Raymond, "or she'll try and go on. Dog like this'll kill herself tryin'. We gotta protect her from herself. How you holdin' out, boy?"

"Better'n Lite, but that ain't sayin' much." The *ain't* had come quite easily and comfortably. He was maybe going to be a woodsman after all.

"He'll git up," Hart said darkly, as if he were privileged to know things Mason Raymond couldn't. "He ain't gonna be left out no way. He'll rest hisself and then he'll try 'nd run agin. He's back there now prayin' our bear'll git away, and it prob'ly will, knowin' the terrible power of a man like that."

He kept comforting the dog. "Cain't leave her 'til she calms herself," he said. "Won't do us no harm neither to git a little wind back. You run pretty good—for a boy city-brung-up. You don't see Young John Buttes runnin' with us, do you? He ain't gonna put hisself out for nobody but hisself—ain't like his Pa no more'n you's like yourn. Put me in mind of myself when I was your length—no sense at all, no more sense than these crazy hounds runnin' their hearts out. You rested enough to run, boy?"

Mason Raymond wouldn't have measured his breathing apparatus in such positive terms, but he was willing to try. They left the whining dog, chained, bleating to be let go, and crashed on through the rough, briared woods. They had lost the dog or Horatio himself had lost the track because they were tracking in silence, the dog somewhere out there in the forest running without a sound. Hart kept calling, hoping Horatio would hear and howl back; Mason Raymond had hauled up alongside a creek, resting, when he looked up and saw the dog streak by. He ran hollering for Hart, floundering up the creek bank. Ahead, the creek widened; he had to cut right to bypass a round little pool; a half mile down the bed, a regular river ran. Mason Raymond kept screaming for Hart to come on. Then just ahead of him Hart ran out of the woods and just ahead of Hart he saw that the bear was swimming at the widest part of the creek, the dog paddling along behind. The bear swam fast, reached the opposite shore and climbed up on a bushy part of the bank and crashed through the brush. The dog splashed out, shook himself, and ran after. Mason Raymond and Hart banged after them. They ran almost a whole hour before Hart called it quits. He stopped suddenly, crimson-faced, chest heaving, looking as if he might topple over. And that's just what Hart did—fall to the ground. He was tuckered out.

Mason Raymond bent over him, too winded to speak. Finally Hart looked up and said, "You jest like Cob, a regular spring off the old tree." In effect he was saying you're a Buttes as well as a Raymond. Mason Raymond didn't even have the breath to say thanks.

The bear was old and wise, running with a plan, treeing two or three feet up to leave his scent, then springing free and running again, trying to throw the dog off or fake him out, circling the whole mountain, it seemed, and now they had lost both the bear and the dog, Hart said, pounding the ground, ready, Mason Raymond saw, to give up, quit, when Lite came limping out of the woods, looking worse than they did, but still on his feet. When Hart caught sight of him, he heaved himself up and stumbled on; God alone knew how much later it was that somewhere in a climb they heard Horatio. They tried to run and couldn't, stumbling and falling, wheezing and heaving, and then stopping to listen and hearing nothing. Another silence. They waited. Hart sat down on an old tree stump and put his head in his hands and heaved. He was so tired that he was sick. Mason Raymond was beyond even being sick; the next step was death so far as he was concerned. "My Gawd!" Hart cried, "there he goes again." He forced himself up and started down the path, a pathetic jog toward the sound of his dog's call.

A pattern was established: a long, semi-silent run, an encounter, another run, another silence, with Hart and Mason Raymond struggling after and Lite tagging along, half the time out of sight.

Then Mason Raymond heard the real thing, the cry the hound makes when he says, I have him. Hart let out a yip and sprinted ahead, jumping from rock to rock, trying to get across a gully, slipping, going down in rock almost waist deep, then plunging up and grabbing hold of some shale, climbing up out of the debris into a big windfall, dripping stones and mud. *They're in there,* Hart screamed, and ran into the woods.

One minute Mason Raymond saw the bear secured to the tree, his arms wrapped around the trunk, his broad rear wedged into a forked branch, the next second he was clawing his way down; there was the harsh, grating sound of ripped bark; the bear made two leaping bounds and disappeared into the brush, Horatio running after, and following Horatio, Hart. Mason Raymond heard him just ahead, but he couldn't see him. "He's treed! He's treed! He's got 'im treed!" Mason Raymond ran, Lite maybe twenty-five feet behind him.

They thrashed into a clearing, the bear backed against a stone wall, up on his hind legs slashing back and forth with his big claws while the brindle leaped this way and that, darting out of his way. The bear was trapped; it saw the men coming and it knew the dog was bedeviling it and it lunged out, striking left and right with its claws.

"Don't move in, don't move in," Hart screamed at Mason Raymond. "You don't have no gun." But Hart and Horatio were moving in, they were exposed, and there was still an open space on the left where the bear might swing free.

Mason Raymond ran to the left to cut the bear off. The dog was in front of the bear, rushing it, Hart coming in from the far side. The bear caught the dog and swung it through the air. Mason Raymond ran but he didn't know what he was shouting; it was *fire* or *shoot* or *raise your gun,* maybe all three.

Lite stood directly in front of the big, shaggy, slashing bear, frozen, unable to lift his gun to fire. "Shoot," Hart screamed, "for God's sake shoot before he gits the dog. My gun's come apart."

Lite stood still, paralyzed, unable to move.

The dog lay on the ground, its whole side ripped wide open and one ear hanging loose. It got up and staggered toward the bear, trailing half its insides. "Shoot!" Hart screamed and then rushed the bear, trying to distract it. The bear held the dog with one paw and lashed out at Hart with the other. It gave Hart a wound almost identical to that of the dog's, a great, slashing gash from the top of his head down to his groin.

"Shoot, goddam you, shoot," Mason Raymond screamed at Lite.

Lite dropped his gun and ran.

Mason Raymond scooted across the space between the bear and where Lite had been and picked up the gun and fired and fired again, and suddenly the bear lay on the ground, its head blown off. There was a fragment of the skull left and possibly a quarter of one side, but the face was gone and even part of the neck. Hart lay on the ground ten feet away, his side open, the intestines tumbling out. He had put his hands to the wound, trying to hold his insides in, but he was too weak, there was too much to take care of. Horatio lay beside him, his back ruptured, his spine broken. Only the dog's eyes moved. They were on Hart.

For a bear, Mason Raymond thought, *all for a bear.*
"Worth?"

Hart's eyes were open, but Mason Raymond wasn't sure he could hear or comprehend. The wound was terrible, there was nothing you could do for a man like that. The stomach was gone, too. Any fool could see that.

Hart raised his hand a little. He tried to talk. Mason Raymond took Hart's hand and put it on the dog's head.

Hart struggled to speak.

"Just lay quiet," Mason Raymond said.

Hart shook his head. His lips moved.

Mason Raymond lifted the dog closer to Hart so that he lay alongside him. He put his head down, burying his head in the fur. He did not want Hart to see he was crying.

"Me and you, we'll—" Mason Raymond could hear Hart fighting for breath. "Ain't fair," he said, "ain't fair nohow."

The dog could not move either of his back legs or his front ones, but he turned his head to press up to Mason Raymond; a low moaning came from his throat. "Ray-shi," Mason Raymond said in a strangled voice.

"Done all he could," Hart said in his broken voice. "Weren't *his* fault."

Without speaking, Mason Raymond nodded, feeling the dog's hair first on one cheek and then the other. A powerful smell came from him—a wet, dog smell that was normal, and the musky odor of bear, and then the stench of bowels. When he had been ripped open, an involuntary muscular spasm had released the wastes inside him. He smelled of dying. Mason Raymond knew this, a scent that was there that had never been before and would never be again—the body fluids pouring out of him, the puslike smell of death; heat, pain, and fear; and the smell of giving up, of letting life flow out without fighting to hold it back.

He raised his head and looked at Hart. He smelled, too—the intestines and bowels and stomach ripped, but there was still a look of life on his face. He was fighting back. Useless, but he was fighting back. He always had. He'd beaten the game when the hired man had taken it into his head to hit him with a hoe and had bashed his skull in and his brains had come popping out, but he wasn't going to beat the game this time.

"Git the gun 'nd put him out of his misery," Hart said.

Mason Raymond stood up. He was shaky and disoriented, but he picked up Lite's gun where he'd thrown it. "It's what we can do for animals that we can't do for people," Hart whispered.

Mason Raymond threw Lite's gun down and looked around for Hart's gun. He wasn't going to kill Horatio with a coward's gun. But Hart's had come apart when it hit the ground; the double barrel lay separated from the stock.

Mason Raymond took it up and worked it back together. He held the gun carefully as he put the bullets in. His hands were trembling and he had trouble loading. The gun would work. It might have grown rusty and disabled in service; the cartridges were homemade and makeshift (like most everything else of Hart's), but if he was careful it would serve his purpose. After all, Hart had been firing and killing with this dilapidated gun for years.

He put a shell in each chamber, checking carefully to see they were in right. If one jammed—

He closed the gun and stood over Hart, pointing it toward the dog. Horatio's eyes were on him, bright, clear, knowing. "I'll talk to him," Hart said. "I'll talk 'nd you—"

There was the report of the gun, the shudder in the dog. Horatio lay still; nothing would ever move him again. How could he have loved an animal so much? But he had. He had

] 369 [

loved the dog and he had loved Hart; they were part of one another, maybe even the same.

He could hear Hart scratching for breath, a low bleat from inside the torn tubing of his body. He moved the gun slightly to the left, closed his eyes, and fired again.

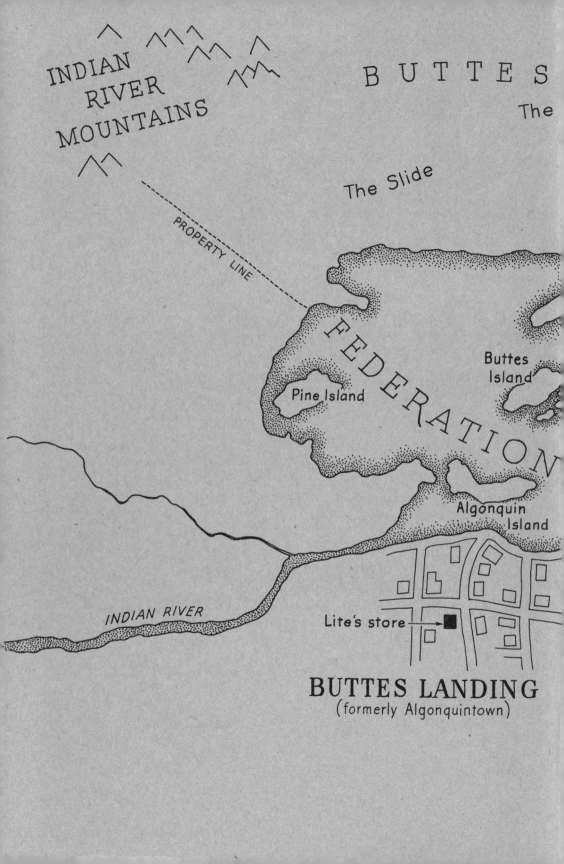

INDIAN
RIVER
MOUNTAINS

B U T T E S

The

The Slide

PROPERTY LINE

FEDERATION

Pine Island

Buttes
Island

Algonquin
Island

INDIAN RIVER

Lite's store →

BUTTES LANDING
(formerly Algonquintown)